Teen
Killers
at Large

Also available by Lily Sparks

The Teen Killers Club Series
Teen Killers in Love
Teen Killers Club

Teen Killers at Large

A Novel

LILY SPARKS

CROOKED
LANE

NEW YORK

Published in the United States by Crooked Lane Books, an imprint of The Quick Brown Fox & Company LLC.

Crooked Lane Books and its logo are trademarks of The Quick Brown Fox & Company LLC.

Library of Congress Catalog-in-Publication data available upon request.

ISBN (hardcover): 978-1-63910-487-1
ISBN (ebook): 978-1-63910-488-8

Cover illustration by Alvin Epps

Printed in the United States.

www.crookedlanebooks.com

Crooked Lane Books
34 West 27th St., 10th Floor
New York, NY 10001

First Edition: October 2023

10 9 8 7 6 5 4 3 2 1

For my mother Barbara,
who taught me to type and got me into mysteries,
and so can be blamed for everything I write.

Chapter One

Surprise

❧

It's embarrassing to accuse someone of murder. Not that anyone who accused me ever seemed too torn up about it. The officers who came to our trailer, put me in handcuffs, and charged me with the strangulation and beheading of my best friend Rose did so with neutral authority. The DA confidently told national news that I was a deranged killer. But by far the most passionate accusation came from the real killer herself, Rose's own mother, Janeane, when she sobbed on the stand that I was "the Girl From Hell."

That time even I almost believed her.

But for me, here, in the nerve center of the Desai mansion, across the gleaming conference table from the immaculately dressed Skye Wylie-Stanton, to actually say the words: *He was going to kill me.*

It's embarrassing. I know I will sound hysterical. They'll tell me I was imagining things; they've been telling me that all week.

But it's the truth.

Aarush Desai, at the head of the conference table, dressed in a simple navy sweatshirt that probably cost three hundred dollars, taps his fingers as if to time my silence.

The defense attorney his father has hired for me, Honor Hadley, widens her eyes: *Well?*

Skye's cashmere sleeve squeaks against the table, his smooth, manicured fingers twitching across his scarred face as if to hide a smile.

"I'd like to make a statement about what happened at the Wylie-Stanton house three weeks ago," I start.

"When you saved Skye's life," Aarush says, in his elegant British accent, "after Erik violently assaulted him—"

"No. After Erik stopped Skye from *killing me*."

There, I've said it.

Aarush cringes back reflexively, but Skye leans toward him, frowning with concern, his voice almost reassuring: "She's been through so much. Going from a year in solitary prison, to camp, to being held captive by my brother for days—"

"I was never his captive. I'm his girlfriend."

Honor ticks her hand under the table: *Stop talking*.

"But of course, excuse me," Skye's eyebrows lift. "I should say, after an extended period of Class A influence, and the raid on camp, she's showing signs of PTSD. You said she had trouble sleeping, that she has a panic attack if she hears a helicopter—"

Aarush's cheeks darken with a blush, long brown fingers suddenly fidgeting with the steel latch of his glass water bottle. He has expressive eyes; large, thickly lashed, and so dark the iris merges with the pupil into a single black gazing pool. He is hiding them from me now, avoiding my unspoken question: *Why would you tell Skye that? Why would you tell him anything about me?*

"With all the mental damage she's sustained, who could blame her for being paranoid?" Skye goes on.

"I'm not paranoid. You put on black leather gloves—"

"Signal." Skye sounds like he's talking a toddler down from a tantrum. "I was closing the windows because of the rain. The hardware is poorly maintained, and my grip . . . is not what it used to be. So I put on gloves."

"You ran down the hall to catch up with me and kicked my phone out of the room—"

"Signal, I'm sorry, but we both know that didn't happen."

"I asked Skye to leave." I look from Aarush to Honor. "Repeatedly. He said it was his house and got in my face—"

"No. I'm sorry, no." Skye shakes his head with authority. His wide eyes catch the rippling reflections cast by the glass wall behind me, which looks into the Desais' pool, and go popsicle blue. "What *I* remember is that we were chatting, everything was fine and friendly, and then I tried to lock the window in Erik's old room." He pauses. "The same window that Erik used to come in, and then to flee authorities later. When I tried to lock *that* window, some switch flipped, and you became hostile."

"Hostile? You *cornered me!* You were going to kill me and blame it on Erik, just like you did with your—"

Honor is on her feet, but her round, dark brown face stays perfectly composed. "Gentleman, I need to take a beat with my client, if you'll excuse us."

Skye and Aarush stand as we leave. I keep my hands in fists until we're out of the room, afraid I'll slap the phony concern off Skye's face before I can stop myself.

"CurtPro was testing pills on minors at camp," I hiss once we're down the hall from the nerve center. The security guy posted beside the hall entrance stares at the white marble between his dark shoes determinedly as I go on. "*That's* why he was going to kill me and frame Erik for it, just like he framed Erik for killing their parents!"

"Can you prove it?" Honor asks.

"I was there."

"So no. The answer is no. You have no evidence."

I lean against the cold marble wall, bracing for the lecture.

"This house may *look* like a five-star resort, Ms. Deere, but you are in custody. Not acquitted. And if Skye changes his story and says you helped Erik escape his family home, the authorities will revoke your house arrest immediately. You'll be back in prison. The only thing keeping you here is Skye's testimony that you saved him."

"Okay, but how can Erik be a fugitive from camp when everyone knows camp was torturing—"

"Camp is a federal detention facility." Honor cuts me off. "Its validity will be determined by a judge, not Twitter, Miss Deere. Besides which, Janeane accused Erik of attempting to kill her—"

"And she's lying! We have her on camera getting stabbed by Kurt—"

"Yes." Honor nods. "And her counsel will be in for a big surprise when the subpoena goes through and we can present that evidence, and whatever is in Jaw's lockbox, at the evidentiary hearing. But *until then*." She looks at me a long time. "You need to learn how to lose a battle so you can win a war." She steps in closer, so close I can smell the expensive perfume rising from her tailored blush suit. "So you will go back in there and say you misunderstood what happened at the house—"

"But it's a *lie*." I shake my head, fighting back tears. "How do I win a war when all I have is my word, and you want me to go back on it—"

"It's your word against his because Erik refused to turn himself in and testify."

"He had no choice. He's under a conservatorship. If he turns himself in, Skye owns him!"

"I wonder . . ." Honor raises one sculpted eyebrow. "What if we made a deal. You play nice with Skye today—" She stops my protests with a single manicured finger. "And I have someone at my firm look into Erik's conservatorship?"

I pause. "You think there's a chance you could get him out of it?"

"We won't know until we look. But until you're fully acquitted, Skye owns you. So, either you play nice, or we spend the next month planning your defense thirty minutes at a time through safety glass."

I take the deal with a nod. But a burning fist of pain gathers under my heart when I follow her back to the nerve center. And as its sensor panel door glides open ahead of us, Skye is murmuring, "—obviously still under his power, if there's any possible contact—"

"Hey!" Aarush cuts him off quickly, nodding to me and Honor. "Everything okay?"

"Signal had a moment of clarity."

"Right." I try for a deep breath, but it doesn't go past the knot under my heart. "Skye, I'm sorry for bringing you here today. There's no point in this conversation. I retract my accusation."

"Because?" Honor prompts.

"Because I . . . misunderstood what happened at the house." The knot incinerates, and Skye licks his lips, like he can taste how much it hurts me to say this.

I misunderstood nothing and we both know it.

"There we are!" Aarush smiles. "Thank you so much, Skye, for letting Honor mediate this quietly."

"It's the least I can do." Skye slowly rises, then makes his way toward me with a pained, staggering step. "My only concern is that we do better to acknowledge how deeply damaged and scarred Signal truly is. Signal—" He puts a heavy hand on my shoulder. "I do not doubt for a moment the fear I caused you was very, very real." He squeezes my shoulder hard. His grip is just fine. "And I hope you can hang onto this clarity through the coming trial."

My fingernails bite my palms until I expect blood to slide through my fingers as Aarush beams at us. When he goes to walk Skye out, I shoot past them down the hall, head down, sick with rage.

I careen around the corner and up the stairs, racing to my room, slam my door, and cry, "Blackout!"

The shade panels whisper closed at my command; the lights dim off. I curl up on my giant bed, pull my lilac comforter over my head, fingers groping through my silky sheets for my phone and clacking wired headphones.

On top of hosting us, arranging for our legal defense, and arranging Zoom tutoring so we can finish our GEDs, billionaire Sonny Desai also provides us with phones and a weekly allowance. I've never been this pampered in my life.

So why am I so miserable?

Our song from *Swan Lake* swells as my eyes close, and I'm back there across from him. In that black room covered in rain and shattered glass, watching his face soften, his cheek against my hand. The only thing that hurts worse than hearing this song is turning it off.

"I'll send you some sign," Erik had said. *"I love you too,"* he'd said.

Three weeks and nothing.

I know they haven't caught him. But I don't know why. I don't know if he's still in the state, in the country, I don't know if he's alive. But I do know if I don't see him again I will die.

Under the music I hear steps in the hall—Nobody and Jada must be done with Zoom class. I crawl out of bed and crack my door so if it's Javier I can quietly retreat. Yesterday he sat next to me during our nightly movie in the Desai home theater and it was . . . too close.

But it's not any of my friends.

It's Skye Wylie-Stanton, not bothering to limp as he creeps past our bedrooms.

He tries one of our doors; fortunately, it's locked. Then Jada comes out of the bathroom across from him. She's in her pink bikini—she always does laps after class—and looking very young with all her makeup washed off. She starts at the sight of the scarred blonde man approaching her, his hand outstretched.

"You dropped this on your way out of the pool!" Skye says, a smile in his voice.

"My earring?" Jada's hand floats to her ear. "Thanks—you didn't have to bring it all the way up here!"

"No worries, it was my pleasure." He leans against the hall, blocking my view of her.

"Jada!" Nobody calls from downstairs. "Our delivery is here!"

"Coming!" Jada yells back. Then, to him: "Thanks again, but I gotta run down to parking level—" She turns away, flip-flops slapping the cold marble. He follows her.

"Headed there myself," he says cheerfully.

I slip out of my room and chase after them, almost breaking into a run as they round the corner into the recessed alcove where the elevator lets off. I land behind them just as the doors swish open to reveal Aarush.

"Signal!" Aarush says, eyes locking on me. "I need to talk to you."

"Sure, how about in five minutes—" I try to move past him, but he catches my arm, stopping me just short of the elevator threshold as the doors close. Jada sees me and smiles. Skye smiles as well: the same expression, the opposite meaning.

"I need you back in the nerve center at once," Aarush is saying. I throw off his hand.

"Skye was up here *trying doors—*"

"I told him to come up here." Aarush rolls his eyes. "He wanted to return Jada's earring. Let's not let our paranoia get the best of us."

I shake my head in disbelief as he herds me down the hall and toward the central stairs. I'm scanning the marble-tiled breezeway between the living area and pool deck for Nobody, for Dennis, for *anyone* to send after Jada. Hadn't I heard them all down here a moment before?

Something is off. I can feel it.

"Signal!" Aarush snaps as I move toward the main elevator.

"I need to run down and check with Jada about something." I press my hand against the inset LED screen next to its doors. Aarush has programmed the house to recognize our biometrics and voices, but his voice can override our commands. So when he calls over my head:

"*Hold elevator.*"

The doors obey. The light above them comes on, so I know the elevator car is waiting behind them, but they won't open until Aarush says.

"Fine." I turn, about to run up the sloping breezeway to the deck, but Aarush sidesteps to block me, and I blurt, "Just because your dad is paying for my lawyer doesn't mean I'm your prisoner."

Aarush's jaw drops.

"I never should have been a prisoner. You know that, or I wouldn't be here, so stop treating me like one. I need to see Jada, and you have no right to stop me."

Aarush staggers back. "I tried." He is disgusted. "I *really* tried." Then, to the elevator: "*Open.*"

The steel doors part with the rubbery thunder of a hundred balloons escaping, every shade of blue, and then a gold "1" balloon and a gold "8" balloon, their ribbons still clutched in Nobody's scarred hands. Javier cradles several grocery bags, Dennis is balancing a pyramid of crepe paper and sparkly bunting, and Jada holds a giant pink bakery box.

"She's RIGHT THERE?!" Jada screams. "AARUSH, what the HECK! You were supposed to get her out of the front hall!"

"How did you know?" I cry, as my friends barrel past me to set their stuff on the built-in bar.

"Your birth date was in your court records," Sonny Desai says, coming out of the elevator last. "I took the liberty of telling them."

Even juggling a grocery bag full of sparkling cider bottles, Aarush's dad looks distinguished: tailored suit, silvery hair, white perfect teeth glowing against deeply bronze skin. His face always has the cheerful certainty of a smile, even when he's not smiling—maybe billions of dollars in your account just has that effect—but his eyes are restless. He's always searching for things to be improved. And the first place he always looks is Aarush.

He gestures at his son now to grab the streamers tumbling from Dennis' arms, but I catch them first.

"This is so sweet," I say, helping Dennis wrangle the bouncy rolls of crepe. "You guys didn't have to do this—"

"Sure we did. Eighteen is a big deal," Javier says behind me, and Dennis adds, "Yeah, they can charge you as an adult now."

"I had no clue! What a total surprise! I'm sorry if I ruined it—"

"It's not ruined! Just stop looking at everything!" Jada frantically waves her hands between me and the mound of decorations. "Run go hide for like, fifteen minutes!"

"Are you sure I can't help in some way?"

"No! No! Just give us a minute, Signal! Maybe there are *still some surprises* you don't know about yet, okay?"

The elevator light comes on again, the house assistant AI voice intones: "Outside guest has arrived."

"*Hold elevator!*" Aarush barks.

An electric current passes through the group as they look from one another to me, a giggle escaping Jada, Nobody's face going as bright pink as her hands.

It couldn't . . . there's *no way*, they would never allow it. But my idiot heart is going so hard my hands shake.

"Who is it?" I ask Sonny.

"Surprise," Sonny says, and the doors glide open.

Behind the doors of the elevator is a frightened old woman with gray bangs and a "FEAR NO DEERE" hoody, clasping my mom's old quilted handbag.

Wait. That's—

"Signal?" My mom's voice wobbles uncertainly into the vast house.

And then all I hear is my own incoherent sobbing, my head heavy against her slight shoulder, my heart pierced through by the familiar sting of her Vera Wang body spray. She feels so much smaller.

"Oh, honey, honey, honey . . ." Mom rubs my back. I can't get any words out when I pull back from her, I just stare. Her hair was the color of milky coffee before I went to prison; now it's shot through with white. There are deep circles under her eyes, face drawn from losing weight she didn't have to spare. But her smile is radiant as she inspects my face. Then she reaches out and plucks at my dyed-black bangs.

"You look so grown up." She shakes her head; then her eyes fall to my side, where I was gouged open by the helicopter shrapnel. "Sonny said you had to get more stitches?"

"I'm fine," I sputter. "Really, I'm fine, Mom."

I hear Jada crying and catch Javier wiping at his eyes; then Sonny sweeps us both onto the deck. Mom and I share one teak deck chair, a space heater glowing above us as the air goes dark, and I try to put the last few weeks into words: signing on for camp, the attack by Dog Mask. The mission Javier and I went on together to kill a cult leader. How Erik saved me from becoming a killer and bought me and Javier time to flee the compound. How Erik and Nobody and I made our way to Ledmonton to confront Janeane while wearing Aarush's camera, and how after my friends showed up, Kurt went rogue, stabbing her and demanding the others kill me. How I'd run back to our trailer, but no one was home.

"The news people were too much. For me and for the park." Mom takes off her glasses to wipe at her eyes. "They'd just let me go at work when the Fear No Deere people reached out. Offered me a place the press didn't know about. They're how Sonny found me, and then he offered to fly me out and . . . Oh, Signal." She shakes her head. "I can't bear thinking of you being alone all this time!"

"I haven't been." I gesture toward the breezeway, glowing gold in the blue dark. The full force of Dennis' immense concentration is engaged in centering the "HAPPY BIRTHDAY" banner, its ends held by Jada and Nobody, both standing on chairs.

"Come on, Mom. I want to introduce you to my friends."

But a few feet out from the entrance, Javier, chasing after a bunch of balloons teased loose by the night breeze, crashes straight into us. His muscled six-foot frame sends my mom staggering back in the dark, and he lets the balloons disappear so he can catch her arm.

"Whoa, sorry, Mrs. Deere!"

Mom blinks up at him with surprised recognition. What's she noticing? His long, handsome face? The earnest apology in his expression? His tear tattoo?

"It's very nice to meet you, ma'am." He steps back and offers his hand properly. "I'm Javier, Signal's . . ."

A fraction of a beat, and then, at the exact same time:

"Friend," I say.

"Ex," Javier says.

"Very nice to meet you too," my mom says smoothly. But as we walk on, her voice bristles. "I remember him alright, from the stream. Forcing that kiss on you out of nowhere! I should really give him a piece of my mind—"

"Please don't. He was on those pills. We're friends now, seriously."

"Friends or exes?"

"Short relationship. Long story," I say under my breath, then louder: "Dennis, come meet my mom!"

Dennis offers a handshake, but my mom hugs him instead.

"Oh, I know Dennis!" my mom cries. He cuts me an awkward look and I pull her away while she's still gushing. "He is a genius, and a hero, and I will never stop thanking him for saving my daughter."

"Yes, well," Dennis says, adjusting his glasses, "it doesn't take much to be a genius around here."

Jada shoves him playfully. "He is a genius, Mrs. Deere, but don't let it get to his head 'cause that thing's big enough already." She undercuts the dig with a dazzling smile. She's put on a girly pink dress and a scent like fresh cotton candy emanates from her still-damp black curls. "I'm Jada, and you have the best daughter. Come here!" She throws her arms around my mom, who responds with a full-hearted embrace.

"Oh, honey, it's so good to see you looking so well! How are you doing now?"

As Jada reassures her the pills are out of her system, I catch Nobody by the sleeve.

"Mom, this is—"

"Nobody!!" Mom screams, like she's recognized her favorite celebrity, and suddenly my tiny mother is wrapped around my tall best friend in the biggest bear hug. Nobody smiles shyly, dipping her head to hide her face behind her blonde bangs as my mom interrogates her about Zoom class.

"Yes, ma'am, we're all on track to be officially graduated by the end of the month, ma'am."

When I can finally drag my mom away, she turns to me, eyes huge.

"That girl is *stunning*. I'd seen pictures, but in person? Holy moly, she is the most beautiful thing I've ever seen."

"I know, but don't bring it up."

She frowns, curious, when Sonny approaches.

"Breann!" He sets a hand on her shoulder. "So glad you could be here."

"Thank you so much for having me, Mr. Desai. Parent to parent, it means everything to be here with Signal today."

"And I want her to have your support throughout the coming trial." Sonny nods. "So I've arranged with my housekeepers to ready a property in Marin City for you to use. My drivers can take you there tonight after the party."

"Oh, I don't want to impose." Mom's voice trembles. "I planned on finding a hotel in the city, but I would be quite happy to rent the space from you—"

"You are my guest," Sonny says firmly. "Anything Signal needs, it is my privilege to provide. And what she needs right now is her family."

Mom sags against me in relief. Without her job, I can't imagine how she would've paid for a hotel for months and months, and she's almost in tears thanking him when Aarush drifts by, frowning at his phone.

"Hey, Aarush, this is my mom," I announce, and he swiftly tucks the phone away. Aarush has perfect manners when he needs to; he's charming with my mom, but formal enough to forestall a hug. Then he locks back onto me.

"Is there *any chance* I could have a *moment* of your time for a brief conversation, Signal?" he says with pronounced formality.

"Of course." I smile too hard and follow him down the hall to the nerve center.

"I'm sorry about before, Aarush," I start. "It's hard to accept, but maybe I have grown a little paranoid."

Aarush lets out a bitter laugh as the nerve center panel door sweeps open for us, then when it falls closed, says, "Perhaps I haven't been paranoid enough."

He walks to the wall of screens with the Destech logo spinning on them and pulls his old chunky laptop from a recessed shelf, jerking more slack from a cord anchored between a rubber plant and small wastebasket. He holds the laptop up so I can see the empty ports down its side.

"Did you take my thumb drive?" he asks. "It's a small rubber hamburger? With googly eyes?"

I shake my head.

"I had really hoped you would say yes." He sighs and sets the laptop down with a curse. "Because that was the thumb drive with the Janeane rant on it. And it's gone."

The attic rant is the only footage we had of Janeane with her mask off, from when Nobody, Erik, and I interrogated her in Ledmonton. We'd gotten her full confession on camera, but the prototype streamed it without recording. Aarush had managed to record his screen the second time we streamed—when she'd lured my friends up to the attic and told them if they killed me and returned to camp, she would clean up my body.

"Gone?" My throat starts constricting. "It's not like, in the cloud or something?"

He doesn't look up from the table, head hanging between his tensed shoulders. "That laptop has always been on a separate, wired network for security reasons, which kept it from backing up to our wireless cloud."

"And the original screen recording?"

"Was erased as well."

I sink into a chair.

"This was deliberate destruction of evidence."

"You think Janeane . . . like, sent someone here? Have you checked the security footage?"

"We don't film in the nerve center." Aarush frowns. "The nerve center and bathrooms are the only places we don't. I'm going through last week's footage of the connecting hallway, but so far no one has appeared who doesn't live in the house full-time, besides your lawyer."

I realize what he's saying and shake my head, my face heating.

"My friends didn't do this."

"I must insist you consider the possibility," Aarush says. "Because while Janeane's rant helps your case against her, it hurts their case against camp."

I keep shaking my head. Frustration flickers over his face.

"Signal, they're claiming Naramauke forced them to murder people against their will. That they had *no escape*. But that footage clearly shows them walking over Janeane's bleeding body *to go back!* Back to the place that 'tortured them' and forced them to go on 'murder missions'!"

"It *was* torturing them, it *was*—"

"They. Went. Back. It's not a good look. Not when camp is claiming they're lying about the abuse to get lighter sentences. And it's why we had to keep your counsel separate from theirs. Your cases have competing interests. And I'm guessing one of them has figured that out."

"Our cases are *not* competing," I insist. "Once I'm exonerated, I'm a witness for their case. I'll testify about the murder missions at camp. But I have to be exonerated first. So why would they hurt my case like that?"

"Maybe they think your case is strong enough without that particular piece of evidence."

"Or maybe, like *I keep telling you*." I struggle to keep the frustration from my voice. "Skye doesn't want me to testify about CurtPro testing pills at camp. And he was in the nerve center today, so he must have—"

Aarush pinches the bridge of his nose. "More paranoid fantasies about Skye. Brilliant."

"CurtPro Pharmaceuticals is Skye's company—"

"No, it's not!" Aarush snaps. "Skye is one member on a *board of twelve*. He doesn't even have a controlling interest."

"It's his family's business. Kids were dying from their pills at camp. And the same day he comes in here, the thumb drive goes missing?"

"Skye *did not know this footage existed*. The only people who knew about this footage are directly involved with your legal defense. Unless *you* told someone?"

His large eyes search mine as he pushes: "Did you, or did you not, tell your 'friends' we had footage of Janeane's rant in the attic?"

I stare back in silence. Of course I did. They're my family. I tell them everything. And who knows what *he's* told Skye? All Skye would have to know is that my legal counsel meets regularly in the nerve center, and he would comb the place the first chance he got.

"From this point forward, you must keep all the details of your case confidential. Do you understand?"

My hands are in fists again.

His phone lights up; he scans it and frowns. "Well. It would appear you have some candles to blow out on the deck."

*   *   *

Jada has Dennis keep his hands over my eyes until everyone has built up a sufficiently loud tabletop drum roll, then cries,

"Ta da!"

I blink down at the cake she's just placed in front of me; a half-dome of elaborate pink frosting and yellow candles with a doll stood up in the middle of it; but not the doll you'd usually see wearing edible formalwear.

"*A Skipper cake?!*" I cry, and Jada rocks forward laughing.

The moment is so perfect it feels like a memory even as it happens. The golden glow of the birthday candles washing over my friends and mom, ringed close around me. I've never had so many people I loved at a birthday party before. But the warmth recedes at Aarush's cool expression, his sharp eyes scanning the joyful faces around me like he's analyzing some masterful performance.

Well, he's wrong. My friends aren't traitors. I'll prove it to him. Somehow.

"Make a wish!" Jada cries.

Send me a sign.

Gold light sputters into gray smoke and Aarush calls for the house AI to play "Birthday Mix." But just as it starts, we all hear the raspy male voice at the same time:

"*Signal.*"

A figure materializes out of the dark, broad shoulders cutting across the reflection of the pool, pale face ringed in a black hood.

"I had to see you—"

But before he can stride toward me, two security guards rush from opposite ends of the deck and pin him to the ground.

Chapter Two
Candygram

Sensor motion lights train themselves onto the writhing crumple of boy under the security guards. As they zip-tie his wrists behind his back, his hood slips away from long, curly brown hair, and his pale blue eyes meet mine.

Nobody steps slightly in front of me and Mom.

"Who is that?" Mom whispers.

"I have no idea," I whisper back.

The trespasser is still screaming my name as he's dragged off the deck. More guards appear from inside, including the head of security, Raoul, a guy who looks like two marines stuffed into a navy tracksuit. Raoul and Sonny consult briefly, then Sonny approaches Mom.

"Would you mind staying the night, Breann? Security has deemed it necessary to lock down the house."

My mom nods and is quickly wrangled away by one of Sonny's assistants. Raoul, head on a swivel, herds me and the other club members toward the home theater.

The opening credits of Hitchcock's *Vertigo* are starting as we file into the rows of white leather seats; once he's done a quick head count, Raoul darts away again. I wait until I'm sure he's not coming back, then leap to my feet.

"Sound OFF," I tell the home AI system. "PAUSE film!"

Jimmy Stewart's swooning face freezes behind me, then fades almost to white as the houselights come up.

Nobody and Jada lounge on either side of my seat, Javier just behind, Dennis in front. We do that now, we huddle together. Maybe because this house is so large, or maybe because there's so few of us left.

"We need to talk," I begin.

"Yeah, we do." Jada crosses her arms, barely suppressing a smile. "You got a stalker for your birthday? I'm jealous."

Nobody reaches across my seat to shove her, which makes Jada's smile break through.

"I'm kidding," Jada rolls her eyes. "But did anyone else think that was Erik for a minute?"

Hearing his name actually hurts.

"I just don't understand how someone got so close to the house," Javier says. "I thought they had laser motion sensors around the lawn and stuff."

"There are lasers along the main gate, yes." Dennis nods.

My stomach sinks at the words. Even if Erik *was* okay and nearby, even if he wanted to give me a sign, how? There's no way. The Desai mansion is basically the most luxurious prison in the world.

"Or at least, as far as I can tell," Dennis goes on. "Aarush isn't exactly forthcoming about security schematics."

"Why not?" Nobody tilts her leather theater chair back with a pneumatic "whoosh" that sends her stocking feet up into the air. "Weren't you two hacking partners for years? Why would he keep stuff from you?"

It's true, Dennis described Aarush as his best friend when he sent Nobody up north to find him. Yet in person, Aarush and Dennis seem to actively avoid each other. And now, in response, Dennis falls silent.

"If there's lasers by the gate, the crowd's going to be setting them off anyway," Nobody continues after a beat, crossing her hands under her head. "It was getting wild out there when me and Jada went to get the cake from the delivery guy."

"Yeah, there's about a million idiots in blue wigs." Jada frowns at her nails. "And all these girls holding up heart hands and wearing T-shirts that say 'we love Erik'—"

"Jada started shouting 'get a life' at them." Nobody laughs.

"Someone's got to wake up these boy-crazy dick-zombies!" Jada insists, and Javier throws his forearm up to catch his shocked laugh. "Boys are dumb, and bad, and I hate them. I'm just trying to share the good news!"

"Boys are dumb, and bad, and you hate them." Javier laughs softly. "When did *that* happen?"

"Don't get mad at me for stating science facts." Jada bats her lashes at him. "And sure enough, the one boy in the crowd threw something at Nobody!"

"What?" I cry. "Are you okay?"

Nobody shrugs. "He did? I didn't notice."

"The guy with the rattail! I should've called security right then and there. Between him and Signal's stalker, it's turning into Medieval Times Dinner and Tournaments around here."

"The stalker was weird. But that's not what I wanted to talk about." I clear my throat. I know Aarush would be furious at what I'm about to do. I just hope he's got his hands too full with house security to listen in on us now as I drop my voice and tell them all about the thumb drive going missing and files being erased.

When I finish there is a long, tense silence.

Dennis pushes his glasses up the bridge of his button nose. "That's not good," he says at last.

"You don't have any backup copies?" Nobody asks.

"No." I shake my head. "That evidence is just . . . gone."

"That sucks, that really sucks . . ." Jada's fine eyebrows come together in concern, but her gaze slides away as she says, "But it won't actually mess up your case, right?"

"Without that footage, everything about the Ledmonton allegations becomes my word against Janeane's."

"But you still have the evidence from the security lockbox," Javier says. "That's the proof Janeane killed Rose, that's what you've always said."

"When are they opening that, anyway?" Jada asks.

"I don't know. But we still don't know what's in there, so losing the attic rant could seriously jeopardize—"

"No, it won't. Because you're not a Class A," Nobody sighs.

There's a ripple of cold through the room. Because it's true. They reran the Wylie-Stanton on me, and I came back a D. The most harmless designation the algorithm can give.

"Yeah. You'll be fine," Dennis adds flatly.

"It's not just losing the evidence that kills me," I go on. "It's the fact he won't even consider that Skye might have taken it."

"Who does he think stole the thumb drive?" Nobody repositions her chair with another "whoosh" so she jounces upright.

"Us. Duh." Jada's eyes flash up to me. "Aarush suspects one of us, right?"

"Yeah, he does," I admit. "He won't even consider Skye could've taken it."

Javier turns to Jada. "Weren't you talking to that guy when you went down to get the cake?"

Jada nods, one manicured hand reaching up to toy with her hair.

"Skye was hitting on Jada," Nobody announces.

"Like it was his *job*." Jada hides an embarrassed smile behind a fist. "He like, practically chased me to the elevator and he like, MADE me take his number—"

"That dude is what, twenty-five?!" Javier says.

"Jada," I say, "Skye is a sexual predator."

"Wow, you think?" Jada laughs. "I definitely didn't get that within five seconds of talking to him, thanks guys!"

"What was he talking to you about?" Dennis asks.

Jada picks at her nails. "I don't know, he was just asking like, how do I like the house, what do I do all day. I said school, he was like, if you get bored, I live close by . . ."

Javier and Dennis exchange a look.

"Are you serious?" Javier's voice is cold.

"And I was like," Jada goes on, not acknowledging him, "'I'm kind of on house arrest but thanks' and he was like, well, you *really* must be bored then, text me sometime—"

"What do you think Aarush would make of all that?" Nobody asks me.

I roll my eyes. "He'd say Skye was offering to tutor her, probably."

"What if I could turn up the charm so high Skye shows his whole ass?" Jada grins. "Get him to lay on that groomer game so thick Aarush has to see him for what he is?"

"Stop playing." Javier sits up in his chair. "You wouldn't. You know you wouldn't."

"Why not?" Jada snaps back. "I'm *single*, Javier. I'm my own woman. I can text with whoever I want, especially if it helps Signal—"

"How." Javier scoffs. "How does texting this dude help anyone?"

"You know," Dennis says, turning in his seat to look at Jada, "if you could get him in the habit of sending links back and forth, I have a widget that would let me remotely clone his phone once he navigates to the link."

"Wait, hold on." Jada blinks at Dennis. "You're telling me you can hack his phone if he clicks on a link?"

"More like mirror it onto a dupe phone. See his texts and emails and incoming calls in real time. Find out what CurtPro is up to." Dennis looks at me significantly. "It'll take me a day or two to set up, but as long as he clicks the link, I can capture him."

All of us stare at Dennis in horror.

"Seriously?" I say at last.

"That just shouldn't be possible." Jada has a hand over her mouth.

"You have seen me use exploits to crash a helicopter, but *this* is what bothers you?" The slightest amusement registers in Dennis' monotone.

"None of us has helicopters," Nobody says. "All of us have phones."

"Seriously," I tell Dennis, "let's do it."

"What? No, no way are we doing any of that. Jada shouldn't be talking to this creep at all!" Javier cries, half out of his seat. "You'd put Jada at risk like that?"

"At risk?" Nobody scoffs. "It's texting."

"We'll start with 'wyd' and go from there," Jada says, tapping at her phone primly.

"Well, count me out." Javier shoots to his feet. "Aarush can suspect me of whatever. My hands are clean, and I'm keeping it that way. I'm going to get my reps in and go to bed."

"Hey, hold on, I'll come too." Dennis is about to follow him when Jada grabs his wrist.

"You're just *going?*" Jada gasps, then turns and glares at Javier. "You're both just *walking out* on Signal's birthday?"

"We hit the gym every night, tonight is no exception," Javier says, but pauses, then turns and steps toward me, one arm out. "Signal knows I care about her," he says, and I acquiesce to a hug. "Happy birthday," he says, holding me just half a beat too long. Then he turns, his face stiff, and heads up the aisle.

Dennis, following after him, gives me a wave before the door closes behind them, and then I look to Nobody and Jada, eyes wide.

"Since when does Dennis lift?"

"Since we got here?" Jada laughs.

"You miss a lot when you go to bed early," Nobody says, pulling a box of strawberry Pocky from her flannel.

"Oooh, did you get another care package from Amy?" Jada squeals, reaching out her cupped hand. "Did she send you any more of those little rainbow star-shaped candies?"

"Konpeitō? Yes," Nobody says, her mouth full. "But I ate them first."

"You know," I point at Nobody. "I looked up Amy's dance company, and *Swan Lake* is still playing in the city. Why doesn't she come drop off the packages in person sometime?"

"I don't feel right inviting anyone by the house," Nobody says primly.

Jada flashes me a disbelieving look and is about to say more when her phone dings.

"Skye?" Nobody leans over to read the screen, which washes Jada's face with blue light.

"Oooh, he got back *fast!*" Jada cries triumphantly. "Okay. So I said 'wyd,' and he says, 'takeout and video games' . . ." She frantically types, narrating her response. "'Nice what game,' send . . ."

We all wait, and the phone pings again.

"'You play?'" she reads, and cackles, pressing the screen to her chest and looking up at us. "You think I can get him to bring a Switch to the house? I bet I could get one here tomorrow . . ." Her thumbnails flash across her screen as she replies, but there's multiple dings from more incoming messages before she can finish.

"Someone's chatty!" Jada rises to her feet, eyes still on her screen. "I might have to bow out of movie night early too and start dialing in on this himbo."

"You're sure you're okay with this?" I put a hand on her arm.

Jada rolls her eyes. "Is the sun okay with shining? Destroying dumb thirsty boys is what I was born to do."

"Just . . . don't ever be alone with him."

"*Signal.*" She smiles. "If he tries to lay a hand on me, I'll make what Erik did to him look like a paper cut."

And then it's just me and Nobody.

"Aarush wouldn't care if you invited Amy over," I tell her. "And we'd all like to meet her. You should totally—"

"Signal," Nobody cuts me off. "No offense, but can we just start the movie already?"

Her face is strangely tensed.

"You *want* to watch this movie," she adds with meaning.

"Um . . . Start film?" I call to the house. The lights dim again. Once I'm cuddled up in the seat next to her, Nobody's scarred hand reaches into mine, something stiff and scrunched up pressing into my palm. Her head turns fractionally, widened eyes glistening in the light from the screen. Whatever it is, I should keep it out of the range of the security cameras behind us.

"It's what the guy threw at me." Nobody keeps her gravelly voice just loud enough to register beside my ear, under the tense background music as Jimmy Stewart stares down at the ground below. "The guy at the gate that Jada saw. I recognized him. He was our driver from Oregon. The one that took us to that secret show."

"*Scraps?*" I hiss, and her hand flickers over her lips.

I'm shaking in my chair as I look down at the thing in my hands.

It's a crumpled packet of Pop Rocks. With a note inside it.

* * *

"I can't believe we're really doing this!" I smile at Mom.

"Me either," she says grimly, knuckles white on the rented SUV's steering wheel.

I squeeze her arm, wishing I could transfer some of the joy pulsing through me. The note in my Pop Rocks packet had been short, but his impatient handwriting was unmistakable:

KINGS CANYON
BLACK MOUNTAIN TRAILHEAD
12/3-12/10
FOLLOW THE BLACK HEART
11-10-33

I'd gone directly to Mom the next morning, and once we'd strolled far enough away from the house so no camera could pick up my voice, I threw myself on her mercy. I laid it all out for her: Yes, it was detrimental to my parole to see Erik, but the note was vague enough for plausible deniability. Yes, the Desais would absolutely forbid me to see him if we asked; I'd have to lie to my most loyal supporters.

And yes, I had to go. It was see him or die.

She frowned at that, but somehow she talked them into it. She told Sonny we needed a mother-daughter camping trip. Honor worked her magic with my probation officer, and now we're flying down a foggy backwoods road, tall trees crowded as close as they grow in Ledmonton but hidden in banks of white fog. I can sense how deep the forest goes, though I can only see a few of their dark outlines break through. The mist turns the forest into a short poem in the middle of a blank page.

SKREEE-**CRAASH**!

I turn to the rearview window in time to see the second black drone crash onto the road behind us, exploding across the asphalt like a tin water balloon. Nausea twists me forward in my seat. Moans that have to be mine but don't sound like me fill the cab as Mom pulls over.

My new scar burns with old memories: Nobody's dirt-streaked face, the high scream of the helicopter engine exploding, my shaking fingertips brushing parts of me not built to feel daylight.

No. *No.*

I am *not* going to see Erik for the first time in weeks with vomit in my teeth.

Mom says gently, "I'm going to get those out of the road—"

"Don't go near them!" I grab her. Her hands go over mine, still and calm.

"They're not going to explode, honey. They're just drones."

I drag my gaze to the machines shattered across the backwoods highway, then get out of the car as well. The monotone *ding ding ding* of the car fades behind us as we hurry across the lane line. I grab one of the two drones by a propeller—a shattered black cow skull of plastic and metal—and see its camera light is still on.

I throw it as far as I can into the brush.

"The Desais must be tracking us," I tell Mom. "Don't put them in the car. We must be far enough out of range they can't pilot them remotely."

Mom checks her phone. "Oh dear, yeah, I've got no reception. Now I can't call Aarush when we get in."

"Oh well," I say with heavy sarcasm.

We drive on in silence, but Mom is growing tenser every moment. If she tries to turn the car around, I'll throw myself out of the vehicle and run the rest of the way. But she doesn't turn. She says nothing. She drives up to the small dirt parking lot by the trailhead and cuts the engine before retrieving a crumpled Aldi bag from the back seat.

She looks at me for a long moment. Her gray eyes are paler than I remember them, as though faded by too much crying.

"Signal, when you asked me to drive you up here, my first instinct was to say 'hell no.'" Mom sighs. "But then I thought, 'don't make her do this without you. Because she'll go, one way or another.' My job is to get you there and back safely. So, before I let you leave this car to meet this friend of yours, I need to make sure you have these, and that you know how to use them."

She fumbles nervously before taking out several gold foil squares, and my jaw drops as I realize they're condoms.

"MOM!" This is not happening. Oh, please, do not let this be happening.

"Hold on, Signal, just hold on a second—"

She pulls out what I think is an electric razor, until she presses a button and an actual bolt of miniature lightning flashes between two metal prongs at its end, making us both jump in our seats.

"A *STUN GUN?!* WHERE DID YOU GET A STUN GUN?!"

"After everything I've heard about Erik," Mom says, "I want you to take both these items."

"Mom, I do *not* need condoms. I mean, I *really* don't need the stun gun, but like—we're not—we've gone on two dates, okay?!"

"Honey. Your grandmother had me when she was your age. I had you not too long after. Better to have them and not need them than need them and not have them. And that goes double for the stun gun. Don't fight me on this one. You know how to use them?"

And I realize, with a fresh surge of horror, that the last item in her bag is a banana.

"They showed us in health class, Mom! Please, this is so unnecessary, I promise you," I mumble, my whole face on fire as I wad the foil squares into one zip-up pocket of my jacket.

She makes a point of showing me the safety on the stun gun, having me slide it off and hit the button. The stun gun pulses in my hand and the hairs of my arm stand on end. I triple check that the safety is on before zipping it into my other pocket, aware of its presence as though it were a live animal.

"Okay, honey." Mom sounds relieved. "I'm going to go check in at the KOA. I'll be back here first thing tomorrow morning."

I nod, my chest tight. "Thanks, Mom."

The air is heavy with mist as I approach the trailhead. There's a wooden box just next to a weathered map with "PCT" etched into it; inside is a notebook with messages from various Pacific Crest Trail hikers. There's also a half-empty box of Band-Aids, a Clif bar with a masking tape label claiming it for "PJ the DJ," and a taped-shut packet of Pop Rocks.

I tear the bottom and a plastic compass slides out.

The bezel has been wiped blank of coordinates or bearings; the only course it can chart is to a heart drawn with black ink.

Dave taught us how to use simple compasses like this back at camp. Once I've gone a few yards down a manicured trail, I "put the red in the shed": I turn myself about until the red end of the magnetic needle tucks inside the directional arrow. Its other end pierces the black heart.

If I follow Erik's black heart, I will have to leave the marked trail for the wilderness.

The air tastes like a coming storm, and everything around me craves the rain, leaves tilting back toward the sky like hands lifted in prayer. Before I duck under a fallen tree, I catch the brown tracks on its green moss. I imagine Erik climbing over it and my throat goes dry.

Thirty more minutes of walking and I run into a chain-link fence. A "PRIVATE PROPERTY" notice hangs from its links. But there's a small black heart dotting the "I" in PRIVATE.

He's really going to make me climb another fence?

I tuck the compass into my jeans and clamber up the wet chain-link, mindful of the seam along my side that's still healing. The soft ground absorbs my leap down, and from here the mist gets even thicker, rolling off a lake just past the thinning trees.

Dark branches part. Below the mist, still black water holds the perfect mirror image of the pines, cut out by white sky. A rotting dock extends far into the mist, something small and rounded at its end. My hollow footsteps ring through the air as I cross its planks and find a waiting red cat carrier. Its door is fastened shut with a combination lock.

I kneel, spots on my knees going instantly wet from the dock, and turn the dial: 11, 10, 33.

The padlock releases; inside is a hefty square flashlight. On masking tape, on the handle, Erik has written: **TURN ME ON.**

Its beam cuts a bright stripe through what might be miles of white fog. I strain forward, trying to make out a far shore, wondering where he could be. I scan for a tent, a car, anything.

I keep the flashlight on and crouch beside it, hands in fists. Then I dig out my supplies from my jeans pockets: vanilla lip balm and cinnamon mints.

I'd imagined kissing Erik again so many times, and settled on this combination for the next opportunity. But maybe I'll be sleeping out in the cold instead? I've been crouched here at least ten minutes. In an act of pure faith, I put the cinnamon mint in my mouth and draw the fluttering lip balm across my lips.

The mist swirling around me is going from white to gray, the bird calls shifting into something plaintive. A few rings break the mirrored surface of the water; I'm trying to believe they're fish nibbles when a fat, cold raindrop hits the top of my head and slides through my carefully styled hair.

I sigh and pull up my hood, wondering for the first time if I should give up, when I see the figure gliding toward me through the mist.

His head is covered by a ski mask but his broad shoulders give him away, the tension in them like he's carrying something heavy no one can see. He stands in a low rowboat almost hidden by the swirling vapors, balancing like a gondolier until he gets to the dock. He sinks down and grabs the plank at my feet, stopping the rowboat's momentum with one sculpted hand.

If the bitten-down fingernails didn't prove it, the torn green eye would.

"Erik!"

He holds up a finger over his hidden mouth, but I can see the smile in his eyes as he helps me into the boat. His hands are burning hot. A shiver goes through me at their brief contact, but there is no prolonged greeting: He settles me on the narrow bench behind him, then turns his back and starts rowing. We move soundlessly away from the shore and into the blank eternity of mist.

I don't try to speak again, but he turns to peer at me in furtive glances, as if to make sure I'm really there. I stare. I watch his shoulders move as he steers us around boulders that seem to rise out of the lake as we pass, their forms clouded by the mist until the last moment. The urge to reach out and set my hand on his back is almost overwhelming.

A motion light snaps on ahead, throwing another dock into silhouette. Erik maneuvers closer, then grabs one of the tall posts, the boat bobbing slightly as he steps out. He reaches for my hands. I take his and stand carefully, the rowboat seesawing wildly in the icy black water with my slightest shift in weight. Once he's got me balanced, and I'm about to step onto the deck, he whispers:

"Sorry."

And with one easy motion, he wheels me out over the black water. And lets go.

Chapter Three

The Lake House

~

Icy water closes over my head; my clothes go heavy as iron. The stitches along my side light up with shock, the new skin unused to cold.

Through the rush of bubbles streaming past my ears one furious thought fires off:

This is it? *This* is how he kills me?

I fight the pull down into the dark, kicking toward the dim gray light rippling above, chest burning with cold and shock. The moment my fingers break through the surface his hand is on mine. He hauls me easily up onto the deck, laughing as he falls backwards, me on top of him, gasping and shuddering violently with bone-deep cold.

"I had to make sure you weren't wearing a camera!" He is still laughing as I fight to my feet, calling him every curse word I know. "I know how Aarush loves a livestream—wait, here, I got a blanket—"

He darts away and is back in a moment with a quilt he had waiting.

"Let's just get you into the house," he says warmly over my continuous stream of invective, carefully tucking the heavy quilt around me. "You can have a hot shower and change into dry clothes."

"H—house?" It's the first non-four-letter word that's escaped me since seeing him.

He nods and pulls his ski mask off, and I can't take it.

His face is not just beautiful, it is *right*, the only thing that fits my brain after dreaming of him so long. Erik registers my reaction and fights a smug smile, but he has no clue. He knows he's hot, but he doesn't understand what the sight of him does to me; even I don't know the word for a joy this painful. But if my heart were a bell, his face could shatter it with its own ringing.

Erik jerks his chin toward something ahead of us, and I tear my gaze away to a black cabin beyond the dock. He all but carries me up a steep flight of stairs to its narrow deck and through its front door. It's so cozy warm inside, my shoulders drop with relief and sensation floods my fingertips.

It's a small space, but lovely. There's a fireplace framed by river stones and a painted black floor with a low couch to one side. A rustic dining table fills the other side, fake candles with plastic flames on the tabletop and mantle, warming the dark walls with bobbing wheels of orange light.

I had been hoping for a tent. This is a vacation home.

"Did you dismantle the security system or something?" I ask him.

"I didn't break in," he says, staring at my face until I look at him. Then he looks away. In the cozy dim of the cabin, the dark circles around his eyes stand out; he's almost as wet as I am from pulling me out of the lake. "The owner knows I'm here. It's sort of a payment for a job I'm going to do."

Before I can ask what job, he jerks his head down and brusquely moves away. "I'm going to put on some dry clothes. You should shower—the bathroom's upstairs."

And he disappears through a dark door without a backward glance.

The stairs are narrow, the corridor that holds them tall and steeply slanted by the A-frame roof. The bathroom is surprisingly modern; the floor heats up with a switch. The soaps all smell like flowers, and there's a rose gold razor in the soap dish and a blush pink robe on the door, so new I feel guilty touching it.

My bandage is waterlogged. It falls away, leaving my stitches exposed when I step in front of the bathroom mirror. Seventeen black stitches, sharp against puckering pink skin, an outrageously ugly seven-inch seam that curves from the back of my lowest rib, around my waist, and down to my belly button.

I was really hoping to keep my bandage on.

I open the medicine cabinet, searching for gauze and tape, but there's nothing. I put on the new robe and cross to the only other upstairs room, a master bedroom with a massive vanity centered under the peak of the A-frame roof and more fake candles wagging their plastic wicks at the ceiling.

Still dripping from the shower, I tiptoe toward the giant circular mirror of the vanity. Laid out below the mirror is a treasure trove of cosmetics: perfume bottles cut like gems, tubes of lipstick inlaid with gold latticework, palettes of eyeshadow the color of butterfly wings.

I think of my dumb middle school vanilla lip balm, still in the pocket of the rainproof jacket in the bathroom, and back away until my legs bounce against the velvet duvet of the bed.

I turn to see rumpled blankets—this must be where Erik sleeps. His worn backpack from camp hangs incongruously off one of the bedframe's elegant golden posts, a large black flannel on the other. I hold the flannel against my face. It smells like him, like rain, something between a freshly sharpened pencil and a handful of dark earth. It makes me a little tipsy.

"Hey," comes Erik's deep voice. "Knock knock."

"Occupied!" I cry.

The door is still closed but quite thin; it sounds like he's right next to me.

"I won't come in," Erik says quickly. "I just wanted to, uh, hang out. I don't know how long I get you for." An anxious beat. "How long *do* I get you for? Can you stay till the tenth?"

"I have to leave in the morning."

There's a soft thud on the other side of the door, as though he's resting his forehead against it.

"But you'll be here all night?"

"Yeah," I almost whisper. "If that's okay?"

"Okay?" He laughs wildly. "Yes, Signal. That's 'okay'!" Then, impatiently, "What's taking you so long in there, anyway?"

"I . . . don't . . . have any clothes to change into."

The beat of silence that follows is just a moment too long. Then he clears his throat and says, "You can wear whatever you find in there, and I'll get the laundry going and clean your stuff before tomorrow. I'm sorry about throwing you in. I would've warned you, but I figured if my voice was caught on camera—"

"I get it," I say quickly, opening the closet doors to find a rack of designer clothes. But whoever they belong to is a foot taller and several inches narrower than I ever will be.

"Whose house is this?" I say. Then, "It's like, my dream home."

"Yeah, same," he says.

"She's got great clothes too," I prod. "Whoever this mystery host is."

"Oh, uh, remember that party at Aarush's house?" His voice moves down; the floor creaks, like he's sitting against the door. "That, like, Russian singer? Nadya?"

"The pop star?" I try to say it casually, but there's a dull beat of panic as I realize who he means. The lady who grabbed his arm, across the pool at Aarush's house, after our narrow escape from *Swan Lake*. I had sort of recognized her then, but after a year in solitary had no idea how famous she'd become. Not quite headlining Coachella, but certainly on the program. "You're working for *Nadya?*"

"When I got low on money, I realized I still had Scraps' business card. I figured he probably made enough money selling that photo of us at the Hopeless show to CNN that he might consider something like that again."

I go to the armoire and tug the drawer open, trying to manifest some sweatpants.

Nope, just lacy lingerie and Skims.

Nadya: what the hell?!

"We worked it out so we'd go to an event, take pictures, then send them to the band or skateboarder or whoever once I was clear of the area, so they could post them. People paid pretty well and it wasn't hard. After several of those gigs Nadya got in touch. She wants to make a music video with us as the theme—"

"Us?" I pull out an entire drawer of lace thongs and bralettes, then quickly shut it again.

"The concept is a couple on the run, like we were, before." He clears his throat again. "So the idea is to do the same kind of thing I've been doing with Scraps. Film shots of me on the set to cut into the video, make people speculate if it's me or not, so it hits bigger. Since I'm uh, 'at large,' or whatever."

"Wow. That's . . . a very bold choice."

"Her dad is some gangster oligarch, so she's pretty fearless. And it'll be a massive paycheck. *And* she's letting me stay here until we do the shoot, down in LA."

"Well, that's great, if you trust her." I cringe, then hurry to say, "I mean, I'm sure you *can* trust her if you've been here this long. I just mean . . . Sorry, my mind is blown! You're friends with a legitimate pop star! What's she like?"

"I only met her that one time at Aarush's house," he says, and there's a small release in my chest. "I won't see her until filming. All communication has been through Scraps. That keeps everybody safe legally, sort of. Not me, obviously, but I'll never be safe legally, so . . ."

"Never say never." I try to keep my voice light.

He doesn't reply.

I walk closer to the door when there's a distant beeping, and the floor creaks again.

"That's the oven timer. Dinner's ready."

"I'll be right down." *Possibly wearing this robe.*

I pull open the last drawer of the armoire in a state of desperation and see something slightly more substantial folded up in the back corner: a powder blue satin slip. It seems old-fashioned, like it's from the '40s, but the satin is surprisingly thick and falls past my knees. I pull it on and check myself out: it *really* fits, looks elegant even. But I chicken out and throw Erik's big black flannel on as well before going out to the top of the stairs.

Erik, returning from the kitchen, stops short at the bottom of the steps. He stares up at me, his face softening.

"Hey," I say.

"Hey." He smiles. "I like you in my flannel."

I smile back and walk down toward him. And though my hair is still wet and I have no makeup on, he looks at me like I'm sparkling.

My mouth still tastes like cinnamon; my heart is going so fast. But just when I'm close enough to touch him, Erik steps away, turns, and hurries into the living room ahead of me. He's wearing his black hoodie with the snags from barbed wire on the back, dots of bare skin visible beneath, and my throat goes dry again.

"I made pasta salad," he says quickly, ducking his head, a spot of color high in his cheeks, and whips a spoonful of pasta on a plate so hard it rattles. "Do you like pasta salad?"

I walk over to the table, waiting for him to look at me. But he glares down at the tabletop instead. And as I approach the chair across from him, he steps back, so far he's practically against the wall.

"Erik . . . ?" He looks at me, at last. "Are you . . . still afraid to touch me?"

Erik throws the spoon back in the pan with a clang, his eyebrows shooting up.

"Yes." He sounds alarmed. "Is that a problem?"

I shake my head, though there's a sudden stinging flash behind my eyes that could become tears if I let it. I won't. I force a tight-lipped smile. "Whatever you're comfortable with. I don't want to make you uncomfortable."

"Well, you're making me *extremely* uncomfortable." He sets the pan down and crosses his arms over his chest, the jersey over his arms stretching tighter. "I'm jumping out of my skin over here, if you must know."

I step back. "It hasn't . . . the injections haven't worn off? You don't feel any . . . any better?"

There is still a raised vein at his temple. Light purple, like fading bruises, circles his eyes, and the muscles of his shoulders seem exaggerated under his hoodie. He's nowhere near as beastly as that terrible night in his parents' house, when he went after Skye. But he's not back to normal, either.

"It's hard to say. I'll think it's getting better, and then something weird will happen and then I think maybe it's getting worse."

"Weird how?"

"Well, like—" He rubs between his eyes with his knuckle, still not looking at me. "When Scraps brought me to this crash pad in LA—truly, a hell mouth of a warehouse—he was giving me a 'tour' I guess. 'Mugs are under the sink, check them for rat droppings,' all that good stuff. Then he takes me through the fridge. He says I'm welcome to eat anything, except the oat milk. That's *his* oat milk, hands off. And I think, 'Huh, oat milk, wonder what that's like.' Then he moves on to explaining how the hot plate works, and I'm nodding along when he goes quiet. And I realize I'm *holding the oat milk*, and it's empty, because *I just drank it all*. Right in front of him." Erik lets out a short, nervous laugh. "I didn't even . . ." He trails off and shrugs, shoulders going just a little too high. "Do you understand what I'm saying?"

I lower myself into my chair. "Am I . . . the oat milk?"

"No! That's just it! That's what scares me! I had *one nanosecond* of sort of wanting that oat milk. Whereas you . . ."—his voice goes deeper—"are all I want, all the time."

I rest my cheek on my hand, turning my face away from him, heart leaping painfully at the words.

"Am I freaking you out?" Erik asks.

"No, I appreciate your honesty."

"But you're disappointed." His voice is rough. "You're thinking, why did he drag me all the way out here—"

"No." I shake my head. "No, you could never disappoint me."

He collapses into the chair across the table, his shoulders at last dropping, and stares at me openly. I keep my eyes on my empty glass, enjoying the warmth of his gaze as though it's a ray of sunlight.

It's sad he's afraid to touch me, but this is what camp did to him. My tin of cinnamon mints proves I had my own hopes for tonight, but I would have walked the woods a thousand times as far to talk to him. Did he really think I would be disappointed? That I wouldn't come if we couldn't touch?

I remember what he'd said before, about girls who'd sleep with him at parties without wanting to talk to him.

"You have to know, Erik, I didn't come here just to . . . Your outside is great and everything. Physically you're, like, perfect, but—" My head is on fire. What am I doing? "But people don't need light bulbs because they want some glass avocado. They need the light. You are a light bulb, okay?" I swallow and meet his stare. "I'm not here for the glass avocado," I finish weakly.

"Signal . . ." Erik blinks slowly. "That is . . . the most baffling thing anyone has ever said to me."

I burst out laughing.

"And I have *lived in an asylum*. What are you *talking* about? *Glass avocado?!*" he repeats louder, delighted. He's smiling his biggest smile, and the air feels looser somehow. "You tell me *I* have bad lines, then drop some surrealist 'glass avocado' game out of nowhere—"

"It's not game! My *point* was you don't have to touch a light bulb to appreciate—"

"*STOP!*" he howls. "You're making it worse! Enough. *Enough.*" There are tears of laughter in my eyes as he bangs the table with mock ferocity. "That bizarre stab at talking me up was as ludicrous as it was confusing, and I am now embarrassed for both of us. It's also *completely* unnecessary, since—" He stops short, catching himself. Then, after a beat, he goes on deliberately: "Since I already love you, way too much."

My laughter trails off in a hiccup as I stare back at him, staggered by the words. He is glowing from the recent bout of laughter, but his eyes are slightly wary.

"I love you too." I reach for his hand without thinking, and when he flinches back the air goes tight again. "I'm sorry."

"Don't be. It's not your fault," he says, then leans forward and says, urgently: "I'm trying to anticipate what you want. But if I'm wrong, if you would rather just . . . let me have my way with you—"

"*Erik.*"

"Didn't think so." He flashes me a grin before leaning forward onto his elbows and raking his fingers through his messy hair; then he sits back, banging his fist on the table so hard the glasses jump: "So! Pasta salad! Do you like pasta salad, Signal?"

I peek into the pan, refusing to acknowledge that the skin from my chest to my scalp is now the color of a severe sunburn. "What have we got here, bow ties?"

"With pesto."

"Heaven and earth have traded places," I say, and he laughs.

After a few moments of forks scraping plates I add, "When we were at your house, that night. Skye said something about how, like . . . any time you wanted to turn it off, all you had to do was ask . . ." Erik doesn't look up from his plate. "Does that mean there's a cure?"

"Who knows." A crease darts between his eyebrows. "Skye will say anything to get me back under control."

"There has to be a way around the conservatorship. If there was some anonymous statement you could make, or—"

He's already shaking his head.

"I could get in touch with Alice. She could finally press charges against Skye—"

"I haven't talked to her in years." He shakes his head harder.

"I could make some kind of press statement or—"

"*Signal.*" His eyes rise to mine, and he starts nervously rubbing his wrist, like it aches. "I appreciate the thought. But people . . . really hate Class As. And I am *the* Class A. There's simply no way around that kind of branding."

"So what, you're just . . . not going to return to like, society?"

"Can you return to a place you've never been? I went from being home-schooled, to living in an asylum, to a murder camp, to an *underground cellar*— I've gone from cage to cage to cage."

And I realize what he's rubbing around his wrist: crisscrossing lacerations, thin rings of scabbed flesh, just above both of his beautiful hands. Like a restraint bit through the skin when he tried to break free, but he kept trying. Zip ties, metal cuffs, something merciless from when Dr. Ledrick kept him down in the cellar.

"Now, for the first time in my life, I'm free. I can't . . ." His face darkens. "I cannot, *I will not,* lose my freedom again. Nothing is worth it."

I stare down at my full plate, the fake candles silently flickering between us, my heart suddenly so heavy I'm surprised I can sit upright.

"However," Erik goes on, "that doesn't mean I intend to let Kurt run around 'killing people willy-nilly up and down the California coast.'"

I recognize the quote, and when I look up at him, he's fighting a smile.

"Did you think I'd forgotten that gem? Oh yes, Ms. Deere. You may have the rest of the world fooled. But I know that behind those haunting eyes lurks the heart of an *absolute dweeb.*"

"What's the plan for stopping Kurt?" I ask, refusing to smile.

"You and I join forces again." He spears several pieces of pasta. "Me by coming up with brilliant insights; you by passing on my brilliant insights to the authorities."

"Is that your extremely arrogant way of asking for my help?"

"Yes, Watson." He smiles, his real smile. "And you'll have an edge on me this time, because I rarely get access to a computer, and we both know your internet stalking skills are second to none."

"Touché," I say, remembering when my printout of his parents' murder case fell to the ground back outside Portland. The thought makes my eyes slide away from his. I haven't told Erik my solution to that last case: that Skye drove his parents' car purposefully into the cliff, killing them both instantly.

I don't know if I ever can. Not because he wouldn't believe me, but because I know he would.

"This is what I know so far," Erik begins, "starting from back in the cellar."

I hug my arms around myself, cold again.

"I don't know how long it was after the injections finished, because I was always in the dark." Erik stares through the table, gripping his wrist. "But at some point, the lights came on, and Ledrick and Kurt came down. Ledrick told me Kurt and I were going on a special mission. There was no route, no profiles, no oversight from headquarters. Kurt would have to call in after each target was finished to get the next one. My job, in Ledrick's words, was to make a mess."

Like the Director told the others to make a mess with me.

"If there was no route, how would you keep from setting your kill switch off?"

"They couldn't put in a second one." He pats the back of his neck. "The tissue was too compromised."

"It didn't occur to him you'd just run away?"

"To what?" Erik says. The words hit me like a slap. "At that point, a mess was all I was capable of." He looks down, a vein ticking in his throat. "Kurt drove us to the first town, then called in to confirm the target's address. He said we'd wait until dark to go out and turned on the TV. And camp was on the news. Your stream—we watched it to the end, when they airlifted you out . . ." He rakes his hand over his hair. "And by then I was capable of anything."

I clench my hands under the table to keep from reaching for him.

"Kurt and I had a little scuffle." The side of his mouth flickers. "I wanted to go to your hospital, he tried to stop me, so I slammed his head into the wall. I'm sort of surprised he got up from that. I was way less, uh, restrained than I am now . . ." Erik shrugs. "But the salient point is that Kurt's first kill couldn't have been Ledrick's target. Because she didn't live in that town, she lived in Bellingham. Here, I've got an article about it—"

Erik gets up and retrieves his old diary from the couch. He flips through to the chunk of blank pages in the back, where new handwriting has started to fill the pages, and finds a yellowed newsprint article:

CAMPUS ON LOCKDOWN FOLLOWING GRISLY HOMICIDE

Bellingham University locked down its campus for twenty-four hours Wednesday after 19-year-old Donna Laguardia was brutally murdered in her own dormitory room.

"There is evidence of an attempted strangulation, and mutilation of the eyes and jaw," the Bellingham coroner's office announced in a statement Friday morning, "Cause of death was a laceration across the throat, made by a straight razor or box cutter."

Laguardia famously testified in the Storybook Murders while in high school, but according to her roommate, had recently moved past the case: "She was finally putting all that behind her, and focusing on her own life. This is so tragic."

Authorities believe Donna knew her attacker, as there were no signs of intrusion or struggle.

I look into Erik's eyes, the torn one always a little startling when he stares full on at me, as he's doing now.

"What were the Storybook Murders?"

"They're why Kurt and Troy went to camp in the first place, a series of killings they were convicted of in high school. But I can't research their case, being off the grid and all." He lifts his chin to indicate the cabin, and the glimpse of his muscular throat stuns me. I stare back down at the article.

"So, if I find something out, how do I share it with you?"

He flips to the next blank page and turns his diary to face me.

"Give me the password of your personal email. Write a draft, and don't send it. When I'm in LA I'll sign in, read it, and write back in the same draft. That way there's less for Aarush to trace."

"You think Aarush is reading my email?"

"You think he's not?"

"I mean, I would *hope* not."

"I need more than hope these days." He stands. "I'm going to start laundry."

"Oh, let me get my clothes. I left them in the bathroom—" I start to get up, almost knocking into him. He steps wide of me, puts one hand out. We both freeze for a moment, the air tight again. Then he looks away.

"Please," Erik says. "Please."

And then he bounds up the stairs.

I sit back down and cover my face with my hands, the diary falling closed. I open it back up a couple of pages too early, and my name in Erik's writing catches my eye. I absorb a line before I can look away:

. . . obsessed with Signal, it's like I'm her hostage. Wherever she is will be the first place they look for me but I can't . . .

I turn the page, breath coming too fast. I stare at the blank page until heavy footfalls, much slower now, bring me back to the moment, and I write out my email sign-in and password with a shaking hand as he approaches.

"Um, Signal . . ." Erik's voice, just behind me, is on the edge of a hysterical laugh. "You want to explain what I just found in your jacket?"

Chapter Four
High Voltage

~

I whip around to see him holding up the stun gun.

I sag against my chair with relief.

"Oh, um, my mom gave me that. Just in case."

"Just in case of *what?*" He laughs, slipping off the safety. "Just in case you decided to join a backwoods militia?"

He presses the button and a bolt of blue lightning leaps between the prongs. He laughs again.

"It still works?!" I'm shocked. "The water didn't short it out?"

"It was zipped up in a waterproof jacket." He hurries past the table and into the kitchen. "I have *got* to try this out."

I drift to the kitchen door and watch him approach the granite counter, his back to me, sidling up to a wooden bowl of onions. There's more crackling, and then a hot smell of the dry peel catching fire.

"I like your mom's style!" Erik says over his shoulder, eyebrows way up, a thread of white smoke drifting up from the bowl. "But this thing is useless. If some animal came at you in the woods, you'd have to get too close to use it. You'd be better off with bear spray."

"It's not for bears." I tuck my hair behind my ear. "It's for you."

He turns away from the counter, smile fading.

"She hasn't met you. So . . ." I shrug. "She thought I needed protection."

He looks down at the stun gun, face contorting in a way that makes my chest hurt, then turns and snuffs the small flame licking the onion peel with his fingers.

"The advice still stands," Erik says, his tone nonchalant. "You'd have to get way too close to . . ." And then he stops. And his eyes go wide.

"Erik?"

"Signal." His smile is huge. "This is *perfect*." And without hesitation he fits the stun gun against his own throat, in the sharp angle between his heavy jaw and muscled neck.

"*Put that down!*"

"Now, Signal, hear me out—"

"That's not funny, Erik, the safety isn't on!"

"Well, I'm not joking. Come hold it—"

"WHAT?!"

"Take a breath. Listen to me," he says, like *I'm* the irrational one, his Adam's apple bobbing beside the silver prongs digging into his neck. "I have been keeping my distance from you all this time because I don't want to—to start something, when we both know you can't stop me. But this—" He holds it away from his throat and presses the button again. The lightning bolt springs to life with a crackle that makes me clench my teeth. "This would stop me alright! Drop me right to the floor. And if I know you can stop me . . . why keep our distance?"

"You're out of your mind." I turn and hurry back into the living room. He practically runs after me, hovering so close now, excitement rippling off him like currents from a Tesla coil.

"What? Why?" he laughs, keeping up with me as I pace the room, green eyes burning into me, the stun gun still at his neck, until I stop and fume at him. His eyes are so laser-focused on my mouth I don't think any other thoughts are getting through.

"It's a *stun gun*, Erik! What if I press the button by accident, or it just went off—"

"Is that it?" He beams. "That's your only objection, that you could hurt me?"

"It's a pretty huge objection!"

"All you do is hurt me, sugar cube," he laughs, his eyes soft again. "You have a gift for it. But if you don't want to make out—"

"I do." I say, too fast, and blush. "But I'm also perfectly happy just talking. You shouldn't put your safety at risk just to kiss me. It's not worth it—"

"Yes, it is," he says, so sincerely my stomach turns over. "It's absolutely worth it, I promise you."

He steps closer, and I sway toward him, involuntarily. Like there's some spirit in me who answers only to him. And she just might be a demon.

I reach out. My hand is shaking, his steady and warm as he wraps my fingers around the stun gun and places it directly on his pulse.

Freed, his other hand tucks my hair behind my ear again. Then he wraps both arms around me in a hug. And for a long moment he just holds me, so close. Like if he could hold me tight enough time itself would stop and keep us together a little longer.

Hot tears slip down my cheeks at the weight of his warm head against mine, the fact of him alive and breathing and here with me.

"Right against my throat, please," his voice rumbles against my chest the instant I try to angle the prongs away from his skin.

I pull back to look at him, and he kisses the tracks of my tears, first on one cheek and then the other, and then we're kissing. And this is what kills me about Erik, this is the hook that has pierced me completely: this secret gentleness that he only seems able to express through touching.

His lips, his hands, are perfectly steady, like the stun gun isn't there at all. But me, the person with my finger on the button, I'm shaking uncontrollably. Half sick with fear I'll hurt him, and simultaneously overwhelmed as all the energy in my body converts to pure joy. I must be infinite inside, to contain so much feeling.

And then running steps fly across the deck, and I shrink into something small and afraid as the front door flies open with a rush of cold night air.

"You're Erik, yes?" a heavily accented female voice cries. "Who the hell is she? I did not say you could invite guests!"

For a moment the young woman standing in the doorway, in head-to-toe beige athleisure, just stares. I'm sure we're quite a picture: me holding a stun gun against Erik's throat, him still staring down at me like if we ignore her long enough she'll go away. Embarrassed, I bring down the stun gun and wriggle back from him. Erik groans out such a heartfelt string of curses I almost laugh.

"Sorry if I'm interrupting," Nadya says, "but I'm afraid this is an emergency and—is that my vintage Dior slip?"

"I told her she could wear it," Erik says quickly.

Nadya tosses her long, red mermaid-wave extensions back from her shoulders. "Listen. Erik. Scraps said he could not get you by phone, so I drove up here myself to tell you, you have to come with me right now. There's police and park rangers all over, they've been calling already to my security. My car is on the access road, we will go straight to LA, but we have to go *now*—"

I'm so jealous of myself five minutes ago I could cry. Erik hesitates, then bites at his nails, green eyes focusing on some spot across the wall, thinking.

"No cars. I'll go into the woods," Erik says. "That's safer if they do roadblocks. I'll smash a window on the way out. That way you can claim I broke in, if they trace me."

He turns away then, all action, catching up his scattered things: his diary, a penknife, a flashlight. We're both watching him, me and the pop star silhouetted by the porch light, the urgency of the moment strangely paralyzing.

Erik turns to Nadya. "You should drop her off close to the trailhead. Don't let them see you together. The sooner they find her, the sooner the search ends."

Then he bounds up the stairs, leaving me and Nadya to stare at each other.

"Cybil—" she says.

"Signal."

"Whatever, Signal, you heard him. We should be going."

But I don't move until he comes back down. There's a backpack over his shoulder and the ski mask hides his beautiful face. I slip off his black flannel and hold it out to him. He takes the flannel but keeps moving toward me, arms going around me, burying his masked face in my hair. Nadya finally gets the hint and retreats to the deck.

I try to make it sound like I'm joking when I ask, "Will I ever see you again?"

"Awww." I can hear his smile. "Missing me already?"

I nod against his neck, not trusting my voice.

"I bet I miss you more."

This is one bet I'll easily win.

"Okay. Go." I step back, but his hand catches my arm, clutches it like a life preserver.

"Drafts."

"Drafts," I promise.

He turns to leave, gets three steps down the hall, and then comes back. With a desperate motion Erik pulls me against him, the black acrylic wool crushing between our mouths, his heart thrashing right above mine.

This is how he kills me. Not all at once, but a little bit each time we say goodbye.

He pulls himself away, turns, and sprints down the hall into the darkness at the back of the house; there's a shatter of breaking glass and then the wind howling in the door, and he's gone.

* * *

I'm in Nadya's massive SUV moments later, sitting in her too-long, too-tight velour pants, half sick from her too-sweet perfume; the whole cab smells like a mall lingerie store.

Her LED high beams wash out the trees ahead to the color of ghosts, jittering out of the dark as we bump along the access road. Nadya suddenly cuts the engine and points to the sweep of a flashlight in the far distance.

"Park rangers?" I whisper.

"I don't know." We both watch the beam of light bounce farther into the trees. "Such a mess," she sighs heavily.

"Thank you for coming to warn us. And letting Erik stay in your cabin."

"I told Scraps it was to be just for Erik." Her expression is cold. "What were you thinking? To get us all mixed up with the police, right before filming! I can't believe he would take such a risk—" She glares at me, her pretty face twisting; it's the kind of pretty that gets planned in a doctor's office. "Just to hook up with some ex."

"I'm *not* his ex. We're very much still together—"

"Together? Don't be stupid, how are you together?" She laughs. "You two go in the same room, they call out the National Guard."

"You didn't even know my name a minute ago—"

"I have trouble with your name, it's a weird name! But I know very well who you are. I know you were the girl he was on the run with, and then left him."

"I *never* left him."

"Well, if you cared about him at all, you would," she cuts me off, turning the engine back on. "You would not bring all this trouble on his head, not make him kiss you with a knife to his throat."

I throw the passenger door open and practically leap out of the car, toward the white arrow trail marker glowing in her headlights.

"Get back here, stop being so stupid!" Nadya calls after me. I don't turn around. I get to the trail, making sure the black heart is right behind me, and head toward civilization.

The first thing I'm drafting Erik is a demand that he never talk to Nadya again.

*   *   *

It seems like forever until blue and red lights splinter between the pine needles. Dry mouthed, feet wet, I stagger into the headlights of several waiting cop cars.

"There she is!"

Rangers, highway patrol, and park authorities close in on me: What was I doing in the park so late? Was I meeting someone? Didn't I know the trails close at dark?

"Honey!" Mom throws her arms around me, then wheels on my interrogators in a fury: "Is she being detained? I thought this was a search and rescue effort. She's been located, so we're going! You want to question her, get a warrant!"

And then my timid little mom, who has never in her twenty years of grocery store work so much as sassed an angry customer, *gives them all the finger.*

Genuinely, I'm touched.

But once we're alone in the car, she crumples forward onto the wheel.

"What happened?" I croak.

"Your probation officer called Sonny to check in," Mom says. "When he told her we'd lost phone contact, authorities came to the campsite. And when I told them you'd gone hiking, they started searching the trails."

"Hoping I'd lead them to Erik."

"Most likely, yes." She leans back against the driver's seat wearily. "That's probably why they let us go in the first place. They figured you'd lead them to him."

"They have no right to use me like that!"

"Yes, they do, Signal. They have a *responsibility* to find him. And it's ridiculous that he would put you through all this, and *still* refuse to turn himself in!"

"He never will."

"Really? What's his plan, then? Let you and the others just fend for yourselves?"

I shrug, face stiff.

"You need him to testify about Ledmonton. And your friends need both of you to testify about camp, to testify that what they say happened, did happen. If they don't have you and Erik, who do they have? And he knows that! He has to know that. I thought . . ." She shakes her head. "I was hoping he'd show up for you. For your friends."

I can't look at her. "It's complicated," I say at last.

Mom starts the car, shaking her head as she pulls out of the trailhead parking lot. The woods fall behind us; the smaller the tree line grows, the hollower I feel. We are not talking about Erik not showing up. We are talking about my dad not showing up, and I know this from all the things we suddenly can't say. My dad's only presence in my life is the way he haunts our silences in these kinds of conversations. We don't talk about my dad for several minutes.

"Sonny asked that we head back tonight," Mom says at last. "I already packed everything in from the campsite—"

"Pull over then," I tell her. "I'll drive."

Mom doesn't resist. She's so worn out she sleeps the whole way back. I punch in the Desai address and lose myself in the double yellow line of the dark road. Tired as I am from the trail, my mind is spinning like an electric carnival ride, sensory fragments looping manically: the sound of his voice through the door, the way he looked at me when we were both laughing too hard to speak, how hard his mouth pressed into mine the last time we kissed.

Probably because part of me doesn't believe I'll ever see him again.

*   *   *

When we get back, I collapse into bed around the time the birds start singing and manage a few hours of the worst kind of sleep. I get up at noon, having missed most of my Zoom classes, and come downstairs to find Aarush talking with Lupin, my old Higher Paths counselor.

She looks comically out of place in the polished Desai mansion, wearing her broken-in hiking boots, a mandala headwrap, and clacking wood bracelets. I slow to a stop on the staircase, unsure why she's here. Aarush and I had to lie through our teeth to get me enrolled in the troubled kids' wilderness program she leads, so I could hike through the forest to Naramauke. She's probably just given a deposition about me being a low-level psychopath.

But when Lupin sees me, a smile spreads across her face.

"Sunshine!" she cries, throwing out her arms, and suddenly she's hugging me, surrounding me with the smell of apple cider vinegar and coconut oil.

"Lupin, as you might remember, is a youth counselor." Aarush smiles. "And I remembered you saying she helped you before. So I thought maybe she'd be someone you'd like to talk to again."

"I'd love that," I blurt. But I feel strangely shy, even after leading her out to the relative privacy of the deck.

Lupin keeps it light, asking me about my classes as she slips off her boots and sits down on the white porcelain tile deck, back very straight. She stretches one leg out and takes her ankle in one hand, nose almost brushing her knee, as I curl up behind her on the padded deck chair.

"I hear you can't sleep," Lupin says, adjusting her pose. "I remember a dream you once shared that was very disturbing."

"Oh, yeah, the body I had to break up or whatever." I pull my knees to my chest. "Yeah, that was the worst one since the Rose dream."

"Rose dream?"

I describe the nightmare I had at camp that woke me up screaming, the night Dog Mask attacked us. By the time I finish, I'm shaking.

"But it turns out that wasn't so much a nightmare," I say at last, "as a memory."

"I see." Lupin frowns, stretching to the other side. Then: "Well. If your dreams are your memories, and you're repressing your memories, maybe you can't sleep because you're afraid to dream. And remember it all again."

"Why would I be scared of my memories?" I hug myself on the deck chair. "It's not like they can hurt me anymore."

She gives me a sad smile. "You tell me."

* * *

That night, I try repeating the affirmation Lupin gave me:

I accept my memories, all of my memories. My past is in the past, it cannot hurt me.

I repeat this for almost fifteen minutes, then give up and turn on my headphones. But instead of relaxing me, the music unlocks visions of what could have happened in the lake house if Nadya had never barged in. I pull the headphones off and tromp down the stairs, heart pounding. I hurry up the breezeway, past the pool and basketball court, to the small white outbuilding at the very edge of the terraced deck.

The clank of weights almost makes me step back through its automatic doors, afraid I'm interrupting Javier. But then I see the flash of Dennis' dark, intent face in the mirrored wall, and continue into the golden glow of the Desais' private gym.

"Getting those gains?" I call, threading my way through the Nautilus machines. Dennis sits up from the bench press and takes a long drink of water.

"I was up late finishing a project." Dennis grimaces. "And Javier says I'm not allowed to skip any days."

"Look at us. A couple of gym rats."

He runs the sleeve of his giant royal blue sweatshirt across his forehead. "It is truly the bane of my existence and I hate every second of it. But it works." His glance cuts just above me, to the security camera in the corner of the room. "Say. Would you mind taking a step to your left so I can show you something?"

I move into place and he retrieves a phone from under the weight bench and hands it to me. The home screen is tiled with various trading and social apps I don't recognize, its background a somewhat spooky picture of a sidewalk that apparently extends straight into the ocean.

"Is this . . . ?" I look at Dennis, who nods. The dupe phone.

"This is amazing!" I breathe, opening Skye's email. "Have you found anything good?" I search CurtPro and 1–20 of 50,000+ come up.

"I only just got it online. It's . . . a lot. I still haven't recovered from the photos."

"Photos?" I click the camera icon and a grid of nude girls leaps to the screen. I yelp, and the phone falls to the rubber matting.

"See what I mean?" Dennis says flatly.

As I pick it up, there's a new text from someone called "Jailbait#3SF":

We playing some switch or not, dude?

"Hold on . . . is Jailbait#3SF . . . *Jada?!*"

"Unfortunately, yes." Dennis nods. "I showed her and she laughed for about ten minutes straight. Also, I downloaded his email archive. I'm currently running it through a filter for mentions like CurtPro and Ledrick and Janeane. Anything else you can think of?"

"Security deposit box," I say quickly. "Ledmonton Bank. And the names Jaw and Itznicki."

Dennis nods, typing a note on his second, personal phone with one thumb. "Will do. Though considering how covert camp was, there could be some shorthand neither of us would know."

"But Erik might?" I drop my voice. "I could ask him about dates or code words—"

Dennis' eyes go very wide. "You two are in communication?"

I lean in closer to whisper, "Through drafts. You know what I mean?"

"Yes, I do." Dennis nods. "That's interesting. That's *very* interesting. They're about to do a big security upgrade through the house, because of the intruder. And whenever there's a changeover in systems, possibilities open up. Possibilities are not without risk, of course . . ." He gives me a small smile. "But look who I'm talking to."

"Whatever it takes, I'll do."

"I know," he says. Then: "Signal, if there's a way to get me in on drafts . . . I could really use his advice on some stuff right now."

I remember, with a pang, how often Erik and Dennis talked apart from everyone else at camp.

"Of course."

"And I could talk to him about possibly coming for a visit."

"Like . . . into the house?" My voice goes up too high. "*This* house? Like . . . sneaking in?"

"I wouldn't try unless the tech was airtight. But Erik is good with social engineering. And he could get more out of this phone than you or I."

My heart is jumping in my chest.

"Let me think about it at least." He lies stiffly back on the bench. "A little puzzle is just what I need to get through this caveman routine."

I hop on the treadmill, keyed up at the thought. I'm fifteen minutes into a brisk walk when Dennis rushes out like he's just remembered something.

But he doesn't share his epiphany until the next morning, minutes before I'm about to go into the nerve center for my first PR meeting.

"Hey." Dennis hurries toward me, legs too straight like he's making an effort not to break into a run. He lands in front of me before the security guard can escort me to the nerve center. "Signal, you forgot your bag—"

He holds out a pale pink leather tote that is definitely Jada's.

"Right! Thanks!" I give the guard an apologetic smile and step aside to talk with Dennis.

"There's a raspberry pi in here. It has an ethernet cable," Dennis whispers, rattling the pink tote, which has several cutesy keychains hanging off its zip pulls. "It has to be plugged in before they transfer the current camera map to the new security server. You have forty-seven minutes."

"Raspberry *what?*"

"It's a computer the size of a playing card. Just plug its cord in where Aarush usually plugs his hardwired laptop—"

I hear Sonny's laughter booming down the stairs, the staccato heels of his assistant scurrying to keep up with him. The elevator doors open and Honor, flanked by security, steps past me with a cheerful wave. Aarush's annoyed voice bounces down the hall: "Where *is* Signal? Everyone's waiting on her—"

"There will be like five other people in the room!" I say under my breath.

"Do you want to see Erik again or not?" Dennis asks.

I take the bag.

"Forty-six minutes," Dennis says. "Good luck."

Chapter Five
Raspberry Pi

～

The sunshine through the pool water sends streamers of blue light floating across the dark conference table. At its far end is Aarush, Honor to his right, and two other people I don't know across the table from her.

Ten feet behind Aarush is the ethernet port. Right between the rubber plant and the wastebasket.

It might as well be across the universe.

Aarush is speaking deferentially to one of the strangers, a middle-aged man with a round face almost swallowed by a shaggy black beard and untidy scruff. The second stranger, a woman with bright red hair, a fuchsia blazer, and statement clear-rimmed glasses, cries as I enter: "Hey, cute purse! Where's it from?"

"It—was a gift?"

"Well, it's *adorable*."

Honor leans in toward me as I take the seat next to her, her voice dropping low. "Signal, I just heard back from my conservatorship person. Skye is *not* Erik's conservator."

"What do you mean?"

"Just what I say. The way it's drawn up makes Erik a ward of Camp Naramauke, as an institution. His conservator is whoever the current director is, and only if camp closes does it default to next of kin. Now, obviously, we're *hoping* camp gets closed . . . but until it does, the current director is empowered to make all legal decisions on Erik's behalf."

"Who's the current director of Camp Naramauke?" I ask.

"No idea." Honor shrugs. "Their structure is . . . opaque to say the least."

Sonny's assistant darts forward then, to place a wide bakery box of croissants in the center of the table as Sonny's voice commands the room:

"So happy to circle up with this team. Unfortunately, I can't stay the whole hour—"

Hour? So much for staying behind once they've all left.

"I've got to get down to LA, so I'll leave you all in Aarush's capable hands."

Aarush nods, quietly proud to be second in command.

"Last week, we ran into a major roadblock in the discovery process," Sonny says grimly. "The feds are refusing to turn over the Wylie-Stanton algorithm. They claim that because Signal was never a Class A, and only 'deliberate human malfeasance' classified her otherwise, the algorithm itself is not being litigated, and will not be submitted as evidence." He looks each of us in the eye. "They clearly want to keep hiding this algorithm. We cannot let them. So here's today's objective: How do we activate the public to join us in demanding they turn over the Wylie-Stanton?"

He looks to the red-haired woman. She sits forward in her chair with a tight smile.

"Is that my cue? Signal, hi! I'm Cassie, your new PR person." Her teeth are so bleached they've gone transparent at the edges. "And straight off, just the fact 'human malfeasance' is possible, when we're supposed to be *dealing with an algorithm*, justifies *serious examination* of the Wylie-Stanton, alright? How it's given, who analyzes it, and yes, its formula."

Everyone around the table nods, except Aarush, who quietly adds, "An algorithm isn't a formula. It's a computational procedure."

"Exactly," Cassie nods. "No one knows what makes this thing tick. And that's a problem. We need to hammer home that everyone in this country is at risk, while whatever that algorithm does is undisclosed. Make it clear that any innocent person could be subjected to Signal's terrifying ordeal. We astroturf the socials. Launch as many human-interest stories as we can with calibrated SEO. Make sure whenever someone searches 'Wylie-Stanton' or 'Class A,' 'Signal Deere' pops up first."

"Talk to our search engine connections," Sonny tells Aarush, who hurries to make a note on his phone.

"And once we know when they're opening the lockbox," Cassie says, "we announce we have a bombshell development, and drop a televised profile." Her eyes flick to Sonny. "Mary Larland is interested."

Sonny cocks his head, impressed.

"I went out to her people with the angle: Signal was forced to live surrounded by Class As, she was deeply traumatized and almost influenced, but now she is bravely ready to bare her scars—"

"But that's not true," I say. "My friends didn't *traumatize* me. They saved me. If there's anything I've learned from living with Class As, it's that they're not bad people. *That's* why the Wylie-Stanton shouldn't be used." I look from Sonny to Aarush. "I thought this was something we all knew?"

"I quite agree with Signal," Aarush says, and my jaw almost drops. "Which is why I've invited my chancer journalist friend, Greg Ballas, to join us today. He's been doing extensive research on the Wylie-Stanton and has a major piece coming out on its history."

"A pleasure, Signal." Greg stands, leaning awkwardly over the table to offer his hand. The cuffs of his jacket are worn, but his handshake is warm and firm, and his eyes are kind.

Sonny nods. "A major piece, great. When is it coming out? Maybe we can help launch."

"End of the month. Barring any major setbacks," Greg says.

"Yes. Well. Signal and Aarush, I appreciate your objections. But we have to be pragmatic here, whatever we personally believe," Sonny says sadly. "The reality on the ground is that the public is *terrified* of Class As. We lead with pro–Class A rhetoric, they will shut down before any arguments can be made. We need to figure out how to use this fear to reach our aim: transparency for the Wylie-Stanton. Because the fear isn't going away. Especially with Kurt on the loose."

"Sometimes you lose the battle to win the war." Honor gives me a significant look.

"Do you understand, Signal?" Sonny says.

And I know I'm supposed to say yes. They are making all of this happen for me—the best lawyers, the best second chance at clearing my name—and I *owe* them. I know I owe them.

But I owe my friends more.

"No." I shake my head, my face burning, my stomach going on sour. "I'm sorry, but I'm just not that good of a liar. If you want me to go on TV and talk about how scared I am of my best friends, I won't convince anyone. But sharing how much they've meant to me, how much they've done for me, maybe that would mean something. Because it's true."

Greg leans forward. "I would certainly like to hear more about Signal's frien—"

Sonny cuts him off. "The public doesn't care about the other kids."

"But they care about Erik," I say quietly. "He's the original Class A. He could tell you everything behind how the Wylie-Stanton was started—"

"Erik is a pathological liar," Aarush cuts me off. Whatever solidarity we had a moment ago shrivels up and dies. But Gary's face lights up.

"Signal, I've been hoping we could talk about Erik. He's the key to all of this," Greg says eagerly. "If there's any way to relay questions to him, I would, of course, treat him as a protected source—"

But before I can open my mouth, Honor answers, "My client has no way of contacting Erik or vice versa."

"But any time Erik is ready to turn himself in," Sonny looks at me, "we're ready to talk."

The bag in my lap is suddenly full of bricks.

"Yes. Well. If this is a sticking point, if you really can't budge for one interview"—Cassie clears her throat—"I can maybe convince the Larland people to frame the profile around the 'bombshell evidence' in the lockbox. Unless Signal has some ethical objections to *that?*"

"No, no, I can do that."

"Great, great." Sonny frowns at his smartwatch and shifts away from the table. "Well, that's my hard out. My assistant will stay to take notes. Aarush!" He nods to the opposite end of the conference table. "Carry on and I'll look forward to you briefing me later."

Aarush clears his throat nervously once his father is gone. He fumbles with his phone as he casts his notes app across the wall of screens behind him and types out:

IDEAS?

The cursor blinks ominously over the table as he looks from Greg to Cassie.

"So. We need a strong angle on why the Wylie-Stanton is a part of Signal's defense. Let's brainstorm. No bad ideas, guys. What comes to mind?"

This is going to take forever. I have maybe ten minutes left to hook up Dennis' computer. I start to push my chair back from the table, and Aarush whips his head toward me.

"Going somewhere?"

"Uh, just to charge my phone?"

"There are wireless charging plates in the center of the table." Aarush raps the tabletop, and I lower myself back into my seat. How do I cross the room if I can't even get up from my chair?

Then Cassie looks up at the window into the pool behind me and freezes like she's seen an approaching meteor. As I turn to see what she's staring at, the entire focus of the table shifts to the massive panel of glass.

Nobody streams through the water, an arc of glittering bubbles trailing her like she just dove in. There's an almost reverent silence as she swims through the bright, wintry sunlight, a neon blue angel. Watching Greg's and Cassie's stricken expressions reminds me of how shocking it was to see Nobody with her mask off the first time. She has the kind of face that only gets more perfect the longer you look at it.

"I mean . . . ," Greg says after a moment, "would it be *that* hard to get the public to care about the other kids, if we shone more of a light on them?"

Nobody slips out of view, then streams back the other way, pushing off from the opposite wall, when suddenly her long body contracts. She sinks deeper through the water until she's level with our conference table, twisting to face us; scarred, slender fingers cupping over her mouth.

Something like brown smoke spills through them.

"Oh no." Cassie grimaces. "Is she—"

A plume of dark brown vomit unfurls between Nobody and the glass, and Cassie gags. A gossamer jellyfish of half-eaten food blooms larger and larger as Nobody kicks away to the surface, streamers of digested material trailing down to the tile.

And then the unmistakable tangy scent of bile fills the room, as Sonny's nervous assistant wretches a bolt of half-digested food straight across the croissants and onto Cassie.

For a moment Cassie just sits there, flecks of brownish green sliding down her clear glasses and dripping onto her bright pink jacket.

Then she screams like she's been stabbed.

Aarush hollers at the house AI to send staff. Greg gingerly covers the stain on Cassie's jacket with a napkin, which instantly goes transparent. Honor gets out of her chair and flees the room, gagging.

And I realize this is my chance.

I clap my hand over my mouth and race to the wastebasket beside the rubber plant. I make retching noises as I rock forward, feeling the wall and shifting my bag forward until the raspberry pi slides out. My fingers find the plug, and I wedge the tiny computer behind the back of the shelving. Once it's securely tucked away, I stagger to my feet. Behind me, staff are sweeping the vomit-soaked croissants into a rolling trash bin.

"The meeting has moved to the north library," a concerned-looking lady tells me, approaching with a gloved hand outstretched. "I can take that if you're . . . done?"

"Better keep it with me," I tilt the empty wastebasket toward me, hugging it into my chest. "Just in case."

*   *   *

I am writing this on a paint-spattered laptop I found in this warehouse co-op where I'm staying. It was abandoned along with a full set of welding tools and an eight-foot-tall scrap metal bust, by an artist who skipped rent for six months. If he shows up, I'm supposed to "break his thumbs," which seems like a standard penalty among Scraps' business associates.

It's an upgrade from the trees and freight cars I've been sleeping in. But wherever I am, sleeping or not, I dream of you. They are not restful dreams.

As cute as it was, we can skip the stun gun next time. Touching you makes me the most aware I've ever been. Of everything. You could stop me with a look. But really, why would you?

Where are you, besides in my head, all the time.

At your computer, I hope?

I almost drop my phone, bolting upright in bed. I read the draft twice before I reply:

Erik!!

Dennis has a plan. I'm going to give him my email pw too so he can jump in & say hi, but he has a way for you to come see US without it being as risky as that sounds. He can explain better than I can, brb

Julius Caesar bust or the Dolly Parton variety?

Dennis opens his door with his glasses off, blinking, after I pound on it for a solid thirty seconds. He looks less baby-faced somehow. Maybe all the lifting is kicking in.

"Drafts," I say.

"Password?"

I hand him a Post-it note folded in half. "Don't hack me into oblivion."

"Don't read what I write to him."

"I wasn't planning to." My eyebrows shoot up. "But now . . . I'm curious."

He gives me a dark look before shutting the door, and I sprint back to my room, where more lines are waiting on my phone:

I pour my soul out and you respond with . . . logistics! You heartless beast. No kind words, no lines of poetry, for a man sleeping beside what is either the giant head of Edgar Allen Poe or Che Guevara? (No hat)
 Not even "Shall I compare thee to a summer's glass avocado?"

Drafts bolds again, and I refresh.

According to Dennis you have been making special agent moves! A woman of action, not words.
 Something about files hidden in a pie?

I smile and type back,

I can't take all the credit. I got a big assist from Nobody.

I want to write something back that's romantic, but I don't know if he can see what I type before I erase it, and I'm afraid I'll go too far, so I type out:

I miss you.

After a few beats, I refresh the page and more lines appear:

This seems like a huge risk to take before your name is cleared.

I frown, when drafts bolds again:

Then again . . . Dennis' plan would include me spending tomorrow night in your room.

Ten minutes go by. I'm sure he's going back and forth with Dennis across the hall but I can't take it, I refresh every ten seconds until finally:

See you tomorrow.

Good thing I'm used to not sleeping.

* * *

"It was mostly chili and Italian dressing," Nobody tells me the next day.

We're sharing a deck chair: she's curled up at the head in a blanket and I'm at its foot with a bowl of popcorn, the lit pool water murky below in the fading light of dusk. Apparently, some chili got in the filter and stalled the system out, cheating Jada of her post-school laps, so she's playing one on one with Javier across the deck. Nobody watches them, waiting for someone to lose so she can tag in.

Dennis is tapping away on his laptop one chair over. He's refused to tell me any part of the plan, except that Erik will be at movie o'clock.

In exactly one hour.

"Foul!" Jada cries, as Javier's arm goes around her waist.

"Hey . . ." I lean into Nobody. "You ever think maybe Jada and Javier would be like . . . cute together?"

"Don't do that."

"Do what?"

"That straight girl thing. Trying to rehome your ex." Nobody scowls. "If those two want to get together, they will. You calling it out will crush it faster than anything else. Just sit back and relax."

I'm trying to figure out how to take this when her phone dings, but she dismisses it without even looking. It starts chiming again, and she turns it off.

"Would this bad mood have anything to do with Amy?"

"I'm not in a bad mood." Nobody glares across the pool.

"Are you two fighting or something?"

"No." Nobody's shoulders rise and fall. "She's just being clingy."

"*Clingy?*" I'm actually offended on Amy's behalf. "Um, she hasn't seen you in a year, right?" And when she refuses to answer, I go on: "I mean it's none of my business, but I didn't know you could *be* clingy, in a long-distance relationship, with someone who's spent most of the time you've known her *in jail*—"

"You're right," Nobody says. "It isn't your business."

I'm about to really get going when the head of the Desais' security, Raoul, leads a scrawny guy in a bright blue Dickies coverall and yellow aviators through the breezeway and over to the massive pool filter.

"Usually we contract through Victor." Raoul is frowning at his business card. "You're . . . Nick?"

"You can call me Scraps," the guy with the yellow aviators says, and I freeze, heartbeat screeching to a stop as I recognize our one-time driver to Portland. His signature rattail is gone, replaced by a fresh crew cut, but he still wears a neon green cast. "Victor likes to throw us the real dirty jobs because me and Dingle, we don't say no."

As though on cue, another guy in a Dickies jumpsuit steps out from under the shadow of the breezeway, several pool skimmers balanced on his broad shoulders, the brim of a neon yellow baseball cap shading a face half hidden by boxy black snorkel goggles.

No. Way.

"We're going to do a manual chlorine shock, filter swap, and spot clean as best we can." Scraps barks over his shoulder, "Dingle, you start sopping up the hot spots while I check this filter, eh? We want these folks up and running by tomorrow morning."

Nobody grabs my shoulder hard. I grab her hand back and *squeeze*.

"Is he . . . wearing Scraps' rattail?!" Nobody hisses in my ear, and I have to bite my finger.

A dark curly rattail is, indeed, sticking out from the back of Dingle's cap as he turns his back on us to run the pool skimmer through a strand of floating chili. It just barely covers the kill switch scar at the back of his neck.

Javier's dribbling has slowed to a stop, and I look over to see Jada, game forgotten, staring. She looks to me then, terrified.

"Dennis?" Aarush calls, hurrying out onto the deck. "Did you invite someone to the house?"

Dingle's pool skimmer goes still.

Dennis sets aside his laptop and springs to his feet. "I booked a session with a personal trainer. He's meeting me at the gym, he's not going in the house—"

"I thought I was your trainer!" Javier calls from under the hoop, and Nobody groans faintly beside me. We're squeezing each other's hands so hard her fingers have gone butter yellow around the scar tissue.

But Aarush doesn't respond to either of them. He's staring at Dingle, who pivots away from him as the stare drags on.

"Why is he wearing goggles?" Aarush says at last. Then, "Hey—excuse me, but I need you to take those goggles off at once."

Dingle leans farther across the pool as Aarush strides toward him, as though trying to hide his face.

"You—" Aarush bats his arm, and Dingle turns, too fast; if I had any remaining hope it wasn't Erik, it dissolves at how gracefully he falls into the dirty pool.

"Sir!" Raoul hurries around the side of the pool filter, Scraps just behind him.

"Is this man with you?" Aarush points to the water just as Dingle comes up with his back to us, spitting water and gasping for air.

"Nah, Dingle's with me!" Scraps snaps his gum. "He used to be a roadie, so his hearing's not great. I wouldn't ask him to take those goggles off, mister, at least not till he's dried off." Scraps points at his own yellow aviators. "Double pink eye. Occupational hazard."

Aarush takes a step back from the pool edge, as though the germs could skip across the surface of the water to find him. "And who are you?"

"Pool cleaner. Sent by Victor." Scraps grins.

"They've been cleared," Raoul says. "They got an on-site parking pass for the van, which has been checked and swept."

Aarush nods.

Dennis coughs into his fist. "So I'm cleared to meet my trainer in the gym?"

"Yes, but he can't park on site. Security stopped him at the walk-up gate so I suppose he found parking in the neighborhood. But I'll be sure to have them direct him to the exterior entrance of the gym . . ." Aarush watches Dingle climb out of the pool, recoiling at the sheets of contaminated water cascading from his tall form.

Scraps holds up a duffel. "Anywhere my boy can change? We always keep dry jumpsuits around. Another occupational—"

"Hazard, yes. Let me see . . ." Aarush bites his lip. He clearly doesn't want pink eye germs anywhere near the house. He points instead across the deck. "There's a water closet in our personal gymnasium."

Dingle takes the duffel bag and squelches away heavily. Dennis picks his laptop up off his chair, flashing a look to me, and heads after him. I rise from the deck chair to follow, but Aarush lands in front of me.

"Signal, with me."

"What?"

He glances toward Nobody, then nods for me to follow him across the deck, like I'm a dog he's training. I shoot a last glance at the gym, then follow him to the glass boundary fence.

"This is entirely confidential," Aarush's voice drops low, "but we just got word from our team in Ledmonton. The subpoena went through. They'll be opening the lockbox tomorrow morning. We'll fly out to Los Angeles first thing to meet Mary Larland for the profile. That way we're in the best position to frame the narrative going into the trial."

"Oh, wow."

"Yes, 'wow' indeed." Aarush smiles. "There's still a lot to prepare. You just be sure and get your rest. Tomorrow is game day. And remember. Tell no one. Keep this entirely to yourself."

"Game day!" I return the thumbs up, as a man in a dry Dickies suit reemerges from the gym, duffel over his shoulder. He's got the wet baseball cap on, and the snorkel goggles, and he gives us a nod before cutting across our path. We both watch him pass, a wet rattail clinging to the back of his smooth, broad neck.

Scraps springs out from behind the filters.

"Don't have that size in my van," Scraps calls to Raoul. "Going to have to head back to the shop, come back through tomorrow with 'em first thing—"

Aarush gives me a nod and hurries into the house, and I all but sprint into the gym.

Chapter Six
Movie O'Clock

❧

Dennis is sitting on a weight bench, fingers flying over his keyboard when I come in.

"Aarush?" Dennis asks.

"Just went back in the house. Is . . . he . . . ?"

Dennis tilts his head toward the single-person bathroom at the back of the gym, and in another moment its door is closing behind me.

I didn't think to knock. Erik is shirtless and soaked from a shower, wearing only Dennis' black sweatpants.

"Oh, I'm so sorry!" I flinch back, but he takes my hand and pulls me into him like we're about to dance, so tight the water on his chest soaks through my shirt. His face so close fades all my thoughts into silence. The only thing is his breath and my breath, faster every moment, the air between us heavy and strange. And then Erik takes a step back and sweeps a potted bamboo and basket of towels off the counter behind him and onto the floor with a clang.

I cry in surprise as he sweeps me up onto the counter and seats me in their place, his eyes on my mouth.

"Hi." Erik says.

And we meet at last in a greedy kiss. His lips move breathlessly across my neck, down to my collarbones, my hands are mapping the muscles of his bare back when there's a polite knock at the door.

"Um, guys?" Dennis says. "We're on a schedule here."

"Cool. Be right out." Erik's voice echoes up the hollow of my throat as he makes no move to stop. I have to be the one to slip down from the table. I grab the fresh white T-shirt hanging over the shower rod and hand it to him, avoiding my own blush in the mirror.

He rolls his head like he's trying to pull himself out of a deep sleep. As he finishes getting dressed, I reassemble the counter—turning the bamboo pot so its new hairline crack faces the wall—every nerve in me attuned only to him, like metal filings pulled by a magnet.

"First the plates at your house. Now flower pots?" I laugh, feeling weirdly drunk. "Something about ceramics. . . ."

"Our next date will be in a china shop," Erik says, and opens the door for me.

* * *

Dennis turns from locking the automatic doors as we come out, and he and Erik clasp hands before bringing it in for a clap-the-back hug.

"You freaking legend!" Erik laughs.

"I owe a lot to Scraps coming in with that double pink eye out of nowhere. And the rattail!" Dennis bursts out laughing. He hasn't laughed that way since Ledmonton, and Erik joins in.

"Did everything work out okay?" I ask. "How long do we have until security realizes three guys came in the house and two guys came out?"

"They won't." Erik squeezes my hand.

"The raspberry pi allows me to insert timed loops in the security camera feeds, from footage I recorded earlier," Dennis explains. "For example, right now, if security were to access the gym security camera, they'd see a loop of me jogging on the treadmill. We have about fifteen more minutes of that, until the lighting no longer matches current daylight."

I nod.

"My 'gym trainer' signed in at the walk-on security gate. This 'Dingle'"—he nods to Erik—"and Scraps drove through the main gate and checked in at the garage as two guys. The trainer changed into Erik's dry jumpsuit, put his workout clothes in the duffel, and became the new 'Dingle' back on the patio. Right now he and Scraps are checking out in the garage, then they'll drive around to a service exit where I have a blank loop going. No one will see the van stall there, until the new Dingle has his workout clothes back on, so he can double back across the lawn and check out via the walk-in gate. Three guys in, three guys out."

"So how does Erik leave the house?"

"Looping footage from your door all the way across the deck at dawn," Dennis says. "I took the liberty of recording fifteen minutes of each person sleeping in their room, so I'll be looping that too, in case security randomly checks in. But unless there's a major disturbance they generally stick to the common areas."

Erik's hand tightens on mine: We have until dawn.

"Yeah, yeah, Dennis, very clever. But can we talk about how *swole* you are?" Erik reaches out and pinches at the slight curve of bicep below Dennis' T-shirt sleeve. "You got jacked."

"Almost two pounds since camp!" Dennis does a half-joking, half-proud flex. "I'm benching one hundred and thirty now. What're you lifting these days? Cars?"

"These things aren't real." Erik looks down with an uncomfortable laugh. "They're just some weird chemical reaction. I've gained zero strength and lost overall mobility, not to mention IQ points. I'm very eager to, uh, deflate."

Dennis rubs his fingers together. "This is me playing the world's smallest violin. Chicks still dig them."

Erik bursts out laughing.

"Yeah, he's just a hunk of arm candy these days," I say. "But let's try and pit his remaining IQ points against Skye's phone anyway."

Dennis hands the dupe to him.

"*Wild*," Erik says, settling down on the bench, thumbs flashing over the screen.

"You can keep that," Dennis says quietly. "I've downloaded his email archive already, and he gave Jada some old Nokia burner to use, so honestly I feel like the creepy one when his texts come in."

"Wait, what? Skye gave Jada a burner?" Erik frowns. "Why?"

"She's running a honey trap operation." Dennis nods. "Since he started tampering with Signal's evidence."

Erik's gaze fastens on me, suddenly on high alert. "Skye did what now?"

"The thumb drive with the attic rant was stolen the day he came to visit. The footage was erased from the computer as well."

Erik scowls. "So Skye has the thumb drive?"

"If he hasn't destroyed it," Dennis says.

"He'd keep it." Erik bites at his nails. "Skye is very aware of opportunities to control other people, and it means too much to Signal—and Janeane—to just throw away. But it kind of surprises me, because he's not, uh, a tech guy. *At all.*"

"I got that from his email password," Dennis says. "Which, yes, is Password1234." Dennis' smartwatch emits a short beep. "We should get over to the home theater. We only have three minutes of treadmill loop left." Dennis rapid-fire taps on his laptop and a grid of camera feeds comes up.

"Home theater?" Erik frowns at me.

"See what you're missing?" I say, as lightly as I can. "Time for movie o'clock."

* * *

The movie is playing when we creep through the double doors: Judd Nelson, in a high school library, explaining how his dad gave him a pack of smokes for Christmas.

Erik laughs. "*The Breakfast Club?*"

Nobody is out of her seat the moment she hears Erik's voice. She gets an arm around his neck and is bearing down with a fierce noogie before the house lights even come up, Dennis calling, "HOLD FILM!"

Jada follows up the aisle after her with a bagged lunch.

"This is for you, Erik," she enunciates very clearly. "It's some food. In case you're hungry."

Erik replies the same way: "Thank you. For explaining food. Jada."

"Hey." She cuts me a look. "I just don't want to flip you into rage mode or whatever."

"I'm ninety-nine percent stable." Erik rifles through the bag. "And one percent angel."

"Oh man." Jada laughs. "I think all of us got stuck with some version of that shirt, back at camp."

"I always preferred the 'you all laugh because I'm different, I laugh because you're all the same,'" Dennis says, and Jada snorts laughing.

"I heard you had a reaction to the pills," Erik says quietly, pulling out a wrapped-up sandwich.

"Yeah, but it's all good now. Thanks to these hot weirdos—" She grins from me, to Dennis, to Nobody.

No Javier, though.

Erik peels back the wax paper and bites into the sandwich with a sigh of appreciation.

"Made by the Desais' private chefs." Jada sniffs. "Every meal is all catered and organic and whatnot. They even do room service—we can call down to the kitchen during Zoom class and order lunch."

"Lots of unexpected perks to a house arrest." I nudge Erik. He keeps chewing.

"How was FaceTiming with Skye today?" Dennis asks Jada, as we all walk to the very first row of the theater and each claim a buttery leather theater chair.

"Slimy," she says, leaning back in her seat. "He brought up Ledmonton Bank."

"How does he know about Ledmonton Bank?" I ask, surprised.

"I don't know." She shrugs. "But he asked if I'd heard about some trip up there and I was like 'nope, boring, yawn.'"

"Are they opening the security deposit box?" Dennis asks, and they all turn to hear my answer.

I know Aarush said this was strictly confidential. But clearly *he's* been leaking information to Skye. And this is Dennis. The person who literally made a helicopter fall out of the sky to save my life.

"Yeah. Tomorrow," I tell him.

Erik's eyes search mine. Then he draws his forearm roughly across his mouth and says, "Don't bother messing with Skye, Jada. Anything you get out of him you will pay for."

"He brings *you* up a lot," Jada says.

"I'm sure." Erik crumples up the sandwich paper and pushes the last bite into his mouth. His jaw works furiously; then he swallows and says, "Let me know the next time you're FaceTiming him, so I can break into his house and wring his neck."

"Well, hell." Nobody sits up in her theater seat. "That's not a bad idea."

"What?!" I cry.

"Easy." Nobody pats my shoulder. "I don't mean the neck wringing. I mean Erik breaking in and getting the thumb drive back."

Erik's dark eyebrows lift very high.

"It's not the worst idea," Dennis says. "Skye has a Destech security app, so he can check the security cameras at his Pacifica house on his phone. You could case the joint right now . . ." Dennis shows him how to pull up the quadrant of camera streams on the dupe phone, and as Erik pores over them a cold knot of dread forms in my chest.

"So many blind spots!" Erik grins.

"Please don't," I say quickly. "Please. It's too risky. If you were caught—"

CRACK. The back doors fly open, and a voice booms down the aisle:

"POLICE! FREEZE! PUT YOUR HANDS UP!"

I whip around to see Javier moving down the aisle, hands cupped around his mouth. They drop and reveal an angry smile.

Erik puts up a hand, nonchalant: "Nice to see you too, buddy."

"I *should* call the police," Javier goes on. "Except they wouldn't believe anyone would do something *this* dumb, sneaking into this house like a little bitch—"

"Javier, let me ask you something:" Erik lets his head fall back on the theater seat and meets Javier's cold stare with an irreverent smile. "Is it *possible* you are *so uncomfortable* dealing with strong emotions toward another male that you default to expressing them as anger? When they're actually concern? And perhaps, dare I say . . . brotherly affection?"

"You can save your little mind games for Signal." Javier glares at me until I meet his eyes, then asks coldly: "So you've been in contact with him this whole time?"

"Yeah, Javier, we're dating?"

"It's almost our seven-week anniversary," Erik adds, and even in the discomfort of staring down Javier, I do the mental math and realize he's right.

"You think this is funny?" Javier cries, a vein fluttering wildly in his neck. "I didn't agree to sneaking him in here. Did anyone else agree to this?"

"The fewer people who knew, the better," Dennis says.

"Yeah? Well, we'll *all* go to prison if he gets caught tonight. You get that, right?" Javier looks from Nobody to Jada. "You're ready to risk that, for a psychopath who won't do *anything* for us?"

"Between the private chef and personal movie theater, it seems like you're doing okay to me," Erik says.

"Camp is denying they ever sent us on murder missions. It's our word against theirs. If you turned yourself in to testify about camp and what the Director did to you, to all of us, that could *free us*. But no way you're doing that, right?" Javier sneers. "No, you're just sneaking in real quick to bang Signal—"

"Hey!" I gasp, but he steamrolls on.

"—and Peter Pan out the window, and if that gets the rest of us sent back to prison, oh well, right?"

"I'm handling the cameras." Dennis says. "If the tech wasn't airtight, he wouldn't be here. We have an exit plan."

"*All* his plans are exit plans. Signal, I can't believe you're even talking to him—" Javier cuts himself off, shakes his head. "When this whole time, you've been acting like we're *such good friends.*"

"Why would me dating Erik make us not friends?" I sputter.

"Because unlike you," Javier sneers, "I have some self-respect."

Erik is suddenly on his feet. Chemical reaction or not, his proximity makes Javier take a step back.

"Don't talk to her like that," Erik says quietly.

"Whoa, easy now." Javier regains his ground. "Signal, you need to put a choke collar on this thing."

Erik steps toward him, but Nobody catches his sleeve, knuckles shining as she pulls him back toward her.

"I want to talk about Kurt," Nobody says. "Not watch a cockfight."

"*Please.*" I look up at Erik.

"Yes. Agreed. Let's get down to business." Dennis gets to his feet. "We have the remaining runtime of *The Breakfast Club* until a loop of us watching a glowing screen ends and we have to clear Erik out of the theater. So, I officially call this meeting of the Teen Killers Club to order."

Javier's gaze finally disconnects from Erik. Jada is pulling on his sleeve, and he sits heavily in the chair beside her.

Erik, still standing, looks down at me, the hot pink that flooded his face in the last few minutes still receding, the vein in his temple standing out sharply. I take his hand, and his shoulders drop as he sits back down in the chair beside me.

"Someone is sabotaging Signal's case," Dennis begins. "One of our members is publicly racking up kills ahead of our trial. All of this will complicate shutting down camp and ending the Wylie-Stanton. Erik, maybe you could tell us what you know about Kurt?"

"Yes. Okay. Kurt." Erik leans forward, looking up and down the row. "As all of you know, Kurt and I were sent out on a mission—"

"To kill a bunch of people for headquarters, right?" Javier says. "Must have been an exciting day for you."

"Eh, it was more like when they sent you out to kill Signal." Erik smiles coldly. "Just a job. And it wasn't for headquarters. Targets came directly from the Director. Kurt drove us to where the first target lived, a town called Little Fern. We checked in at a hotel, and he called the Director shortly after dawn."

"Wait, hold on," Jada says. "If it was after dawn, the Director was already dead."

I turn to her, surprised.

"When he clicked the fob at me," she goes on, "I remember the sun was like, rising behind him. I'll never forget. Cause I had the thought, *this is the last thing you see*, and I was like, well . . . at least it's pretty. But then . . ." A dazzling smile spreads across her face. "Dennis came through. And the new recruits turned the Director into a pile of hot dogs."

"And Kate was tied to a chair," Nobody adds. "Gagged real good, too. She didn't talk to him."

"So that leaves Dave, right?" I say.

"Unless headquarters got hold of Kurt somehow?" Dennis frowns. "Do you remember someone calling his burner phone?"

"We didn't have burner phones. Kurt used the hotel phone to call a number the Director gave him," Erik says, "though the Director did say something about it being a 'last resort.'"

"Interesting." Dennis frowns. "Because if he wasn't using something super private, like a burner, the best alternative would be something super public, a number anyone might call from a hotel room, to hide in plain sight. Was there a code interface, at least?"

"I . . . don't remember things from then as well as I should." Erik's shoulders are very high. "But I remember Kurt listening to a recorded voice menu for a really long time. "

"So, the Director sent you two to one place, then *Dave* sent him to kill the girl in Bellingham?" Nobody cuts in.

"Or," Erik bites at his nails, "the girl from Bellingham was Kurt's own personal target. Because the girl, Donna, testified in—"

"The Storybook Murders," Nobody finishes.

"Which are?" Dennis looks at her.

"Why Kurt and Troy got sent to camp in the first place. Three girls they killed in high school." Nobody's voice is hard. "Their bodies were found in a condemned kiddie park called Storybook Village. All strangled, all hidden in the attractions. One in Sleeping Beauty's tower, one in Snow White's glass coffin, and one down Cinderella's wishing well."

"You've been looking up the case?" Erik sounds impressed.

"I'm in front of a screen all day for school." Nobody shrugs. "Beats more geometry proofs."

Jada has gone absolutely silent. When I look over at her theater chair, she's curled into herself like the top of a fiddlehead fern.

"You okay?" I ask her under my breath.

"Kurt and Troy killed three girls?" Jada asks the group, her brow furrowed.

"That they know of," Nobody says grimly.

"Hedonistic process killers," Dennis adds. "Remember?"

"No, I *don't* remember! I never asked!" Jada snaps. "What I remember is Princess Signal insisting we all needed a *fresh start*." She shoots me an accusatory look. "Just because she didn't want to admit she was a zero—"

"Yes. Okay. That's fair." My face heats. "I was afraid to admit I was innocent. But Kurt said he hadn't killed anybody either, back in Ledmonton. At least, he'd never killed anyone before his mission. Why would he lie to us about that? What was the point?"

There is a moment of quiet consideration; then Javier clears his throat and leans forward.

"One time in the boys' cabin, our first week, before you two came?" Javier looks from me to Nobody. "Troy made some joke about them double dating a girl named Donna, and Kurt got mad. *Real* mad, not just joking around mad. Like they were fighting on the floor and stuff."

"What led up to that?" Erik bites his nails.

"Hmm." Javier rubs at the scruff along his jawline. "Now that I think of it, they were talking about *you*, man. About you and Jada hooking up all that first week of camp, before more girls showed up."

Erik glares at him and Jada chokes back an outraged laugh.

"But that's the only time I heard them mention someone named Donna." Javier shrugs, then turns to Jada. "Can I leave now, or what?"

"Kurt is out there killing girls," Nobody says through clenched teeth. "If you have any other information—"

"I don't know what the hell Kurt is doing. And neither does he." Javier stares down Erik. "And if he did, he should go tell the police. Turn yourself in. Testify in Signal's case. She could use the help, too. If that matters to you at all."

The cords of Erik's neck are standing out from his jaw to his shoulder, but it's not until I see his hands, fisted tight, that I realize how close he is to losing it.

"But of course it doesn't." Javier gets to his feet. "You're here to get what you can and get out. And you just . . . let him." Javier looks at me with disgust. "So you know what, Signal? The next time someone asks, tell them I'm your ex. Because you and I are not friends."

Javier turns from us then and moves in momentous silence up the aisle and back through the double doors. Once they fall closed, Nobody leans in toward Jada.

"Troy never talked to you about his murders? At all?"

But Erik is not listening. He is staring at me like we're the only ones in the room, his jaw as clenched as his fists. I widen my eyes at him: *Yikes.*

It's more glib than I feel—I'm almost nauseous after Javier's remarks—but Erik's jaw softens. One reddened hand rubs at the back of his neck as he ducks his head down, his searchlight gaze breaking away and falling to the floor.

"We weren't together that long. A couple of days, not even," Jada says, then stops, and I realize she's barely holding back tears. "Guess I dodged a bullet, right? But I really . . . I really liked him. I didn't—I had no idea that . . . there must be something seriously wrong with me—"

"Nothing's wrong with you," I tell her firmly. "We *all* liked Troy. He was extremely likable."

"How else could he get all those girls to meet up with him in an abandoned kiddie park?" Nobody adds. "Donna must have testified against him and Kurt back in high school, and this was Kurt's revenge. Anybody know a site that might have transcripts from the trial and stuff?"

Erik looks up at me then, and we both smile.

* * *

Every aspect of my bedroom is making me nervous. While Nobody navigates Armchair.org, Erik peers around the blue dark of my room, lit only by the laptop screen and tiny blue LED fairy lights strung around my bedframe. He squints at the spines of my latest library stack: *Predators* by Anna Salter, *The Gift of Fear* by Gavin de Becker, and Sylvia Plath's *The Bell Jar*. He teases a page of my AP biology homework from the notebook on my desk to examine, stares at the *Unknown Pleasures* poster pinned up beside my desk, and even pinches my lilac duvet cover between two fingers, peering at it for a beat before smiling wickedly. When I give him a look, he steps closer to where I perch, at the edge of the bed, and leans down so his head is level with mine.

"Purple," he whispers in my ear, "is the color of sexual frustration."

"Excuse me?"

"Okay, here we go . . . ," Nobody says, and starts reading aloud the list of threads on the Storybook Murders: "Sadistic twin killers; fire alerts authorities to remains; Cinderella's wishing well glows in the dark from luminol; phished for girls online—no Donna coming up . . . wait, here we go—screengrab of Donna's page for Troy . . . ?"

She clicks on the last link and a wall of pictures of Troy comes up: at lunch in the sunshine scarfing French fries, face painted at a basketball game, sprawled out over the hood of an unimpressive car with a knowing smile.

Under the wall of images is the headline:

We Will Always "B" Here for Troy!

"A couple of these are definitely Kurt." Erik sets a fingertip, nail bitten to the quick, on a supposed Troy playing guitar.

Nobody reads Donna's statement aloud:

"'My boyfriend Troy is the kindest, funniest, best guy I've ever known. I testified in court that he was WITH ME every time one of his alleged victims disappeared. But the jury still found him guilty of homicide! Now Troy is serving a life sentence for a crime *I know for a fact* he did not commit, and is not allowed to appeal, because his brother KURT is a Class A! Troy's parents shared THIS PICTURE of Troy's Wylie-Stanton results with me; he is a Class B!!! And as such should be allowed the right to appeal!!!

"Sign this petition & help us bring Troy home!'"

"Huh." Erik blinks at the screen. "Donna was actively campaigning to get them released."

"Huh," Nobody agrees, leaning back in her chair. "Let's see what she said at the trial."

Erik navigates to the Armchair.org transcripts archive folder, and Nobody hunkers down over the finely spaced text before searching Donna's name. Dozens of yellow highlighted boxes light up along the page.

"Says here," Nobody's finger drags along the screen, "Donna testified, under oath, that she and Troy were playing putt-putt golf until eleven PM the night of the first murder. Then she said they were watching Netflix until three AM the night of the second. And they spent the whole night together when the third victim disappeared. Giving him an alibi for all three murders."

"Why didn't the jury believe her?" I ask.

"There were no social media images of them together on those nights," Erik says, "though she habitually documented their dates. Prosecution claimed she was lying to protect her boyfriend. She said Troy just happened to be feeling camera shy."

"*Camera shy?*" I pull a face. "Didn't Troy take a picture of his butt with Dave's phone?"

"Quite so, Watson," Erik says, the side of his mouth twitching. "But what I find most interesting is the modus operandi. In all the Storybook strangulations, the marks left behind indicated the victim died face to face with her killer. You remember how Troy watched Jada's face, during color wars?"

My stomach twists. "You're saying . . . they liked to watch girls die?"

"Watching someone die is the whole point for a process killer," Erik says casually, like this is common knowledge. "They kill to *possess*, to have complete power over someone. Like Bundy said, 'a person in that situation is God.'"

"I sure wish a trash truck would've swept these two jokers to Kingdom Come before they got to high school," Nobody mutters.

"Sure. But if we go back to the coroner's report on Kurt's kills—" Erik's shaking fingers twitch across the trackpad. "He can't seem to kill someone face to face. He tried strangling Donna but apparently couldn't finish. What he ended up doing with her, and has gone on to do with all the others, is get their back against his chest and slash their throat—"

I quickly look away from the image he pulls up: Kurt's second victim, the cashier at their hotel in Little Fern, face down in a pool of red. When camp's card was declined at checkout, she'd tried to call the police. Kurt had snuck up on her while she was dialing the phone.

"And if he can't turn them away, he cuts out the eyes," Erik goes on, Nobody nodding along.

"Like with the chemical wholesaler—"

I look away as another photo fills the screen. "How did he know a chemical wholesaler?"

"Don't know. Wholesaler's name doesn't come up in connection with Storybook," Nobody says. "And she'd recently moved to NorCal from Arizona, so no hometown connection."

"I don't understand." I look up at Erik. "The wholesaler seems like an obvious camp target, but camp is fully under investigation. We know they're not funding Kurt, because his card was declined. All the kill switches were disabled—he watched the stream, so he knows that too. So why take out targets for camp, unless it's . . ."

"For fun?" Erik offers.

"But he's *not* having fun, like you said." Nobody frowns at Erik. "He didn't get in on Dog Mask that time. He doesn't *like it*, you know?" She holds his gaze, and I lean away from them, back on my elbows. "My take on the eyes is that he was doing something ugly in a hurry. Like he was told to make a mess."

Erik sinks onto the bed beside me with a big sigh, and my body tilts toward the sudden weight, rolls so close our shoulders momentarily brush, and I flood with panic. It's too surreal, halfway between a dream and a nightmare, to have Erik actually be here sitting on my bed. To have his arm casually brushing mine, like that's our normal when we could barely touch before, and then, simultaneously, to have to focus on these senseless murders.

I jerk away from him before my brain fully breaks—too fast: my stitches scream in protest.

"Dave is the most likely person to call these targets," Erik says. "But Dave was putting out a real 'last day at the office' vibe in your stream, Signal. Why would he risk getting caught up in the investigation now, supplying targets to Kurt, when he clearly wants out of camp himself?"

I remember Dave pocketing Clif bars in the pantry after he'd dragged me in from the girls' cabin.

"I wish they would hurry up and identify the fourth victim." Erik yawns then, stretching his arms out until a pale strip of abdomen appears above his jeans. I sit up abruptly and shift back to the edge of the bed.

"Fourth victim?" I clear my throat, addressing Nobody. "I thought there were only three victims: Donna, the hotel clerk, and the chemical wholesaler."

"This one turned up yesterday," Nobody pulls up a news page: an unidentified body was found near Bridgewood. The city right next to my hometown of Ledmonton. "In her thirties, but no positive ID yet. On account of her head's still missing."

"Kurt, Kurt, Kurt." Erik bites at his nails. "What're you up to, buddy?"

"Nothing good." Nobody pulls her knee up to her chest and rests her chin on it. "What about the thumb drive? When are you going to go get it?"

"He's not doing that," I say quickly, looking to Erik. His forearm angles across his face, hiding his expression. "It's too dangerous."

"He broke in here okay," Nobody points out.

"Signal's afraid I'm going to kill Skye." Erik lifts his forearm and stares me down. "That's the issue, isn't it? Because I scared you so bad last time."

"I mean—I just—" I don't know what to say.

"So what if he does?" Nobody scowls at me. "I'd say Erik's within his rights, considering Skye drove their parents into a cliff."

Erik freezes, arm still in midair, like he's just heard some distant explosion. I freeze too, and the silence between us goes on so long Nobody turns around in the chair, sees my face, and instantly realizes what's happened.

"It's late. I'm getting tired," she says quickly, standing. "You guys have a good night."

She flashes me a look of abject apology before she closes the door. But even after she's gone, Erik continues to stare at some indeterminate point in the air, like words are hanging in the dark only he can read.

"Erik—"

"Skye didn't kill my parents," he says quickly. "He's a psycho, but he's a self-serving psycho. My mom bought his act, she always took his side, why would he—" He stops. "I don't think you have means, motive, and opportunity with Skye. What would the means even be?"

"He was a stunt driver, right?" I say quietly. "He wanted to crash cars for a living. Taking his chances on a hard turn makes more sense than someone figuring out how to cut the brake lines."

"Still no motive." Erik shakes his head. "My mom chose him, always. She was his biggest supporter and the one in the family holding the purse strings."

"Now he's holding the purse strings. He owns the Wylie-Stanton algorithm, which has a big government contract. And a substantial share of CurtPro."

Erik keeps shaking his head, face stiff, refusing to look at me. "It's not just money, though. Skye would always have money, but my mom—you don't understand. She was the smartest, funniest—and *good*, like, a completely good person. And she *chose him*." The corners of his mouth are twitching down. "She *always* chose him. Who would give that up?"

"A nice guy, maybe?" I say softly. "Especially if his little brother was about to expose his sexual misconduct. And then your mom would've realized how she'd misjudged him."

He turns glittering eyes on mine, and his bottom lip jerks. "So it's *my* fault."

"No, Erik, that's not—"

"That's what you're saying. He killed them so I couldn't tell on him."

"Erik, no."

Erik sits up, but he can't seem to stand. He falls back on the bed and turns away from me, his broad shoulders tensing. Like he's hiding from me. I reach out and set my hand against his back, and realize Erik is sobbing.

"No, no, no." I wrap my arm around his side. "I'm sorry, Erik, I'm so sorry . . ."

He turns to face me, then crumples around me like a car on impact. His cheek is wet against mine, chest tensed like he's bracing for a punch, body racked by sobs he's fighting with all his strength to keep down.

"I'm sorry you lost your mom and dad," I say against his neck.

He lets out something between a cry and a laugh, and shakes his head.

"You're the first person who's ever said that to me." His voice is very deep and tight. "At the funeral, Ledrick took me out of the receiving line. He said no one believed that I . . . I hate crying, okay? It only makes things worse . . ." He passes his hand over his face. "No one believed I was sad. All their friends thought, they *still* think . . ."

"And if you'd cried, they would have said you were faking," I say quietly.

"Exactly! *Exactly.*"

"Every time I cried at Rose's trial, they said I was 'trying to manipulate the jury.' And when I didn't cry, I 'had no remorse.' You can't prove yourself to people who hate you. So. Cry all you want, or not. You've got nothing to prove to me."

He takes my hand, and runs his thumb along the back of it for a long time. Then he lets out a deep sigh, his muscles releasing.

"Why didn't you tell me before?" he says at last.

"It never seemed like the right time. And you seemed ready to kill him anyway—"

"I am going to kill him."

"No, you're not." I grip his shoulder. "Stop playing into his hands—"

"How does killing him play into his hands?" He rolls his glistening eyes.

"Because it would be the thing that finally destroys you, the real you, *my* Erik. I won't allow it, alright? Skye *deserves* to be exposed for what he is. It's not fair, that he's—he's running CurtPro Pharmaceuticals, and cashing checks off the Wylie-Stanton, and living in his *mansions*, after all he's done! While insisting *you* get hunted down like an animal! It's so wrong it makes me sick."

Though the room is dark I feel his eyes burning into me.

"But if you kill him, he wins," I go on. "He wins, because you *prove him right.*"

It takes a long beat for him to speak, and when he does, his voice is dripping with sarcasm.

"I know you're a five-foot-tall sentient lollipop, but if you're counting on the good guys winning here, you don't know the story we're in. I'm not some cursed prince, Signal. All of that—CurtPro, the mansions, the 'checks off Wylie-Stanton'—that exists because *I am the bad guy.* So Skye, and everyone else getting those checks, will make sure I *stay* the bad guy—"

"Erik, listen to me." I clutch his hoodie. "My lawyer looked into your conservatorship. Skye is not your conservator, alright? Whoever holds the position of director of camp is. So unless camp is dissolved, Skye can't touch you."

He stops for a moment, considering.

"Okay, but then if I testify against camp and it 'dissolves,' I'm under Skye's conservatorship again."

"Or a next of kin," I say quickly. "Surely there's someone in your family who could qualify, an aunt or uncle, a cousin even. *Anyone . . . ?*"

"Skye is the only family member who doesn't think I killed my parents." The saddest smile flickers across his face. "And now I know why."

My heart incinerates.

"You remember the reporter Aarush wanted us to talk to," I try again. "The chancer guy? I met him. He's writing about the history of the Wylie-Stanton. And he wanted to talk to you, as a protected source. You wouldn't even have to turn yourself in—"

"But you *want* me to turn myself in," he says, annoyed.

"Yes," I admit. "You know I do. It would really help our friends."

He tenses, about to make some reply, when the door flies open, and I wince from the flood of bright light. Javier is looming over the bed, a queasy expression on his face as he lunges toward the still-teary Erik.

"Enough is enough, man." Javier grabs Erik's collar. "Time to go—"

Erik's eyes lose all expression. Any control he had before is gone. Before I can cry out, he's on his feet and Javier is tumbled backwards into my desk, the laptop sliding off its stand, my homework washing across the floor.

"Finally," Javier cries. "An excuse."

"*Stop!*" I hiss, but it's too late now. I just have to try and get Javier out alive.

Erik flashes forward, striking like a snake, and Javier wheezes as the air goes out of him, face momentarily unrecognizable from pain. Still recovering, Javier throws out a powerful right hook. Erik dodges and continues the momentum straight forward, knocking Javier against the wall with a hollow thud that lands in the pit of my stomach.

My Joy Division poster crumples, rips from its pins, and floats to the floor as footsteps hurry up the stairs and down the hall toward us, the slap of security's hard-soled shoes unmistakable.

"Stop! Stop!" I hiss, panicking.

Erik's hand is wrapped around Javier's face, pressing his head against the wall. Javier is punching wildly at Erik's side, connecting hard each time, though Erik barely seems to notice.

Knocking rattles my door.

"Under the bed!" I try with all my might to pull Erik away from Javier.

"What's going on in there? Signal!" Aarush calls.

It's Aarush's voice that finally registers. Erik sinks under the bed as Javier and I stare at each other in the middle of my trashed room.

"Signal! Open this door at once!"

"Take off your shirt," Javier says, voice low and rough, unzipping his own hoodie.

No. I curse him out under my breath, scanning the room, trying desperately to think of another way to explain the mess as I pull my sweatshirt off, but we're out of time. He picks me up and braces my back against the wall just as Aarush yells, "We're coming in!"

As the light snaps on, Javier's face meets mine. I try to turn my head away, to fake it, but he doesn't let me. He grabs my chin and holds me in place as he kisses me hard, enjoying it way too much, though he knows Erik can see. *Because* he knows Erik can see. And I hate him for it. I hate him with all my heart, as we passionately kiss up against the wall.

Chapter Seven
The Penthouse

Aarush clears his throat, and Javier at last pulls back, letting me slide down onto my feet.

Aarush's face has the fullness of deep sleep, but it's getting sharper every moment as he surveys the scene. Javier and me against the wall, the torn poster, the fallen homework.

The security guard behind him steps farther out into the hall, talking fast into his headset mic; my friends' faces bob in and out of the doorframe.

"It is almost midnight. We're up in less than six hours." Aarush's voice is acid. "Tomorrow is the most important day of your life, Signal. And you're spending tonight doing *this?*"

I stare straight down, terrified to even glance at my bed.

"I guess you can take the girl out of the trailer park," Aarush sneers, "but you can't take the trailer park out of the girl."

I don't care, I don't care, let him think whatever he wants, as long as he leaves without checking under my bed.

"Javier, get out of here. All of you—" He turns to the others, gathered around my door. "Back to your rooms at once. Signal, go to sleep," he says, and hits the light.

I don't look up until Javier has moved past me. I don't exhale until the door clicks shut. Then I stumble to the bed and drop to the floor, sitting with my back against my lilac duvet in the ruined dark.

Am I supposed to apologize to Erik? Because I didn't ask for any of that. Does he understand how much I did not want any of that? Even if I had to act like I did? I don't know if I can make this better for him when I'm still choking on rage about it myself.

Finally, I reach under the bed. In the dark, his hand takes mine without hesitation.

That's when I start crying.

The door clicks open, the blue LED lights a tiny galaxy in Dennis' glasses.

"Just started loops from here to the deck," he whispers. "You have four minutes."

Erik's shape moves from under the bed as soundlessly as vapor. He's past Dennis and out of the room before I can get to my feet.

I stare down the hall as he disappears, listening to his footsteps hurrying down the stairs and up through the breezeway, fading across the deck and into silence. I slide down against the wall outside my room, ending up in a heap on the floor of the hall.

He's gone. He's safe. It's a relief. It's hell.

Javier's door opens down the hall. He comes out, still in his undershirt, and stares down at me until I finally look up at him.

"He did the same thing to me, back in Ojai," Javier gloats. "So now we're even."

My chest drowns in heat. I'm on my feet, but Jada is faster. I hadn't noticed her coming out of her room, but now she's slamming her fist into Javier's chest like she's holding a knife.

"What the hell is your problem?" Jada shrieks.

"We were just faking, Jada, get a grip." Javier tries to grab her wrists, but she rips them away, breathing hard. "Just like when you talk to Skye all night."

"*Faking!*" Jada's eyes go dark. "I'm not talking about the kissing, idiot, I'm talking about you going in there and acting like you own her! That wasn't fake! You think you own her! *You think you own her!*"

Jada, more beautiful and terrifying than I have ever seen her, lunges at him. She shoves Javier, who is a good head taller than she is, almost off his feet. She's about to lunge at him again when Dennis' hand lands on her shoulder. She whips around, still furious, sees him, and bursts into tears.

Dennis, his voice low, lets her collapse against him, then deftly leads her back to her room.

"Wait—Jada! Jada, what the hell was that?" Javier follows after her, but it's too late. Her door closes after them, and we hear the lock click. Javier turns to me, bewildered. "Signal, can you talk to her? See what's gotten her back up—"

"No. You were right," I cut him off. "We're not friends."

And I close the door hard on whatever he's about to say next.

* * *

Aarush is still bristling when I meet him in the elevator, wearing my head-to-toe black sweats. He makes no greeting as the elevator takes us to the garage; he only says, once we're in sight of a gleaming red Aston Martin, "There's no eating or drinking in my car."

I put my full paper cup of green tea in the trash without argument. But he still seems to shudder as I slide into the caramel leather passenger seat, as though my trailer-park essence might enter the grain by osmosis. I hug myself as small as I can beside him.

"Play classical list," Aarush tells his phone as we pull out of the garage.

And that is the last thing either of us says, all the way to the airport.

Luckily, Honor is already on board the Destech private jet. She absorbs Aarush's attention while I bundle my hoodie under my head and pretend to sleep. But as we reach LA airspace, the sunlight turns the inside of my eyelids the color of orange juice, and I sit up and stare out the window as we land, watching a smiling mosaic of red tile roofs and aqua blue pools tilt below us. Los Angeles looks impossibly happy from a distance.

It takes us almost three hours to get from the airport to the hotel downtown where Mary Larland is waiting. When we finally arrive, Aarush all but sprints through the lobby. I pause a moment to take it in, overwhelmed: the floors are black marble, the walls stone carved in the style of ancient Mayan stelae, white flowers dripping from tall golden vases. The lobby is populated with very tanned people, many of whom seem vaguely familiar, like I've maybe seen them on TV; they lounge on low couches and frown at their phones, unimpressed by the opulence.

"Signal! Let's *go!*" Aarush shouts from the private elevators. Everyone turns to look as I duck my head down and hurry after him, face going red. I don't look up until he's ushered me and Honor to the double doors of the penthouse suite; the entire floor has been rented out for the filming.

I'm struck by a jacket of brilliant puce: Cassie's blazer, her back to us, deep in conversation with a short woman with a giant strawberry blonde bob. I know it's Mary Larland before I see her face; the hair is iconic enough. She's been Very Concerned on prime time longer than I've been alive. When I do see her famous face at last, I'm surprised at her anxious expression, totally unlike her TV persona. But when her eyes land on me and Aarush, she breaks into her familiar smile.

"Signal Deere!" Mary Larland shakes my hand. "It's a pleasure."

Behind her, several men are setting up giant lights on tall stands, throwing sandbags at their bases to keep them upright, taping blackout curtains over the panoramic view of downtown LA. Nestled between the stage lights are two cozy leather chairs, a table of candle holders without candles, a sweep of maroon organza. An intimate setting superimposed on the starkly minimalist hotel suite.

"Mary's team is prepared to do the full hour-long with you today, Signal!" Cassie gushes, waving at the set. "Can you believe it?"

"People want to hear from you, young lady!" Mary wags a finger at me. Then her voice shifts into Very Concerned mode: "Your resilience has inspired so many of my viewers. And you really haven't had a chance to share that journey."

"My journey is whatever. What I'd like to talk about is the importance of ending the Wylie-Stanton."

"Sounds like a solid angle to me," Greg Ballas says, landing between me and Aarush. There are a few croissant crumbs in his beard, but he gives me a real smile.

"Mary, have you met Greg Ballas?" Aarush says. "A brilliant journalist I very much admire."

"Ballas?" Mary smiles at him blankly. "I don't think I've had the pleasure—"

Cassie whispers something in her ear and she starts, turning to Cassie. "Oh, that was very controversial, wasn't it?"

"Well, I hate to break up the party, but they need this one in wardrobe!" Cassie says, making a show of looking at her smartwatch. "Follow me, Signal—"

Cassie leads me to a woman all in black with purple spiky hair and a headset. She scans my body with the business-first gaze of a mortician before offering a selection of hangers to Cassie. Cassie points out a plaid skirt and black blazer.

"And for her hair and makeup?"

"I usually do like—" I start, but Cassie interrupts.

"Keep it natural. Do what you can to soften the hair, make it more schoolgirl, less e-girl. I know our time is limited."

"Got it." The woman with purple hair nods and hands me my chosen wardrobe before pointing me down the hall.

Once I'm changed, more stylists come and tailor the seams in closer to my waist with safety pins. A bib is tucked around my neck and I'm led to a director's chair, where a hyper-focused man takes a straightener from a leather holster and starts styling my hair.

I pull my phone out and angle the screen so he can't see it before checking my drafts. Nothing new yet. So I start:

Erik, I am so sick and sad about how things went down last night. I couldn't sleep after you left, thinking about the way you found out about Skye. And the stuff with Javier. Obviously, that was not a reflection of what I wanted or how I feel, I just didn't know what else to do. But knowing you had to watch still makes me sick & please tell me if you're mad.

I'm about to paste this from my notes app to my drafts, when the draft folder bolds:

Last night probably could have gone better. Glad I got to see you though.

I almost laugh out loud, and close the note before writing back:

Last night was ROUGH. Where are you? Are you okay?!

Erik writes:

In LA still just wrapped pick-up shots

I frown.

I'm in LA too!!! Oh yeah, I never got to ask, how did Nadya's video thing go?

My hairstylist's assistant has enough time to go get drinks and come back before his response pops up.

It was a long day. But it paid well.

I type back:

So are you guys friends now?

Another pause, then:

Yeah I'd say so. She's cool.

Cool. *Cool.* Why is that the worst thing he could have said?

So what did you do in the video? Wear a T-shirt with her name on it?

Another long pause. To the point where I almost send a row of question marks, but then:

More or less.

There's a knot in my stomach, but I hear Honor approaching and darken my screen.

"Getting close now!" Honor squeezes my shoulders. "This is where your case truly starts, Signal. We've got two paralegals on-site at Ledmonton Bank. They'll alert us the moment the security box is opened. Depending on what's inside, Janeane's counsel could try and plea out by end of day. Cassie has some statements prepared for the Larland thing I'm about to look over. We'll obviously refrain from getting too specific, but we *can* use the words bombshell, breakthrough, and game-changer."

Honor's phone goes off and her eyes widen. I recognize the Oregon area code as she pivots away from my makeup chair.

I pull out my phone again, my drafts folder bolding with a new message:

How is the "big day" going?

"What?!" Honor cries, voice so sharp even Mary Larland's head snaps in her direction. Honor puts her finger in her ear and paces, head down, talking fast in a hushed voice, striding back and forth across the pearly silk carpet.

In another moment she lands in front of Aarush, her voice low and fast. He leans in, then staggers back, his huge eyes going wider still.

"Empty?" Aarush's cry silences the room. "What do you mean it's *empty*?"

"The lockbox?" I stand, pulling the bib from around my throat, my stomach a balloon of ice water. "Jaw's lockbox is empty?"

"But we can still do the sit-down, right?" Cassie looks to Mary.

"About *what*?" Aarush says.

"Well—" Mary's grimace is back. "Signal's fears about being sent back to prison?"

The balloon of ice water breaks. Coldness shoots through my veins, all the way to the ends of my fingertips. The room falls away, all the people in black blurring into shadow, the walls of the penthouse fading into dark. All of it an illusion, a thin projection, playing forever on the wall of the black shed, where I still am. Where I will always be.

"You didn't think you could get away that easy, did you?" Rose whispers.

I realize I'm heaving over the toilet only when my reflection goes still in the water below. Nothing came up, I was already empty. When I step out into the hall the crew members walk around me like water moving around a rock in a stream, their eyes straight ahead. The crew is now striking the lights they had just set up, a man in a Patagonia vest and baseball hat talking with Mary intently. When her eyes meet mine, they immediately bounce away again.

"Hey." Greg's hand closes on my shoulder. "I understand if now is not the best time to talk. But you can always reach me at this email." He presses a card in my hand. "Because trust me: this fight isn't over."

Of course it's not over. Does everyone else think it's over?

Is it over?

I float down the hall, toward the kitchen suite, where Aarush's voice is going back and forth with Honor's.

"You're telling me Jaw came in and emptied the security deposit box this morning and nobody stopped him?"

"We've found the community to be . . . extremely antagonistic. Local PD has essentially made themselves part of Janeane's counsel. The DA practically ran on Girl From Hell and is terrified it'll be overturned. And look at *this*—" She hands him her phone. "Janeane's holding a press conference in Ledmonton. Someone on the force tipped her off."

"Or one of the maniacs living at my house."

"If one of Signal's friends had a hand in this, they're being played. Because if we can't exonerate Signal, they lose the only surviving camper willing to back up their claim against camp—"

If they can't exonerate me.

A tinny voice playing off a phone becomes blaringly loud. Aarush has turned the volume all the way up, and now Janeane's teary voice claws through me:

". . . want to thank everyone who's been holding me up during this difficult time. A few weeks ago, I was brutally attacked in my own home and lost my husband to Class A violence. I will never recover from the mental and physical wounds. But the hardest thing to take is the accusation that I could ever, *ever* have hurt my precious daughter, Rose. An accusation that has won Signal Deere supporters from the very naive and the very cynical. But not from *anyone* in our community. Not *one person* has come forward to defend her."

I curl in on myself against the cold wall.

"Because *we* know Signal Deere," Janeane continues. "We know she's a sick, broken individual who has been influenced by some of the most dangerous and volatile Class As in our country. And my hope, my prayer, is that we can protect others from Class A influence. We deserve a world where no one is a victim, like Rose, or a cowardly accomplice, like Signal—"

A talking head interjects, and the volume goes back down.

"'Class A influence,' what does that even mean? Why is that term suddenly everywhere?" Aarush snaps.

"It was in the camp files recovered after the stream." Honor sighs. "One of the campers wasn't a Class A but was marked as 'Class A influenced.' Protectionists are having a field day speculating. And I'm guessing it's how the prosecution plans to sidestep Signal's actual Wylie-Stanton score at her retrial. Damn, damn, damn . . ." I've never heard Honor sound so tense. "The attic rant is gone. Whatever was in the security deposit box is gone. Jaw himself is nowhere to be found. This case is starting to boil down to Signal's word against the mother of the victim. And we all know how that went last time."

I slowly back away from the kitchen and down the hall. I don't stop until I'm through the penthouse's double doors and out in the dim empty quiet of the hotel hall.

Standing there, trying to catch my breath, black lace fans across my eyes, my field of vision popping and snapping with thin dark threads. I move one foot in front of the other down the telescoping hall, not sure where I'm headed except away. Through the shifting lace a door stands open at the very end of the hall, and I go toward it.

Fire stairs?

I pull the heavy door closed behind me and stare down. Under a single fluorescent bar, concrete steps lap back and forth into darkness.

I bet they go all the way down to the lobby.

I pull up the drafts thread again and answer his previous message:

"Big day" could probably be going better. Where are you?

Instantly, he replies with an address and:

come here

I'm down the stairs and sprinting through the lobby. Icy air that tastes like expensive perfume gives way to the thick, hot air of downtown Los Angeles as I run out into the street.

Here the people are no longer beautiful and well-dressed but bowed under the sun and scowling, sunlight thick as honey streaming between slabs of blue shadow across four lanes of racing traffic.

The wheeze of pneumatic brakes pulls my attention to a long red bus shimmying to its stop. I sprint to catch it, thin ballet flats dodging piles of unidentifiable muck and stomped-flat roaches. Without even knowing where it's going, I get on.

Some kind of air filtration device is droning overhead as I take a seat at the way back. It almost drones out the constant alerts from my phone, now Aarush has caught on that I'm missing. I fire back:

Felt sick back soon battery low.

Then I turn off my phone.

It's slow going through downtown traffic. I use the time to navigate the bus routes posted overhead and figure out where I am in relation to Erik's address without turning my phone back on.

I get out at a CVS halfway there, starting to glow white and red against the burning sunset. I spend the rest of my cash on a disguise: a giant black Hollywood sweatshirt large enough to wear like a dress, opaque black tights, slip-on white sneakers, wraparound sunglasses, and a Dodgers hat. A pack of makeup wipes, vanilla lip balm and cinnamon mints, and one last item it takes all my bravery to buy.

The expensive TV clothes I cram into the bathroom trash.

* * *

Hollywood is as depressing and beautiful at once as a place can be. You can tell it was built by people dreaming about everywhere else, the original apartments dressed up like split-timber cottages, Spanish missions, and ancient Egyptian temples. There are more LED billboards in three blocks than I've seen in my entire life, their sterile glow warmed up by the neon curlicues buzzing around marquee after marquee. White marble stars under my feet honor every famous dead actor I've ever heard of, when they aren't covered up by nameless heaps of living humans.

The address Erik gave me belongs to a giant construction site, something I figure out only after circling it twice. I stare up at the half-finished skyscraper; it has to be at least twenty stories high, each of its exposed beams twinkling with streamers of silver like some strange Christmas tree. It's enclosed by a chain-link fence that's draped with dark green netting.

"How the hell do I get in?" I mutter to myself.

A deep voice answers, "Follow me."

Erik's dark silhouette is on the other side of the fence across from me.

"I saw you coming from, like, halfway down the street." He laughs, excited. "One of the many advantages of staying at the future Ritz-Carlton Hollywood."

"Is it really?" I say, following him along the chain link.

"I have no idea. There's some kind of legal dispute going on with the site, no one's actually worked on it in like two years. Here, this way . . ."

The fence runs into the side of an automated parking lot, its metal gapping. He pulls it open further, I wiggle through, and in another moment, he's holding me.

The smell of rain, the warmth of his chest, the gentle rock as he hugs me. These things are real, and while they are real, I can't despair completely.

"Thanks for dropping by." I feel him grin against my neck. "How long do we have until the police get here?"

"I kept my phone off since our last draft and changed clothes before I switched buses," I say into his shoulder. "We might have two whole hours."

"I'll take it."

He leads me to an upright crane that runs the height of the skyscraper. From it hangs a coffin-sized milk crate. He pulls up its plastic grate door and waves into the cell.

"Ladies first."

I get into the construction elevator first, and Erik pulls the door down behind us, then steps past me to reach into a nest of cables. He hits a switch, pulls a lever, and the car lurches upwards with a high, alarming whine and a roller-coaster clatter of gears. Usually an elevator is enclosed; this one is not. We're being hoisted up through the air by the crane, with only a red plastic grid between my feet and the headstone-gray ground below, falling away faster every moment. The horizon rolls and swells out the higher we rise, wind pulling through the plastic harder and harder the farther we climb, rattling our little cage until the gears shriek in protest. Unbothered, Erik adjusts another lever to brake, turns off the switch, and throws the door open.

"Welcome to my penthouse!" he announces.

There are no walls, just the bright steel beams that will one day brace them and a floor of rough cement; it looks like a fun house mirror maze without the glass. There are dim work lights every ten feet, so I can just make out a sleeping bag anchored by pieces of brick. It's huddled up against a short stretch of unpainted particle board he must have brought up to fend off the wind, which rolls through the open beams in waves.

The view is one of the most amazing things I've ever seen. Below us the sweep of the city zooms out into a glowing galaxy of red and white freeways and golden streetlight supernovas. Compared to the ground, the constellations above are just pinpricks that barely register through the sky's purple haze. Los Angeles outshines the stars.

"It's better than stars. I like it better, at least." I drift closer to the edge, where the cement gives way to night. "They always say, every star you see could already be burned out a million years ago. But every light down there is a sign of life."

"Or it's a streetlight." Erik gently pulls me back toward him. "Careful, the wind is really strong this high."

I nod and turn to him. And with a surge of panic, I take the final CVS item and shove it into his hands.

Erik stares down at the three-pack box of condoms for a long moment, spots of color rising in both his cheeks, then looks up at me, bright green eyes very wide.

"Way to wine and dine me, Signal."

It's worse than when he threw me in the lake.

"Forget it," I mutter, horrified, and try to grab the box.

But he snatches it away, leaping back with a wild laugh.

"Hey, hey, no take-backsies!" His gaze is an electric current; I can't meet it. I turn away but he spins me back toward him, his hands hot and shaky. "That was not a rejection, by the way. Not in any way, shape, or form, alright? I just—" I watch him as he looks from the box, to me, to the sleeping bag on the cement floor. "I'm *surprised*. But it's a good surprise, it's a very good surprise! You've *swept me off my feet*, Signal!"

"Shut up," I mumble, mortified.

His arm goes around me then, and I hold still. Too still, I guess, because he tilts my chin back with a look of concern, like he's trying to read my face. My eyes slide away, cheeks burning unbearably. He keeps staring until finally I meet his gaze, and then the tears come.

"Signal," he says gently. "What happened?"

I push away from him, crying harder now because I'm so angry I'm crying.

"Aren't you supposed to, like, always want to do this? No matter what, as soon as I say?"

"No, actually," he says, the spots of pink growing. "Not if you're in the middle of a nervous breakdown."

"Wow!" I blink at him. "Well, you figured it out, Sherlock. I'm going through something, and I just wanted out of my head for a while, okay! But you're not in the mood so, whoops, just kidding. I need to go—"

"Now now now," he says quietly, catching the sleeve of my sweatshirt and pulling me back into him. He catches a strand of my hair and tucks it behind my ear. "I can't take the suspense. Tell me what's wrong."

"I'm going back to prison, okay?!" I sob. "There was nothing in the security deposit box! They opened it up, and there was nothing in there, and now everyone's decided I'm a bad bet. Because it's just my word against Janeane's now, and why would anyone believe trailer trash!"

The wind pours through the steel tower, and Erik shifts us so he's taking the worst of it, his back to the open starry horizon, me huddled against him, unable to stop crying. But he doesn't seem to mind. He strokes my hair slowly, arms tight around me, letting me cry.

"Sometimes, in solitary," I whisper, "sometimes I started thinking I was still in the shed? Like everything around me was . . . just a projection, just some weird movie playing over the darkness I was floating in. The dark was the only thing that was real. Because I had died with Rose, and I was watching myself from hell."

"Seduction complete," Erik says gruffly, and I laugh before I can stop myself. "No, seriously, you've convinced me. Enough chitchat." And there's a heat in his voice that makes me shiver as his face lowers to mine. "I'll get you out of that head alright."

And that's when all the LED billboards start flickering behind him. All of them at once glitching, ads pixelating and washing into digital snow at the exact same time.

Then they all fade into the same clip of footage: a girl with blue hair, passionately kissing a young man with one torn green eye, the top of his face hidden by a ski mask as she presses a stun gun into his throat.

Blue CGI lightning haloes around them and then, after far too long, the kiss fades to white with OUTLAWS in red blood spatter font, and below it:

NADYA 12.10

Because, of course, it's Nadya.
It's Nadya kissing Erik.

Chapter Eight
The Proposal

～

I stare, open-mouthed, as the title glitches out and the kiss begins again.

I stagger back from Erik. He reaches out, but I bat him away. "Don't touch me!"

"What? Why? Did I do something?" He actually sounds scared.

"You kissed Nadya!"

Confused, he follows my gaze to the sea of LED billboards across the intersection and all of Hollywood, playing the kiss again in high res and slow motion, blue-bright screens as large as stadium fields broadcasting the evidence on a loop.

It's worse every time I see it. The first time was excruciating, and each loop is like a thumb jammed into an open wound.

"Signal—" Erik starts.

"Get away from me!" I turn and hurry through the steel beams, toward the elevator, but he's much faster. He grabs my shoulders and spins me to face him, pinning me up against the unpainted particle board.

"We. Were. Acting."

I laugh in his face, laugh so hard it's almost a sob.

"How is that"—he points behind us with one hand, the other still anchoring me in place—"any different than what you and Javier did?"

"Javier wasn't wearing an Erik costume! We weren't on billboards! And I didn't *hide it from you!* Let go of me!"

"No," he says. "There's a lot of rebar and sudden drops around here, and we're not done talking. You don't get to announce you're going back to jail and then just take off."

"And you don't get to make out with Nadya and not tell me! Why didn't you tell me?!"

"Oh, I don't know, maybe I was worried you'd *overreact*?" The thick cords of his neck pulse with the too-fast beat of his heart. "Yes, okay, we kissed. In front of a green screen, while thirteen crew members stood around to make sure her wig didn't slip. It was a *job*, Signal. It wasn't real, like what happens with you. *Nothing* is as real as what happens with you."

"Yeah?" I say gently. "You mean it?"

"Yes." His arm softens. "Now can we please go back like two minutes ago when—"

I lunge forward, tear the box of condoms out of his hoodie pocket, and sprint for the edge of the floor just as he lunges to stop me. For once, he's too late. The golden box twinkles cheerfully as it sails into the dark, arcing twenty stories as it falls to the street below.

Erik lets out a bellow of frustration that rings down to earth and back again, so anguished I can't stop laughing. He sinks onto his knees, face like I've punched him in the gut.

"She's trying to kill me," he says to himself. "She's got to be trying to kill me."

But I feel much lighter now. Maybe it's seeing that clip, but I know with perfect clarity I cannot handle moving forward that way when he is always, always leaving.

I sit down on the icy cement next to him, pulling my knees up and crossing my arms over them, making a place I can hide my head from the deep, slow-motion kiss still looping in front of us.

"I knew she liked you," I tell him.

"She doesn't, not really."

"Uh huh. Sure." I try to swallow past the knot in my throat. "Anything else juicy happen? Onscreen or offscreen, with Nadya?"

He hunches forward and starts biting at his nails. Never a good sign.

"Well," he says at last. "She did ask me to marry her."

"Seriously."

"So I could get Russian citizenship? Through a marriage visa." He is still biting his nails. "She was saying I could be a Russian citizen by marriage and live in Bali. Her dad has a house there too, apparently."

"Oh."

This is how he kills me. He leaves me for a pop star.

After a long moment I manage, "Could you at least wait until after I go to jail?"

He reaches out and pulls me into him, and I don't resist. I let him cradle me against his chest, my head fitting perfectly between his neck and shoulder, legs spilling over his lap, his heavy arms holding as much of me as he can gather.

"Let's go," he says. "Tonight. You and me. Let's disappear."

The only part of me moving is my heart, but it's thrashing so hard.

"I have a ton of money from the shoot. All cash," he goes on, dead serious. "We could be in Mexico City by tomorrow. Then we could jump trains down to Costa Rica. We could hide out for years, and they'd never find us."

For a moment I let myself imagine it. The two of us haloed in golden dust from the road, how bright his smile could be under new kinds of sunshine.

Then I take the reins of my heart and pull it back in.

"I can't do that to Mom," I admit. "Or Nobody, or Dennis, or Jada, or . . . All of our friends would be guilty by association if I ran away. What about them?"

Erik closes his eyes.

"What about justice for your parents?" I go on. "And stopping Kurt from killing more people? And ending the Wylie-Stanton? What about telling the truth, and fixing the world?" I wind my arms around his neck. "Who will do that, if we run away?"

"There is no fixing the world," Erik says. "*That* is the truth."

"You don't believe that."

The distant thrum of helicopters makes us both go still. Erik rises, hand still in mine, and leads me into the shadows past the work lights. For a nauseating moment the helicopters seem to bear toward us; then they pivot west and grow smaller. As their engines recede his head drops, his profile black against the purple night. He peers down into the city, his gaze sinking through the ground like none of the light registers. Like the dark is all he sees.

"I keep hanging around," Erik says, his expression blank, his voice pained, "hoping something pushes you far enough to give up. But if this doesn't do it, nothing will."

"Give up on what?"

"On the good guys winning, I guess. On fixing the world. I keep waiting for you to just choose me."

"Of course I choose you."

"Sure, once all our friends are happy. And the mansions and the money are back in my name, and the article comes out so everyone knows I'm the good guy! *I was always the good guy*, right—"

"I don't care about money, Erik. But yes, I'm worried about our friends. I care about what happens to them." My voice is getting too fast; this feels like a conversation that only goes in one direction and I am desperate to turn it around. "And they are relying on my name being cleared—"

He cuts me off. "I'm going to get caught. Maybe tonight's the night."

"Then *turn yourself in.*"

His head falls back with a groan.

"The more you run the worse it gets. But if you turn yourself in, and tell everyone the truth—"

"That's not how this works. You think good guys always win, Signal, because no one tells the bad guy's side of the story. I am the bad guy. My only way out alive is *leaving the story completely.*" He looks down at our clinging hands, and his gaze is furious. He pulls his hand loose, thrusts it deep in his pocket. "I think you can either love someone, or you can be free. But not both."

". . . And you want to be free."

He is quiet a long time. Then he nods. "Yes. More than anything."

"Right," I say thickly, stepping back from him. "Loud and clear, Erik. Have fun in Bali."

"Signal, that's not what I'm saying—"

"Yeah, you're being real flowery about it, but that's what it boils down to. You got a better offer so you're going to take it." I wave at him kissing Nadya, which is still nightmarishly looping. "But, you know, you could have brought all this up before—" I flounder for words. "Before I stupidly offered you *everything*—"

"*Everything?*" he sneers. "What are you talking about? You mean when you threw some condoms at me?"

"Don't worry." I turn away, mortified. "That will *never* happen again."

But he's too fast. His arm snaps out and he spins me into him, holding me by my elbows; he holds me gently, but I can hear how much restraint he's using in his voice.

"'*Everything,*'" he repeats. "You think sex is everything now? Well, it's not, not compared to what I want."

"A Russian visa?"

He can't contain his laugh, a spasm of equal delight and outrage passing over his face.

"You *are* the girl from hell," Erik says. "Sent here just to torture me! No, demon, I don't want a visa. I—I want—" The high spots of color flood back. "I want the seat next to you, anywhere you go, to always be mine. I want to know for a fact, every time I see you, it's not the last time. I want to get sick of you, alright? I want to get so sick of you I could die—"

I am holding him back now, holding him with all my might.

"And *you* come here and offer a one-night stand as some parting gift. Like I'm something you need to get out of your system—"

"No! That's not what I want! *I love you.* How many times do I have to tell you?"

"Then *choose me*. Me, as I am, right now. Come with me, tonight." His eyes harden as they scan my face. "Or tell me to go. It's your choice."

"My choice?! 'Screw over everyone in your life, or you never get to see me again' is not a *choice*, Erik!" I swear, there is blood at the back of my mouth, seeping up from my heart. "You just want to leave me and blame me for it at the same time! I'm *forcing you* to go live in Bali with your rich pop star, right? Such a liar. You're such a liar!"

I thrust him off and half run, legs shaking, back to the elevator, very aware of him closing in behind me. I rush into the elevator car, determined to make it out without openly bawling, but he grabs the plastic door before I can pull it shut.

"You want to be free?" I snap, yanking on the strap harder. "Be free! But it doesn't work like that for me, Erik. *I* can't just desert the people I love—"

"Just me, right?" he yells back.

I bring the door down between us with a slam, then turn to the brake lever. But it sticks; even with me straining with both arms I can't budge it. He quietly opens the door and comes on beside me, arm brushing mine as he effortlessly pushes it into place.

"Weakling," he says under his breath, stepping away again.

"Are you—" It's so stupid, but I can't stop myself. "You aren't going to say goodbye?"

He turns and glares at me, then storms back into the elevator car, backing me against the plastic grid wall so the car tilts wildly. He hooks his fingers into the grate, his face just short of mine, heat rolling off him so high he seems feverish, his torn-eyed gaze unreadable.

And then Erik's eyes fall closed, and he kisses me with all his heart. Tenderly at first, but as I kiss back, something savage creeps in on both sides: It's not enough. We clutch each other, frantic. My hands slip inside his hoodie, his teeth tug at my bottom lip like he's considering biting a piece of me off, his weight pressing into me so hard there's going to be marks across my back, if the cable doesn't snap and send us plummeting first. I don't care, I don't care, if this is our last kiss, what do I have to live for?

The rest of my life, of course. Even if I have to spend it in prison. It's more than Rose got.

It takes all my strength to stop. But at last, with a shaky breath, I break off the kiss. I put my hands on Erik's shoulders and gently push him back out of the elevator car. And I pull the door down between us again.

A look of frank pain crosses his face, but he shakes it off and laughs. A cold laugh, nothing like his real one.

"You know, I should really thank you," Erik says, "for showing me I'm not missing out on the whole 'being in love' thing after all. It's just pointless suffering, like *everything else*."

"Yeah, well, maybe you weren't as in love as you thought."

And I hit the switch that will take me in the opposite direction from his black heart.

* * *

The moment I'm out of his sight, I start bawling. Ugly, uncontrollable sobs pile one on top of the other until I'm gasping for breath before I reach the ground. Traffic smears across my blurred vision as I wait for the bus. All I want to do is run back, to try to convince him one more time, but the billboards above me steel my resolve. Erik has made it clear what he wants: to help himself. To *marry Nadya*. He loves me, but not enough. He loves me, but not like I love him. No one should have to love someone that much.

I cry in the back of the bus all the way to the hotel. And when I stagger back into the lobby, eyes swollen almost shut, I practically walk into the waiting phalanx of police officers.

The crackle of walkie-talkies rebounds through the lobby as police circle me. I don't answer any of their questions until Honor comes down, Aarush right behind her. They're both furious, but they withhold from openly yelling at me until we're back in the penthouse, where Sonny himself has recently arrived.

Aarush and Honor hurry me into the luxury business suite where he's waiting. Sonny greets me with a weary smile and I collapse into a chair, mortified. Only a true crisis would put me at the top of his list of priorities.

"LAPD was minutes away from a full-scale citywide manhunt," Honor tells me. "This was not the day to play games, Signal."

"What were you thinking!" Aarush cries. "Where did you go?"

"Just sightseeing," I mumble.

They all stare me down, their disapproval giving every moment of silence an almost unbearable weight.

"I kind of snapped, okay?" I admit. "I figured I was going back to jail so I wanted to be . . . out in the air, I guess. I just started running and wound up on a bus and . . . got lost. Then my battery ran out."

Aarush snatches my phone and holds it up so I can see the screen, shaking with rage.

"Do you see this? This icon right here? The one shaped like a battery?!" He pushes it closer to my face, "See how it says *fifty-four percent* right next to it?!"

"Aarush . . . ," Sonny warns.

"You're grounded." Aarush doesn't raise his voice, but he makes every word sting. "For the rest of your time with us, however long or short that might be. You may not leave the Desai property from this point forward. You will have a curfew, and no guests in your room after lights out—"

Sonny puts a gently restraining hand on Aarush's arm.

"It's been a long day," he says quietly. "Get some rest, son."

Aarush's mouth opens and closes; then he pushes back from the conference table, shaking his head, and lets the door fall behind him with a clap.

"Will she have an ankle bracelet?" Sonny asks Honor after a beat.

"No injunction yet. But she's formally a flight risk now. The bail will be higher."

I cringe.

"Understood," Sonny says. "I'd like to have a few words with her, if you don't mind."

Honor nods, stands, and walks evenly to the conference suite door. She turns to close the door softly, but the look on her face when our eyes connect hurts worse than anything she could have said.

Sonny stares across the lacquered table at me for a moment, and it's all I can do not to start begging. He's going to tell me he won't pay the higher bail, that I will be taken from the hotel and put straight into custody, that he's spent enough on such a bad bet.

"I received a very strange call this morning," Sonny says, "from our opposition. That is to say, Janeane Rowan. Not her counsel, but Janeane herself. I have no idea how she got my number, which in itself is a little unsettling."

I blink at him, surprised.

"She told me she wants to see you," Sonny goes on, "face to face and 'off the books,' in her words. No lawyers, no mediators. Just you and her."

"Why would she do that?"

"I have no idea." Sonny shrugs. "If she wanted to settle, she could go through your counsel. And she has no reason to settle now. You're the one at a disadvantage, going into this trial with no evidence to back up your defense." He sits back in his chair. "Which is why I wanted to give you the choice, Signal. If you want to meet with her, I can make that happen. You and I would take my private car and stop at a halfway point between LA and San Francisco. But we'd have to leave first thing tomorrow, before my son gets wind of it." He rolls his eyes, but there's affection in the gesture. "Aarush takes this 'flight risk' business—Aarush takes *everything*, frankly, a bit more seriously than I do. He is highly conscientious. Which is usually helpful. But sometimes not so much."

"Should we . . . ask Honor first?"

"Ms. Hadley would tell you not to do this under any circumstances." Sonny smiles. "Because this is highly unconventional, unorthodox, and risky. But ultimately, this is your case. This is your life. So the question of whether or not to meet Janeane is one only you can answer."

The last time I saw Janeane, she told my friends to kill me, with my blood on her teeth. Moments before, she had tried to bite through my Achilles tendon. That is what Janeane does, she goes after weak spots. And right now, I am pretty damn weak.

I try to read Sonny's expression.

"But you think I should do it."

"Everything I have, I've acquired by being unconventional and unorthodox and taking calculated risks, Signal. I think you and I are a lot alike in that respect."

Calculated risks. What is the risk in meeting with Janeane? What could she possibly want from me? Right now, she has the upper hand. And even when she was zip-tied to a chair, I wasn't able to stay in control across from her.

"*That's the point*," I can almost hear Erik say.

Janeane wants the chance to twist the knife. To taunt me about Rose, to break my heart until I snap again, but *this* time she'll be ready. If she can get me to attack her on camera, that would hand her a decisive victory. But if I could get her to slip, to talk about her crime, that would be all the evidence I need.

"Whatever she wants to say, I would record of course," I tell Sonny.

He puts up a finger in warning: "Officially, I didn't hear you say that."

"Then my answer is, let's go."

The scales that always seem to be weighing me in the back of his mind seem to tip in my favor, and Sonny smiles.

*   *   *

Ragged Point Inn sits about halfway between Los Angeles and San Francisco, on cliffs overlooking the Pacific Ocean: a restaurant, a rest stop, a nexus of earth, and sea, and sky. Its little red cabins circle a broad green lawn with a looping stone path and some of the luckiest flowers in the world. Beyond the lawn, past the edge of the sheer cliffs, the sky and the sea gaze into each other for so long they bleed into one horizon of perfect blue. I wish I could be happier while I was here, but its beauty only reaches my eyes; my heart feels full of broken glass.

Sonny and I walk in silence along a cliffside path. Just past the broadest, most ancient tree, one point of stony cliff juts out into the ocean, the world dropping away so the only thing between you and forever is a wood fence with chain link in its gaps.

This is where we're supposed to meet Janeane. I struggle to get the small streaming camera to work, the upgraded version of the prototype I broke into camp with.

"I don't think it's storing as it streams."

"She might have planted a jammer," Sonny suggests. Then, "Look out, I think that's her now, under the trees—"

I follow his gaze to a lanky figure in the shadows under the redwoods. She wears a dark visor, oversized black sunglasses, and an unnerving smile.

"Try recording on your phone," Sonny says quickly, his hand on my shoulder. "If you need help, I'll be close, just wave for me."

Janeane is within arm's length of us now, close enough I can see the way her pearlescent foundation has melted into the fine lines of her face. Sonny glares at her, and her smile deepens.

"You can leave," she tells the billionaire. With a final squeeze of my shoulder he retreats, and it's just Rose's killer and me.

Janeane holds out her hand, palm up, like a teacher demanding I spit out my gum.

"Phone."

"That's not—"

"Phone or I leave."

Hot anxiety spiders up my neck, but I hand her the phone. She turns and throws it underhand past the tree. It cracks against a boulder with an unmistakable shattering sound.

"*Hey!*"

"Oh stop." Janeane takes a pack of cigarettes from her pocket and shakes one loose. "Have Daddy Desai buy you a new one. He's paying for everything else these days, isn't he?"

"Why am I here, Janeane?"

She cups her long thin fingers around the lighter. After a moment a curl of smoke flies by on the wind.

"Because I've got some very good news for you." She exhales. "And after yesterday, you need good news."

I glare at her.

"I came here," Janeane says, "to tell you I'm willing to testify about my time at camp."

Chapter Nine
Grounded

For a moment all I can do is stare.

"I'm ready to come forward. About the torture." Janeane puts her hand to her chest, voice racked with sudden emotion. "About the murder missions. About being sent out against my will to take down grown men and women. How my blood would turn to ice every time I had to call in for conditions on the next target. How we buried some of our own friends during training! As the last surviving camper of our class, it's my duty to tell the world!"

She smiles again, raising her eyebrows above her sunglasses: *How'd I do?*

Mary Larland would love her.

"You're bluffing," I say slowly. "Why put that out there, that you went to camp, when that only supports my testimony?"

"Because your testimony is going to change," Janeane tells me. "Right now, your friends' suit against camp? It sounds like a conspiracy theory they cooked up in the back of a squad car. They need someone who can testify camp was training kids to take down targets before the Wylie-Stanton. Someone who has something to lose, not something to gain. So your little stream looks more like a rescue mission and less like a prison riot. And I'm the only one who can do that, Signal. Because I'm the last adult camper."

"No, you're not—" I sputter, horrified. "What about Kate?"

"She's taken off somewhere." Janeane frowns, tapping her cigarette against the wood rail. "I thought she went over to your side maybe? Or maybe she went to find Mutt. She was always crazy about him."

"If you mean the guy in the Dog Mask, we already killed him."

"You *killed Mutt?*" Janeane drops her jaw dramatically. "Shame on all of you! He was just a big old *sweetheart!*" She shakes her head. "Yeah, you can forget

Kate helping any of you little stinkers, then. But if I testify about camp forcing kids out on murder missions, your friends will win their case. You agree?"

I nod.

"And you'd like that, wouldn't you. Watching all those little rascals walk scot-free?"

I nod again.

"Well, there you go." Janeane leans back on her elbows. "Then I need you to do something for me. Remember that nasty little shed, behind that seedy little park you used to live in . . . ?"

I can feel her watching me through her dark lenses; my skin crawls.

"Did you know," Janeane grins, "my husband used to go to that shed all the time?"

"What?"

"Rose's stepfather had chronic pain from an old football injury. When the prescribed pills ran out before the end of the month, he'd figure something else out. Go to buy unprescribed stuff from that one drug dealer kid who used to mow our lawn. Don't remember his name now. Never liked him much myself."

Her smile curls up on one side.

"I wouldn't be surprised if that's what my dear departed husband was doing in the shed that night. Dropping by late, to make a score. And what does he find? Rose, with that awful boy! It'd be enough to drive any father to his breaking point. Especially one going through withdrawal."

Even knowing the truth, even having had Janeane say to my face that she killed Rose, for just a moment my brain makes this fit. Lets me believe this is some miraculous secret that will set everything in my life back on track.

But it's not true. It's just what I would rather believe.

"You want me to 'remember' that your husband killed Rose?"

"Bingo." She exhales smoke. "I'll testify to the drug use, obsession with Rose, yada yada . . . I've got plenty of receipts, believe me."

"And Halloween?"

"We just tell the truth. With a few edits." She winks. "You and your little Class A pals broke in to interrogate me. When Kurt got carried away and stabbed me, I confused him with Erik because of all the masks. Kurt finished off Tom, who'd been passed out high the whole time, and he went down the drain while I bravely fought my way through the house to a phone."

"And you get away with everything."

"So will your friends," Janeane says coolly. "And your little boyfriend. A victimless crime!"

Because she doesn't count Rose. She's erased her from her mind as completely as she erased her from life.

"Who told you," I say after a long moment, "about the security deposit box?"

She laughs. "Oh, honey. You don't get to ask questions." She tips her shades down and bares her teeth in a smile. "But I'll say this much: It was the last person I expected to hear from."

I grip the rail of the wood fence between me and forever, and my eyes fall closed.

"You will remember what happened that night and alert your legal team to the fact, Signal. And *no one else*." Her eyes flash to Sonny. "Before the evidentiary hearing. Or any future for you little losers is off the table."

I have no idea what to say.

"Or I can just put you away for life again." Janeane shrugs. "It's up to you, honey." Then she flicks her cigarette butt out into the horizon and strides off without a backward glance.

* * *

"Well?" Sonny asks "What did she want?"

"Just tried to convince me she's innocent." The words come out thick. He's not buying it. He starts to say something, then stops himself and puts his hand on my shoulder.

"Honor says sometimes you have to lose the battle to win the war," Sonny says. "But in my experience, for that strategy to work, you have to know *exactly* what you're fighting for."

Back in the limo, I email everyone I can think of on my shattered phone, anyone who might be able to testify against Janeane: Mike, Vaughn, randoms from their church. I pull out Greg's crumpled card and email him too.

Nothing new in drafts, of course. Not that that keeps me from checking every five minutes for the rest of the limo ride, and every two minutes during Zoom class once we're back at the house, back in my beautiful cell of a room, unable to bear the silence. Then somewhere around three, halfway through AP biology, something new finally does come up. An error message.

Mandatory Update: Password

I pound on the door to Dennis' room.

"How do I get around this?" I say, holding out the phone.

He frowns at the screen, T-shirt damp like he just got out of the gym. "You change your password."

"No, I mean, how do I keep from changing my password?"

"Let me see . . ." He perches behind his laptop, pulls up his email, and gets the same prompt. He pulls up the code panel of the browser while I look impatiently around his room. Dennis has several computers in different stages of unmaking all over his desk, stacking bins of hardware and wires and hard drives lining the wall. Whatever isn't covered in electronics is compulsively neat, his shoes lined up on shelves, bed precisely tucked in at the corners. He's taped an Excel spreadsheet to the back of his door, covering his full-length mirror, which seems to plot out his workout routine and calorie intake for the next twelve weeks.

"This is a very simple command applied universally across the server. There's no way around it that doesn't involve an administrator," Dennis says at last. "My guess is, Aarush picked up on our security breach. You just have to change the password."

"But then Erik can't get into drafts anymore!"

Dennis shrugs. "You'll have to find a way to get him your new password, then."

"I can't! He'll think I changed it to lock him out!" My voice is too high.

"Erik can handle a couple weeks of the silent treatment." Dennis shrugs. "But we should definitely go get the raspberry pi back before Aarush finds it."

"Oh boy." I sink onto his bed. "I don't think the chili trick will work again."

"Chili might not be necessary," he says, and pulls a canister from beside his computer. "You know where the concealed door to the nerve center is, you've been through it enough times."

I nod.

"If you spray this along the seam of the door, as close to the side that retracts as you can, it should open automatically."

I take the canister. "Keyboard cleaner?"

"Compressed air can open a locked motion-sensor door. Passive infrared sensors read it as motion coming from inside the room and release the locking mechanism. Automatic doors rarely prohibit egress, due to fire codes."

"And if it doesn't work?" I ask. "And Aarush catches me just frantically spraying the wall of the nerve center with this?"

"I don't think Aarush can be any madder at you than he already is." Dennis shrugs.

* * *

"Signal!"

Jada calls out to me from one of the low leather couches under the staircase. She's giving herself a manicure. When I approach, she flops back the corner of her thick knit blanket and smacks the seat next to her with the palm of her hand, fingers fanned to protect the lacquer.

There's enough security guards milling around the nerve center I'm happy for somewhere to stall.

"Soooo . . . ," Jada says as I settle in beside her, the sweetness of her body spray mixing with the sting of acetone. "How was your trip to LA?"

"One of the single worst experiences of my life, basically."

"Noooo. Yeah. Well, Skye told me about the lockbox." She widens her eyes at me. "Ouch."

It's a hell of a lot worse than ouch, but I just nod.

Jada sighs. "That's all three of us girlies going through hell right now. I wonder if luck can sync up, like periods? You know Nobody dumped Amy?"

"WHAT?"

She shushes me, and I whisper: "Nobody broke up with Amy? What happened?"

"I don't know, I can't get her to tell me. But last night she was sobbing so loud I heard her through the wall. Got her to the kitchen and she ate a lot but all she'd say is 'it has to be this way.' And she missed all her Zoom classes today."

"I'll try and talk to her."

"*Please* do." Jada fans glossy paint over her thumbnail. "You're always so good at the touchy-feely stuff."

I lean my head back on the wall and watch her paint a moment, then ask, "Why are you going through hell? Is Skye giving you trouble?"

"Skye? What? No. Only trouble Skye gives me is if Dennis clowns on him so hard I pull a muscle laughing. That kid is *funny*. I never realized before."

"He's very dry."

"Yeah, exactly! Like, he says these things where they have to sink in for a while, but then you're like, wait, that was *amazing*. Like a good deep conditioner. Anyway, Skye's not my problem, my problem is Javier. *I'm* still in a rage about the other night, so I'm sure you're furious at him too."

It takes me a beat to remember what she's talking about. Then I say quickly, "Oh, yeah, I guess so. But I was such a jerk to him when we broke up—"

"No! Do not make excuses for what he did!" Jada turns on me. "And since Javier was petty enough to bring it up, let me just say: Erik and I *never* hooked up, Skipper." She holds up a fanned-out, freshly painted hand, like she's taking an oath. "We're both hot people, so there was a vibe, sure. But after you showed up, he dropped me like a hot rock. On to the next thing."

On to the next thing. I wince as the words land.

"And okay," Jada goes on, "maybe I didn't handle that in the most ladylike fashion—"

"You mean when you jumped me and *slashed my face?*"

"Every time you describe that you make it bigger, geez." Jada rolls her eyes. "But in *reality*, did I carve you up? No. Did I make a scene every time everyone was together? No! I moved on. Javier needs to move on already."

The stiff tread of a security guard clips down the breezeway. Once he's past, I slide my keyboard cleaner from the pocket of my hoodie to just inside my sleeve.

"You sneaking into the nerve center?" Jada whispers, and I look up at her, surprised.

"You know the compressed air trick?"

"Dennis is always showing me his cute little hacks. Want me to distract the guards?"

I nod, smiling for what feels like the first time in days.

"On the count of five," she whispers with a wink. "One . . . two . . ."

I get up from the couch and sidle closer to the hall that leads to the nerve center. A security guard is just around the corner from where I'm standing; he clears his throat as I inwardly count five, and a nail polish bottle goes shattering across the floor.

"WHAT THE FRICKIN' HELL WAS THAT!"

The security guard runs to the stairs, and I sprint down the narrow hall to the hidden door.

"Pigeon? That was no pigeon! Pigeons have WINGS, that was a RAT!" Jada is shrieking.

Hands shaking, I run a stream of compressed air down the wall, just beside the biometric pad, and instantly the concealed door sinks open in front of me and retracts, and I duck into the room.

* * *

"Signal! What can I do for you?"

Honor, at the head of the conference table, looks up from a sea of tabbed documents as I stop with a jerk just inside the door.

"Oh, I didn't know you were in here!" I gasp, holding the compressed air as casually as I can.

"We only have three weeks before your evidentiary hearing." She raises her perfectly shaped eyebrows. "Where else would I be?"

"Actually." My stomach goes sour. "About the hearing, I wanted to ask you something."

Her eyebrows go even higher: *Yes?*

"If I remembered something from the shed that was different than what you and I have previously discussed, what would I do about that?"

A long beat. Too long.

"Something different?" Honor repeats in disbelief.

"Like . . . if I remembered that the killer wasn't Janeane after all."

Honor sits back in her chair, then surveys her piles of tabbed documents like she could sweep them all to the floor.

"*If* that were the case," Honor says, "first, it would be stupendously unfortunate timing. Second, Janeane's counsel and the court are aware of our fiasco with the lockbox, so some last-minute revelation would open you up to accusations of opportunism that I, personally, would find hard to counter."

I feel myself going the guiltiest shade of red.

"*But*," Honor continues, "if you were *absolutely certain* about this . . . memory, we would take your statement and present that at the preliminary hearing."

"Okay." I nod, too fast. "Good to know."

"Why do you ask, Signal?"

"I just . . . I had a dream but it might not have been a dream." I falter. "I just need to sort out what I remember, I guess."

"Yes. Well. Why don't we table this until tomorrow." Honor pinches the bridge of her nose. "When we're both a bit more rested and have more space from yesterday's events. And then, if this dream of yours is something you want to base a new defense on, we'll talk about that."

"Thank you, Honor," I mumble, and back out of the room and down the hall, hot shame seeping from the inside out until it burns the back of my eyes. I can't look at my own hangdog reflection in the darkening windows. And this is just the start, this is just the first taste of what a lifetime of lying will feel like.

* * *

"Nobody home," Nobody croaks when I knock on her door.

". . . Hey."

It's bad.

Nobody is sprawled out on her bed, under a panoramic poster of the skyline of Manhattan, her unopened care package snacks from Amy cradled to her chest like a pile of baby ducklings. She is, unsurprisingly, an extremely pretty crier. The blush of pink around her eyes makes them an even brighter blue; her lips are swollen like she's gotten injections.

The floor is blanketed with dirty dishes ordered up from the kitchen, crumpled clothes, and ragged Kleenex. As I start picking up the mess, I realize the Japanese pop song she's blasting is on single repeat.

". . . Jada told me you broke up with Amy."

"She didn't lie," Nobody chokes out.

"I'm sorry, but . . ." I set a stack of plates on her desk with a clatter. "What the hell were you thinking?"

Her head jerks like I've slapped her.

"What the hell, Signal?" She props herself up on one arm.

"I'm sorry! I'm *sorry*." I put my hands up. "You're my best friend, I love you, but—*you* broke up with *her!* And she stood by you through everything. Even when we were on the run—"

Nobody saws her melted forearm under her perfect nose. "You don't know what you're talking about."

"Nobody! Like, the first thing you ever said to me was that you had a girlfriend you loved very much! I know you love her, and I know this hurts you, so I just need to know what the hell all this pain is for!"

Her eyes narrow. "Let me guess. You saw Erik in LA, huh?"

"This isn't about me."

"And he dumped you."

"Why would you . . ." I choke on the rest of the sentence. We glare at each other across the room, my face getting hotter and tighter until finally I can't hold it back. I burst into ugly tears.

Nobody throws out her arms and waves me in. I curl up against her on the narrow bed, and she hugs me, and I ugly-cry on her shoulder as she pulls an old knit blanket, sent from her gram's house, over our heads. The light that filters through the squares of faded color is a dim, warm pink.

"Seriously," I say, "what happened with Amy."

"It's like what you said." Nobody's voice is so quiet I don't think I'd hear her if the blanket wasn't over us. "She'd stand by me no matter what. And if we don't have any witnesses and our case fails, I don't just go back to prison. I go back to death row."

My insides turn to ash and suddenly I'm gripping her wrists very tight.

"If I gotta die, I gotta die." A tear flashes down Nobody's cheek, her eyes staring right through me. "But I'll be damned if I let Amy watch."

She breaks off then with a long sigh, her burnt hands covering her face, her shoulders right up by her ears.

"You're not going back. I promise you," I swear.

"You *can't* promise that. There's nothing you can do."

"Yes, there is. I met with Janeane—"

"What?"

"We made a deal. You can't tell anyone. But she's going to testify about camp."

Nobody's eyes widen, a spasm of relief flitting across her face. Then she frowns.

"What do you have to do for her?"

"Whatever it takes," I say, gripping her hand. "To keep that promise."

Her chin dimples again as she squeezes my hand, and her hot blue eyes close. I wrap my arms around her, and her lanky frame releases. I think of Kurt, crying over Troy by the side of the lake back at camp, and ask, "Any more news on Kurt?"

"He popped up on some security footage." She sits up with a lot of effort, pulls her phone off her desk, and falls back on the bed, holding it over us as she shows me a map where she's marked each place Kurt has been sighted: Little Fern, Bellingham, Bridgewood. And another place she's marked with a pin labeled "Snow?"

"Snow?" I ask. "What's that?"

"He was caught on camera going into a dollar store in Bridgewood. He bought some food and asked the cashier when snow season is over. Cashier told him whenever it stopped snowing."

"Huh."

"That's the closest city to camp that has a snow season," she says, tapping the pin, and the map zooms in on a dot marked "The Summit at Snoqualmie."

"But there've been no victims there yet?"

"No confirmed victims at all since the headless lady in Bridgewood." And when I cringe, she says, "Not exactly dinner date conversation, huh."

"It is with me!" I tell her, flopping onto my back. "Let's order pizza up from the kitchen and fuel up before movie o'clock."

* * *

Nobody and I walk into the theater arm in arm, the blanket still draped around us like a shared cape. Dennis and Jada are laughing as we come in. They turn to us, Jada smiling up at me hopefully.

"Feeling better?" she asks Nobody.

We both give her teary nods. The real proof is that Nobody is eating Amy's care package Pocky, like she's confident there will be more, and she no longer has to save everything Amy once touched like sacred relics.

Javier stands in front of the theater seating and beams at us as we sit beside Dennis and Jada, for once excited to be here.

"Tonight, for my movie choice, I got something special planned." Javier announces. "I worked out the AV details with Aarush so we could see a *very special* world premiere—"

"If you're about to show us footage of you humping an ottoman to slow jams," Jada says flatly, "I'll pass."

Nobody chokes on her Pocky.

"You wish." Javier rolls his eyes but gives up the rest of his speech and calls for the show to begin before settling in his seat, a couple down from mine.

The lights go down, the red curtains retract, and then the first bolt of pale blue lightning flashes across the screen.

"OUTLAWS" a robotic voice announces, an extreme close-up of blue-haired Nadya filling the screen.

The Pocky turns to wax in my mouth.

Chapter Ten
Outlaws

～

The shots in the music video cut on the beat: Nadya leaning out of a car window as a masked Erik drives. Nadya with her hands up Erik's shirt, making out in a stairwell. An Erik lookalike with long styled hair, a better match for his mug shot, running down an alley with Nadya. A blurred shot of the lookalike and the guy in the balaclava—who I recognize, who *we all* recognize—sitting on the stairs, passing a flask back and forth. And then their stun gun kiss starts; the billboard clip was definitely a more clothed, more PG version.

Nobody is balling up in her chair with discomfort. Jada has both hands clapped over her mouth. Dennis is frozen. Javier doesn't even bother looking at the screen. He just drinks in my reaction.

I make it exactly one second into the kiss before I stand up, head down, and head for the aisle. Nobody moves back in her chair to let me through, the reflections of the blue lightning onscreen pulsing under my feet as I break into a run.

I burst out onto the deck, doors swinging shut on the music behind me. Drool pools in the back of my throat: I'm going to hurl. I should get to a bathroom or in range of a potted plant at the very least. I stumble into the house.

"Signal!" Aarush barrels toward me. "What the hell do you think you're doing?"

I veer away from the rubber plant.

"I just spoke with Honor." Aarush lands in front of me. "Don't you dare try any of this 'recovered memory' drivel with me. I watched Janeane's attic rant, in real time. I know what she did and *so do you.*"

I have no defense to offer. I just stare at him, willing myself not to throw up.

"I know you hit a setback with Jaw's security deposit box. But to scrap your whole defense and claim you had some revelation in a dream is *sociopathic*, Signal."

I try to sidestep him, his arm shoots out, blocking me.

"Honor said you had a can of compressed air when you barged in on her. Who taught you that little trick?"

". . . YouTube."

"Oh, alright. And the raspberry pi I found behind the shelves?"

Oh no. He already found the raspberry pi.

"I suppose you just picked up some higher function exploits online as well, in the last couple of days or so?" Aarush goes on, mockingly.

"I don't know what you're talking about," I bluff.

The anger in his eyes detaches from something and cools to contempt.

"I have been helping you, Signal," Aarush says, "because I thought you were willing to stand up for the truth, no matter the cost." He shakes his head. "What an utter disappointment you've turned out to be."

There's nothing I can say. I made a deal with the devil back at Ragged Point. For Nobody, for all of them. This is my war; this is what I'm fighting for: to keep them safe.

"I will be advising Father that we need to break off all ties with you at once—"

"No, you won't." A flat voice comes down the hall. Dennis walks toward us quietly, both hands tucked into his red hoodie pockets, one gym sock slightly higher than the other. At his approach, Aarush nervously crosses his arms.

"Don't run to your dad on this one," Dennis says. "Just put it on my tab."

"You really think that tab is *endless*, don't you?" Aarush shakes his head. "Just because there's no legal charges against you—*yet*—do not suppose for one instant you're invulnerable."

"I am absolutely invulnerable," Dennis cuts him off. "Because I have nothing to lose."

Aarush looks ashamed for a moment; his large expressive eyes soften, and he hangs his head. But when he looks up at me again the softness is gone.

"Very well. I will not 'run to my dad' ahead of the hearing. But you had better believe, Signal, the first moment it's possible, I will see you turned out of this house."

"That seems a bit harsh." Skye's voice rings out from behind Aarush. He lands beside us a moment later, face almost sunny at the sound of emotional abuse. "What'd she do now?"

"Skye! Hey!" Aarush covers, startled. "You heard that out of context. It's—just a little inside joke between me and Signal."

"You really had to be there," I add flatly.

"Don't tell me we had a dinner and I've forgotten?" Aarush goes on, ignoring me.

"I'm actually here to see your old man." Skye shrugs. "But he's nowhere to be found."

"He had to jump on a call to Singapore. But he shouldn't be more than an hour."

"I see," Skye nods. "I'll just have a drink and wait on him, if you don't mind?"

"We've a bar cart in the west library. I still have some projects to close, but you're welcome to wait there."

"Mind if I join?" I ask, and they both turn to me, surprised.

"Maybe when you're twenty-one!" Skye shoots Aarush a knowing look.

"Not to drink." I smile a tight-lipped smile. "Just to help you kill some time."

Aarush fumbles for an excuse, but Skye nods, a sly smile in his eyes.

"Why of course, Signal." And he adds, as we start down the hall, "If you're sure you feel safe with me?"

"With all the cameras in this house?" I smile, "Please. Take your best shot."

*　*　*

The west library has a giant blown-glass sculpture installation that takes up one wall; something like a flock of blue jellyfish fighting their way through party streamers. The glass is thin as crepe and apparently ridiculously expensive. Skye examines it while sipping his highball. I spray some seltzer water into a tumbler and wince; it tastes like medicine.

"So." Skye holds out his crystal tumbler. "What are we toasting to?"

"My hearing!" I smile. "Finally, I get to present my evidence and clear my name." I hold up my glass, watching his reaction. His eyes flash as our glasses clink, his expression stiff.

"What a validation that will be. And, of course, you're in great hands with Honor. She's a wonderful lawyer. I've used her many times."

I try not to let my surprise register, but it must because he adds, "At this level, paths tend to cross quite a bit. There's only so many truly great lawyers, and so many billionaires in San Francisco. We all tend to live in each other's pockets."

"It *is* funny, how paths can cross." I nod, taking a deep breath before I go for it. "Like you and Janeane Rowan. You've gotten close, haven't you?"

This is why I came here with him, to see his face when I say her name. Since he stole the thumb drive and watched the rant, he knows Janeane is guilty. He knew about the lockbox, so he must have tipped off Jaw. He was the only one who could've given Sonny's number to Janeane. And he is the one she would least expect—Erik's brother—reaching out to team up. Skye is obviously orchestrating all of this. To protect CurtPro.

I just need one shred of proof.

But Skye doesn't react at all. He bobs his shoulders in a neutral shrug. "That lady Erik stabbed? I think I sent her a muffin basket when she was in the hospital. One must go the extra mile when you have a psychopath in the family."

"Erik's not a psychopath. That's why he scares you so much."

"No, no. I'm not scared of Erik, please. I'm *wary* of him. For the same reason you're wary of me." And Skye leans in, so fast I don't have time to dodge him, so close his breath brushes my ear as he whispers: "Because I know how bad he wants to kill me."

I don't let my expression change, though my heart jerks in my chest. I know the cameras are all around us; he can't touch me. He just wants a little hit of humiliation. So I force a big, angry smile once he's leaned away from me again. He returns it mockingly, before shoving his hand in his pocket and limping toward the jellyfish sculpture, gesturing with his half-empty glass.

"An original Chihuly, of this size, made in the last ten years." He squints. "What do you think it's worth? Half a million?"

"I have no idea."

"No? No clue? Really?" he says with mock surprise. "A girl from your background, not appreciating fine art?" He gestures wildly at the jellyfish. "Next you'll tell me you didn't summer in Provence, or spend your ski seasons in Leysin! Like *our* family would, before Erik got all—" He makes a stabbing gesture. "It's really a miracle you held his attention for so long, he's so *chatty*. Well. Not like he had a lot of options!" He sips his drink, considering me. Then: "What do you make of his new girlfriend?"

I'm getting nauseated again.

"Because she won't stop calling me. Wants to patch things up between us brothers, she says, since we're 'all going to be family.' Isn't that sweet?"

A flash of pain shoots up my jaw, I'm clenching my teeth too tight.

"I did warn you, Signal: Erik's sexual obsessions fade quickly. You wanted to bang a psycho killer so bad, now you're shocked he *hurt your feelings?*" He leers at me, and I stare straight forward. This was a mistake. I'm not made to spar with sadists. It's taking everything in me not to knock him backwards as he looks away and prattles on.

"Well, rest assured, Erik will get what's coming to him once he's back in my care."

"And what's that?"

Skye lets out a little laugh. "What he's *always wanted*, actually." And he laughs again, harder.

". . . I don't get it. What's the joke?"

"Oh, it's not a joke." He blinks at me for a moment, then puts on a concerned expression. "I just finally appreciate what an exceptional specimen my brother is. And I'm ready to devote every possible resource to helping him reach his *full potential*." The scarred corner of his mouth twitches at my glare and then his phone chimes, drawing the last of his attention from me. "Well, it's been nice talking." He drains his highball glass before slamming it onto the bar cart. "Let's never do it again, huh?" Skye points a finger gun at me and limps out of the room.

* * *

I lie in my bed in my silent room, the past few hours swirling and fragmenting in my mind, faster and faster, but the same patterns. The same questions.

Why had Kurt asked about snow? Skye had taunted me about ski seasons. I never went skiing; I don't know when a ski season is. Was that what Kurt was asking? What, he wanted to go skiing?

Erik had said the Director told Kurt to call in only as a last resort. But Kurt had called first thing when they got to the hotel room. Erik, in his haze, had to have misunderstood.

Janeane had made some offhand remark about calling in to check conditions on a target, back before camp had been operating with burner phones. When Janeane and Dave were teens, cell phones had been a luxury.

Dennis had said if camp was using a dial-in, it would be something that wouldn't draw attention, something it would be okay to dial from hotel rooms or public phones. In a time before ubiquitous cell phones, what would be more innocuous than calling in to check ski conditions from a hotel room?

I search "Last Resort" and "snow" and "ski conditions" on my computer.

The first result is 1-LST-RSRT. A hotline to call for ski resorts all over the US.

My heart starts pounding as soon as the long prerecorded menu starts.

The young woman speaking has an old-fashioned, over-articulated cadence, like the girls in *Charlie's Angels* reruns, and a popping hiss threads through her voice as though it's been transferred from ancient cassettes.

"If you're looking for a quick getaway, Last Resort can provide your ideal escape! Skiing or surfing? Press one for tide charts, press two for snow conditions—Snow conditions. Please select your destination. Press one for east coast, two for west, three for—West coast ski resorts. Press the first letter of your destination—"

Snoqualmie.

Another whirr, and then:

"Conditions are prohibitive. Repeat, further action is prohibited. For more specifics, press one for the resort line, or two to consult with a private instructor—"

I am on my feet as the recording gives way to live air. Someone has picked up the line and is listening.

"Dave?!" I whisper.

There's no answer. But whoever it is doesn't hang up.

"It's Signal. I'm about to give a statement clearing Janeane as the killer. And I really don't want to. But I don't have any evidence against her anymore, and she's the only one left who can testify about camp. *Unless you can help.*"

There is a sound on the other send of the line, like someone swallowing.

"Come on, Dave," I plead. "You know what she is. And if you don't help, she walks. She *walks*, Dave! Don't let her get away with this. You can call me at 415-543-7271."

I repeat the number slower one last time before hanging up, and throw myself down on the bed, staring up into the blue dark.

* * *

I wake to heavy knocking, though I don't remember falling asleep. A security guard waits at my door while I throw on clothes and shuffle after him to the nerve center, my brain racing even faster, as it tends to do when I lose sleep.

Honor is waiting at the head of the conference table in a flawless navy pant-suit, flanked by two sharky paralegals. Sonny is behind her, immaculate as ever. Aarush is to his left, eyes trained on his phone.

At the opposite end of the conference table a single chair waits for me, a small camera on a tabletop tripod facing it, already running. When none of them stand or greet me as I take my seat, I feel contagious.

"Signal," Honor begins. "We want to talk you through your recent revelations. And when you're ready, we'll swear you in and take a new deposition."

The camera lens swivels slightly forward, auto-focusing on my face.

"I understand you had a dream," Honor says. "Why don't we start there? When did this dream happen?"

I picture Nobody on a bus back to Tennessee, head bowed, wrists cuffed. Jada swallowed up in a beige jail uniform. Javier drawing a gang tattoo on his arm.

"We were driving down to Los Angeles—"

"Really?" Aarush interrupts. "Because I don't remember you sleeping."

"I'm sorry, back up from Los Angeles, I guess is what I mean."

"You *guess* that's what you mean?"

My phone lights up: Unknown caller. I take it, over Honor's objections.

"Good morning, Signal." Dave's voice is unmistakable. "Got time for a chat?"

"*Dave!*" I'm on my feet, the room erupting into whispers. Honor leans forward, eyes wide.

"Because I would be more than happy to testify to what a psychopathic bitch Janeane is," Dave goes on, tone flat, "but I'm going to need some kind of immunity around the whole changing your Wylie-Stanton score thing. Have you got a lawyer?"

I hold the phone out to Honor. "He wants to talk to you."

Their conversation goes on for hours. Honor passes notes the whole time to her paralegals, taking Dave on and off speaker. I down a croissant and two cups of hot milky tea, suddenly ravenous. Aarush is uninterested in his phone for once, watching Honor's face intently. Sonny sits back with his hand over his mouth, saying nothing. But every time his assistant leans forward with a call, Sonny shakes his head.

At last Honor hangs up and stares across the table at me.

"Looks like we'll be bringing in a surprise witness to the hearing. A *federal employee* who knows *exactly* what was going on with the Wylie-Stanton, who is *Rose's dad* . . . and who just confirmed everything about Janeane's involvement in your incarceration. *And* he's ready to repeat it all before the judge! You're not going to have a trial, Signal. You won't need one!" Honor beams at Sonny. "Honestly, I wouldn't be surprised if they just settled with the other kids after this." Honor looks back at me, knowing. "Unless you still want to change your statement?"

I shake my head and she bursts out in giddy laughter.

* * *

I float out of the nerve center, a dance hall in my chest. I'm practically skipping down the hall, when I see my friends on a low couch across from the TV in the west library.

"Nobody!" I cry, "You'll never believe—"

Javier shushes me and points to the screen: They're in a Zoom conference with our head tutor.

"Signal? Are you here too?" The tutor, an older woman with large glasses and a white pixie cut, peers down from the flat-screen mounted above the travertine mantel.

I step in range of the webcam and wave.

"There you are! We're all talking about graduation coming up in a few weeks. You should all feel very proud of yourselves!"

"We really do!" I cry too loud and Jada shoots me a look: *Girl?*

"Glad to hear it, because Sonny wants to have a graduation ceremony that all your families can watch—"

This is met with clapping and whoops from the couch.

"Oh man!" Javier is tearing up. "Amazing!"

"My family can't come," Dennis says quietly.

"It's a video conference," our tutor says, confused.

"We're no-contact," Dennis says in his usual matter-of-fact voice. He's sunk low in the couch, and his face is hidden from my view by the curve of his white hoodie.

"Oh. Well. Just—forward the emails of anyone who might want to attend to Sonny's assistant." Our tutor moves on, embarrassed.

As the others ask follow-up questions, I slip closer to Dennis and set my hand on his shoulder. He cranes his head back to look at me.

"What?"

"Just saying hi."

Beside him, Jada's Nokia dings strangely, and we both look over at Skye's latest text:

So sad. Looks like my brother has found a new victim.

Victim? What does he mean, victim?

Heart pounding, I skirt out of the library and sprint up to my room, where I immediately search Erik's name online:

NADYA COURTS CONTROVERSY WITH OUTLAW BOYFRIEND

Popstar Nadya's surprise release of her latest music video, *Outlaws*, has gone viral, racking up 120 million views in its first 24 hours, thanks to internet rumors her costar is the fugitive Erik Wylie-Stanton!

Nadya fans were quick to spot that there are two actors portraying the star's love interest, despite the single credit. The steamiest moments involve the masked actor, and screencaps of what appear to be his coloboma have flooded social media.

Nadya set off a further cycle of speculation when she commented on one image, "Whoever that was, he's a good kisser." The tweet has since been deleted.

Nadya, a Russian national, was seen entering the LAPD Central Bureau with lawyers in tow early Wednesday morning, fueling the rumor mill further.

"If it's just an impersonation, then it's in incredibly poor taste," said Skye Wylie-Stanton, Erik Wylie-Stanton's brother. "And if it is [Erik], then Nadya will be held accountable for aiding and abetting a fugitive, to the furthest extent of the law."

I scroll down to the comments:

There's a picture on Nadya's Instagram RIGHT NOW from two nights ago—EWS is next to her at a rooftop party, it's TOTALLY his hand with the super short nails like in the video.
127 👍

So the Girl From Hell is single you say? I can fix her
111 👍

If they are together . . . that is a serious upgrade lol . . . Signal is painfully mid
99 👍

<3 Nadya standing beside the man she loves against the world <3 true love is beautiful <3
85 👍

The wormhole yawns. I analyze Nadya's Instagram, shots of a weekend in Bali with what is either definitely Erik or another guy with broad shoulders and very bitten nails, face ducked out of frame. I find thread after thread of her fans speculating about their whirlwind romance, wedding rumors, and the universal consensus that Nadya and Erik have "incredible chemistry."

Eventually I find myself typing in Armchair.org, where I know the "Girl From Hell" and "Who Killed the Wylie-Stantons" cases have been moved to the "active" page, as though they will know us better. Wanting someone, anyone, to point out that Erik doesn't love Nadya. That he just needs a way out of the country. And so what if she's a gorgeous, famous, rich pop star.

Anyone. Please.

> GIRL FROM HELL: THE ROSE ROWAN MURDER **NEW UPDATES**

>> **FEAR NO DEERE: Third person in shed? New witness comes forward**
>> **ERIK & NADYA: Viral video "Signals" break up?**
>> **LOCKBOX FIASCO: Signal's claims fall flat, Clatsop County DA not amused**

Caught off guard, I click on the first link:

With the GFH case possibly going into retrial, new witnesses are coming out of the woodwork in the Ledmonton area. Most aren't credible, but one statement has gotten serious attention: one of the residents of King's Gardens Trailer Park, walking their dog between one and two AM, saw Jaw exit the woodland path that connects to the shed the night of the murder.

When he asked Jaw if he could buy something from the shed, Jaw explained he couldn't go back there then but would help him in the morning. The next morning, Rose Rowan was dead and the shed was a crime scene.

The witness did not come forward before as buying drugs would have violated his parole. But if true, this statement upends the cornerstone of the prosecution's case against Signal Deere, namely that no one else entered the shed the night of Rose's murder.

"See?" Jada sighs as my door flies open. "It's time for an intervention."

I look up at them, face puffy with tears and washed blue from my computer screen in the dark.

"You missed dinner," Nobody says.

"Dinner?" I look at the clock, shocked to see it's almost nine.

"Nobody told me about you and Erik breaking up," Jada says quietly, shutting the door behind them. "So this is really not the time to be sitting in the dark listening to old people music."

"*Swan Lake* isn't old people music—"

"Change it," Nobody tells Jada.

Jada squeezes me out of the chair. Nobody assists by pulling me to my feet.

"You guys, really, I'm fine," I sniff.

Jada flashes through my thirteen tabs, twelve of which are articles on Nadya and Erik, six of which are scrolled through to the comments section.

"Girl." Jada sighs, closing each of them. "This is not how you do it when you're fine. Honestly, it's like you and Nobody never went through a breakup before or something."

Nobody and I exchange a guilty look as Jada pulls up a playlist on a streaming music site called "DANCE URSELF CLEAN" and turns on an insanely upbeat dance song.

Jada launches herself out of my chair and takes our hands.

"So here's the deal," Jada half-screams over the music. "The worst has happened. It's over. He's never coming back. Your heart is broken. Right? Broken! Completely! Forever!"

Never coming back. I remember her collapsing beside Troy, moments after he died.

"Well, look at this." Jada points to my feet. "Do you see what's happening right now? Do you understand what you're doing?"

"What?"

"You're STILL STANDING!" Jada cries. "The next step is dancing."

"I really don't feel like dancing."

"That's *exactly* why you have to. We gotta make some happy chemicals! That frown isn't turning upside down with you just sitting around, bitch!" Jada says, and turns up my computer's sound bar what has to be all the way, music ringing through the room and down the hall.

The drum machine is a pop dance beat, but the lyrics are weirdly sad. Nobody, jumping up and down, still has puffiness around her eyes from crying all night. But she's waving her arms overhead. Jada, who was punching Javier in the chest on my behalf a couple of nights ago, hops up on the bed. She jumps up and down like it's a trampoline, a smile on her face, head wagging back and forth, then reaches down and pulls me up beside her.

"LIKE THIS!" she says and starts explaining an incredibly complicated arm dance.

"Like *what?!*" Nobody calls up, climbing up beside us, and the mattress seriously starts to sag. But tilting and swaying, we follow along with Jada. It takes us about fifteen times to get in unison.

"Okay, now here's the next part—" Jada goes on, and Nobody and I both burst out laughing.

"NEXT PART?!" I yell.

And I'm not happy. I'm dancing, I'm laughing, that's not the same as being happy. But who's happy? Maybe no one. How many hearts are broken, badly patched and deflated, and still going? Everyone's, surely. But the music is still playing, our hearts are still beating, we can still laugh too loud when the mattress sags and sends us crashing into each other. Maybe we laugh harder when we're sad. Maybe we jump higher when we don't care where we land. So many times, I've curled up in despair and waited for it to go through me. But tonight, I will meet it standing. I will go through the pain dancing.

And when they finally leave, close to midnight, I sleep like a baby.

Chapter Eleven

Fear No Deere

❧

Three weeks later, Mom and I follow Honor through the echoing marble courthouse. Honor strides like a gladiator approaching the arena: shoulders back, head high. "We'll bring Dave up first," she says smoothly. "After his testimony, the court may even throw out Janeane's counter charges on the spot. Be ready for anything. There's our team!"

A group of junior attorneys are clustered around a bench just outside the courtroom. They are debating something intensely, all of their phones out. As they greet Honor, Mom adjusts my collar, hand fluttering nervously as she pulls the white points from under my black cardigan. I've got on a pleated skirt with black tights and ballet flats, all chosen by Cassie, who seems hell-bent on convincing the judge I'm secretly attending prep school.

"This skirt is so loose," Mom frets. "You've lost weight."

"From nerves." I shrug. It's not true. I just keep forgetting to eat. Whenever Jada and Nobody aren't actively keeping me busy, like two kids bouncing a balloon back and forth, I get in bed and search for news about Erik on my phone and forget everything else I'm supposed to do. Like eat. Or shower. There are rumors, but no new photos. Nadya's stopped posting personal stuff on social media. There are no candygrams from Scraps. Nothing in drafts. When we said goodbye, I didn't fully realize he was going to vanish off the face of the earth.

"So?" Honor scans her team. "Where's Dave? I'd like to go over a few things."

A terrified hush falls over the junior attorneys, and my phone goes off in my hand.

"Hello?" I step away from the others. Staring down the hall, I see a flash of blonde hair, a certain, almost exaggerated limp hurrying through the crowd.

"Signal." It's Dave's voice. "I won't be able to testify today. Or any other day, I'm afraid—"

His words are swallowed by a siren as a fire truck flies by the courthouse. I hear the unmistakable clang echo through on his end of the line.

"You're here," I say through clenched teeth. "You're here right now, aren't you?"

"You won't find me."

I scan the hall, furious tears blurring my vision, when the blonde head turns and I see Skye's face flash over his shoulder, his eyes connecting with mine.

"Who got to you? Was it Skye?!"

"Just do whatever Janeane says," Dave answers coolly. "That's the only way this is going to end, no matter what you or I do."

And he hangs up.

"Amira," Honor says sharply. "We have to be in court in five minutes and you're telling me no one knows where our key witness is?"

Sonny and Aarush have joined us, with Nobody, Dennis, Javier, and Jada all in tow. I can't bring myself to look at my friends, all dressed so neatly and brimming with doomed hope.

"We came early for a probationary check-in, and thought we'd stick around to watch you drop your bombshell!" Sonny's smile has already started to fade. "What's wrong?"

"—never appeared," Amira hisses to Honor. "His contact number redirects to some kind of ski resort—"

"He's backing out," I tell them, my voice so small in the vast marble hall of the courthouse.

Honor whips her head in my direction. *What did you just say?*

"He just called me. He won't testify."

Honor pinches the top of her nose for a moment, nostrils flaring. Aarush fidgets with his water bottle; Sonny's broad square jaw flares wider, as though he's clenching his teeth.

"Alright. Here's what we'll do. We go in," Honor says, after a long moment. "We present Signal's sworn statements about camp and Ledmonton, and Skye's testimony that she helped him during the break-in to reinforce that she's not a flight risk. We let the prosecution bring out whatever they have, and we try and counter it at the appeal."

Mom frowns. "What about bringing an indictment against Janeane?"

Honor shakes her head. "Breann, at this point? We'll be lucky if they let us take Signal back to the house."

All the blood drains from my mother's face, and the crack of the doors being thrown open by the bailiffs makes us all turn to the courtroom.

The vaulted ceiling is embedded with fluorescent lights, but the space is so massive, the lights so high, they can't seem to fully illuminate the room. The spectators' faces are hollowed by the shadows into skull shapes. The judge, an elderly man with cotton candy wisps of white hair, scowls over the tall redwood bench at us as we enter.

Janeane and the Clatsop County DA are already at their table. I refuse to look at her, but I feel Janeane's gaze scorch my face.

"Dave is in this building right now," I tell Honor as we take our seats. "Someone or something scared him off."

"Well, unless you can stick your hand up his ass and make him talk like a sock puppet," Honor snaps open her briefcase, "I fail to see how that helps."

A junior lawyer from the prosecution ducks over to us, arm darting past Honor to show me a note that reads simply "New name" before flitting away.

My eyes connect with Janeane's. It's like putting my hand in a flame.

She mouths: *JAW.*

Then she looks back significantly toward the crowd still taking their seats: There's some of her church friends from Ledmonton, an old man in a fishing hat turning up his hearing aid, some bloggers, a very tan little woman in a bright pink pantsuit who winks at me when our eyes meet, and Skye at the very back, jagged lines of pearlized flesh dragging down the corners of his eyes and mouth. But Janeane isn't looking at them. She stares past all of them, at the bench with my friends.

At Nobody, Jada, Dennis, and Javier, sitting so close their shoulders brush. They all immediately shoot me quick, hopeful smiles.

I grip the sides of my chair like it's swinging.

Janeane must want to get ahead of the witness statement from the trailer park. Instead of framing her dead husband, she wants to frame Jaw. Same deal, new victim: throw Jaw under the bus or else.

It was bad enough, the idea of bearing false witness against a dead man. But Jaw is still alive. I know what it means to be framed. I can't do that, not even to my worst enemy.

But then I turn back to look at my best friend. Nobody, holding her head high in public without a mask, her long blonde bang tucked behind one ear. And I start shaking.

I will do whatever it takes to keep her safe. But there's got to be another way. Anything. Like, maybe I could even . . . I could confess? End all this the way it started. With me as the Girl From Hell.

I turn around to the bench behind me, and Mom leans forward like I've called her name. The dim light makes her hair look almost white, her face even frailer. And I know in that moment, from just the set of her narrow shoulders, if I confessed it would kill her.

"—Calling you to the stand, Signal!" Honor shakes my shoulder. "They just called you to the stand as a witness for new evidence for the prosecution."

I blink at her. "Do I go up?"

"Just say you do not recall, whatever they ask," Honor hisses. "The judge is not hearing my objections on this one."

The floor tilts under me as the bailiff escorts me to the stand; I fist my hands to hide how hard they're shaking. There's the crunch of the microphone as they tilt it toward me, and I swear to tell the truth.

Black lace washes over my vision. Good, maybe I'll faint. But my brain refuses to fully disconnect, and now Janeane's lawyer is at the rostrum, shaking the long pieces of her talk-to-the-manager haircut out of her face.

"Ms. Deere, did you, or did you not, recover new memories at camp, which you then discussed with Janeane Rowan when you and your associates held her at her home?"

"Objection," Amira breaks in. "Compound."

"Ms. Deere, did you or did you not recover new memories at camp?"

My mouth is very dry. "Yes. Yes, I did."

"Did you, or did you not, discuss these memories with Janeane Rowan?"

"I did."

"Did you not come to the conclusion there was a third person in the shed, the night Rose Rowan died?"

". . . I did."

I look at Nobody. I look at my mother. Janeane's face floats in my peripheral vision like a grinning skull.

"Who was the third person you saw in the shed?"

My throat is constricting so tight. I want to scream "Janeane," but I can't. I can't say anything.

"I don't recall," I whisper.

"Really?" Janeane's lawyer snaps. "After breaking into Jarrod, aka 'Jaw' Itznicki's house, as you yourself have testified; after taking a security deposit box key from his home; after demanding a subpoena to open that security deposit box, you are telling this court you don't remember who the third person in the shed was?"

"I do not recall," I repeat, staring down at my hands.

"Ms. Deere, may I remind you that you are under oath. Was Jaw Itznicki in the shed the night of Rose Rowan's murder? Yes or no."

"He came into the shed, yes, but—"

Honor is staring hot flames at me like she will come jerk me off the stand if I say anything else. Aarush's head is in his hands. At the very back of the gallery, Skye's hand creeps over his face to hide his smile.

"Ms. Deere, you have taken an oath before this court. Please answer the question. Did Jaw Itznicki kill Rose Rowan?"

What my story should be whirls in my skull like white plastic in a snow globe. I don't even know what I should say, all I can remember is the truth.

"Jaw didn't kill Rose," I whisper into the mic. "He came into the shed, but Jaw did not kill Rose."

"Thank you," a voice calls from the back of the courtroom. "I appreciate that."

A ripple of gasps chases through the gallery like fire through dry grass. Chairs squeak, cameras flash, as everyone turns to see Jaw Itznicki himself, stepping through the double doors at the back of the courtroom.

And then Erik walks in behind him, and the gasps become cries and yells.

It can't be him. He's in Bali. Am I hallucinating? Maybe I fainted and I'm hallucinating.

"This is an evidentiary hearing, right?" Jaw says, holding up a long yellow envelope. "Well, I got some evidence here. I got some pictures y'all need to see!"

Janeane's face withers, upper lip pulling back to bare her teeth.

"MURDERER!" she screams. "*MURDERER!*"

"I don't think so, babe." He grins at her. "Nice try, though."

"Order!" The judge cracks his gavel. "I will have order!"

Feedback from the walkie-talkies whines around the edges of the room. I'm not the only one who sees him, then. He's not some personalized hope breaking out of my brain into reality. He's really here. He came.

Erik's eyes connect with mine then, and I'm on my feet.

"Signal Deere!" Erik calls to me, moving past Jaw now, past Honor. "I need you to answer a question!" He neatly hops over a table, sidesteps another bailiff with quicksilver speed, and puts a piece of paper on the stand in front of me, some manic energy behind every motion, his face stiff from struggling to keep it at bay.

"Will you marry me?" Erik asks.

Maybe I fainted before the first question after all. This has to be a dream.

Behind him, Skye is on his feet, screaming, *"Don't let her sign that!"*

But I have the mic. So I duck forward and say: "Uh . . . yes?"

He scrawls on the paper. His signature is atrocious, his hand is shaking so hard. And what he's just signed is a marriage license.

"Cool, thanks." Erik smiles, eyes bright, his dimple going deeper as one of the bailiffs pulls him away from me. "Clerk?" he calls over his shoulder toward the spectator benches. "Where's my county clerk?"

The small woman in the bright pink suit, the one who winked at me, pops up.

"You mind witnessing this real quick?" Erik calls over the bailiff's arm as he's herded back toward Jaw. The clerk hurries past Honor, who looks like she's about to blow a vein, and hands me a pen.

"This is an *absolute circus*," the judge groans into his hand.

"This is no marriage! This is a fraud!" Skye screams. "Tear up that license!"

And I realize, staring down at the marriage license, that if I marry Erik I will be his next of kin. His conservator. And Skye will lose all claim on him.

My hand jitters wildly as I sign my name on the line for "bride."

"Is that it? Are we married now?" I ask the clerk over Skye's shrieking and the hubbub of the courtroom.

"There's a little more to it than that, honey. *I* sign as witness . . ." The clerk adds her signature. "And then the judge signs as officiant, and then you have to file it, of course."

She holds the license out to the judge. He takes it, but he doesn't sign it, doesn't even look at it. He's watching the scene unfolding in the center aisle.

The bailiffs have encircled Erik and Jaw. Erik's smile is gone, and Jaw is fanning his photos, but they flutter to the floor as both of them are seized, the glossy paper crumpling under the bailiff's thick-soled shoes. Jaw screams in protest:

"DUDE! THAT'S EVIDENCE!"

"Arrest them both at once," the judge orders.

Four bailiffs are wrestling Erik toward the doors, though he's not resisting. And then the smallest one hauls back and punches him right in the stomach, hard; Erik's breath rattles out of him.

"DON'T TOUCH HIM!" I scream. "DON'T YOU TOUCH HIM!" I leap over the stand and run toward them.

"No." Honor gets in front of me. "Signal, no—" One of the larger male junior attorneys clotheslines me around the waist, sending a sharp pain up my stitched side, but I throw myself forward, screaming.

"Let go of him!"

"Have these disruptors taken from my court immediately." The gavel clacks again and again. "Ms. Deere, I order you be held in contempt—"

"Your Honor, please! Hear them out!" The bearded old man in the fishing hat is suddenly on his feet, hands clawing at his face. His voice is jarringly young, and as the fishing hat falls from his head a brown thatch of hair scattered with gray is revealed, a sharp contrast to the white beard that used to be on his face. Now it's half ripped away, fake skin curling around his mouth like dried Elmer's Glue as he addresses the courtroom:

"My name is Dave Keogh," Dave says. "I am the director of Camp Naramauke. And I can back up their evidence with my own testimony."

Chaos. All the phones that are supposed to be off are now angled on him, recording as the judge orders Dave to the bench. Honor and Janeane's lawyer approach as well. The bailiffs still holding Erik sweep him out of the courtroom, and I sprint after them.

"Where are you taking him?" I cry.

"Next door for questioning," a bailiff answers without looking at me, his hand around the back of Erik's neck, so he can't look up from the ground. Erik walks with a little hitch in his step, like he hasn't quite gotten his breath back, but he calls: "Get there before Skye does when they release me, okay? I'm counting on you, *wife*."

And they sweep him through the side exit and into daylight.

* * *

The top of the judge's head is glowing red through his liver spots as he stoops over the photos Jaw brought in, retrieved from the floor and now tiled across his desk. He's been looking at them almost the full fifteen minutes we've been in his chambers.

Amira is off following up on Erik. And I'm jumping out of my skin. I'm why he turned himself in, everything that happens to him now is my fault, I cannot let him down. Honor promised that Amira could handle everything, that the best thing I can do to help is to stay in the judge's chambers until a decision is reached on my retrial. At first, I didn't think I'd be able to contain myself. But seeing these pictures has frozen me with shock, wave after wave of memory rising up inside me, the only response in my head Lupin's mantra:

I accept my memories, all of my memories. My past is in the past, it cannot hurt me.

But it's not true. These photographs are unbearable.

There we are, Rose and me. Drunkenly dancing together in the last hours of her life, cheeks pressed together, laughing with each other. There I am passed out against the wall with my old, bright blue hair. There's Jaw, his mouth over mine, the flash so close it almost washes us out. Another picture, taken from farther back and in focus. I'm clearly unconscious, hand limp at my side, but Jaw's mouth is still latched onto mine, though his eyes stare through the camera to Rose: *Happy now?*

"Fakes," Janeane insists. "Photoshopped or generated, who knows."

"Then why did you pay for them so long?" Jaw asks her.

"I did no such thing."

"Guess we'll see when you finally turn over those bank statements," Honor adds, not missing a beat.

"The time stamp is right on the edge, because they were taken with one of those old-fashioned cardboard cameras," Jaw says, pointing to the glowing white and orange letters that display the night of Rose's murder. He looks back to the female bailiff holding his elbow. "You know what I'm talking about?"

"Disposable cameras?" Honor offers.

"Yeah, those things. Rose brought one to the shed and we were taking pictures when Janeane came in, right there . . ."

He sets his fingertip on the center photo. A blurry image of Janeane just as she's coming through the door, a melted Halloween mask version of her face twisting in undisguised rage. Bright red dots glowing from eyes otherwise hooded in shadow, a streak of teeth bared in a scream.

Undeniably her and yet not her, the part of herself she never lets anyone see.

"She went wild at Rose right then, told me to get the hell out, and sad to say, I scrammed. But I still had the camera with me, and after I heard what happened I held onto the negatives. When she found out I had them—" He doesn't elaborate on how. "She offered me money to get rid of them. I took the money but kept the negatives in the vault."

Janeane shoots him a look that could take his head off.

"Those pictures are completely inadmissible," Janeane's lawyer insists. "The chain of custody of evidence is completely unclear—"

"This is evidence. He just presented it," Honor says. "Seems straightforward to me, Tiffany."

"Young man, may I ask why you're presenting these photos now?" the judge asks Jaw.

"Okay, so, I was hiding out at my dad's when that Erik kid just comes walking into my house. Like, I still have no idea how he got in. But I'd seen him and Signal on the news, and he reminded me of something important. Namely, the rule of three—"

"Are we supposed to just stand here and listen to this junkie?!" Janeane interjects, but the judge silences her with a glance.

"In my faith tradition, which is Wicca," Jaw solemnly addresses the judge, "we believe whatever you put out in the world comes back to your threefold, or times three. Erik told me Janeane killed her husband and melted him down the drain of their tub, and once she fixed up Signal for all that, she'd come after me next. 'Cause I was her last loose thread. Welp, dude was right! She's straight up trying to hang Rose on me now?" He sneers at Janeane. "Rule of three, bitch. Rule of three." His eyes dart to me then, and he adds, "And on that note, Signal, I want to be sure and apologize for kiss—for *assaulting you*, in those pictures. I really mean that. It was wrong, it was so wrong, what I did. And I am so, so sorry. Alright?"

I nod, startled.

"Well," the judge says at last, "the negatives will be analyzed, of course, and verified by experts, ahead of trial. I must insist on that. But even without expert authentication, this is more than enough evidence to justify a full retrial."

Honor squeezes my shoulder.

"Until then," the judge adds, "I suggest Ms. Rowan be held in custody. As for you, Ms. Deere? A word."

He motions me closer and taps the marriage license.

"If this young man is under a conservatorship, this will be null and void unless you get the conservator to sign it first. No officiant will solemnize this without the conservator's signature. Myself included."

"But . . . it's an emergency?" I whisper, face heating.

He slides the license toward me, face stern. "Good luck, Ms. Deere, on your emergency marriage."

* * *

The mass of people outside the courthouse is almost terrifying when we finally leave. The crowd swells up and down the block and rushes up the courthouse steps toward us like a stormy tide. My own face stares up at me from so many chests, the Fear No Deere mug shot printed on T-shirts and signs of every color. There's a roar as I appear and the crowd surges, people shrieking my name the whole walk to the limo. I try not to resent them for slowing me down.

"*SIG-NAL! SIG-NAL!*"

Mom at least finds it gratifying; she pumps her fist until we're herded into the limo. Aarush and Sonny are inside, both glued to their phones.

"What's happening with Erik?" I beg them.

"He's being deposed." Sonny looks up from his phone. "You know how long it took making your own statement. It'll be some hours if not days before we know what they're charging him with."

"And the fact you'd *want* to see him after the stunt he pulled today!" Aarush adds.

"He saved me."

"He's just trying to save himself." Aarush's tone is sharp. "Erik tried the same fatuous trick Ted Bundy pulled on a Florida courtroom, when he married Carolyn Boone on the stand, during a murder trial he *lost*—"

I laugh. "Well, Erik is a big Ted Bundy fan—"

"Do you *hear yourself?!*" Aarush screams. "Do you even hear yourself when you talk about him?! You are *not* legally married to Erik, thank God, and it boggles my mind that you would want to tie yourself to such a depraved—"

"Let's keep our eyes on the prize." Honor puts her hand on Aarush's wrist to forestall more screaming but keeps her eyes on me. "We need to get Dave's deposition as soon as possible. Through Dave, we can tie the Wylie-Stanton to the federal case."

Sonny's well-shaped eyebrows go up. "If that's true, I can cover his representation as well."

"And they'll give me time to talk with him if I'm his counsel," Honor points out.

"Consider yourself hired."

"But Erik—" I press.

"Is in capable hands with Amira." Honor looks back down at her phone, scrolling through her messages. "He just needs someone advising him on what he does and does not have to answer. I'll have her stay with him until you're done talking with Dave and we'll go from there—"

"*I'm* talking with Dave?"

"My gut says he'll open up more across from you. Then I can follow up."

"Alright . . ." I nod, then: "Will there be a printer there I can use?"

Aarush frowns, looking wary.

"I just want to, like, have what I'm going to ask him in front of me?" I blink at them innocently.

"Sounds good." Honor nods, not looking up from her phone.

* * *

The interview room is small and white. A table and chairs in front of a mirror the size of a blackboard. When I walk in, Dave is cuffed to the table, still in the tan Members Only jacket and Dockers he wore pretending to be an old man, flakes of prosthetic skin still clinging to the stubble of his square jaw.

I set a cup of cocoa in front of him, then pull back the heavy chair across the table from his with a long screech. I shuffle my papers in front of me, still warm from the printer.

"Well, Signal." He looks down into the cocoa, then looks up with a cold smile. "How's that plan to appeal going?"

"I just got one." I fold my hands in front of me. "Things are starting to look up, Dave."

"No, they're not." He leans in toward me. "Believe me, Mrs. Wylie-Stanton, you're in greater danger now than you've ever been before."

Chapter Twelve

Daddy Issues

∽

"Is that why you backed out of testifying?" I lean toward him. "Who threatened you?"

He sits back as far as the cuffs will let him, his generically handsome face giving me nothing.

"Camp is going down," I tell him. "But if you testify, Sonny can protect you—"

"No one can protect either of us." Dave shakes his head. "You better start waking up to that."

"But you still came to the trial."

"I was hoping you had something else up your sleeve. If I'd been the only witness your whole trial hinged on, I would've been too clear a target. But when Jaw and Erik came in, the situation changed. It became safer to spill what I knew, so I wouldn't be silenced later."

A wave of vertigo makes me sway in my seat. If Erik and Jaw hadn't burst into the courtroom, Dave would've stayed hidden. Or if they had come, and Dave hadn't been there, Erik would've been arrested for nothing and I would've . . . what?

Confessed? Collapsed?

"Who is silencing you?" I push. "Headquarters? Are they still—are they still sending out Kurt? We know he's not on Ledrick's mission, whatever that was—"

Dave's eyebrows go up at my use of the Director's surname.

"You and Erik really *are* together. How cute." He doesn't smile. "I never particularly liked Ledrick, but you can't say he wasn't focused. He'd worked his whole life to chemically engineer a perfect assassin, and he got damn close with Erik. But some kind of self-preservation instinct kicked in right before we finished."

"What do you mean, finished?"

"Erik had a series of injections that helped heighten his natural neurochemical makeup and allowed us to map his brain. The new money behind camp was getting excited about our progress and made it clear Erik was a high-priority asset, not to be expended. But Ledrick started to drag his feet as things got more, shall we say, heated between them. I think he realized the moment Erik got to the point headquarters wanted him, Ledrick would be a dead man. So, before the last round of injections, Ledrick sent Kurt and Erik out on a suicide mission. What we call a 'public clean up'—call authorities in on the last target so your agents flame out as spectacularly as possible."

I swallow hard.

"Ledrick also violated protocol," Dave shakes his head, "by having them call the 'last resort' number my class used to organize missions back in the day, to circumvent headquarters." Dave sips his cocoa, makes a face, and pushes it away. "When you ran into me at camp that morning, I'd just reported Ledrick to HQ and was planning to get out of Dodge until he was neutralized. Instead, you came in and turned over the apple cart. Now they're all scrambling."

"But you're the director now, right?"

"Unfortunately, yes. I was 'promoted' for informing on Ledrick." He nods, rattles his cuffs. "And all that means is a lot of fun new charges."

I nod, not letting my face show my mounting excitement. "And Kurt?"

"He kept calling in and calling in to the point I thought someone would pick up his calls and trace me. So I gave him the direct line to headquarters."

"Then his targets are from headquarters?"

"I highly doubt they're improvisations." Dave frowns. "Because when I looked into the twins' case, it was abundantly clear Troy had racked up all the kills himself."

"But headquarters is being actively investigated. How can they support a mission and deny they exist at the same time?"

"They can't get him money. But that doesn't mean they aren't dangling some carrot to keep him in line," Dave says. Then his mouth sets like he will not say more, though he could if he wanted to.

". . . Like . . . the injections Erik was on? Is that what Kurt wants? Does he want to take Erik's place as their perfect assassin or something?"

His expression is too practiced to flicker, but his eyes gleam knowingly.

"CurtPro is the new money behind headquarters. That much you can confirm, right?"

He shrugs, and starts to whistle, glancing over at the two-way mirror.

I pivot. "What about Kate? What's happened to her? Will she testify?"

He stops whistling, tilts his head back. "Have you tried tracking her kill switch?"

"Kate has a kill switch?" I say, startled. "Do you?"

"Of course I do," Dave snaps. "You sign on for something at seventeen, sometimes you change your mind before thirty-five."

And it hits me then, that at one point Dave was a camper. That he survived years of missions only to have a kill switch installed after his friends were all "retired."

To make sure he went through with taking them all out.

"Dave . . . I'm so sorry."

"Could you please focus, Signal?" Dave snaps. "You're missing the point. Headquarters has all but shut down since your stream, but I can still log into my camp profile and track the switches that weren't deactivated by Dennis: my own, and Kate's. Now, Kate is a lot more tech savvy than me. She installed some kind of ten-hour lag on her kill switch. So I can tell you where Kate was ten hours ago. But the woman moves fast."

Kate had been looking for a way to escape? And here I'd thought she had so much control.

"Okay," I nod. "Maybe Dennis can do something with that."

"Yeah, he probably could. You little assholes turned out to be pretty exceptional."

I feel strangely heartened by the unexpected praise and lean forward, hopeful. "Please, Dave. If you know anything about CurtPro, it could save Erik's life if you just—"

"You're terrible at this, Signal." Dave shakes his head. "Stop trying to appeal to my sympathy—I have none. You incentivize a subject like me."

"Fine. Name your incentives."

"Immunity and a lifetime supply of big fat checks." Dave raises an eyebrow. "Got any of those?"

"I can tell you what I'm authorized to offer you, once you sign this NDA." I keep my face straight, tapping the stack of papers on the desk before sliding them in front of him.

He scans through the first double-sided pages, brow furrowing.

"You have five minutes to sign," I say calmly.

"Five minutes?" Dave gives me a hard look. "I gave you fifteen to sign on for camp."

"Then you know this is pure pageantry, Dave. I didn't have a choice then, just like you don't have a choice now."

He rolls his eyes, then heavily goes through and signs everywhere I've flagged with a yellow tab. He's almost to the last line when the intercom crackles overhead.

"Okay, Signal," Honor says, quickly. "Dave, you don't have to—"

"Just a second, Honor!" I call over her last words.

"What'd she say?" He looks up at me, face tense, pen hovering over the line.

"Just a second!" I cry at the mirror, in a whiny voice, then lean into Dave. "The lawyer's supposed to swap in with me once the NDA is signed. But I have all these questions I need to ask first, so hold off on signing the last page for a second."

He signs, hard and shoves the pile back at me. "No thanks. Send the lawyer in."

"Thanks, Dave," I say, and exit the room with my prize: a sample NDA I found on the internet on the way over, a credit card contract, and finally, at the bottom, the marriage certificate.

*   *   *

I step out into the hall and immediately text Dennis everything Dave said about Kate's kill switch while I still remember. I'm three texts in when Sonny's nervous assistant approaches me, haloed by the pale light from the narrow windows.

"Hey, Signal, exciting day, right!" The assistant taps her iPad, and I struggle to remember her name. "So it looks like your bail requirements have changed, yay! Which means you're off house arrest, very cool . . . and free to move in with your mom at Sea View!"

"What?"

"You'll be moving into Sea View today! And don't worry about stopping by the house. We'll pack your things up and drive them by. You and Breann are welcome to stay at the property until the fifteenth of next month, and then if you want to apply as tenants—"

"I don't understand. What's happening with Erik?"

"Let me see . . ." The assistant taps on her iPad. "He's in a secured part of the station that we can't access, but I can text you after he's released—"

"After? No. I need to be there when he gets out."

"You're welcome to try getting into building B of the station." She gestures at a building identical to ours through the window, smirking but not looking up from her iPad. "But you won't get far past the metal detectors without some kind of clearance."

I turn and try the door of the interrogation room; it's locked automatically. I hurry down the beige linoleum hall, to the entrance of the viewing room, the assistant's heels clacking a few steps behind.

"Signal? Signal, where are you going—"

I throw the door open, but the dark viewing room is empty. The glowing window into the interrogation room presents a striking tableau: Honor and Sonny across the table from Dave, who is leaned back in his chair, a smile on his face.

The assistant speeds ahead of me and stabs the button of the intercom.

"Honor! Signal is in here? She wants to talk to you before leaving?"

Honor jerks back in her chair. Sonny nods to her, and she moves toward the door out into the hall. I race to meet her there.

"I thought you were going to help with Erik?"

"Erik does not require representation, as there will be no charges against him at this time."

"*What?* No charges at all? So—so what're they going to do with him?"

"He'll be released to his next of kin."

"To *Skye?!* No, I promised him—Honor, we need to file a restraining order or something—"

"I'm really sorry to tell you like this," Honor says, "but Sonny has asked me to move over to your friends' trial. Now that Jaw's evidence is in, he thinks they're a bigger priority."

"You're—not my lawyer anymore?" My throat constricts.

She shakes her head, coolly but firmly. "But I can forward you the names of some really great public defenders—"

One of Sonny's security guards comes around the corner, hand to his earpiece.

"Ms. Deere!" He smiles at me. "You need help finding the car?"

I turn on my heel and sprint down the hall.

* * *

The alarm goes off as soon as the fire door handle sinks below my hand. I sprint up an echoing set of cement stairs, the security guard's footsteps just behind me: "Where're you going, that's the roof—"

I burst out into the open air and almost slam into the chain-link fence hemming in the fire exit. But thanks to camp, I get over the fence quickly and drop lightly onto the gravel on the other side.

We're ten floors up, but the space between the two police station buildings is tantalizingly narrow, and some painter has left his equipment leaned up against the ledge of the roof. Drop cloths, paint cans, and a long workmen's ladder. I tuck the marriage license down the front of my tight undershirt and roll up my cardigan sleeves.

"Ms. Deere! Get away from there!" The security guard rattles the chain-link, having tried to climb up twice unsuccessfully in his slick-soled patent leather loafers. "What are you—? Put that ladder down!"

I balance the ladder along the lip of the roof, and unlock the second length of rungs, cocooned in its aluminum frame. Carefully, I turn the aluminum ladder so it's perpendicular to the roof's edge, cantilevered out into the air, then dip it forward enough the second set of rungs rushes forward, extending another four feet.

"Oh no, what are you—if you're doing what I think you're doing—" The security guard sounds genuinely horrified as I hoist the ladder farther over the low cement edge of our building, so it's tottering three-quarters out into space. "Are you trying to get yourself killed?!"

It takes all my weight to keep the ladder sticking straight out in midair between the two buildings, and all my strength to shove it so the far end of the ladder goes sailing and catches across the top of the building across from us with a rattle. I've got about two feet of ladder balanced on each building now, and nothing but wind whistling through the rungs between.

But it might actually be easier than climbing the obstacle course ladder at camp, I tell myself: It's level, and shorter, and should hold still. I hope.

I start crawling out onto the ladder and the security guard screams:

"She's climbing?! SHE'S CLIMBING!!" The security guard is practically hyperventilating. "YOUNG. LADY. *Spider-Man* is a movie! They use special effects, okay?! They tried that in real life, on Broadway, and it was NOT pretty! *Turn Off the Dark?* Hello?"

The ladder wobbles under my hands, slick with sweat against the ridged metal rungs, my whole body tensed as I fight to maintain my balance.

"Oh my Lord, oh my Lord, this girl's going to make me watch her fall to Kingdom Come. I can't! I can't! *Ma'am*, you are *traumatizing me!*"

Traffic noise washes up from the street as I crawl forward; the farther I go, the more the ladder reacts to my weight. There are scattered yells below me, cries up and down the street, but I refuse to look down. No fainting this time, no fear allowed. I keep my eyes trained on the far wall, but I can hear:

"SIG-NAL! SIG-NAL! SIG-NAL!"

I can't believe I'm doing this. But I know I can.

Until my tights snag on the metal lip of one of the rungs. When I bring my knee up, the side of the ladder is pulled with it, the sky and ground suddenly sliding, the ladder pulled onto its side. The crowd below emits guttural sounds of dread as one of my ballet flats falls into their midst.

But I've done this before. It feels almost familiar, gripping the rung and sliding my weight the way I used to when someone would climb over me on the rope ladder. The metal ladder stops dancing on its side and flips over, becoming a grid between me and the white sky. My stitches hurt, hanging this way, from my fingertips. But hey, now I've got a set of monkey bars between the buildings.

So what if I hate monkey bars.

Erik. Erik is waiting.

I reach out for the center of the next rung, my shoulders aching, my fingers screaming, my feet pedaling the air. Blocking out the cheers from below, I keep my eyes on the cement lip of the roof until my hand cups its cold curve. I kick out until my stocking foot brushes the brick window ledge, then swing forward enough to step onto it. In another moment, I'm hauling myself up onto the roof like a kid pulls themselves out of a swimming pool. I get upright, and as I pull the ladder after me, the street below explodes in wild applause.

I finally look down: The crowd from in front of the courtroom is massed below, hands all outstretched like they were ready to catch me if I fell. And when I wave, they all start cheering like I've won the Olympic gold.

The security guard, across the way, is clapping too, clearly relieved.

But under the cheering I hear rough shouts, doors being thrown open. I run to the far side of the roof. Below, dozens of wary police are escorting a figure in a straitjacket with a broken halo of dark blonde hair.

One officer gestures to a Mercedes van at the intersection ahead; two officers open up a back gate: It's Skye and his driver.

Twelve feet below me the fire escape starts.

Luckily there's a rain gutter that leads to a drainpipe—old-fashioned, good gussets. I step over the side of the building, testing the bracket with one foot; it handles my weight well, so I scuttle down to the top level of the fire escape.

Skye's Mercedes van pulls in, the officers rolling the covered chain-link fencing just enough so it can fit through. The police pull a stiff Erik toward the van, Skye's driver stepping out to open the side door just as I reach the ground, and then I lose him in a knot of officers. I duck behind the police vans parked directly behind the building and run around the back of Skye's van, huddling down by the sliding door on its other side.

Through the tinted glass I watch them force Erik into the back, thick red hands steering his head, pushing his shoulders, his mouth muzzled with a strange opaque plastic mask, his eyes wild. The moment they slam the passenger side door shut, I pull the driver's side door open.

Erik turns to me, blinking, and I hold out my hand. In another moment he's leaped down beside me, wobbling a little in his straitjacket, and I brace his elbow. Then my arms are around him.

"What the hell," Skye's voice rings out, "do you think you're doing?"

Skye is leaning over the middle seat of the van, a Taser gun out, jaw flaring as he levels it with Erik's throat. I get in front of Erik, blocking Skye's shot and fumbling with my shirt.

"I got all the signatures. Even the conservator's. The *real* conservator's!" I pull out the marriage license. "He's mine."

"Officers?" Skye turns his head slightly over his shoulder without taking his eyes off me. "I need some assistance in the transfer of this juvenile."

The knot of glowering officers fans out from the other side of the van.

"This man is an important witness, and my husband!" I tell them, the license fluttering in my hand. "He's coming with me. Skye has no right to him."

A look of uncertainty flashes through the group, but one of them, the short bailiff who punched Erik, sidles forward.

"We've been searching for this prick for weeks up and down the coast," he says. "He made a fool of us with that damn video, then struts into our courthouse like he owns the place. And now they're not even charging him! So he's important to someone. But not you, kid."

He cuts a look to my other side, to another officer sidling around me, moving toward Erik in a pincer movement.

Even with his face masked, Erik's expression is clear: *I told you so.*

"Hold on," I whisper, then slip through the policemen, race to the chain-link fence between the van and the street, and haul the fence open as I scream at the top of my lungs:

"IT'S ME! SIGNAL DEERE!" My voice echoes down the street. "THEY'RE TRYING TO TAKE ERIK! THEY'RE TRYING TO TAKE MY ERIK FROM ME!"

Wild yells, a thunderstorm of racing footsteps, and a flood of young people wash toward the fence, my own black and white face twisting across their torsos.

"Erik's here?! For real?"

"Hey! They got married in court; we all saw! Back off!"

"Sign my shirt?"

Skye's van is immediately penned in by the crowd, and he hurriedly gets in his seat and slams the door closed as fists start drumming on his windshield. Our fans surround the van, one especially energetic girl in raver boots vaulting onto the hood and trying to kick in the windshield as the others start rocking the vehicle back and forth. The police struggle to clear the vehicle as wave after wave of teenagers floods their back parking lot.

Erik, eyes laughing now, nudges me along with his shoulder, away from the crowd and back into the street. We run upstream against the steady flow of protesters pouring in, ducking and dodging through the mass of people, who scream cheers of approval in our faces as we run by. Even with his arms strapped around his sides, Erik's able to sprint faster than me. But I keep up and we don't stop until we've put several blocks between us and the carnival of screams and whistles and honking erupting now from behind the police station, ducking into a gray stone stairway.

Erik bends toward me, tilting his head so I can unstrap the muzzle from his burning face. He shakes his head hard, gulps down air, and turns on me, his eyes and smile so bright:

"Could you have cut that any closer?"

"You're one to talk!"

A battered bronze sedan slows at the curb, axles screaming, and a kid who looks about sixteen leans out the passenger window and yells: "Hey! Erik! Signal! You two need a ride?"

"Yes!" Erik calls back. "Take us to the nicest hotel in town!"

* * *

The driver keeps glancing up in the rearview as I work to unstrap Erik from his straitjacket, swerving abruptly to stay in his lane. The two guys up front are delightedly eavesdropping as we wheel out of the crowd and farther downtown, the faint sun climbing down behind the fog.

"*Ouch!*"

"Hold still, this buckle is weird—"

"Maybe I should just keep this thing on," Erik snaps. "Seems like suitable attire for what we're doing."

"Getting married?" I laugh. "Hey, this is *your idea.*"

"It's my idea of the punishment *you deserve*," Erik says, dimple flashing as he tries desperately not to laugh. "After the way you trapped me into turning myself in—"

"I told you you were free to go!"

"But I wasn't, was I?" he says, pulling one arm loose. "No! You came at me, with your tears and visions of hell, and roped me in! Made me skip out on a flight to Bali to keep you from going back to prison—" He pulls his other arm loose, and then they're both around me. He pulls me down into his lap, bending down so close our noses brush, his eyes bright green against the high spots of pink in his cheeks. His voice drops, confidential: "You realize you almost killed me, right? Dumped me in a skyscraper. Locked me out of drafts. Cut off all contact. Are they *sure* you're not a Class A?"

"Hey, man—" the driver calls back to us. "Any of these hotels what you're looking for?"

Erik cranes his head out the open window to investigate, hair blowing back in the wind, then ducks back in again, unimpressed.

"No, no, I want the kind of place where the doormen dress like admirals," Erik explains.

"Like *what?*"

"Like Cap'n Crunch, my good man! Like Cap'n Crunch!" And then he smiles at me, his most wicked smile. "It *is* our wedding night."

"Not *really,*" I say, my stomach flipping over, but Erik leans forward to pound excitedly on the driver's headrest with his fist.

"There! Right there! That's the one!"

An ornate building rises before us, covered in flags and flourishes of stone, fountain sounds washing over us as we hurry into the lobby, running like someone's chasing us. Erik offers a non-driver's license with an outrageously good photograph and starts pulling hundred-dollar bills from a thick wad dug out of his pocket, topping the crumpled heap with Nick Scarpelli's Discover card.

A few moments later, we're stepping into a brass elevator that glows like a beam of sunshine, when the tiniest, most darling little old couple gets on as well.

We stand in the back corner, so close yet not touching, the old couple looking back at us politely whenever the elevator dings. Erik nods back each time with reflexive politeness, and I bite my lip to keep from laughing.

"You do realize you've got a straitjacket tied around your waist?" I whisper to Erik.

He leans down and whispers back, "Yeah, well, you're missing a shoe."

"Hey, so, are those jeans back in style or have you fallen on hard times?"

The corner of his mouth twitches. "How much of a fight did he put up?"

"Who?" I whisper.

"The husky tween boy you stole that blazer from."

I burst out laughing as the elevator bounces to a stop and cover my face as we pass the darling old couple out into the hall. Erik finds our door and turns to me, eyes very bright.

"I should carry you over the threshold."

"Do *not!*" I step back.

"It's really bad luck if I don't." He puts out his arms, but I bat them away.

"No, it's not, we aren't even technically married. Save *something* for the actual wedding day."

"That's all we're saving," he says under his breath, and throws the door open to a vast and dimly lit room at the very top of the building.

The buckles on his straitjacket jingle as he gets it loose and kicks it to the floor of the closet. I spin around dreamily, taking in the room. The floor-to-ceiling windows are hung with red velvet curtains, the bed a broad plane of white. I place the marriage license carefully in the top drawer of a gleaming black armoire, and when I close it Erik is hovering just behind me.

"It's really something," I say.

"Uh huh." He pulls his hoodie over his head and throws it to the floor.

"What do you think?"

"Of what?" He's watching my mouth like he's lip reading.

"The room. You were so particular about the hotel . . ."

He finally breaks off staring at me, scans the space, and nods, indifferent. "It'll do."

Then he picks me up like it's nothing, and a shiver of nervous energy passes between us before he sets me in the middle of the glowing white duvet. Everything goes silent then, like when the world is muffled by new-fallen snow.

Erik slings himself on top of me with careless grace, but it's an ease at odds with his tight expression.

I know this face. It's the same face as when he stepped through the smoke after killing Angel Childs, fighting some battle inside himself more urgent than the fire around us.

It frightens the hell out of me.

"Erik?"

His lips momentarily tighten, like his body is fighting to keep the words in.

"What's wrong?" I ask gently.

And his head drops, his shoulders sink in defeat.

"Signal," Erik says, "I've got to tell you something."

Chapter Thirteen

Honeymoon

❧

"What happened?"

Erik shifts his weight so he's leaning beside me.

"They didn't charge me with anything, back at the station." He peers into my eyes like a cat watching for mice.

"I know. Is that a bad thing?" I prop myself up on my elbows.

"*Yes.*" He claws his hand through his wild hair. "They should've hit me with grand theft auto, at least. Evading arrest, coercion, kidnapping, attempted murder, *actual* murder—all of those would've been fair." He bites at his nails. "But that cop was right. Someone cleared the way for Skye to take me home."

"Like . . . headquarters?" I swallow. "Dave said they consider you a high-priority asset. That they want to finish the series of injections Ledrick was giving you."

"I see." Erik nods, staring at the sheet between us like it's a map, and he's lost. "And they can't haul me back to camp while it's under investigation, or a CurtPro facility, because that would be too incriminating. But it would only be natural for me to go back to *Skye's house*, being his incompetent little brother . . ." His eyes are very green as they lock with mine. "So now you're the only thing between me and Skye. Which means our union will have to be a short one."

". . . How short?"

"However long it takes for me to give evidence. A couple of weeks. Then I'll leave the country for good."

I fall back against the duvet, stunned.

He shifts his weight again, rests his forearms on either side of me and balances on them, one knee between my knees, eyes level with mine. He's still a lot heavier than I would've guessed, his body dense and radiant with heat as he says, "But while we're married, you will enjoy *all* the perks, I promise you."

And before I can recover enough to say something, he kisses me, so perfectly.

It's the kiss in the part of the dream just before you wake up. And I kiss him back without hesitation. It's like the room is underwater and he's air—the fact he's running out doesn't make me need him less. And though what he's said is slowly and certainly collapsing my heart, the little demon in me just wants him closer. I claw at him, and he meets, then escalates my intensity, ladders racing down my tights as his fingers dig at my hips. I go for his beautiful throat and he groans and pins me down with a kiss that exorcises all words from my head completely. The room dips and spins like the bed is a carousel as he sits up and starts deftly unbuttoning my blouse.

And then a silent alarm goes off inside me:

He's just told you he's going to leave you. His exit strategy is Nadya, you realize that, right? So get your hands off of him and his hands off you and get a hold of yourself.

But I *can't*. I don't care how much it hurts later, I have lost all allegiance to my future self. Am I seriously about to do what I think I'm about to do?

. . . Maybe?

Then his hand slides under my undershirt, toward the curve of my waist where my stitches lie, and I jerk upright.

"No, wait, stop."

Erik stops immediately. I push up on my elbows and half-crawl out from under him until I knock against the leather headboard. Both of us are panting hard, staring at the other like we're aiming dueling pistols. He's shirtless, which is my fault, and I have no idea where his shirt went. I just hope it's not in pieces.

"Leaving the country?" I gasp. "You mean, running off with Nadya?"

He stares at me, eyes glazed over, lips slightly swollen, like he doesn't understand the language I'm speaking.

"And this whole 'wedding night' setup—" I sit up, adjusting my blouse. "Is just practice for your honeymoon with Nadya in a couple weeks, right—"

"No! No, no, no." Erik shakes his head. "It's not like that with Nadya, it's a business arrangement. I'm an *employee*, okay? I don't—I *can't* like her that way, I've tried and—"

"Tried *how?*"

"I tried to let you go." He looks so sad. "And when I couldn't, I thought there'd be, I don't know—a parole officer, a case worker, *something* between me and Skye, other than my five-foot-tall sugar cube." He kneads his face with his hand. "But what's to stop Skye—and whoever helped him clear my charges—from going after you?"

Coldness steals through me.

"I brought Jaw back to clear your name. And I will testify about camp for our friends. I can do that if you're my conservator. But then I have to go. Or you'll be in danger."

"So tonight is just to 'get me out of your system'?"

He sits up, and the tall glass bedside lamp becomes the equivalent of a Renaissance sculptor as its rays carve his torso from the dark.

"I mean, I *hope so.*" Erik moves lightly over and next to me, leaning back against the headboard so we're eye to eye. "Wouldn't it be easier if sex could cure these feelings? Can you tell me with a straight face you *enjoy* this?" He waves one hand between us, sneering. "Because I don't. Love is worse than fear, love is the worst thing I've ever felt. Constantly swinging from euphoria to depression, the obsessive thoughts, and I have to be in love with *you* of all people." He shakes his head, disgusted. "I'm *aware*, at least, when I'm being evil. You have *no clue*, no idea what you do to me—"

"Excuse me, *what?*"

"The look on your face." He bites at his nails. "When you pushed me off that elevator! You didn't want to leave any more than I wanted you to go. But you *still could*. You could! You have this cold little thing in you—"

"A conscience?"

"—that means you can just stop loving me any time you want, and go comfort yourself with your perfect little soul." He glares at me. "But the only good thoughts I have in this world are of you. The only relief I can have is seeing you. So excuse me if I'm looking for a way to cure these feelings, but I'm the one who's trapped by them."

I'm about to protest how completely not fair and untrue all this is when I notice a strange shadow under his rib cage. Not a shadow, a bruise: dark purple, shot through with red where the bailiff punched him. Much harder than I realized. He came back, though he thought he'd be charged. He came back, when he was almost free.

I take his hand; he immediately presses the back of mine against his heart, beating too fast under the warm muscle.

"Don't we owe it to ourselves to try? To get sick of each other, I mean."

I wait until I'm sure my voice won't break. "I don't think it works that way for me."

He scans me then: my loose skirt, the circles under my eyes, and looks down at my hand, blistered from my climb across the ladder. He traces the ridge of my knuckles, thinking so intently. He starts to say something, then stops, as if coming up with an argument and then dismissing it. He leans his head back and stares at me, and I can feel his heart thundering. Then at last his shoulders drop. "Fine, then. I didn't come back for the glass avocado." Pink spots rise in his cheeks. "You're a light bulb, too."

My fingers go through his when the phone I didn't know he had starts chiming.

He pulls the dupe phone from his pocket, his other hand still in mine, and tilts the phone so I can read along:

Where are we on my brother and the skank?

The response is from someone labeled "Eyes":

Some hotel downtown.

You got that tracker app on her phone like I told you to?

Of course

Good. They cannot get married. License is not filed yet. It CANNOT be filed.

What do you expect me to do about it?

whatever it takes, just stop them. youre supposed to be my eyes in the house, that's our deal. you keep them from filing while I see about a 5150

And then the texts disappear before our eyes, as Skye deletes them.
"5150?" I ask Erik.

"It lets your family put you in a psychiatric hospital for seventy-two hours." The crease is back between his eyebrows. "'Eyes in the house,' huh?"

". . . I should probably get another phone," I say dully, powering it down. I don't want to think what 'eyes in the house' means. But of course, I can't help but think.

"What do we need to do to file the marriage license?" Erik asks lightly.

"We need to get an officiant to sign it and, like, marry us?" I can't even say the word without making it a question. "Then we file and we're official."

"We should probably get going on that . . ." Erik reaches over me, pulls his shirt off the nightstand where it's hanging from a drawer knob. The neck is incredibly stretched out. He plucks at the distended collar while giving me a wry look.

"Sorry." I cringe.

"You should be. What kind of noodle-armed weakling can't even rip *cotton*?" He falls back against the bed. ". . . Anywhere in particular you'd like to be married?"

I sit up, slip my foot into my single ballet flat, frowning down at my shredded tights. For a moment, despair uncurls through me, like black ink drops in still water. "The main thing is just to do it as soon as we can. Anywhere that's open twenty-four hours works fine for me."

He laughs, but not his usual laugh.

"What?" I ask.

"Signal, you're doing me a huge favor. And I'm sure it's made things weird with Aarush." He stares at the corner of the bed just past me. "If there's anything I can do to—"

"Introduce me to Alice," I say immediately. "And we'll call it even."

"Alice?" He frowns. "I haven't seen her in years. It might be kind of awkward."

"You think that scares me? I *invented* awkward," I say eagerly. The black despair flooding my chest slows, some reckless hope rising to chase it away.

Erik looks at me a long moment. "Okay," he says at last. "She's down in Pacifica still, I think. It's an easy drive. Just . . ." He catches my hand, his thumb tracing a slow circle in my palm that makes me flush helplessly. "You're sure there's *nothing else* you'd like to do, in this incredibly sensuous bridal suite, before we check out?"

"There is *one* thing . . ." I lean over him slowly, placing my hand in the center of his chest, and his whole body goes tense as I drop my mouth to his ear and whisper, "*Take all the little soaps from the bathroom.*"

He throws a pillow at the bathroom door just as I close it.

* * *

Luckily, Scraps has a friend with a car he's looking to sell fast, who would prefer cash and no questions. The late-'90s Volvo V70 is already a good deal at eighteen hundred; Erik gets another five hundred knocked off the price by posing in a photo with the seller.

We stop by a Target, and I get the cheapest pay-as-you-go phone they have, as well as a giant army-green raincoat, black leggings, a navy sweater, tall socks, cheap rain boots, and a thick plastic file folder, to keep our marriage license in. All of which Erik vehemently insists on paying for.

My old phone I tuck into someone else's shopping bag as they buckle their kid into a van with out-of-state plates.

"Well, Watson!" Erik says as we pull forward out of a small twenty-four-hour coffee drive-thru, pausing at the hazy street for passing headlights.

"Any thoughts on who this 'eyes in the house' person might be? What is, quite literally, their 'deal'?"

"Well, Sherlock," I sigh, "I'm guessing it's the same person who stole the thumb drive. And that the deal was to help sabotage my case, so I couldn't testify against CurtPro. In exchange for . . . any of the things Skye could offer. Money, a job, a better lawyer? Who knows."

He sips from a small cup of heavily sweetened coffee before slipping down an exit onto a highway that feels abandoned, faded gold stripes of streetlight sliding over our laps at regular intervals as we bear toward Pacifica.

"Aarush told you the only people who went near the nerve center when the thumb drive was stolen lived in the house full-time, yes?"

"Yeah, and my lawyer, Honor."

"But if I remember correctly from our visit back in October, wasn't there a touch pad by the door? Wouldn't Aarush have to have let our saboteur in?"

I shake my head. "Actually, there's a trick to get around the touchpad. All you need is keyboard cleaner. Dennis showed me."

He looks excited, the blue dash light carving his profile out of the dark. "Interesting! So, Watson, now we go down the list of full-time inhabitants of the house and assess means, motive, and opportunity for each one." Erik glances at me. "Starting with you—"

"Me?!"

"Suspect: Signal Deere." He doesn't look away from the road. "This sexy little dweeb was savvy enough to install a mini-computer during a boardroom meeting, so she could've easily handled pocketing a thumb drive and erasing a few files. She was in the nerve center quite a bit during the period the drive went missing and also, apparently, knows some shady keyboard cleaner trick, so she had means *and* opportunity. *But* destroying the footage has all but wrecked her case, so . . . no motive. Signal is officially eliminated. We move on to Aarush."

"Okay . . ." I nod, getting into the game of it. "Same profile as me—"

"Sexy little dweeb?"

"No." I bite the inside of my cheek. "He had the means and opportunity, but no motive. What could Skye offer him?"

"Evidence," Erik says quickly. "Aarush is strongly against the federal use of the Wylie-Stanton. He could want Skye, as the face of the Wylie-Stanton, to testify in the federal case badly enough to offer some bread crumbs in exchange."

"The thumb drive isn't a *bread crumb*. It's a key piece of evidence!"

"In exonerating you, yes." Erik shrugs. "But as we've seen in the last twenty-four hours, that's *not* Aarush's biggest priority."

"Yeah, but at that time, he was investing so much money in Honor's counsel—"

"Not *his* money, his father's money. Ask any rich kid if they're rich, they'll tell you: 'no, my parents are.' Which brings us to Sonny." I protest, but Erik goes on. "We're doing this for *everyone*, no exceptions. Suspect: Sonny Desai, billionaire altruist. Did he have the means to steal the thumb drive? Yes. Sonny knew about the attic rant and where Aarush kept it. Opportunity, plenty. Motive? Same as Aarush, he's dedicated to striking down federal use of the Wylie-Stanton—"

"But with the added complication of, why put so much of *his* money into my defense, then try and sink it?"

"One would *hope* he has more business sense, but the ways of businessmen can certainly be counter intuitive. *However*—" He bites at his nails. "If Sonny wanted to share information about the case with Skye, why all the subterfuge? Why be the 'eyes' in a house he *owns*, when he could just have Skye over for a drink and tell him anything he pleased?"

"Which he was basically doing already," I grumble. "Because he and Aarush are convinced CurtPro would *never* be involved with illegal activities, because Skye is just *such a good guy.*"

"Hilarious," Erik says coolly. "Moving on to our next suspect: Honor Hadley. World-renowned super-lawyer, full time snappy dresser."

"She's worked tirelessly on my behalf, but if we're really doing *everyone*—" I sigh. "Means: Honor knew about the attic rant, she'd seen it many times. Opportunity: the nerve center is basically her office. She's in there all the time. But I don't see a motive. And she was really horrified when Jaw's lockbox ended up being empty."

"It's worth mentioning she's done legal consulting for CurtPro."

I blink at him. "She works for CurtPro?!"

"No, slow down, Honor works for an independent firm, and CurtPro has probably employed every decent lawyer in California at some point or other. That doesn't mean she's under the board's control."

"Who is on this CurtPro board again?" I squint at him. He shrugs.

"It used to be my grandfather and his five favorite golfing buddies," Erik says. "But who knows how much Skye has sold. It's still a private company, they don't have to disclose. *Here's* a question: Is Honor tech savvy enough to put a tracker app on your phone?"

"I've left it charging on the nerve center table like, dozens of times. When all three of them were in the room."

"Alright. So, aside from you, no one can be eliminated. On to the next suspect."

Meaning, one of our friends.

"Let's start with Dennis. I'm going to go ahead and just rule him out completely," Erik says, "since Dennis would never have to physically enter a room to erase the footage."

"Actually, this time he would," I laugh, "because Aarush kept the laptop air-locked and on a separate wired network."

"You *vicious harpy*," Erik says through clenched teeth in mock anger. "Fine. Suspect: Dennis. Knows all about compressed air and deleting files and phone tracker apps. *However*, Dennis doesn't have any actual criminal charges against him. Much like myself, he's an innocent man. So he doesn't have a real motive to risk your life to win the camp lawsuit. Unless he's *that* whipped over Jada—"

"*Wait. What?*" I jerk upright so hard my tea splashes up out of the drinking hole of the lid and sloshes down my hand. I say, in between licks of my wrist, "Dennis *likes* JADA?!"

"Is this news?" Erik glances at me a beat too long. "He's had a crush on her since the first week of camp."

"I had no idea! That's—*that's* the 'guy stuff' you two have been drafting about?"

"Among other things." He frowns. "I thought you knew. Don't tell her, he'd never forgive me."

"I won't! I would never! I just . . . my mind is blown!"

"While we're on the subject: Jada. Means, motive, opportunity?"

"Hmm." I sip some of the escaped tea out of the lid. It needs more honey. "She *did* know about the compressed air trick," I admit, then brighten. "But she's in Skye's phone as JailbaitSF#3, right? So it couldn't be her."

"*Gross.*" Erik cringes. "Not Jada, I mean Skye using—Jada's a cutie, obviously. But I don't like her. Romantically, I mean. I like her as a person—"

"I know what you mean."

"The first week of camp we met up after lights out twice. Kissed once. No tongue."

"*Erik!*" I gasp. "That is *really* none of my business—"

"It was super awkward, too, because she was wearing this bucket hat?"

I pummel at his dumb, muscly arm. "*Seriously!* Enough!"

"Like she didn't tell you all this anyway—"

"No, no, she did not! Like a *real friend*, she said you two just flirted!" I cry, filled with gratitude for her discretion. I never asked to picture any of this, but it's too late now. ". . . A bucket hat?"

"It was like, pink with like, a fringy kind of brim? Kind of killed it for me."

"No. You know what? No. Moving on!"

He grins, then, "Nobody."

"We can go ahead and rule her out completely."

He bursts out laughing. "Oh, come on! I had to do Dennis. Let's hear it: means, motive, opportunity."

"Okay, fine. There's no point, but fine." I take a deep breath. "She could have learned the compressed air trick from Dennis, when they were on their mission together or something, who knows. She knew about the attic rant, and she also knew about Aarush's special laptop and where he kept it." My face is starting to heat. "But come on. We can rule her out."

"Just to be fair," his voice is too casual, "for the same reason Dennis has less motive, she has more. Since she came to camp from death row."

I stare down at my tea. "Moving on."

"*To the foul culprit himself!*"

I roll my eyes.

"Means, motive, opportunity for Javier. How about I go first?" Erik says. "Javier didn't even *need* the compressed air trick. He just punched the door open, threw the laptop against the wall, and slobbered all over the screen until the footage erased, since that's his go-to solution for everything. Obvious motive: If he can't have you, no one can—"

"Now that you've gotten that off your chest—" I am going to bite through my cheek soon and it still won't stop me from laughing. "I don't know how Javier would know the compressed air trick. He knew about the attic rant, but not about Aarush's special laptop. And I think the retrial has like, an ethical significance for him—"

"*Ethical significance?!*" Erik chokes. "Are you *high?* Signal, how do you not see what's going on with him—"

"What's going on with him?"

"He's a borderline *Nice Guy*, Signal! He *acts* nice to make you feel *obligated to do what he wants*—then punishes you if you don't!" Erik keeps whipping his gaze between me and the road. "Why do you think he walked in on us? What did you *think* that was?!"

"I think he got jealous," I say, tucking my arms around my chest. "And I know how that feels."

"No, you *don't*," Erik says savagely. "Because you actually *liked him*, back at camp. And you have *never* seen me like another girl, and you *never will*."

"For you to have the audacity to say that," I shake my head, "when I had to watch you make out with Nadya half naked—"

"*I don't care about her!*"

"That *makes it better?*" I snarl. "I'm just supposed to think, 'Wow, I'm so lucky Erik likes me more than whatever woman is currently chewing on his mouth'—"

"Remember, back at camp?" Erik's voice is shaking with anger. "When flower boy was drawing twee blossoms on your arm and making you dandelion crowns? You think I couldn't have beaten him at that game? I can be cute as *hell*, Signal. Some coy lyrics, a pair of friendship bracelets? You don't even know. You would've met me after lights out all night, every night, and forgotten Javier existed—"

"Uh huh."

"But I needed you to be honest with me about your case. So I tried to be honest and open with you. And since all romance is basically bullshit—"

"*Excuse me?*"

"I tried to treat you as an equal, not a mark. So imagine what it was like," he lifts one hand from the wheel, then grabs it fast again, "watching Javier pull his dollar-bin Edward Cullen routine—"

"Someone's been polishing that gem for a while."

"Yes! Yes, I have!" he half shouts, half laughs. "It was *unbearable* watching you fall for his act at camp. But I didn't take it out on you, or him. I was prepared to stay just friends—though, *believe me*, there are things I wanted to do to you in that open grave that would have shocked the living and the dead—"

"*Erik!*" I choke on an outraged laugh.

"I was just *myself* with you. I'm more myself, with you, than I've ever been." His eyes flash to mine. Then he looks back at the road, swallowing hard. "And you still *chose him*."

"I'm sitting next to you right now."

"Yeah, and slut-shaming me, *again*," he snaps, "for acting in some dumb music video, when I was *broke and homeless*. You act like I directed it. I just showed up at an address. There was no script, I did whatever Nadya said, because she was paying. I have absolutely no feelings for her *whatsoever*—"

"So don't marry her!" I cry. "Don't *sell yourself* to someone you *don't love*, Erik!"

"I know this concept is unfathomable to a walking, talking gumdrop." Erik's jaw flares. "But transactional relationships are *easier for me*. They are *less confusing*."

"So selling yourself to Nadya is easier than being with me? Cool, thanks."

"I am not 'selling myself,' Signal," Erik says sharply, "because I don't *exist* as myself with anyone but you."

I stare back at him, stricken, and he looks away, rolls his neck, shifts his broad shoulders unhappily. He pulls onto an unlit cliffside road, shoulders high, the silence thick between us. The straight black ocean opens out on one side; the car becomes a bubble of blue dashboard light floating through the dark.

"Someday," I say, "you will fall in love again."

"God, I hope not," Erik says quietly, slowing to a crawl along the private road before nodding his chin at a high gate. "That's Skye's house, by the way."

* * *

Skye's mansion is backed right up against the highest point of the cliffs at the outskirts of Pacifica, its façade lavender in the moonlight, hidden behind the ragged trunks of the ghost gum trees and encircled by a high, starkly minimalist stucco fence, ringed with floodlights and prominent security cameras.

"Hard to climb." Erik frowns through the windshield. "And there won't be any easy access points into the house, no conveniently unlocked windows. My parents really drilled it into him to keep everything locked tight while we were growing up."

"Stop casing the house," I say darkly. "You are *not* going in there."

"I am not casing anything. Though if I were, I'd take note there are no neighbors." Erik keeps scanning the street. "Since most of the properties over here got condemned due to cliff erosion."

"Can we please go?" I say tensely.

"Didn't Skye check in on you about this time of night, when we all got together at the house? Seems only right we return the favor . . ."

"Start driving or I will grab the wheel."

Erik gives the house one last lingering look before drifting down the block, away from the pools of white light that slant down the fence.

Erik parks at a spot just overlooking the shore, and despite the rapidly bluing light and having recently ingested coffee, he throws his car seat back and instantly falls asleep. But his words loop in my head until I'm balled up like a fist. He hates being in love and blames me for it, which is sick. I used to think in terms of a good Erik and a bad Erik, but he's both at once: deeply disturbed and definitely brilliant, my black-hearted light in the dark, the boy from hell for sure. The urge to reach out and trace his cheek is almost overwhelming, I fist my hands. Maybe he's right about love. Maybe we both are seriously unwell.

I quietly slip out of the car and sit on its warm hood, pulling my raincoat over my head and making some calls on my newly charged phone. Mom first. We have a long conversation about where the hell I am. She's furious about me losing my lawyer and all my things showing up at Sea View in trash bags and blames Erik for all of it. When she starts using words like curfew, I explain these concepts simply don't apply to our lives anymore, and she sighs and says, "I really, really, really do not want you to marry this boy, Signal. But so help me, if you think I'm going to miss the wedding—"

I promise I will alert her to whatever McDonald's we sign the papers in. Then, after we hang up, I focus on setting up my email on the new phone. Once I do, a shocking number of unread messages load. Almost all of them are several days old, replies to my emails on the way back from Ragged Point; the desperate cries for help to Rose's ex-boyfriend, his boyfriend Vaughn, all their church friends, and Greg, and anyone else I could think of. *Everyone* I reached out to wrote back, within hours if not minutes of my initial emails.

But it's the pitch from Greg Ballas that really makes me sit up:

Signal, my offer to do a profile of Erik still stands. The public has a right to hear the origin story of the Wylie-Stanton. If Erik can talk to me, in any way he's comfortable with, I will protect him as a source. I am happy to work directly with you on this, despite Honor and Sonny's reservations and without their consent. Please know there are people just as passionate as you are about bringing the truth to light, and hopefully we can figure something out before my deadline.

Why are these coming in so late? Of course: Aarush's security update must have blocked them.

I respond to all of them, but start with Greg:

Greg, hey. I know your piece comes out soon, but since Erik has turned himself in, he is very available to talk! When can we make this happen?

When I return to my inbox I notice my drafts folder is also bolded, with new messages from Dennis:

Hey Signal,

Writing to let you know everyone's sad you've left and sorry they didn't get to say goodbye. What's going on with your trial? Honor's firm seems to have moved on to our case. She says they're closing in on a settlement with USG, which means Dave must be talking.

"USG?" I say out loud, then realize he means the government, and feel a flash of wild relief. A settlement? That's the best possible conclusion to their suit. I read on:

> They'll reach out to Erik to take his deposition. That might be what puts us over the edge.
>
> Thank you for the texts re: Kate's kill switch.
>
> Aarush and I are teaming up to try and cut down the lag. Kate's programming is quite the puzzle box, and we've had no luck yet. But at least ten hours ago she was in San Francisco, close to the court-house. Sort of a weird coincidence, if you ask me.
>
> How are you guys?

I quickly reply:

Dennis!! Hey!!

That is amazing news about the settlement!! & yes, weird about Kate??

I'm about to tell Dennis about the "eyes in the house" text, but my thumb hesitates over the screen. I don't know how to explain without making it sound like an accusation.

So I go on:

We're doing some wedding planning today. Know any good places to get married?

The folder bolds again.

Not really. I'll ask around.
Are you coming to grad nite?

I laugh.

If I'm invited, sure.

I hesitate, then add, **I'm sorry your family can't be there.**
It's very much their choice. Dennis writes back.

If we were in person, I would probably drop it. But I suspect he's the type who opens up more online. And if I told my friends repeatedly that my family had cut me off, I would want someone to ask me why.

So I put the question out there:

I totally get it if your answer is no
But would you feel comfortable telling me more about that?

Enough time passes that I start to get embarrassed, but then just as I'm about to get back in the car, drafts bolds again.

At camp I was known as Dennis the Non-Menace because my body count was zero. But that's not exactly true.

As you know, I volunteered to take the Wylie-Stanton, never suspecting I would rank as a Class A. I had no idea the kind of impact my classification would have on my family. From the moment I took the test, a circle of so-called concerned community leaders started calling for me to be forced out of the school district.

My father and mother had worked their entire lives to secure a house in our very exclusive neighborhood. They refused to pull up stakes and give way to pressure.

What ensued was an all-out bullying campaign against our entire family. I was harassed at school. My mother's accounting clients disappeared overnight. My father lost a valuable promotion. Dealing with all this, none of us saw how much my younger sister was struggling at her middle school.

Danielle was sensitive and emotionally intelligent, but something of a misfit. You remind me of her in a lot of ways. Maybe you can relate to what it feels like to be cast out and bullied in middle school. But our family didn't see the warning signs. We were all completely blindsided when she took her own life.

Since her funeral, my mother has not spoken to me. Because if I had not taken the Wylie-Stanton, Danielle would still be with us. I went to camp not to get out of a prison sentence but to get out of my house. And after what happened, I didn't see much point in my life.

This was something Erik recognized immediately, somehow. I don't think I would have made it through camp without him taking me under his wing. He's the only other person I've told all this to.

But now with this trial, my life has a point again. To stop people from using tech to justify their worst instincts.

Anyway. You don't have to reply to this if it's too weird.

I know it's a lot.

* * *

I call him immediately. Twice. I think he feels weird picking up the first time.

"Hello," Dennis answers, his voice flat.

"Dennis, I love you," I sob.

"Signal, please. You're engaged," he says dryly.

"Like a brother, I mean, don't get flustered." I laugh through my tears. "But I needed to tell you how deeply sorry I am to hear about your sister. I can't possibly understand how much that hurts, but I know, I *know* it's not your fault, and it's *ridiculous* that anyone could blame you, let alone—"

"Um. Signal," he whispers. "I'm currently at the breakfast table and you're kind of shouting."

"I'm sorry," I whisper back. "I'm terrible at this, okay. But I know this counselor named Lupin, she's really helped me in the past, and she helped Erik a lot too. She's really good at just like, listening, if you want her number or something?"

Dennis pauses a long moment. ". . . Okay." Flat, but accepting. Then, "Let me guess, you also have some plan you need tech for too, right?"

"No." I sniff. "I just wanted you to know that you're one of my favorite people in the world, and no matter what I will always be there for you."

"Oh." Dennis sounds uncomfortable. Then he says, "Same."

"Okay." I wipe at my face. "Get back to breakfast, and I'll put all of Lupin's info in drafts."

The passenger door slams, and Erik hops up onto the hood beside me as I put the phone down. His arm goes around my shoulder, and I lean against him.

"Dennis told me about Danielle," I sputter, and his lips press the top of my head as I wipe my eyes. "It sucks. It just sucks."

"I know," he says, and we watch the tide for a long moment, his arm around me, so warm. Then he says, quietly, "Did you sleep at all?"

"Sleep isn't really my thing anymore."

"Why not?"

I make a joke of it. "Fretting about my big day, of course."

"Well," he shoots me a look, "we've got a lead there. I texted Scraps, asking if he knew any officiants, last night. And it turns out he *is one*."

"What?"

"Yeah, he says it's his spring side gig, marrying people around Portland and, uh, at Burning Man—"

"Of course." I laugh.

"He's up in Portland now, but he can be back down here tomorrow, which gives us about a day to get everything else together."

"Everything else? Like what?"

"I mean, we'll need some witnesses. I was thinking we could ask your mom . . . ," Erik says quietly, biting at his nails, and when I look at him, surprised, he adds, "So I can talk shop with her on stun guns. Maybe Alice, too."

"Did you hear back from her?"

"Yeah," He frowns, looking away from me and then back again. "How would you feel about brunch?"

Chapter Fourteen

In-Laws

～

"This isn't her place, she's house-sitting," Erik explains, as we walk up a winding path to a large, pink Victorian house, covered in white gingerbread trim. It has an actual tower on one side, with a big picture window and a pointy roof like a witch's hat. When we get to the bottom step of the porch, he stops short. I go up to the door alone and knock, and after a beat he follows me up the stairs heavily, standing beside me with his head ducked.

One of the two glass-inlaid doors starts to pull back, then sticks. There's a stream of hearty Spanish curses, then the door bursts open, and a little blonde terrier leaps for Erik's knees, jumping up and down with trembling excitement.

"Snickers?!" Erik laughs, crouching down. The dog is practically going to pieces in his hands. "He remembers me!"

"Of course he does," Alice says.

She's tiny, shorter than me, with a heart-shaped bronze face and cautious black eyes. But when she pulls back her jaw-length black hair, my heart twists: it's Erik's exact same gesture. She must be where he got it from, and as a smile pushes across her face she looks years younger. "You were always his favorite, duh."

And then they're hugging, her hands in fists against his shoulders, which for once seem to completely relax.

"Come in, come in, take off your shoes," Alice says quickly, waving me in after him. "I set up a floor picnic in the living room."

"Floor picnic?" I smile, stepping out of my sandy rainboots.

Erik takes my hand as we follow her through the narrow, walnut-paneled hall. "My mom's go-to way to serve food."

"It's *genius*." Alice waves us into the jewel-tone living room, all gold lamps and lace curtains, an ornate Persian carpet covering the floor with warm pink tones. On top of this rug a cheerful cotton quilt has been laid down, a haphazard feast toppled onto a tray at its center: crackers and cheese, veggies and hummus, a giant bowl of cherries and peaches, and pink glass tumblers full of lemonade and water.

"You don't have to cook and you can shake out all the crumbs after." Alice shrugs and sits cross-legged beside the tray, offering me a brightly colored plate.

Erik leans back and hits a concealed switch just inside the plaster lip of the fireplace beside us. A cheerful blaze snaps up from cast-iron logs I would have sworn were real.

"Whoa, you just like, switch it on? How'd you know?"

"This house was our second home, when Erik was little," Alice says. "The family who lives here, the Nortons, their kids were around the same age as the boys, so we practically lived here in the summer. Until around the end of middle school, I think?" Alice tilts her head and squints at Erik.

"Yeah, once, uh, homeschooling started." Erik pulls Snickers onto his lap. "Then I was at Higher Paths during the summers. Though when Mom started in with the algorithm stuff, that was her big carrot: 'Help me with three more sessions, and you can go to the Nortons' Fourth of July party.'"

"You were always pretty down for those sessions, if I remember. *You'd* be reminding *her* about them." Alice stacks her plate with cheese and crackers.

"Yeah, well, you know . . ." Erik's brow furrows. "She wasn't—" He looks to me; then his gaze cuts away. "My mom wasn't big on eye contact. But her professional training would kick in when she was interviewing me. She'd look me right in my eyes, the whole time. Sometimes she'd even like, hold my wrist to track my pulse . . ." His voice trails off. Then he scruffles Snickers' stiff fur and looks slowly around the room. "Yeah, this is sort of wild, being back here again."

Alice nods. "It's been too long."

"How are you doing?" he asks her.

"Really good. Got married!" She holds up her hand, a gold band flashing.

"Congratulations!" I say quickly.

"Nice." Erik nods. "Anyone I'd know?"

"My boyfriend, actually, who uh . . . who picked me up that time, at your grandfather's house." Alice pulls her knees up to her chest, her face suddenly tense. Then she says, fast: "Rique, I really owe you an apology for not coming to your parents' funeral. It's one of my deepest regrets, that I wasn't there—"

"No, hey." He shakes his head quickly. "Funerals suck, I get it."

"You know how much I cared about Monica and Todd. And my mother loved them too. She's always asking about you, still. We were both following everything . . . on the news." Her eyes cut to me then.

"This is Signal, by the way," Erik says, eyebrows leaping up. "Her reputation proceeds her, I'm sure."

"The Girl From Hell, right. Nice to meet you," Alice says, not really selling it.

"We're getting married," Erik adds, so casually I almost choke on my carrot stick. "If you want to come?"

Alice blinks and leans forward, horrified. "I'm sorry—*what?*"

My phone starts ringing. It's Greg Ballas.

"I have to take this," I say apologetically, and as I step out of the living room Alice leans forward and starts hissing at Erik:

"You're going to marry *the Girl From Hell?* The chick who cut off *some girl's head?!*"

"Shared interests are important," Erik says, straight-faced, and then Greg's voice is in my ear:

"Signal! I got your email. I can head down to Pacifica right now and be there in about an hour, if you and Erik can talk then?"

"Yes, perfect," I whisper, heart beating wildly. This was exactly what I was hoping for, that I could get not just Erik, but also Alice, across from Greg. "Let me tell them you're coming and I'll drop a pin your way . . ."

After we hang up, I'm trying to figure out how to pitch a surprise visit from a journalist before I go back in, when I realize Alice is still talking, voice hushed:

"How do you *know* she's innocent?"

"How do you know *I'm* innocent?" I can hear his smile.

"Because I've known you your whole life, maybe? How long have you known this girl again?"

"*Several* weeks."

"Why do you have to make everything a joke, Erik? This is serious."

"Believe me, I take it quite seriously. She's marrying me at great personal risk so I can testify about camp and Ledrick." His voice gets deeper. "I can't keep her in that position, obviously, so we'll have to get it annulled, I guess. And then I'll leave the country, and Skye can't bother any of us again."

"Well . . ." Alice sounds reluctantly impressed. "That's nice of her, to put herself in Skye's crosshairs like that."

"Yeah, well." He clears his throat. "I was hoping you could be a witness. When we meet with the officiant tomorrow."

Alice pauses a long time. "I'm really sorry," she says at last. "But tomorrow is my last day here before the Nortons come back. I need to have everything ready for them. So. It's just bad timing."

"Yeah, no, I get it," Erik says casually.

It's worse than if he'd sobbed, and my hands become fists. There's no use asking for favors, and I'm done asking for permission. Alice can take Erik's side when Greg comes. Or she can kick us out.

*   *   *

Greg's knock at the door makes me jump, though he arrives exactly on time. Alice's tone when she answers the door makes Erik sit up, anxious. She returns to the floor picnic glowering, Greg Ballas in tow, wearing a clear plastic drugstore rain poncho.

"This is a friend of yours, Signal?" Alice asks.

"Yes!" I'm on my feet. "Erik, Alice, this is Greg. He is an award-winning chancer journalist about to file a major investigative piece about the Wylie-Stanton—"

Alice curses under her breath, but I don't stop talking.

"And I was hoping that we could all have a discussion about the Wylie-Stanton, and CurtPro, and Erik's parents . . . and then maybe, *just maybe*, we can get Erik's conservatorship revoked? And he won't have to marry anyone, or flee the country, he could just be . . ." I look at Erik then. "Free. Free to do whatever he wants."

"Signal likes to cut through the small talk," Erik tells Alice, his eyes not leaving mine.

"Well, so do I." Alice turns on me. "This isn't a brunch, it's an ambush. How goddamn dare you."

Before I can reply, she turns on her heel and exits, leaving Greg Ballas smiling uneasily.

"Greg, I'm sorry—" I say quickly.

"Don't be." Erik stands and holds out a hand to Greg. "Nice to meet you."

"Likewise." They shake.

"I'll go talk to Alice," I tell them.

I close the living room door softly behind me and follow Snickers down a long hardwood hallway and into a massive kitchen with a black and white tiled floor. There, Alice is angrily pulling out the ingredients for a stiff drink and slamming them on the vast granite kitchen island.

"You've got a lot of nerve," Alice says, not looking up at me, "inviting yourself over and then calling in a journalist? You don't know me—"

"I know you're the closest thing Erik has to a sister."

She blinks up at me, surprised.

"So I'm sorry if I stepped over the line," I go on, "but I'm terrified of what Skye could do to him."

"You should be terrified of what Skye could do to you," Alice snaps. "Believe me, I am."

"My hope is Greg's profile piece could shine a light on who Skye really is—"

"Skye isn't one guy, Signal." Alice speaks slowly, like she's explaining something complicated to a child. "He's the face of CurtPro. He's the first official Class A victim and heir to the Wylie-Stanton. There are hundreds of very smart people who do what needs to be done while Skye provides a front. They aren't going to give that up!" She furiously spins the screw top off a rum bottle, pours an inch into a glass, then says, voice softer, "Erik said I was like his sister, huh? All this time, I was so sure he hated me now . . ." Then, her eyes wary, "What else did he tell you?"

"He said you gave him a book about Michelangelo?" *That's how he knew you wanted to kill yourself,* I don't add.

"He was always staring at that one sculpture." Alice sets the bottle down gently, eyes far away. "The *Pietà*. It's Mary holding Jesus after he's just come down from the cross." Alice swirls her drink with a glass swizzle stick. "A name that has its roots in both 'pity' and 'piety.' 'Mary's face, as she regards her martyred son, holds both infinite compassion and devotion' . . . At least, that's what the book said." She sets the swizzle stick onto the counter with a clack. "Did he tell you about me and Skye?"

"Skye told me you were high school sweethearts."

"*High school sweethearts?*" she repeats, lips twitching. "Skye said that, really?!" A furious smile blooms across her face. "No. Absolutely not. He is a *predator*—"

"Have you ever thought about reporting him?" I perch on the high stool across the countertop.

She shakes her head.

"But if Greg could protect you as an anonymous source—"

"Signal, stop," Alice says firmly. "It's out of the question. Skye would know. And he would make sure my clients, my coworkers, my husband saw things . . . that they could not unsee." She takes a long sip of her drink, her face hardening. "I'm very sorry you and Erik have to break up. But you probably would have anyway in another six months at your age and—"

"There are other girls," I tell her, unable to contain myself. "Skye is *still hurting other girls*—"

"And wolves are out there eating sheep. And bridges collapse, and murderers lurk in dark alleyways. I know, okay? But I can't save the world. I can barely save myself—"

"I'm not asking you save the world; I'm asking you to *tell the truth*." I let out a long breath. "But . . . I understand why you can't. And now I'm just sorry. For you, for Erik. Sorry I even asked, I guess."

And, not wanting to pressure her any further, I leave the kitchen. I slowly make my way down the dark hall back to the living room. I wait for a pause in Erik's low, thoughtful voice before walking in.

Greg is perched on an ottoman, frantically scrawling notes. Erik hasn't moved from where he was before, but now Greg's phone is just below him, recording.

"I want to go into the first time you questioned your mother's diagnosis of you," Greg prompts. "You said it was when she came to visit Ledrick's outpatient facility? While Skye was having his face reconstructed—"

"I snuck into the office bathroom, yeah." Erik's got his chin on his fist, and speaks in a low, emotionless tone. "I wanted to hear when I was going home. Instead, Mom asked Ledrick to keep me a couple more months. Because she said . . ." His eyebrows draw together. "She didn't want to be around me." His eyes flash to me and away. "And I had a reaction to hearing that. The kind of reaction I was not supposed to be capable of. But I processed it as a thought."

"Do you remember the thought?"

Erik's lips tighten momentarily. Then he says, "I remember thinking, it's a good thing I don't have feelings. Because otherwise I'd be the saddest guy in the world." He shoots me a quick, mocking smile. "Hot, right?"

I'm unable to speak, but Alice's voice cuts over my shoulder.

"What's this piece called, anyway?"

She walks in, drink almost empty.

"'The Mother of the Wylie-Stanton.'" Greg adjusts his blocky glasses with the end of his pencil. "The true history of the algorithm that increasingly runs our justice system."

Alice grabs a leash from a side table and Snickers bounds into the room.

"You'll never find a place that will publish it."

"I have an editor waiting for me to file at *The Meridian*. His fact checkers have been triple-checking my research all year—"

"What research?"

"I began with Monica's original proposal for government funding. But I've also spoken to her colleagues and former federal employees. And what has been reiterated again and again is that Monica meant for this algorithm to find *minors*, minors who *could be rehabilitated*. Young people with specific undesirable traits—"

"Did she ever list them?" Erik says, head ducked so his eyes are in shadow. "These, uh, undesirable traits?"

"Oh, well." Greg looks momentarily awkward, then seems to default to treating the question as a memory test, tucking his notepad under his arm and ticking the traits off on his fingers: "High fear threshold. Tendency toward calculated violence. Profound social distrust. High empathy alongside low conscience. Familial alienation."

Erik's face doesn't change. He doesn't even blink. But Alice claps her empty glass hard on the coffee table.

"But then, after Monica's death, the proposal for funding was heavily revised," Greg goes on. "Ledrick pitched the algorithm as a predictor for recidivism, the potential of a criminal to return to prison. Courts were already using algorithms to help set bail limits and sentences. But because those algorithms were trained on datasets with racial bias, there was a valid concern they would *perpetuate* that bias. And it's not like the politicians legislating around these algorithms were *tech people*—"

"Yeah, the Boomers at my work need an intern just to attach a zip file." Alice snaps her fingers at Snickers until he sits and lets her put on his harness.

"Right." Greg sighs. "So the big selling point for the Wylie-Stanton was the *story*. A mother made this for her son. The thinking was, any bias would be in the subject's *favor*."

Alice lets out a sharp laugh. Erik's expression is frozen. And though I stare at him, his eyes stay on the rug.

"So how did that turn into using it as a . . . as a psycho detector?" I ask.

"Only convicted criminals could be tested, right? Well, it turns out, adult criminals with the same psychological profile of a troubled fifteen-year-old are . . . very scary people."

This gets a dry laugh from Erik.

"So it developed a reputation for being effective at 'detecting psychos.'" Greg sighs. "But it's only been run on a *very biased sample* of people. And rather than perform control experiments, it's been more politically expedient to sell it as a silver bullet for social ills: the problem isn't *us*, it's *them*, all these Class As and their Class A influence. People see algorithms as being objective; but they are a set of priorities made by a person, and enacted mechanically—without judgment, or mercy, or any real accountability. So the Wylie-Stanton keeps chugging along, putting the kids who need our help the most behind bars. And if the violent crime rate is still exploding, well, that just means we haven't found all the Class As yet."

"Why doesn't someone else test it?" I ask. "Analyze the algorithm, or make it process piles of old profiles to show its predictions are inaccurate—"

"The Wylie-Stanton is highly confidential. Even Skye couldn't access it if he wanted to. Its status as a state secret has only been meaningfully challenged in the last few weeks, by the kids' lawsuit against camp, which may not be successful."

"Bad times," Alice shrugs, steering Snickers back toward the door. "We're going for a walk. Why don't you come with us, Signal?"

I nod, surprised at the offer, until she mutters in the hall, ". . . Give Rique some privacy while he spills his guts."

The sky is eerily dark when she throws open the front door. I follow her along a little side path behind the neighbor's garage, and down to the beach.

The tide is crashing in fast, the sky groaning with unspent thunder. Alice unclips Snickers and we walk side by side in silence as Snickers barrels in and out of the pale foam that whispers up sand the color of concrete.

"All this trouble over one damn eye." Alice's face is stiff as the wind whips her black hair around her. "You know, if she'd based the algorithm on Skye, maybe it would work. But Erik had the same eye thing as Monica's dad. So here we all are."

I remember the picture in Erik's bedroom of the grandfather with the two torn eyes, the grandfather who sold him out to Ledrick. And the portrait in their abandoned living room: the mother and son with the same angelic smile, beside the skulking twelve-year-old Erik with his long hair hanging in front of his face.

"Monica talked to me about her dad once. *Only* once," Alice goes on. "Right before she asked me about Skye. And if my dad had been like that? And I had a child who looked just like him?" She shakes her head. "I'm sure it was hard. But when she would talk about, why can't Erik feel more, why can't Erik feel love . . . I think what she meant was, why can't *I* feel more about Erik. Why can't *I feel love* for my son."

I shiver.

"I wanted to tell her the truth, Signal. I almost did, so many times. But you'll see when you're older." Alice's face is hard. "For most people, the only truth that matters is what they already believe. Take Erik, for example." She looks back toward the house. Greg and Erik are winding down the path to the beach now, bowed lines in the distance. "He's always believed his mom devoted her life to saving him. If I told him the truth—that he was abused by a parent because she could not love him—would that *help*? . . . Or would it just make him worse?"

And then she bends down to clip the leash back onto Snickers, shivering at our feat, covered in salt water. When she stands again, we can hear the guys' voices and I know the conversation is over.

"This is *exactly* what I needed to finish this piece." Greg shakes my hand goodbye, the strings of his poncho hood tight under his round face, a shiny pastry in a cellophane wrapper. "I truly believe we have a shot at changing things."

Erik takes my hand as we walk behind Alice and Snickers farther down the beach. He is unusually quiet as the breakers push us right up under the cliffs, rain spotting the sand faster and faster. I want to tell him he can say anything in front of me, he can reveal any old wound or hurt and I won't flinch. But instead I hold his hand, its warmth precious in all this cold.

"Look, up there—" Erik says, pointing skyward, voice just audible through the receding tide, the rain starting to bead on his face. "That's the back of Skye's house."

A slab of pale sidewalk juts out into the air from the cliff overhead, braced into the cliff by a grid of rebar. Scattered pieces of stucco wall glow bone white as broken eggshell among the black volcanic rock below; a back section of fence must have already been swept out to sea. An arch of the same craggy black material rises from the pounding tide, hunched like the back of a dragon. Thunder rolls, too close, and the rain breaks in earnest, coming down all at once with a sound like applause. But Erik doesn't move. He just keeps staring up at Skye's walk. And then one hand floats up, as though to test the scaffolding, when Alice doubles back to us, looking nervous.

"Come on, let's go back already," she calls over the rain. "This is too far."

"You mean too close?" Erik asks.

"I'm getting soaked." I put my arm through his. "Come on. It's freezing out here."

Erik reluctantly lets me steer him away from the path up to Skye's house, and Alice and I share a brief glance of understanding.

* * *

The old-fashioned double doors stick again, but with a good wrench of the handle from Erik we burst into the house. Snickers slips his leash and makes a beeline for the living room, Erik racing after him and catching the little dog up before he gets to the rug, all four of Snickers' sandy paws wiggling skyward.

"You're as bad as the dog!" Alice cries at Erik. Then she looks at me. "You're all soaked. Did you bring overnight stuff to change into?"

Erik shakes his head and she lets out a frustrated sigh. "Okay, come with me. There's tons of stuff in Bryan's old room—"

We follow her through a labyrinth of walnut hallways, up two flights of creaky steps with ornate handrails, and through a narrow door bearing an ironic Garfield poster.

Inside is a young man's bedroom, abandoned for college and being stealthily taken over by sewing equipment, a poster of LeBron James staring sternly over a white plastic rack of rainbow thread spools and quilt scraps. Alice searches through a stuffed closet of outgrown boy's clothes and fishes out a Sonic the Hedgehog hoodie and knee-length nylon basketball shorts for me.

"Thanks," I say, not really selling it.

Erik is allowed to select his own sweatpants and hoodie before going to change in the en suite bathroom.

"I'll take the wet stuff to the laundry." Alice puts out a hand. But as I pull my soaked sweater over my head, she gasps. "*¡Que mierda!* What happened to your side?"

"It's nothing." My hand fastens over my stitches.

"Nothing? Are you kidding? It looks like you had a rib removed!"

"I just had some stitches that got torn out. So they had to sew up the same area twice and . . . it's kind of a mess." I jerk the orange hedgehog sweatshirt down over my hips.

"When was this?"

Erik's voice startles me—I didn't hear him step out of the bathroom—and my head floods with panicked heat. If he was behind me, he couldn't have seen the worst of it. Still, he looks sick.

"Was it at the house?" he says. "Was it when you got between me and Skye?"

Alice's eyes go wide. "You were in the same room with Skye?"

Erik doesn't seem to hear. He's reaching for my sweatshirt. I knock his hand away.

"You're *hiding them from me?*"

"It's not a big deal—"

"Yes, it is!" Erik is furious. "It was when you cut down the sail, wasn't it?"

"The regatta sail?" Alice gasps. "She *cut down Todd's regatta sail?*"

"To save Skye," Erik tells her, but he's still staring at me. "She trapped me under the sail so I couldn't jump him—so what, you were just *bleeding* that whole time after?"

Alice grabs his sleeve and jerks him around to face her. "Rique! You *swore* to your mom that you would never hurt Skye again—"

"He's above ground, isn't he?" Erik snatches his arm back.

"Only because Signal tore herself in half! You would've let down your mom like that?"

"My mom is *dead*." Erik's voice is ragged. "*Because of Skye*. I should've taken him out on the bike trail, God I wish I had! But I'm not *thirteen* anymore. This time—"

"No." Alice shakes her head, tears starting to spill down her face. "Don't be like this, don't say these things—"

"You want him dead too! Stop *lying, Alice*." Erik turns on her, and she shrinks back, and I grab his arm.

"If you kill him, it will destroy you. The real you. My Erik."

"'Your' Erik!" He laughs. "Who is that? Me when I do what you want? Me without the bad parts? Me when I'm *fixed?*"

"My Erik doesn't *kill his brother!*" I snap. "My Erik doesn't *scare his sister!*"

Erik turns to Alice and registers how she's retreated. He looks almost ashamed. Then his upper lip jerks and he gives me a wounded look, like this is something *I've* done.

"Well, 'your Erik' is nothing like me, then," he says. "So don't call me that again."

And he leaves the room, letting the door slam behind him.

Alice turns to me, shoulders sagging, and wipes her eyes with her sleeve. "I don't know how you put up with that."

"Oh, I don't," I say grimly, and hurry through the door after him, just as another slam echoes down the long, dim hall. I wrench open the narrow door onto a spiraling wood staircase. The temperature drops; the air tastes like cold water. Its smell makes me think of crumbling love letters.

At the top of the stairs is a small rotunda room with a lofted ceiling, the inside of the witch's hat tower. It's not insulated, so the tide sounds clearer here than the rest of the house; it rolls through the steady patter of rain like a giant's heartbeat. A four-poster bed with a white lace quilt glows under the oval stained-glass window, its jewel tones dark from the storm. Erik lies across the middle of it, legs hanging off the side as though he sat down and fell back, his forearm across his face.

"I get to call you my Erik," I announce. "I'm not asking you. I'm telling you."

My tone surprises us both. His forearm slides away, and he sits up in one quick, fluid motion; if he'd ever gone to Gym he would have gotten an A+ in sit-ups.

"And I'm telling you: I don't know what 'my Erik' means," he says. "I haul Jaw in for your trial. I come back to testify like you wanted. It's never enough. No, now I have to promise not to kill *my* brother—"

"I'm not debating the inherent dignity of human life right now." I wave a hand. "'My Erik' means: you're mine. *My* Erik. Is that a problem?"

His eyebrows go all the way up. "Uh, we are getting married tomorrow, so no."

"That's a *joke*," I say flatly. "We both know we're getting it annulled. We're going to meet Scraps and my mom at whatever Starbucks is closest to the court-house and sign a piece of paper. And my mom isn't exactly *thrilled*. It's going to be a bummer, the annulment will be worse, and then you're going to *marry a pop star and move across the world*."

He kneads his temple, like I'm giving him a headache. "She's the fastest way I have out of the country, I told you—"

"Stop. It. Are you kidding me?" My hands are in fists. "Her side of your bar-gain is she gets more famous. So you will have to 'act' like the marriage is real, because that's what her corny fans want—"

He narrows his eyes at me. "You read the comments on the video, didn't you?"

"*Of course* I read the comments!" I cry. "And I will read the comments when your wedding pictures come out, and when your honeymoon in Bali is 'leaked,' and meanwhile, for the *brief period of time we're together*, you say 'don't call me your Erik' in front of Alice!?"

"Did you want me to put an announcement in the papers?" The side of his mouth jerks and I lose it.

"*It's not funny!* Because that's what *Nadya's doing!* You don't think, if I had her *daddy's money*, I wouldn't do the exact same thing? Loop us making out on billboards to claim my territory—"

"Miss *Deere!*" Erik's eyes go wide.

"That stupid video is just her *marking you!* And I *know* you didn't direct it!" I squeeze my eyes closed; this is so messy but I can't stop. "I *know* it wasn't up to you, but *come on*. You two were kissing fully shirtless, okay. *We* haven't even done that—"

"That can be corrected," Erik is on his feet, "any time you want."

"No, it can't." I cross my arms as he approaches. "Someone needs to look out for the future version of me, because she is going to be *crucified next month*. I already know how much it kills me to miss you. You think this is easy? That night, in the skyscraper, I sobbed the whole way down. I would rather tear these stitches out, right now, with my *bare hands* than go through that again! You have no idea how close I came to turning back around."

"You should have." He hovers across from me now, one more step across the threadbare Persian carpet and our faces would brush, and he's staring so hard. But I can't meet his stare. I'm too much of an open wound.

"And then the video came out. And it ruined me, alright? I couldn't *eat*, I couldn't *sleep*, all I could think about was her—acting like you're—you're just some hot guy in that video. You're *not* a hot guy—"

"No?"

"Not *just* some hot guy. And for her to treat you like that is *unbearable*—like watching someone—roll up the *Mona Lisa* and use it to scratch their back or something. It's a *sacrilege!*"

He bursts out in the loudest, most delighted laugh. It breaks through the fog of my rant, and I register that he's leaning slightly forward. When he speaks again, his voice is almost a purr.

"I want to hear more of your thoughts on the video. Maybe I can talk you through this."

He likes it. He *likes* that I'm jealous!

What the hell, Erik?

I bite my lip and shake my head, at the edge of tears. He's hurt me so deeply, and when I tell him, he *likes it?* And now he thinks he can just apex manipulate his way out of this. If I call him out, he'll just deny it. I wish I could apex manipulate *him*. It would serve him right, someone breaking into his beautiful head for a change.

If Erik were a keypad, what would his three buttons be?

A pins and needles flush spiders up my chest as I decide to find out.

"Talk me through what?" I ask innocently.

"Your jealousy. Is it centered on Nadya?"

He *really* likes me being jealous. Is that the first button? Let's punch it a few times and find out.

"No. It's centered on *you*. Someone else touching *your* mouth." I let my eyes travel to his mouth. I'd swear he's getting warmer. And it's the truth, it's how I really feel. I just never expected to say it out loud. "Your hands," I go on. "That dimple you make every third smile. The veins inside your wrists and the way you smell like rain . . . if I could have anything in the world, that would be my list."

". . . Say more," his voice is rough.

So one button is definitely possessiveness. What else?

People tell you their weaknesses all the time, he'd said.

How many times has he gotten angry that I was scared of him? That's why he went up on the roof at the haunted house back in Portland; that's why he's up here now, because he scared Alice.

He needs to know I'm not intimidated.

So: what's the last button? What does Erik want most from me?

"Do you know how many days I lay in bed missing you?" About three weeks is the answer, in dirty sweats, a greasy topknot, and cried-in makeup. But I try to say it like silk sheets were involved. "It was like being delirious. I couldn't sleep, but I still had these like, waking dreams? They were so vivid and . . ." I look up at him then and instantly regret it. His eyes are molten, lips slightly parted, like he's trying to taste my words. "*Obscene.*" His eyes flicker. ". . . you really don't want to hear about it."

"Sure I do," he says quickly. "What kind of dreams, Signal?"

"Not restful ones . . ." It's like being across from a hypnotized cobra. I wait for the tide to retreat in the distance, and then drop the knife. "How much worse would that get, if we slept together?"

"You say that, but—" He frowns, putting one finger up, and from the impatience of the gesture I understand at once: Sex is not the right button.

There's something he's *pining for,* that he cannot have. Sex is easy for him to get, but this is something he's been denied by everyone.

And then, I think I know.

"I have my limits." I lean closer to him, watching the impact of each button as it hits. "Don't drive me to the point where I hunt Nadya down, tear her throat out, and *drag you home.*"

A smile flashes across his face like a gleam of sunshine; he visibly glows.

That's the third button. A home. I've been in his house, seen his cell of a room. His mom farmed him out to Ledrick. He wanted to live with his grandfather and got turned over to camp instead. Erik has never really had a home.

I almost wish I didn't know.

"Now *that* would *actually* be romantic." Erik bites furiously at his nails. "But inherent dignity something something. What if I just never talk to her again?" And he pulls out his phone.

". . . What?"

"Is that what you want?" Erik asks.

"Well, I mean . . ." Is he serious? "You'd still have to *leave,* so even if you broke it off with whatsherface, I wouldn't just—jump your bones, if that's what you're asking."

"I am asking *what you want,*" Erik presses. "No strings. What would make you happy, Signal?"

"Don't run off with Nadya," I say quickly, heart leaping. "Please don't."

Erik steps back from me, and starts tapping, fast and focused.

". . . What are you doing?"

He hits send and tosses his phone on a nearby desk with a clack. I pick it up before the screen goes dark. He doesn't stop me from reading:

SCRAPS—No longer avail for Nadya/Bali thing. If they counter still a hard pass. Fake marriage stuff 2 much 4 me man. Other offers outside the US? Will work for visa, sooner the better. See u tomorrow.

XX ya boi EWS

I look up at him, shocked.

"I hate the beach." Erik shrugs. "Sun? Sand? Get me out of there."

"But . . . isn't she your only way out of the country?"

"She's the fastest way. Her team had the visa paperwork ready when she pitched it at the shoot. And the sooner I'm gone, the sooner you're safe. But we'll figure something else out."

I can't believe he just did that. Gave up living in a Bali mansion with a pop star. Did . . . did I make him do that?

Good.

An evil surge of triumph washes through me. The pins and needles flush sweeps through my entire body on a wave of relief. I'm practically tipsy with it.

". . . Thank you," I manage at last.

"Thank *you*"—a suppressed smile ticks at the corner of his mouth—"for asking for something for yourself, instead of the deserving children of the Teen Killers Club."

I laugh and gently shove his shoulder, and this is the contact he's been waiting for: He catches my hand and pulls me into him slowly and deliberately, like winding down a kite from the sky, until our chests touch. His smile comes loose then, beautiful and wide and as giddy as I feel. Like he's relieved too.

"Why are you smiling like that?" I smile.

"Why are you a walking, talking packet of Pop Rocks?"

And then he's kissing me like I really am his favorite kind of candy. The tide sounds like it's beating against the house. Maybe it's just my heart drumming too fast as his hands grip my waist. Then he flinches back.

"Whoa, are you okay?" His eyes are so wide. "Did I get your stitches?"

"Look, I'll . . . I'll just show you, alright?" I take a deep breath and lift the hem of the sweatshirt.

Part of me was hoping it won't look so bad in the half light. But the shadows make it worse, emphasizing the crude black stitching, the jagged hook curving around from my back to almost my belly button.

"Hot, right?" I yank my sweatshirt down. But he jerks it back up again, and then peels it off with an impatient gesture. Then he's on his knees, pulling me into him.

Goosebumps break out across my stomach as his breath brushes my skin. He places a first burning kiss between the stitches and my belly button. I look down, and the sight of Erik drunkenly kissing the space between my stitches and my hip bone goes through me like lightning.

This is how he kills me. Two kisses.

He stands, but his eyes don't rise from my white cotton bra.

"You know what we 'haven't even done' yet?" He murmurs, and yanks his shirt over his head, so close it grazes me as it falls to the ground. I'm right across from his bare chest, his heavily muscled arms and neck tensed, like he's waiting for my reaction. It was always a struggle not to stare when he was shirtless at camp; now that he wants me to, I can look long enough to see his scars. A half-moon stab wound in the wiry muscle just below his collar bone. Faded stitches following one curve of his developed shoulders, which round forward protectively, like natural armor. And floating across the ridges of his abdomen is the bruise from the bailiff. It's hard to consider the number of people who have tried to destroy this body. Or exploit it. Sex and death are what Erik knows. All I know is how to love him, no matter what.

He tilts his head back: an invitation.

"Wait," I say. Then I pull my bra over my head.

He sways forward slightly and my eyes drop to his throat, too shy to register his expression. I have thrown myself in the deep end, and the air is suddenly so cold. When I put my shaking arms around his neck, nothing but skin between our hearts, he's so warm I shiver. He draws me in gently, buries his face in my hair. We sink onto the bed with a creak, and time zeroes down to right now.

There is still an ocean outside, but it's drowned out by the silent music that keeps us moving together as we kiss. I'm shaking too hard at first, but what calms me down is how *here* he is. His skin is slightly rougher than mine and so warm, like stone in afternoon sun. He makes my hands hungry, but I'm so overloaded with newness I can only move slowly. He matches me. Everything stays sweet and slow and gold as though we're swimming in honey. He's so heavy, every time he rolls over, I get pulled along like a giggling undertow. When our eyes meet, we laugh: *How is this so intense?* And when I can't meet his eyes, I still feel him watching me, like his life depends on it.

But when his hand moves to my waistband, I shake my head.

". . . I'm sorry," I say.

"Nothing to be sorry," he says incoherently. He rolls onto his back, flushed, staring up at the eaves like they're spinning, and covers his face with his hands.

"Thank you . . . for never being . . . pushy about stuff."

"Who pushed you about 'stuff'?" He rises up on one elbow, cheeks filling with color like I've slapped him. "Someone up in Ledmonton? Javier?"

"No one! Really. This is all new to me. But Rose used to say . . . the further you get, the harder it is for guys to hear no."

"You mean *rapists?*" Erik says. "Rose was abused. The second someone doesn't hear no, get out of the room. Believe me, I had some words with Jaw about what went down in that shed." Then, rougher, "Did he apologize to you?"

I realize where Jaw's stilted apology came from, and take Erik's hand, nodding. But he is still wild-eyed. Somehow, I've scared him.

"You *have to be selfish* about 'stuff.' You wanting it is the whole point. The second you don't, we stop. And the kind of sharks who won't stop, any kindness is just blood in the water to them—" He looks nauseated, his lip curls with contempt. "I can't take the thought. Some sad-eyed soft boy using *his feelings* to bully you into—"

"Sad-eyed soft boys are *not* my type," I laugh, turning on my side toward him, arm across my chest.

"Your '*type*'"—Erik chokes on the word—"can *burn in hell!* You don't need a type, you have a *husband!*"

"Ha ha," I say flatly. "Erik, you're *leaving.*"

"That doesn't mean I can't come back," Erik insists. "We could figure this out. It might take a couple of months, and the visits couldn't be long, but in a year or two—"

It feels like cold water closing over my head, just the words.

"I am, forever, your personal ghost," he promises, small muscles pinging in his chest and throat. "Please do not complicate that by—by getting in some 'relationship' with a dipshit who *spoils his cats* and takes you out for *pickle fries* and *begs for sex*—"

"Um, *what?!*" I lean back, wrinkle up my nose. "Uh, that's not my type either."

"You're highly susceptible to phonies, you established that with Javier—"

"Javier wasn't a phony."

"Yeah, okay," Erik snarls. "He just faked his entire personality so you would like him, and you fell for it. I never hid anything from you, and you hated me for it."

That's . . . extremely dramatic. Javier had been a little too gallant in his flirting, but he'd never lied about anything, to either of us. And Erik's issue has always been that I was scared of him at camp, not that I *hated* him.

Across the white quilt from me, he's all clenched up. Shoulders high, hands in fists so the veins stand out along his forearms. What is he bracing for? What he's said isn't shocking, it's just wrong. That's not what happened at camp.

. . . But it is what happened with his mom.

Skye faked being the perfect son while Erik let her vivisect him. And she still trusted Skye over him. Maybe he projected that onto us at camp? Or maybe it's just coming up, after talking to Greg. Or after me punching all his buttons. My heart is racing, watching him hurt like this. And all I can say is what I wish his mom had said.

"I'm sorry I misjudged you," I tell him. "I'm sorry you had to do so much to prove yourself." I look straight in his torn eye. "But I know you better now. And I love you with all my heart, Erik."

I put my hand over his. He grips it back so hard, his face so relieved, and pulls me into him, so fast the quilt burns against my bare skin. As we kiss, I can feel his heart flinging itself at his ribs.

"I would trade days with you," he says, "over years with anyone else."

This is such wishful thinking, I can't even get mad.

"Life doesn't work that way," I explain as kindly as I can. "Days turn into years pretty fast. You can't put someone on hold like that."

"So what," Erik says, "you'd rather spend your days and years binge-watching crap with some *vegan dude* with ear gauges and a *sound project?*"

"Still not my type." I bite the inside of my lip. "Since you're dying to know."

"Just tell me, so I know who to kill." His voice drops low. "Besides your stalker, of course."

"Oh no." I cover my mouth. ". . . You heard about him?!"

"Oh yes." He is matter-of-fact. "I plan on popping by his condo and dislocating his elbows when they release him from the psych ward."

"You have his address?"

Erik nods. "They doxed him on one of your fan sites."

"*Fan sites?*" I sit up, needing to focus on where this is going. His eyes immediately drop down from my face, so I grab the pillow behind me and hug it to my chest. "I have fan sites?"

"And a subreddit," Erik says bitterly, still watching me like his life depends on it. "And message boards, and a discord."

"But I don't do anything, except trial stuff. What are they fans of? Jurisprudence?"

The side of his mouth twitches. He squints at his nails. "Oh, you know. They share pics and post news and thirst for you like the damned do for ice water." His eyes turn on me again, his stare a beam of pure focus that moves along my bare spine, to the pillow, and then hovers on my lips. ". . . So, not nearly as much as I do."

I clear my throat. "You go on these sites a lot, then?"

"To keep an eye out for stalkers." He throws his forearm over his face. "They all *loved* the music video. They figured you'd dumped me."

"You mean they're not rooting for us?"

"They think I've ruined your life," he says coldly. "Like your mom, right?"

". . . My mom doesn't think that."

"But if I found a way to stay, and we were getting married for real," Erik says, and I go very still, "she'd try and talk you out of it. Because she's scared of me. Like everyone else."

"What do you mean, 'everyone else'?"

"Everyone with internet." He starts biting his nails. "A bunch of articles keep coming out. About me being the original Class A, and my parents' crash. Things that were supposed to be sealed. Maybe Skye unsealed it all, I don't know."

"Well, whatever you told Greg this afternoon, he thinks it could make a real difference."

"Would it make a difference with your *mom*, though?"

"Erik, look." I tuck my hair behind my ear. "It's nice of you to offer to come back for a couple of days every few years or whatever, but if there's one thing my mom taught me? It's that love means *being there*. So if she had an objection to our 'marriage,' it wouldn't be so much about you as your complete and total absence from my life—"

"I'm right here," Erik's voice is very alert. "Who are you talking about?"

And it's like a punch to the gut. Because he's right.

It's not our marriage I'm talking about at all, is it?

I push myself off the bed, grab his T-shirt, and start pulling it on, more to hide my face than anything else. The unmistakable itch behind my nose means tears. This is what I get for gleefully punching his buttons: He's in his rights to punch right back. And there's no arguing my buttons hurt more, but God, I wish they hurt less. All he has to do is say one thing about my dad, and I'll start bawling.

The bed creaks, and I know he's standing just behind me. I brace myself for what he'll say next.

But all there is, for a long moment, is the rain overhead.

"You already have enough ghosts," Erik says at last, and his warm hand lands softly on my shoulder. "Is that it?"

I turn around and face him.

"Ghosts are not my type," I manage.

"Your type. Yes, your type . . . I'm really going to get it this time." He narrows his eyes, as though diagnosing me. And I realize, with a wave of relief, he is *changing the subject.*

"This jackass is probably a Class D," Erik starts. "And safe, definitely. He's always available to hang out or give you rides. Not to protect you, just because . . . he *wants to* . . ." He tilts his head back, as though struck by the thought. "*Your type* is your best friend. You tell him everything. Show him your wounds, because he stays steady when you need him to. Your type insists on a big wedding, so all your friends can come, because *they all approve.* And on your wedding night, you'd let him carry you over the threshold. Because when *he* does it, it doesn't feel like fairy tale bullshit. It feels true . . . Because your type is *such a good person.* Just like you."

"He sounds very nice." I take his hands. "But still not my type." I slide my hands up his arms, along his shoulders, and interlace my fingers behind his neck. "Which is bad boys. *Obviously.*"

And he laughs, really laughs, before we kiss.

* * *

"I should make a few calls before it gets too late," Erik says a while later, when he catches me yawning. I can't help it, the temperature has dropped enough we've crawled under the covers, rain still distantly drumming along the roof; it's so cozy. "But first, I'm going to tell you a bedtime story. See if I can get you to sleep. Close your eyes."

I do, relaxing against him with a sigh. This won't work, but I love hearing his voice so close, blending with the rain and the tide.

"You are walking through the woods. Do you smell the pine trees?"

"Not really—"

"No talking." His voice is neutral but full of authority. "Just answer in your mind. And keep moving through the trees."

I picture Naramauke; leaves glowing red and gold. Those woods will always be *the* woods, to me: the most beautiful, the most dangerous.

"You know the trail. But it's been long enough you've forgotten where it ends. Who are you walking with?"

Nobody lopes alongside me, mask over her face.

"As you walk, an animal steps into your path. What kind of animal?"

A bulldog appears, his blue-white shape standing out sharply in the shadow under the trees and tilts his head.

"What do you do with the animal?"

Nobody looks at me, and I understand. We have to charge at him. As soon as we do, he turns tail and runs.

"You see a shape through the trees, some kind of building . . ."

A shed. It goes down on one side, like its back is broken.

I am not afraid of my memories. I accept them. The past cannot hurt me.

Nobody and I walk inside the shed, her ducking a little for the low door like Rose always did. Beside the door is a card table, laid out for the ritual. The cupcakes, the saw, the Marilyn and Elvis figurines. But something else too: Jaw's photographs, in a circle, no clear end or beginning. I stand over them, staring down at the flash-bleached image of Jaw kissing me.

And then it's not the photo I'm seeing. I'm back in the moment itself.

The skin-crawling sensation of Jaw's lips squirming against me, the earthy, too-sweet taste of pot smoke. I turn to Nobody, begging for help. She takes off her hood, and long dark hair tumbles out, Rose's face glaring back at me. She holds up a camera, and everything goes white.

As the mist of white recedes from my vision, I see Janeane looking in the window, eyes wild between her hands, fingers distended against the glass, lips parting in excitement over red teeth, panting to get in.

Rose hurries to shut the door, but it's too late, Janeane is too fast; she gets down on her hands and knees and scrambles in as Rose screams. I can't watch. But when Rose goes quiet at last, my eyes crack open to see Janeane crouching, her back to me. The knobs of Janeane's spine are bone white through her blue-pale skin, and her long dark hair swings across her back, back and forth, back and forth, as she rocks side to side, a low moan rattling at the back of her throat.

"*Rose?*" I whisper.

Janeane turns, and I close my eyes. But it's too late. Even with my eyes shut, I can see her bare her red teeth.

"No—" I say out loud.

Erik's voice cuts through the dream: "Signal. I'm here. I've got you—"

His fingers tuck my hair behind my ear, and this makes the shed rattle around us. Janeane scuttles back into the shadows as I burrow into his side, my cheek against his throat. The beat of his heart as steady as the tide.

"I'm here." Erik's voice rumbles like thunder against my chest, and the shed breaks and shatters. The tide pulls it away like sea foam and leaves me on the shore. Warm and free as sunshine.

* * *

I wake in a pool of rainbow sunlight, streaming down from the stained-glass window above me. I'm damp and heavy from the deepest sleep I've had since before Rose died. The sun feels thick, like it's late morning, the white sheets a riot of jewel-bright colors. On the pillowcase beside mine there's a folded-up note, but the bed is otherwise empty, and someone's knocking hard down at the bottom of the attic staircase. I pull on the hoodie, grab the note, and stumble to the door. Alice is on the other side.

"Sorry if I missed breakfast. I must have slept in," I yawn. "What time is it?"

Alice gives me a look. "It's eleven thirty, and we have quite the drive ahead of us."

"Drive?" I yawn helplessly. "Drive where?"

"Your wedding?"

I look down at the note, and read Erik's hurried writing:

I'M NOT JOKING.

Chapter Fifteen
Bonnie and Clyde

～

Alice cuts the engine. "Okay, you can remove the blindfold."

I pull off the black bandanna and blink up at the War Memorial Opera House in disbelief. Apparently, after his hypnotic story knocked me out, Erik made those calls.

"You're supposed to go with her . . ." She points to a tall and intensely grace-ful girl coming down the stairs in a black leotard and brown tights the exact shade of her slender arms. "And I'm going to park and find the groom."

The tall girl waves shyly as I get out. "Signal?" she says. "Hi, I'm Amy—"

"Nobody's Amy!?" I cry, and her warm smile flickers.

"Formerly Nobody's Amy, sure." Her nose scrunches a little as she laughs, a halo of natural curls peeking over her broad headband. "Come on, they're all waiting—"

"All?" I find myself automatically whispering as I follow her through the glowing, white marble lobby of the War Memorial Opera House. "What is *happening* right now?"

"You're getting married? That's what *I* was told."

"Yeah, but I thought we were just signing something."

"Well, I think it might be a little more involved than that, because I was instructed to reserve the space for as long as possible. We've got it until five. But if anybody comes in early, you never met me, alright?" She laughs, nose scrunching again, and leads me into the decadent women's bathroom. Its spa-cious, velvet lounge immediately rings with Jada's shrieks:

"SKIPPER!!!! IT'S HAPPENING!!!"

I actually scream back when I see Jada with Nobody right behind her, both in T-shirts with "99% BRIDESMAID" written on them in black sharpie. We

grab each other's elbows and start jumping up and down, smiles cast in tripli-
cate by the floor-to-ceiling gilt-edged mirrors, and I realize their shirts say "1%
KILLER" on the back and burst out laughing.

"This is so wild!" I look back and forth between them. "What is happening?
What is happening right now!"

"Surprise wedding, bitch! And your groomzilla knows how to do it, because
he put me on snacks." Jada waves at a row of plastic champagne flutes, bottles
of Martinelli's sparkling cider, and giant iced sugar cookies with pink sprinkles.

"For the record," Nobody says, arm still around my shoulders, "this doesn't
sit right with me."

"Says the girl who got us the venue!" Jada laughs, and my heart melts, imagining an overwrought Nobody asking Amy a favor for me and Erik.

"So, wait, how are you here?" I ask them. "Are you done with house arrest?"

"Honor is just *that good!*" Jada fans herself. "I am in love with that woman.
Sonny says it's possible there could just be a settlement instead of a trial. They
still have to negotiate our individual sentences—and being Class As and all,
those negotiations will be tough—"

"But Dave must be spilling his guts." Nobody smiles.

"Is Honor *here?*" I ask, because I can smell the same distinctive scent that
always wafts from her tailored suits. "Because something smells great—"

"Oh, that's just me." Jada flounces at her hair jokingly, then drops her voice
low. "Skye hooked me up with some Givenchy perfume. *L'Interdit?* Ever heard of
it?" She holds the inside of her wrist up to my nose. It's definitely the same thing
Honor wears. "You want some? I brought it, it's in my makeup bag, which, we
should be getting you ready, come on . . ." Jada leads me over to a low red couch
beside a mirror-topped table, where she's already set out combs, hairclips, and
makeup palettes. Nobody plops down onto the couch next to me, dragging one
scarred fingertip curiously across a square of eye shadow.

"It's really nice of Amy to help with this." I elbow her. "Have you been talking through things with her?"

"Because if you don't lock it down, she's going to get snatched up fast," Jada
adds.

"Would you two shut up?" Nobody nervously scratches the back of her neck
as Amy floats back in, holding a garment bag. Nobody devours every flourish of
her movements, though she seems incapable of meeting Amy's eyes.

"I thought this could work as your dress—"

"Dress?" I look around. "You mean I'm not wearing a 99% Bride T-shirt?"

"Erik asked if we had any costumes in your size, and it turns out the Opera
House recently did a production of *Giselle.*" Amy takes out something made

of white tulle, so delicate it catches the air like a spider's web. "So I wrangled a willis dress."

It's a dress from another world, an A-line sheath of ethereal white fabric with a sweetheart bodice. I can't believe I get to touch it, let alone wear it.

"That is *gorgeous!*" Jada breathes. "I don't know what the hell a willis is, but I'm into it."

"Oh, they're so cool." Amy smiles. "They're the ghosts of girls who were jilted on their wedding day, right? And they all rise up at night and dance any man they find to death!"

"*Love* that." Jada nods. "Sounds like my kind of party."

Amy's huge eyes flash back to me. "Just hand it off to Lark when you go back to the Desais, and she'll mail it back to me." Amy walks away quickly then, and Nobody seems to deflate.

"Mail it?" She looks stricken. "I told her I'd bring it to her and take her to lunch, since I can leave the house . . ." She gets up and starts pacing.

"Signal, your phone!" Jada draws my attention to the glowing screen in my hand: Greg Ballas.

"Hi!" I say, stepping out of the carpeted waiting area, into the tiled space of empty stalls. "Today's the big day! Is the article out?"

"That's why I'm calling." Greg sounds pained. "We've hit a setback."

I lean against the wall. "Oh?"

"My editor was apparently fired this morning. Her boss offered to pay me a wildly inappropriate amount of money for the rights to the unpublished article. I told them I'd rather take it elsewhere. I'm talking to a few spaces. We'll find a good home for it, eventually."

". . . Oh."

"But I don't know when that will be, and any new masthead will likely want to do their own fact checking, so it could be several more weeks before it's up."

Not before Erik has to leave. I huddle against the wall, the cold of the tile bleeding through my thin shirt.

"Anyway, I've got another call coming in. But when we find a home, I'll let you know."

And he's off before I can say goodbye.

I cover my face for a moment before I can return to the foyer.

"You should come to grad nite!" Jada is saying to Amy as I walk back in, an ancient Nokia phone in her hands, the kind that's only good for texting and playing snake. She slips it back into her makeup bag. "It's at the Desai house tomorrow night. Then you could just get the costume there, the Desais could launder it—"

"Oh, well." Amy blinks at Nobody. "If that's easier?"

Nobody says, too fast: "It sure is."

"There's our briiiide! Time to strip!" Jada and Nobody take the dress off the hanger. The dress slips over my head easily and fits me well. But I can't unsee it: it's a dress for a broken-hearted ghost. I hadn't realized how high my hopes had gotten, and now they're gone. I want to go hide in a stall and cry, not stand here and smile.

"Guys . . ." I start, "I'm sorry, but—"

"Oh *honey!*" Amy leads in my mom, her jaw hanging open as she takes in the lounge, my dress, my friends. "I thought you said we were going to a McDonald's?"

The room bursts out in laughter, and Jada scrambles to get her a plate of snacks. Nobody helps her find a place for her jacket and quilted bag.

"You're a vision." Mom takes my hands and holds out my arms, scanning the dress. "Where did you get this dress? It looks designer or something."

"Amy is letting me borrow it. It's a costume from—*Giselle*, was it?" I ask Amy.

Amy is right behind me, tying up the complicated laces of the dress.

"Oh, how nice. Is that a love story?" Mom smiles at her.

"Sort of?" Amy frowns. "Giselle is in love with a noble gentleman, but he jilts her to marry someone else, and she dies of a broken heart. He goes to visit her grave, and the willis come to dance him to death. But Giselle refuses to let them and helps him get away. And because she didn't give in to jealousy, her soul is freed, and she can find peace."

A cold weight settles in my chest.

"So . . . not a happy ending," Nobody says, voice rough.

"Great art is like real life," Amy shrugs, not looking at her. "No such thing as a happy ending."

Then she hurries toward the lobby again, just as Nobody breaks off her pacing to walk toward me. They should knock into each other, but as if in a dance, Nobody and Amy coordinate perfectly: Nobody pivots and Amy slows to let her pass. Amy's trailing hand comes within an inch of Nobody's elbow, but they pull it off without making contact; each acutely aware of every atom of the other, without having to look.

"Signal, can we talk for a second?" Nobody asks. I've hardly nodded when she grabs my hand and pulls me to the farthest stall.

"I can tell you're upset," she says, once the stall door is closed.

"Oh, come on, no." I force a laugh. "What are you talking about—"

"Of course you are. You're letting a man ruin your life." Nobody frowns. "You got kicked out of the house. Honor dropped your case. No lawyer right before your trial." Nobody shakes her head quickly, her beautiful face very serious. "I wanted to let you know, we can go right now. Run down the fire stairs to the parking lot, like before. I took a lot of money out in case you wanted to—"

"Nobody, what are you talking about?"

"You don't have to go through with it."

"Yes, I do, if you want Erik to give that deposition!"

She blinks at me. "Deposition?"

"After the ceremony?" I repeat what Alice explained to me on the drive over: "After the ceremony, we're going straight back to the Desai house so he can give evidence about camp for your trial. About the Wylie-Stanton and Ledrick and everything." My hands find their way to her wrists. "Everything is going to work out! Just like I promised. Okay?"

But Nobody looks horror-stricken, and then someone pounds on the door.

"What're you two doing in here?!" Jada squeezes into the stall. "Thinking up more moves for your *secret handshake?!*"

"Nobody was trying to get me to run out on the wedding."

Jada rolls her glitter-lined eyes. "Her mom got married at your age. It's been sending her through a loop."

"Is that true?" I ask Nobody.

"Ruined her life." Nobody pulls some toilet paper off the roll and wipes at her face. "And *not* in a good way."

"Well, then, you will be happy to hear this marriage is only temporary," I tell her. "We're getting it annulled once Erik is deposed. And then he's leaving the country, so—"

"Wait, *what?!*" Jada gasps. "Okay, no offense, but what have I said from the start?! That boy belongs to the streets! Erik is, was, and *always will be* a *player*—"

I shoot her a hard look.

"I love you both," Jada adds with the sweetest smile.

And then my mom's voice echoes down the tiled walls:

"*Girls!* They're ready!"

"Come on." I put my arms around their shoulders. "I need my two best women today."

* * *

We stand in front of the double doors to the auditorium when at last we hear it: a piano breaking into the last movement of *Swan Lake*, and Amy carefully walks the doors open.

Nobody and Jada go down the darkened aisle first, Nobody with her hands in her pockets, Jada holding a couple of pale pink roses from the grocery store bouquet my mom brought. The rest are clutched in my hands, dripping onto my high-top black Vans. Mom's elbow is threaded through mine.

Ahead of us, past the gilded proscenium arch, the painted backdrop from *Swan Lake* glows through the dark: swirling mist over a black lake where the couple go to die together. Standing in front of it, in a white spotlight, is none other than Scraps, dressed as a monk.

No, not a monk. He's wearing an inexpensive Obi-Wan Kenobi Halloween costume.

To one side of him, an older man in a gray sweatshirt and jazz shoes is wringing every dramatic note of the *Swan Lake* finale from an upright piano.

To the other side of Scraps, Dennis at his side, is Erik. He's all in black, hands in tight fists. When our eyes meet, two bright spots of color rise in his cheeks, but he doesn't smile.

I'm really not sure what to do when I get to the orchestra pit. Nobody and Jada are up onstage somehow. I set down my flowers and start to hoist myself on stage. Erik's hot hands pull me up almost too fast, lifting me above the stage so high my feet leave the floor completely. But once I'm back on solid ground, all the confused nerves evaporate. All my awareness narrows to his hand in mine.

And I can't believe he did this. I can't believe how *sincere* it is. How one single gesture, like the perfect note coming in at just the right time in a song, can change my entire life into something so much more meaningful than it was the moment before.

Scraps clears his throat and surveys the echoing dark of the opera house, the rows and tiers and terraces of empty red velvet seats.

"Fellow burners," Scraps starts, reading from an index card curled damply against his palm. "I mean, um, fellow ballet fans . . ." He scratches the back of his head with his neon green cast. "There was this one time, I was driving up to Portland, and I gave this beautiful couple a ride in my car. They were asking me about career moves, as people tend to do—I consult for brand management, at a reasonable hourly rate. And I certainly helped these two! Got them on a little network, maybe you've heard of it, called CNN?"

Nobody suppresses a laugh behind me, and Scraps continues.

"So, during this conversation, we got on the subject of Bonnie and Clyde." Scraps blinks out at the small group standing at the edge of the stage: my mom, Amy, and Alice. "Why did people love Bonnie and Clyde so much? I'll let you ponder that for a moment. But first, the rings! Are you exchanging those? If not we can just skip this section—"

"Yes, we are," Erik says, very composed, and turns to Dennis, who offers up a narrow gold band with a diamond that would be way more convincing if it weren't so large. But before Erik can get it on my hand, it slips from his shaking fingers, bounces off the stage with a merry twinkle, and rolls into the curlicued heating grate in the floor of the orchestra pit with a distant *tink*.

"That could have gone better," Erik mutters, Nobody already leaping down to try and retrieve it.

And I realize I don't have anything for him.

I turn to Jada. "Do you have a pen?"

The guy in the sweats at the piano stands and offers a fine-tipped Sharpie.

I take Erik's beautiful hand and carefully draw a black heart on the knuckle of his ring finger.

He stares at it a long moment, the corner of his mouth curling.

"How about a flashlight? Anybody got a flashlight?" Nobody calls up from the orchestra pit. Dennis gets down off the stage and shines his phone through the iron grate in the floor, while Nobody turns a paper clip into a fishhook.

"You need something longer!" Jada, hand at her neck, hops down herself. "Here, see, string the paper clip onto my necklace chain—"

"Oh, it's okay!" I call down from the stage. "We don't need it, we got a pen—"

"Yes, we do," Erik says quietly. "That's my mom's ring."

"... It's what?"

"That was my mom's engagement ring." Erik stares down at our friends trying to fish the ring through the scrollwork of the vintage grate. "I found it in my dad's safe, back when we first stopped at my house."

"... Oh." I swallow, hard, now terrified. "Is it just for the ceremony, or did you want me to wear it until you leave?"

"Wear it always. If you want," he says, not looking at me. "It's yours."

"Got it!" Jada cries from the orchestra pit, Dennis throwing us a thumbs-up as Nobody holds up a paper clip hook on a gold chain, the giant diamond ring dangling off it like the world's most expensive bait.

Erik crouches to retrieve it, rainbow flashes pinwheeling across the boards as he stands, takes my hand, and slides it easily onto my ring finger.

"So. Bonnie and Clyde," Scraps goes on. "Why did people like them so much? Why do they still remember them at all? I thought about that a lot. And I think it's pretty simple. I think that we'd all like to believe, if the whole world turned against us, the person we love most would still take our side. That beyond what society deems right or wrong in our time, no matter what we test as, deep down there is a more eternal human understanding of good. Which is an inviolable loyalty to those who love us, and to those we truly love. And these two got that. So they've got enough to take on the world."

Nobody lets out a long wolf whistle.

"So. Do you, Erik Wylie-Stanton," he points a finger gun at Erik and winks, "vow to take this woman, to have and to hold from this day forward, for richer or poorer, in sickness and health, to love and to cherish, until death do you part?"

Erik blinks, looking a little alarmed. "I . . . do?"

"Signal Deere." Scraps turns to me then, his large dark eyes very intense. "Same question, but swap out 'man' for 'woman' in that one part."

"I do." I bite the inside of my cheek.

"Beautiful. So by the powers invested in me by the state of California and our sacred Playa, I now pronounce you man and wife: Mr. and Mrs. Wylie-Stanton!" He looks back and forth at us. "This is the part where you kiss, so. Make it a good one."

Everyone starts clapping when it happens. And I swear I can hear the full orchestra version of our song from *Swan Lake*: swirling strings, delicate harps, throbbing timpani. I hear it so heartbreakingly clear, all around us.

* * *

Immediately after the ceremony, Erik walks me backstage while our guests go out to the foyer. He keeps scanning my dress, like he wants to feel how soft it is.

"I can't believe we just got married *at the Opera House*," I gush.

He tilts his head and lifts his eyebrows just a little. "You thought I'd tell our grandkids we got married at a *Starbucks?*"

I burst out laughing, but it quickly sputters out, a spasm of sadness chasing my smile away. He takes my hand.

"I wanted you to have one good day with me, at least," Erik says.

"To the extent that life is made of days," I keep my voice as light as I can, "all my best ones have been with you."

We walk hand in hand along the painted backdrop of the lake, slipping around the buckling canvas into the yawning black behind the stage. The inky dark soars up past catwalks a city block overhead. He scans carefully, then turns to me and steps closer, once he's sure we're alone.

"This is where it gets dangerous," Erik says. "Scraps is going to go straight from here to the courthouse to file the marriage license. Once it's filed, by the terms of the conservatorship, I will literally *belong to you*, Signal."

I nod, overwhelmed.

"Which is why," he goes on, his eyes hard, "while I'm being deposed at the Desai house, *you must not go off alone with anyone*. Not Nobody, not Dennis—not anyone."

"Erik—"

"I know you love your friends." He looks grim. "Fine, cool. But *do not trust them.*"

I put my hands on his shoulders; they're high, tensed.

"Is part of this, maybe, that you're a little freaked out we just got married?"

He doesn't smile. He reaches up and takes my hand. His mom's ring glints in the dark as he presses his mouth to the inside of my wrist, as though he wants to kiss not my skin but my pulse, the fact of my heartbeat itself.

"Promise me," he says, voice very deep, "you won't go off alone with anyone in that house."

"I promise."

And then voices float out from the lobby: our wedding guests, calling for Mr. and Mrs. Wylie-Stanton.

*   *   *

When we get to the Desai house it's close to sunset. I convince Jada and Nobody we should stay out on the patio while Erik goes into the nerve center to testify, to watch the sky change colors from under the heat lamp.

But in all honesty, I'm avoiding Javier. It wasn't lost on me that he skipped the wedding. I also don't need to run into Aarush any time soon. Jada and Nobody are obliging, and come back from the house with blankets, a bottle of sparkling Martinelli's cider and plastic champagne flutes, and Jada's laptop. We cuddle up onto one lounge chair together.

"I bet we have time to watch a whole series," Jada says, navigating through several open tabs. "Depositions always take forever. And I saw Honor in the hall—" she leans past me to tell Nobody.

"Yeah?" Nobody's eyebrows fly up.

"She says, depending on how well what Erik says matches up with Dave, prosecution might offer a deal as soon as tomorrow."

"If we don't go to trial, will Honor be your lawyer again?" Nobody asks, and I let out a weary laugh.

"I couldn't afford her."

"Signal *Deere* couldn't. But Signal *Wylie-Stanton?*" Jada elbows me. "Know your rights. You didn't sign a pre-nup! Erik better pay you out for being an eighteen-year-old divorcée. That's a long-ass story to have to tell, on like every first date, for the rest of your life—"

"You know," I sigh, winding my arms through theirs and pulling them closer to me, "today has been such a beautiful day. Do we really have to ruin it by talking about tomorrow?"

Jada and Nobody exchange an eye roll, and then I see the hashtag bolded on Jada's computer screen.

"What's #WylieStantonMom?" I cry, too loud. Is it possible Greg's piece was published somewhere else already?

Jada clicks on a link, and a clip of Janeane comes up, in full hair and makeup. Mary Larland sits across from her, her expression Very Concerned.

"I have your Wylie-Stanton results right here, which you yourself have not heard yet. Are you ready?"

"Yes, Mary." Janeane nods tearfully.

"You are classified, by the Wylie-Stanton, as 'Class B.'"

Janeane clasps her hands and squeezes her eyes closed.

"How does that make you feel, Janeane?"

"*I* knew. I knew I wasn't *evil*." Janeane smiles tearfully. "And now, so does the world."

The clip cuts abruptly and starts again.

"What the hell is that from?!"

Jada looks at me, concerned. "You didn't hear? Janeane did a big interview last night."

"What?" I look from her to Nobody. "Did a lot of people watch?"

"Just everybody who speaks English," Nobody says.

"Okay. I need to see this—"

"Oh, come on, now—" Jada turns the laptop away from me. "What did you just say about not ruining today?"

"If every potential juror is going to hear her side first, I have to know how bad it is."

With a look of misgiving, Jada navigates to the site where the whole interview is streaming. A very official brass chryon glides onscreen with a flourish, and then Mary Larland stares down the camera.

"Tonight, I'm joined by grieving mother, recent widow, and *alleged murderer*, Janeane Rowan. Janeane, thank you for being here."

Janeane nods. I wonder if her outfit was chosen by the same purple-haired woman who chose mine.

"You have been accused of the *unthinkable*. The murder of your daughter and husband. Why do you think Signal Deere would accuse you of such a heinous crime?"

There's a crushed tissue in Janeane's hand that she passes close to her eyes, but not close enough to disturb her makeup.

"No one who knew Signal personally ever questioned her conviction." Janeane sniffs. "I understand she has a lot of support from people who've recently heard about her. And I know there's money behind her, from people invested in ending the Wylie-Stanton. But I always knew Signal as a deeply disturbed individual. And after being tortured and left for dead by her *gang*, I can tell you the Class A influence hardly *helped*."

Mary Larland frowns. "So you believe Signal is the camper who was marked as 'Class A Influenced' in the camp intake form?"

Janeane shrugs. "It's the only thing that makes sense. Class As and their influence are very real. When we limit or disable tools that can identify Class As, like the Wylie-Stanton, we are playing dangerous games with the lives of our children."

I stand up, stomach twisting.

Nobody reaches out for me. Jada says, "Let's just change it—" But I'm already moving fast across the deck, racing the Martinelli's sparkling cider that's burning its way back up my throat. I bolt past the dark basketball court and through the automatic doors of the gym. Ke$ha is blaring over the still machines as I scramble into the bathroom.

I bend over the sink, waiting for something to come up. But my breath only gets faster and faster as I avoid my own panicked face in the mirror.

The bathroom door creaks open. There's slow, shuffling steps, like a very old man's, and a disturbingly familiar smell fills the small space. A smell that makes me reflexively turn to face the figure just behind me in the mirror.

"Hey, Signal." Kurt smiles, a smile that doesn't reach his eyes. "What the heck kind of getup is that?"

Chapter Sixteen

Eyes

❧

A metallic sound goes through my head as our eyes meet, like the sing of metal when a sword is pulled from its sheath. Kurt's skin has a grimy sheen, darkest around his nails and mouth, pieces of dry skin like clear cornflakes crusting his lips. His hands are at his sides with the fingers slightly fanned, apprehensive. The smell of old blood deepens every moment we're across from each other and the bottom of his backpack is black with it, the bulging weight of whatever is inside digging the straps deep into his shoulders.

"Kurt? W-what are you doing here?"

"What do you think?"

I measure the distance around us. The small bathroom keeps me in arm's reach of him, anywhere but where I'm standing.

"Are you . . . on a mission?"

"Yes. The final mission."

"For who? Camp is over."

"Camp is not over, Signal. Camp is just getting started. Camp is going to be everywhere, and every Class A is already trapped. But *not me*. Because I won't be a Class A anymore."

He thinks he's going to be some super assassin after camp is closed down. But he's just going to be a test subject at best, if they even keep him around once he's finished taking out his assigned targets.

There's no point riling him up, though.

"Kurt, this can't be what you really want." I keep my tone placating and survey the room for anything to use as a weapon. "You didn't kill anyone before camp, you said so yourself." The bamboo vase I cracked is gone; there are rolled up towels in a wicker basket and a small, useless plastic trashcan. "Troy killed all your victims. But you still took half the blame, didn't you?"

Kurt's smile seems to flicker at the edges.

"Is that why you killed Donna?" I push. "Because she couldn't tell the difference?"

"Whoa, come on, Signal." Kurt sounds offended. "I know you never completed a mission, but you know how they work. We don't pick our targets, headquarters does. I didn't *want* to kill Donna. I always liked her."

"Donna was a *target?*"

"The first target of this final mission, yes. To test me. To see if I could really go through with it."

He's raving. I glance over his shoulder to the door, and he bobs toward me. My eyes flash to his, and he freezes again.

"That doesn't make sense, Kurt. There was no reason for headquarters to kill Donna."

"Sure there was. She kept telling everyone Troy wasn't a Class A."

"Headquarters would kill her for that?"

He shrugs, one grimy hand dipping into the pocket of his weathered red hoodie.

"It's not my job to question orders," Kurt says. "Just carry them out."

His hand comes out of his pocket, clutching a long silver straight razor, folded into its handle. He turns his hand and the blade falls out.

"Turn around," Kurt says softly.

Erik's voice rings through my mind: *"Kurt can't kill someone while looking in their face."*

I lock my eyes with his.

"Turn around!" Kurt cries.

I shift my weight to the foot facing the door, and the moment I do, he lashes out. I kick at his knee and the blade flies at my face but I throw my arm up. The tip of the blade catches in the tender skin just inside my elbow.

There's a moment's surprise, both of us startled by my red blood exiting the split flesh. This same arm that held him when he cried over Troy, when he was my friend. But that friend is gone, or never existed. I don't know who this is.

Kurt's eyes move away from mine. He carelessly carves a streak down the inside of my forearm as I jerk past, sprinting out of the bathroom.

The cut is clean, but the feeling is mayhem. Churning flames of pain burn from the knob of my wrist to my elbow, hot blood running down my cold skin as I sprint through the empty weight machines, Ke$ha still singing overhead.

"KURT! IT'S KURT!" I scream when I'm close enough the doors open to let the words ring across the pool: *"SOMEBODY HELP ME!"*

In another moment Javier runs into the gym. Kurt, racing in after me from the bathroom, sees him and stops in his tracks.

Javier bends to pick up a twenty-pound free weight and flings it at Kurt's head. The mirrored wall becomes a spiderweb of fractured glass, and in another moment security is running across the deck. But Kurt is too quick, he melts into the dark as someone yells, "FREEZE! STOP!"

"Over here!"

"LOCKDOWN PROTOCOL!"

Javier's fingers dig into my shoulder, but everything below my shoulder is numb.

"Signal, what did he do?"

I look down and realize Javier and I are standing in a pool of my blood, the whole front of my wedding dress has gone red. Black lace floats over my eyes, and everything goes dark.

* * *

My head rolls back and forth on a slick leather cushion. I blink and a far-away ceiling comes into focus. I turn my head with a throb of deep pain to see dozens of floating glass jellyfish. I'm in the library, stretched out on the low couch. Stiff bandages are wrapped tight around my forearm, an all-too familiar burn pulling at the flesh inside them.

"Signal?" Javier is just beside me, leaning forward in his chair. "You awake?"

"Yeah, I'm up. What happened?"

"You fainted from blood loss. The Desais' private doctor had to give you some stitches."

"Right." I sigh. "Where is he?"

We're all alone in the large library, I realize, trying to sit up. My head throbs again.

"Security escorted him to his car before you woke up. He left me some pills to give you. Here . . ." Javier takes my uninjured hand and carefully dispenses four white pills into my palm. "He said to take them as soon as you woke up."

". . . What are they?"

"Painkillers and a general antibiotic."

"Security escorted the doctor out? Why?" I blink at Javier, not getting it. "Where is everyone?"

The room is so dark.

"The others are out on the patio. They brought us in here so the doctor could sew you up, and Raoul locked us in while security finishes their sweep. We're supposed to stay put till he gives us the all-clear."

The window down the wall goes momentarily bright white, as though swept with a flashlight from outside.

"So Kurt's still somewhere in the house?"

"Guess so." Javier holds my gaze. Then: "You should really take those pills."

"Right." I push them into my mouth, almost coughing them back up again. I wish I had water, but I get them down and grimace from the bitter aftertaste.

"Thank you," I say after a moment, "for helping me back there. You must be pretty sick of saving me."

Javier shakes his head. "I'm sick of you sticking your neck out, how about we leave it at that." He does not leave it at that, though; he adds a nanosecond later: "Especially for people who don't deserve it. That's all I'll say." He leans back in the chair, then goes on. "But I really can't believe I didn't get invited to the wedding. I just hung around the house all confused while everybody else got ready."

"Would you have wanted to come?"

"Sure." He is just holding back a sneer. "If only to object—"

"Thanks."

"I'm sorry I'm the only one who will tell you the truth. But that maniac is using you! Why do you think this happened, with Kurt?" He waves at my dress and I look down and immediately feel awful. Poor Nobody. This ruined dress is going to be what really ends things with Amy. The fine material is so soaked with blood it looks dyed red, the drying hem the color of rust.

"He put you in Kurt's way. He made you unsafe." Javier's expression is intense. "And if you're not safe in *this* house, with all these cameras and security guards, what happens when you walk out of here? I am begging you, as your friend—"

"We're not friends, remember?"

He pulls back, face stern. "You're still going to be like that, after I just saved your life."

"Javier, come on!" I cry, exasperated. "I can be *grateful* and still believe that what happened that night was *not okay*—"

"Jada just got in my head," Javier says. "We were texting and she kept saying how she could hear Erik moaning through the wall and I just . . ." He shakes his head. "He's made you his human shield. As long as you're with him, you're *not safe*. Being next to the wrong person can ruin your whole life. I've seen it happen, alright?"

And I realize, with a lightning bolt flash, this isn't about me. This isn't about Erik.

This is about Mateo.

This is about the fact that Javier—the most protective member of our group—couldn't protect his little brother, and still blames himself for Mateo getting killed. Because he let Mateo be around "the wrong person" on the way to the corner store. I'm still choking on the realization, trying to find the words, when footsteps fill the hall.

Multiple security guards are thundering along the marble passage outside the door, shouting into their walkie-talkies. I actually hear one say "Red alert." They race down the hall and toward the other side of the house, like they're falling into formation. The crack of light at the bottom of the door starts to strobe, some silent alarm going off through the house.

"You think they found Kurt?" I whisper.

BANG! BANG! BANG!

Someone on the other side of the door is knocking like they're willing to break their hands to get in. Javier scans the room for some kind of weapon as the door rattles in its frame; then there are heavy falls of something blunt and metal.

"Signal," Javier leans over me, his hands on my shoulders, "listen to me. If you still got the license, you could tear it up right now. Slide the pieces under the door so he can see—"

"*What?!*"

"He's only doing this because you're married to Erik," Javier pleads. "Listen to me—"

Then the door flies open at an angle, broken at its hinges, and Erik bursts into the room, the fire extinguisher in his hands hurtling to the floor. He locks in on me, cringing in pain when he sees the new bandage.

"It's bad, okay, but not like, dying bad." I totter to my feet. "Kurt cut me, he didn't hit any major arteries, a doctor stitched me up. I don't know how many— we'll check when we're at home. Just don't freak out, okay?"

The muscles of Erik's contorted face stand out as clearly as though he's been flayed. His deep voice strains as he turns on Javier: "*What are you doing here?*"

"He got me away from Kurt." I stumble between them. My dress, so fluid and airy before, clings to me like it's been dipped in oil, and at the sight of me wobbling, Erik flinches. "I know you're upset. But do not take it out on him."

Erik nods stiffly. Then he turns, walks to the fireplace, and pulls out a poker from the marble stand beside it with a clang. He hoists it in both hands, swinging the long poker over his shoulder like a baseball bat.

"Dude." Javier sidesteps away from him. "What are you—"

But Erik walks past both of us, over to the glass sculpture. And then, with a monumental crash, blue jellyfish shiver and shatter down the wall. Glass rains onto the marble floor, bouncing and pinging across the polished tile louder and louder as Erik, cool and focused, slams the bar of iron into the delicate glass, again and again. He wrings himself in half with the motion, the armature rattling all the way up to the ceiling as broken blue glass rains down with a sound like raucous applause. He doesn't seem to notice the sharp flecks of glass that shower into his hair, that wash across the shoulders of his black shirt; he just keeps wrecking the thing, until the poker is scraping the marble wall itself, the wire armature jangling and breaking, his shoes squeaking against inches of broken glass carpeting the floor around him like blue hail.

At last, he turns to me, breathless. Veins stand out along the inside of his wrists and forearm even as he lets the fireplace poker clatter to the floor. A chip of marble flooring bounces up after it falls.

"Okay." Erik walks toward me, hand outstretched. "I'll be steady now."

A knot rises in the back of my throat at the word. I take his hot hand with both of mine. I hold it as tight as though I could keep it. Then I see the gleam.

"Wait!" I say. "Close your eyes!"

His eyes fall shut, and I put my hands on his shoulders and rise on tiptoe to blow a particle of blue glass from his eyelashes. His shoulders sink, releasing with a sigh. I take his too-hot face in my hands, tilting it carefully, catching the sharp glints of glass caught in the divot above his upper lip, his eyebrows, the edge of his hairline. The more I inspect him, the more his breathing slows.

"Lean back . . . ?" I murmur, and I sweep the glass from his hair before brushing every little shard from his collar and shoulders and the lines of his face, until I'm satisfied nothing will hurt him.

"There . . . ," I sigh.

And when he opens his eyes again, his gaze is calm and soft.

"You gave me a scare." He ducks down, one hand drifting up to my cheek, like I'm precious. And when he kisses me, it feels like I'm covered in glitter instead of blood.

He puts his arm around me, and I lean into him, bloody dress pulling and sticking as I wrangle my stiffly bandaged arm around his neck, but he's right. We're steady now.

Erik calls over his shoulder to Javier as we leave, "Thanks, man."

And I look back to see Javier standing, speechless, in half a million dollars' worth of broken glass.

* * *

Erik hugs the wall like a shadow as we climb the stairs, white marble going alternately neon blue and dim gray around us as silent alarms strobe from above. He waits until we are out of the eyeline of the security guards before showing me the dupe phone.

"More texts came in," he says, and I take the phone from him. "I took screen shots before Skye deleted them."

It's Eyes again:

This wasn't part of our deal

Skye's response is simply: What are you talking about

The attack on Signal

What attack

You sent Kurt after her

Kurt? who? I have no idea who you're talking about lol

Yes you do. Who else would send Kurt after her?

Not exactly my department. But glad HQ is finally pitching in to clean up this mess.

Erik just gave his deposition about camp.

Yeah? Well don't think for a second you can make up with Signal. Not after the way Janeane humiliated her at the hearing. We stick with the plan. The house is ready for Erik so get him ready for me.

I've just finished reading when Erik throws open the door to Nobody's room, hitting the wall light so the skyline of Manhattan jumps up in full color over a bed covered in pink Pocky wrappers. He nonchalantly lifts her mattress with one hand, exposing a flattened glossy magazine of girls in bikinis.

"*Erik!*" I try to press the mattress back down, horrified. "You can't just go through Nobody's room!"

"You're one to talk," he says. "Finish the texts?"

"Yes."

"Then you know I'm done playing around." He opens Nobody's computer and scrolls rapidly through her internet history. "CurtPro and headquarters have merged and are calling the targets for Kurt. One of our friends is helping them. Skye is dumb enough to try and be in the same house with me, and I'm tempted to let him—"

"Erik."

"The part about Janeane and the hearing, though, I didn't understand."

"That was when we weren't talking." I frown. "Before the hearing, Janeane got in touch with me, and offered me a deal—"

He turns to me, stricken.

"She said if I helped throw someone else under the bus, she'd testify about her time at camp. Back when she was part of the Teen Killers Club with Dave, in the nineties or whatever."

"No way." Erik is stunned. "There's *no way* she'd do that."

"Well, she did, I was there—"

"No, I mean"—he bites viciously at his fingernails—"Janeane has been building up her 'Nice Mom' persona in Ledmonton for decades. If she came out and admitted she'd *murdered someone as a teen*, her dominant persona would be destroyed, and she's too public now to build a new one. She would only offer that sort of psychic death if she knew it was going to happen anyway."

"Like, if Skye was holding the thumb drive over her head? 'Make a deal with Signal or I leak this to the news'?"

"Skye wouldn't do that." Erik frowns. "My brother would just destroy you. But Eyes is your friend . . . so while they wanted Janeane as a witness, they also wanted a way out for you. But if Eyes was holding the thumb drive over Janeane's head, then they didn't give it to Skye. And it's still here in this house. Probably in one of these rooms . . ."

He pulls out Nobody's desk drawer. I slam it back in place.

"Not this one." I shake my head. "Nobody refuses to kill girls. She was exploited by her uncle. She would *never* make common cause with Skye, not out of loyalty to us but because he's a predator—"

"You need that thumb drive for your trial," he says quietly. "You don't have to help me search these rooms. But you can't stop me."

He pulls the drawer out, rifles through it, then stalks out into the flashing hall. After a moment's hesitation, I hurry after him to Javier's room, cursing under my breath.

It smells strongly of laundry detergent; there's an open box of All at the bottom of Javier's closet when Erik flings open the door and rifles through his jacket pockets.

"Javier did say something weird," I tell him. "He told me to rip up the marriage license when we were in the library before, and slide it under the door. When we thought you were Kurt."

"Really?" Erik turns to me, eyebrows very high, before ransacking the jeans on the plastic shelving below.

"Do you think that . . . means something?"

"Well. It *could mean* he's been working with my brother to get me thrown in prison so you're forced to date him again. Just spitballing here." Erik pulls a charcoal pencil out of the last pair of jeans, scowls, and puts it back. "But then again, he could've told Aarush I was under the bed and he didn't . . . he covered for us in the most ass-headed way possible, but he *did* cover for us."

Erik turns to Javier's neatly made bed and raises the mattress, Javier's red duvet crumpling down against the wall.

Several pencil portraits stare back up at us, all renderings of a sad girl with straight black hair and large, dark eyes, dressed in my favorite outfits. And though they're ridiculously idealized, Javier is skilled enough the resemblance comes through.

"Oh—it's me!" I laugh, embarrassed.

"I've had just about all I can take with this guy." Erik's hand contracts around the portrait, but he can't seem to bring himself to crumple it. He lets the mattress drop back in place instead, turns to Javier's desk, and yanks open the drawer. More drawing pencils and a sharpener rattle beside a neatly coiled cable and small Wacom drawing tablet.

"Though it's hard not to admire such a Spartan level of tidiness," Erik says, closing the drawer. "Credit where credit is due. I've been in here two minutes and feel like I've seen everything."

We move back out into the hall, and he almost passes right by Dennis' open door, but then Erik stops, and backtracks with a sigh. He approaches Dennis' desk, still piled with electronics, and slides out a small cardboard box from behind the monitor. I have no idea how he noticed it from the hall. He frowns as he pulls out a shipping slip from the box and unfolds it. I look around at the weights on the floor, the obsessive measurements of Dennis' gains on the spreadsheets taped over the mirror.

"An order from Knife Barn?" He reads aloud, "'Knife and blade wholesalers. Custom piece . . . blade retracts from handle . . . eighty-eight dollars.'"

"Like a switchblade?" I frown. "Doesn't seem like Dennis' style."

Erik turns to me, eyes fastening to my bandaged arm. "What happened"—his voice is cold—"with Kurt?"

"I just kept looking in his eyes." I shrug. "I think it threw him."

Erik pulls me into him and kisses the top of my head, hard. Then he tucks the invoice back in the box, resting both broad hands on either side of it, and stares down, hanging his head, lost in thought.

"Whoever Eyes is, I don't think they're helping Kurt kill people," I say quietly.

"Our friends? Involved with murder?! What could I be *thinking!*" Erik laughs unhappily.

"Not Dennis. You said yourself he's an innocent man. And he knows you have the dupe phone. Would he be having these conversations with Skye, knowing you could read them?"

His shoulders release. "An astute point, Watson . . . And honestly, I can't get myself to suspect Dennis of anything. Not to mention the impossibility of looking for a thumb drive in *this* room. But I can't afford to miss something again, I can't . . . if Kurt had . . ." He looks sick, and his hand floats up to cover his face, the black heart on his ring finger just over his mouth, his eyes glisten. ". . . It would be like someone turning the world off."

I take his hand. "Not sick of me yet?"

"I don't think it works that way for me either," he says sadly.

We walk hand in hand into Jada's room. The walls are covered in fake flower LED lights, which blink up the walls and around the ceiling. Jada's bed is piled with pink throw pillows, strawberry plushies and pink squishy animals. The glossy pink tote Dennis gave me sits by her laptop, the Givenchy perfume bottle jutting out from the top. As Erik lifts her mattress, I pick it up, uncap it, and spray a little in the air. Erik makes a retching sound.

"Is that *L'Interdit?*" He says the word like a curse, forearm pressed against his nose and mouth as he turns to me.

"It was a gift from Skye, Jada said."

"Figures. He gave Alice some too." He snatches it from my hand, holding it away from him like he's afraid it'll explode. "*L'Interdit* is French for 'forbidden,' which fits on the bottle better than 'Here's a Giant Red Flag You're Being Groomed.'"

He punctuates this statement by dropping it in Jada's pink trash can.

I loyally fish it out again. "Well, Jada likes it. And so does Honor Hadley, and she can afford *anything.*"

"I knew I felt sick in the nerve center . . ." Erik frowns then, bites his nails, eyes going through me. "Honor said they had everything they needed. Sonny said it would be over for the defense . . . That's the thing! That's the thing, though . . ." He sits heavily on the edge of Jada's bed, his long, all-in-black figure stark against Jada's cotton candy pink covers. Pink LED flowers light up around him in a halo, as spots of bright color rise in his cheeks. He takes the dupe phone again, his bright green gaze sinking through the screen, cat's eye cutting as a buzz saw.

". . . Maybe I got it backwards."

"Got what?"

"The whole deal with Eyes. I've been looking at this as Skye wanting access to me, through them . . . to drag me back to his house and finish the injections."

"Turn you into a super soldier."

"But *Eyes wants that too*. Because if all they needed was my testimony, they just got it. So why would Eyes want to turn me into a super solider? It doesn't make sense—"

"Unless they want the injections themselves," I point out. "Kurt said he wouldn't be a Class A anymore once he finished taking out targets. Like head-quarters could . . . reclassify him somehow."

"Great, let him have them," Erik says angrily, then frowns and claws his hand through his hair. "But it has to be me. That's why Skye still has power over Eyes. If I finish Ledrick's injections, CurtPro can reproduce them, but with Ledrick dead, they need me to finish his work, they can't just start again with someone new. If they're going to use the algorithm based on me to find potential super soldiers, they need me to test whatever they shoot them up with. Because I'm the only dataset for the algorithm, I'm *the* Class A . . . but if Eyes knew what the injections actually did? If they'd seen what a mess I was that first night? . . . But Skye's scamming them, of course, overselling what it could do. Just like with the Wylie-Stanton." He shakes his head. "But I can still fix it. *I can still fix it.*"

"Erik." I clutch his sleeve. "You know who Eyes is, don't you."

"I do." Erik nods, shaking now. "And I'm almost positive they would turn over the thumb drive tonight if I agreed to finish the injections."

"Finish the injections!?" I cry. "Erik, *no*—"

"I can handle them, now I know how long they last."

"But then CurtPro will have a new weapon—"

"No, they won't." Erik laughs unhappily. "The injections don't work the way Ledrick promised. And once they see that, they'll *truly* be done with me. CurtPro and Skye. And I . . ."

His hand travels to where I'm gripping his sleeve; his fingers interlace with mine.

"I will be free to stay with you," he says, and my eyes blur.

"Erik," I say as calmly as I can, "tell me who Eyes is, right now."

"I will once we're out of this house. But you won't be able to keep a straight face when you see them if I tell you now. Just hang out on the patio for an hour. Trust me."

There's noise down the stairs, voices floating in from the deck as the security guards return to their posts. The house must be cleared; our friends will be coming back up to their rooms. We hurry for the second-story elevator, tucked behind the little alcove at the end of the corridor. The alarm abruptly flickers back to steady light overhead.

"You realize this is our wedding night?" Erik murmurs, steering me to the elevator. "I know just how I want to celebrate." He stares at my mouth. "Clue board game, all night long. *Oh yes.*"

"Let's just go, then! Why do this now? Can't we talk it through for a few days—"

"Kurt almost killed you, Signal. The sooner I do this, the sooner you're safe."

"What about *your* safety?" I shake my head. "Eyes could be dangerous. What if they—what if they try to hurt you when you confront them, or—"

"Eyes is literally the last person in the house who would hit me." He laughs at the thought, and punches the first story button on the elevator, overjoyed. "I'll be fine, I promise. Cross my heart and hope to die."

I shiver as the doors part behind me, and he kisses me then, hot and fast and shaking, before gently backing me onto the elevator. Black ink starts uncurling in my veins as the doors close. This is wrong, *this is wrong.*

"No. Stop. *Wait!*" I bang the buttons, "Open! Open! Go back up!"

But this house no longer obeys my voice. It doesn't stop at the first floor, it pulls me down into the dark of the parking garage, where security is waiting. I plead with a burly guard as he hustles me toward a fleet of waiting Ubers.

"All visitor passes are revoked until morning, no exceptions—"

"I'm not a visitor, I was on house arrest here! Please, I'm begging you, *my husband* is in danger and—"

"Raoul!" the security guard calls toward the elevator, and I see Aarush and Raoul turn around. "She still on house arrest here?"

Aarush answers for him. "Miss Deere is not a prisoner here," he says, staring straight at me. "Please see her safely off the grounds."

* * *

The Uber takes me to Sea View, a dark shingle complex of condominiums. Mom's unit is small, but tidy. She's horrified by my new bandage, and immediately puts the willis dress to soak in the bathtub, while I joylessly ingest the cold Chinese food she'd ordered for our wedding dinner.

Erik is not home in time for the coffee I brew him. He's not back by bedtime, either, not that I go to bed. I'm sitting up at the glass-topped dining room table when Mom goes to her room for the night, and I'm still there when the morning birds start to cry outside the windows, and the call comes in.

"Signal," Scraps croaks. His voice makes my heart shrink. "I got some bad news."

"Is Erik alright?!"

"I don't know about Erik, but I just got out of the emergency room. Buddy gave me a ride down to the impound lot. My car got sideswiped, on the way to the courthouse. *Bad.* And . . ." Scraps lets out a disbelieving laugh. "You know, I think it was on purpose. And it wasn't someone I've worked with, the car was too nice. But the upshot is, I'm over at the lot with my totaled car, and I know I had your marriage license in this big old envelope in the front footwell, but it's gone—"

". . . They crashed into you before you could file it."

I hear Mom's bedroom door open, the vertical blinds shivering as she pads down the hall to the dining area, where I'm hunched over the glass-topped table.

"I'm going to keep looking. Tell Erik I'll fix this, alright? I'm having trouble getting hold of him . . ."

"Of course . . . ," I say, as Mom pulls out the chair next to mine. The phone slides from my ear as I turn to her. "Mom—I think something's happened to Erik."

"Honey," Mom says gently. "After the ceremony, I had a chance to talk to your friend a little. And he promised me, if the marriage put you directly in danger . . ." She looks down at my bandage. "He would leave immediately. To protect you."

"That's *not* what's happening."

"I know, *I know* how this hurts. But I'm grateful he's keeping his promise. Sometimes leaving is the kindest thing you can do."

"No, Mom!" I shake my head, "No, it's not. There's *nothing* worse he could do to me than leave like this. And you—" I cut myself off. I will not say *you should know that.* But I think she hears it anyway, because she just holds me then, and lets me cry.

Erik miscalculated. One of my friends either couldn't or wouldn't help us. They knew Scraps was getting sideswiped and turned Erik over to Skye. And I have no way to get into Skye's house, or the Desais'.

"Just promise me," Mom says after a long moment, "that you won't miss your grad nite, waiting around for him to turn up again—"

"Grad nite!" I sit up with a start. "When is that again?"

Mom retrieves a heavy, gilt-edged invitation from the fridge, hands it to me. Eight o'clock, tonight.

Chapter Seventeen

Grad Nite

❧

The elevator doors part on the Desai mansion, revealing a heaven of gold- and champagne-colored balloons. GRAD NITE! hangs in sparkling bunting across the breezeway, and an actual DJ is under the stairs, spinning Doja Cat in and out of *Pomp and Circumstance* as I step into the house. I look out of place in my nylon raincoat and black party dress.

But I'm not here to party.

As my mother breaks off to join a ring of adults, Aarush lands beside me. I'm expecting something snide, but he hands me a champagne flute full of sparkling cider, then holds his own glass up, as though in a toast.

"Congratulations, Signal," Aarush smiles. "I want you to be the first to hear this. The settlement on the camp suit includes ending federal use of the Wylie-Stanton."

"What?!" I blink at him, stunned. "Just like that? No more Wylie-Stanton will be run on juveniles, or—"

"On anyone. Largely due to Erik's deposition!" he laughs. "He was a tremendous witness. You were right about that. The kids' individual sentences are still being negotiated, but their Class A status will not be a factor. And Honor is arguing they can fulfill them through restitution centers or residential correctional facilities, after the trauma they endured. A complete win, all around."

My mouth has gone dry. "I wonder if you had a chance to speak with Erik after his deposition last night, or if you know if he spoke with anyone else after I left?"

Aarush shakes his head. "I'm afraid I had my hands full with security after the Kurt break-in."

"Maybe there's some footage of Erik leaving the house?"

"There wouldn't be." Aarush shakes his head. "We had to turn the server over to a police technician, so they could review the footage of Kurt."

I nod, my stomach going cold.

"Why do you ask?" Aarush frowns. "Where is Erik?"

And then Jada yells from above, "*SKIPPER!*"

She clomps down the stairs in gold stacked heels and a sparkling champagne dress, a beaded clutch in one hand, her other arm through Nobody's. Nobody is in a handsome corduroy blazer and white tuxedo pants, her hair pulled completely back from her features for once, which look strangely colorful. "Look what she finally let me do!" Jada waves at Nobody's face. "Like, am I a professional makeup artist or what, because look at her!"

Someone calls to Aarush; he steps away as my bridesmaids hug me. And for the first time in their presence, I feel my smile falter. Because how else would Skye know Scraps was our officiant, unless someone who was there told him? Which of them is the last person I'd expect to hit Erik? Which of my friends betrayed us and how the hell did they manage it?

I don't say any of this.

"You both look incredible." I smile as hard as I can, and turn to Nobody. "How are you since yesterday? Any better?"

"One hundred percent." Nobody grins, and Jada cuts her a knowing look and laughs into her hand, then ducks toward me.

"She was out all night," Jada whispers. "Meeting up with Amy! She didn't come in till early this morning!"

"Oh?" I keep my smile on. "Wow, that's . . . I mean you guys just seemed sort of at odds yesterday, but you worked things out?"

Nobody shrugs and rubs the back of her neck, unable to suppress her cocky grin. "Something about weddings, I guess."

Jada roots through her clutch as the Nokia buzzes inside it, her expression somber as she reads a message and begins to tap out a reply.

"Is that Skye's burner?" I ask, stomach twisting.

It hadn't occurred to me before, but her personal number was listed as Jailbait#3SF in Skye's phone.

But the burner he gave her would be something else.

"Why are you even still talking to him?" I go on, voice thin. "The case is settled! Tell him to get a life."

"For you." Jada blinks at me. "Duh. The whole thumb drive thing?"

"What made you think of that?" I ask stiffly.

"Uh . . . you're my friend? And you have a trial coming up?" Jada looks genuinely confused. "Damn, Signal, are you like, mad at me or something?"

"Mad about what?" a handsome young man asks. For a moment I don't recognize him without his glasses, only registering broad shoulders emphasized by a sharp black suit, baby-faced good looks heightened by a precise fade haircut and a certain new definition around his neck and jaw. Dennis looks transformed—how?

"Um, what just happened." Jada's eyes have never been this wide. "*Dennis?*"

"Looking *good*, man." Nobody nods, impressed.

"I'm trying out contacts." Dennis blinks. "So far, I hate them."

"And I took him to a proper barbershop." Javier throws an arm around Dennis' shoulder, a champagne flute in his other hand. Javier is in a similarly dashing suit, his own hair recently trimmed.

Javier, at least, I don't have to suspect at all, as he's the first person I would expect to hit Erik.

Not that I have any reason to suspect Dennis, though I hear myself asking, a little too brightly, "So what did you get up to last night?"

"Me and Aarush were up late cutting down the lag on Kate's kill switch." Dennis' hand darts up toward where his glasses should be, then continues down the side of his recently styled head. "It's quite interesting. Apparently, Kate's kill switch interacted with the house Wi-Fi at around the same time Kurt was in the house. Meaning *Kate* was somewhere on the grounds as well."

This I was not expecting. I step back from our circle, my eyes wide. "*Kate* came to the house?"

Is it possible that Erik ran into Kate before he was able to confront whoever he thought Eyes was? That she—what, wrangled him into a van? There's no way, Erik is much stronger. But if camp is settling the case like Aarush said, what do they even need Erik for? They won't be making super soldiers at Naramauke any time soon if they're shutting camp down. What is going on?

"What's up with you?" Nobody squints at me. "Are you going to puke again?"

I can't keep it back anymore. I dart a look at Aarush, in a circle of adults but staring at us through the breezeway, then herd my friends into the west library.

The glass from the destroyed jellyfish structure has been swept up, and its armature removed. The room looks better without it.

"I need to tell you all something . . ." I look from Nobody to Jada. From Dennis to Javier. "Erik didn't come home last night and I have no idea where he is."

"You checked in with Nadya?" Javier sneers.

"Javier, this is serious, alright?" I glare at him. "The guy who married us got sideswiped last night, and our marriage license was stolen—"

"Good grief," Dennis says quietly.

"Erik said he was going to hang back and—talk to one of you guys?" the word comes out too high, but I push on: "None of you talked to him last night?"

"What, you think one of us took Erik?" Nobody says flatly.

Jada's face hardens, her grim expression at odds with her glittery makeup. Javier shakes his head, furious. Only Dennis stares at me without any evident reaction.

"I think that somehow he got from here to Skye's house, and I need to break him out. That's all I care about right now."

"Skye's house?" Jada grabs my arm. "You don't need to be married to Erik to get into Skye's house. He's only asked me over every five minutes since house arrest ended."

A prickle creeps up the back of my neck.

"Would you go?" I watch her face. "Because if you were in there, you could just open the back door and then—"

"Oh boy." Nobody shakes her head. "Here we go."

Javier leans forward, shaking his head, "You are not seriously asking Jada to invite herself to that man's house. At *night?* No way, Signal."

"I'm a grown woman, I can handle myself," Jada snaps at Javier, then turns to me. "Say no more, girl, I'll text him right now—"

"Are you sure?" Dennis asks her, and without his glasses there's nothing to mask his concern as he watches Jada's face.

"It's ten minutes in Skye's house! What's the problem?" Jada shrugs.

"You know damn well what the problem is!" Javier explodes. "The problem is Erik will get loose and tear his head off! That freak's been plotting to kill his brother since before he got all roided out!"

"Erik won't hurt Skye," I tell Jada. "He promised."

"Oh, he *promised*, okay," Javier says sarcastically. "The fool who smashed up a glass sculpture yesterday, you're counting on him to be cool, calm, and collected, huh? You let him loose, you and Jada will just be trapped in a house with *two* psychos—"

My eyes narrow. "Why are you so against helping, Javier?"

"Because I beat Erik up, stuffed him in a barrel, and sold him to CurtPro," Javier glares at me. "Is that what you think?"

"Just hold on now," Nobody says, waving a scarred hand between us. "Signal, Javier has a point."

My heart drops into my stomach at her words.

"You're going to need a getaway driver," Nobody adds. "Want me to drive?"

I smile back, relief washing over me. "*Please.* We'll also need a car—"

"The Desai garage has a couple extra." Dennis nods. "And I happen to know the security code for the key safe."

Nobody reaches over and makes me do our special "Ridin'" handshake, and I could honestly cry.

"Fine!" Javier bursts out. "Fine, I'll come too. Just in case that cockeyed freak gets out of hand."

"You don't have to," I say quickly. "If you'd rather stay home, that's—"

"I'm coming," he says darkly. "I'm not asking you, I'm telling."

I'm not sure how to reply.

"Signal, I want to help as much as I can." Dennis frowns. "But it might be difficult. Aarush and I were going to really attack Kate's kill switch once we'd made the rounds tonight. So I'll be around for texts, but if you need any programming, he'll be right over my shoulder."

"Got it." I nod. "Well, hopefully no one needs to bring down a helicopter this time."

"The layout of the house, if I remember from the dupe, is pretty straightforward. First story is open concept, so Erik's probably up on the second floor, where he can be secured."

I nod, though the idea of Erik "secured" makes me ill.

"And if you're going to be in person with Skye while Signal goes looking for Erik, then you should have this." Dennis turns to Jada, pulling a small box wrapped in bright pink paper out of his jacket pocket.

"What! For *me?*" Jada smiles, gleefully tearing the gift open. "You shouldn't have—" She shakes out a long pink tube of lipstick. But when she opens it, instead of a tube of color rising from the shaft, a razor-sharp blade telescopes out.

"Dennis!" Jada breathes, mesmerized. "This is . . . perfect."

"What is?" Aarush's voice booms through the room. Jada caps the stiletto lipstick knife with a loud click. Aarush and Honor stand in the door. He's in a suit; Honor's gown is a subtle shade of gold.

"Our—after-party plans!" I say quickly.

Aarush's eyebrows go up. "After-party?"

"Fun." Honor smiles.

"Yeah," I nod. "I was just telling them, you know, if we could borrow a car we could all go out and get milkshakes! At a diner!" And then, with a pang in my chest: "Meet Erik."

"You got a hold of him? Glad to hear it." Aarush's jaw sets. "But I don't know if that's such a good idea."

"Why not?" I ask, cold sweat breaking out across the back of my neck.

"There's a storm coming in." Aarush nods toward the window. "Seems like you're asking for problems, driving out in all that."

"You forget where I come from. It rains all the time in Ledmonton." I shrug. "I can handle it."

He holds my gaze as Honor sets her hand firmly on his shoulder.

"You worry too much, Aarush." Honor smiles. "Let them have a little adventure. They deserve it."

A distant roll of thunder breaks through her words. But she keeps smiling.

* * *

"Any reply from Skye?" I ask Jada, peering through the stolid Ford's windshield wipers as they fling rain furiously across my view of traffic.

"Not yet."

"Glad to hear it!" Javier calls from the back. He's loosened his tie and can't seem to stop rubbing at a line of scruff the barber left under his chin.

"Maybe I should get a little spicier?" Jada's thumbnails start flashing again, and Javier jockeys over the console to read over her shoulder.

"Spicier?! What are you saying to him?"

"Whatever it takes to speed things up, since we only got two hours or whatever."

"We only have two hours?" Nobody leans against my headrest.

"Till the tide comes in," I say.

"Here we go!" Jada smacks my leg. "Look!" She holds the phone to Nobody, who reads Skye's text aloud:

"'I'll get the fireplace going, see you soon.'"

"*Fireplace?*" Javier half-shouts. "Jada, did you have to whip him up that much? You're going to open the door and it's just going to be a trail of red rose petals over to some sheepskin rug—"

Jada turns in her seat to give Javier a sly look. "Is that *your* move? Signal, is Javier a rose petal type of freak or what?"

Nobody smothers a laugh.

"Look, don't worry about me, alright?" Jada says to Javier, her voice softer. "I'm not going to eat or drink anything. And I've got my fun new lipstick. I'll be perfectly fine."

My hands tighten on the wheel, wanting so much to believe her.

"You know, it might be best if we drop you off a couple blocks away and let you Uber to his house." I say after a beat.

"Just find a place I can wait inside, please." Jada crinkles her nose up at the rain pelting the windows. "It's really coming down."

I pull off beside an all-night diner, hugging her fast before she dashes out and into its warm glow. There's no space to park, so we leave her there to call the Uber. I pull back onto the glistening street, passing Skye's house so Nobody will be able to find it later, then park in the same space Erik and I slept in before, beside the beach.

We're just waiting now for Jada to give us the cue. Then Nobody will take the car and keep it idling in front of the house in case Jada needs a fast way out. Javier and I will go down to the cliffs, I will climb up to Skye's backyard.

The rain drums harder against the roof of the car, and I hear Javier pull the zipper of his raincoat under his chin, face ill in the dim light.

My silenced phone lights up with a text from Jada:

On your mark

* * *

The waves heave themselves through the dark as Javier follows me down the trail of switchbacks, past the scrubby ice plants, and to the cliffs. But when he sees the scaffolding across from the dark arch of rock, he stops.

"No." He shakes his head at the scaffolding. "No way you're climbing that."

"It's my only way up. I just need a boost." He makes no move to boost me. "*Please*," I add, then: "I thought you were here to help—"

"I'm not helping you get yourself killed!"

The surging waves break against the black arch of rock down the beach behind him in a silvery halo, the spray forceful enough to spatter his poncho and dot my cheek. The tide feels angry, the storm chasing it hard up the beach as I stare back at him, aware of every second that ticks by.

"You have saved me so many times," I tell Javier. "On the obstacle course, at the Star Barn, in the attic—and I thought it was because I was—special, or something. But I'm not the special one. You are, Javier. You're like, a real-life superhero."

He blinks at me, startled.

"And if it had been humanly possible to save Mateo, you wouldn't be here now. Because he'd still be alive. Because you would have saved him. Because you're always looking out for the people you love."

"What is this, one of Erik's head tricks?"

"No, it's the truth. And you need to hear it. Because I know you want everyone to be safe, but no one gets to be safe tonight. Because if I don't climb this cliff? Jada is left alone with Skye."

"Yeah, and she wouldn't be in there at all, if Erik hadn't—"

"Come back and testified?" I finish, and Javier looks down, his jaw work-ing, his nostrils flaring. "If Erik had had an older brother like you, none of us would be here right now. But he grew up next to the wrong person and it ruined his life. I'm not the one who needs saving this time, I promise you." I shake my head. "I just need my friend, one of the best friends I have ever had, to give me a boost. Please, Javier."

Javier shakes his head, takes a step back like he's ready to walk off down the beach. But I think he knows I mean it. Because then, with a beleaguered curse, he steps forward, sinks down on one knee, and holds out his linked hands.

"On three," he says angrily. "You ready? One, two—"

"Three—" I step into his hands, and he stands all at once, sending me straight upward. I wrap my hands around the iron rods. Freezing rainwater slips over my fingers, bathes Erik's ring, and runs straight down my sleeves, soaking my bandage.

The cold is shocking, but I block it out. I set my feet along the sandstone of the cliff wall for balance. My right arm screams with pain, my fingers are freez-ing, but I reach and hook and claw at the scaffolding above me until my ballet flats land on metal crossbars. When I look up, my eyes fill with rainwater, so I move half-blind, groping carefully for each hold. It takes forever, but I've never been less afraid. I'm just relieved to be getting closer. At last my fingertips scrape against the concrete of the sidewalk, then sink into the neatly trimmed grass that grows right up to the edge of Skye's lawn.

I haul myself onto the grass, then turn and look down at Javier. He waves his arms over his head, grinning like he's thrilled for me. I wave back down at him, all of me freezing, except my heart. We made it this far. I turn back to the house.

It's a pristine backyard. There's a koi pond, a birdbath, and a white concrete path to the back door. When I look toward the beach, the entire black swollen sea, bearing one hell of a coming storm, bears down at me.

I duck down past the large bay windows, pressing my back against the stucco as I dig into my pocket for my phone. Jada's sent another text:

Go

* * *

Pulling my rain hood over my head, I creep to the back door. The handle gives, and with a surge of gratitude I find myself in Skye's humming kitchen. I care-fully close the door, muffling the thunder behind me.

The kitchen smells like lemongrass and bleach; its spotless appliances are showroom clean. There is neatly sorted mail on the counter, a bowl of lemons, and a cork still stuck in a corkscrew.

I scavenge three paper clips from the mail and start straightening them; whatever door Erik is behind will be locked.

I keep close to the wall, as the flooring there is less likely to squeak, but then the entire floor seems brand new. There is no give underfoot; my biggest tell is the plip-plip of rain falling from the sodden hem of my party dress, and the swish of nylon at my sides when I let my arms move.

I pad down the short hallway toward the redwood landing at the foot of the stairs. If I were to go straight across the landing, the glow of firelight and Jada's soft laughter tell me I'd be in the open concept living space, where Skye and Jada are sitting.

I pivot left instead, so the shadow along the staircase swallows me. The banisters of the staircase open onto the living room; I'll just have to pray Skye doesn't look up.

With agonizing slowness I move from the landing to the first step, bringing my foot right against the redwood molding, hoping no creak gives me away.

Below the stairs Jada and Skye sit across from each other on Javier's feared sheepskin throw rug, Jada facing the stairs, Skye across from her, a tray with a bottle of wine and two wineglasses between them. Hers full, his empty.

Skye's voice is giddy. "So this is your first time at a boy's house since you were what, fifteen?"

Jada has her knees pulled up to her chin, beaded dress sparking in the firelight. "Um, I was not going over to boys' houses when I was fifteen!"

"So this is your first time over a boys' house ever?"

"I wouldn't call you a boy, exactly."

Skye laughs, then says seriously: "Yet I have no problem calling you a woman."

"Damn right." Jada picks up her glass and clinks it against his, then sets it down without drinking from it.

"I have a gift for you," Skye announces. "For your graduation."

A rustle of paper.

"More perfume? Thanks."

The step under me creaks. Jada's eyes cut to me, then bounce back to him as his head begins to absently turn. She reaches out, manicured nails flashing.

"Hey, you got something—"

She takes his chin, and her thumb wipes firmly just below his bottom lip, the air going heavy between them.

Skye flinches back.

"What are you doing?" He pushes her hand away roughly. In the silence that follows, there is only the faint drumming of the rain against the window and my heart racing as I freeze against the wall, holding my breath. "Don't touch my face."

"No worries!" Her tone is expertly girlish. I stare down at Jada through the banisters as she holds up her graceful hands in a placating gesture. "I guess I was just trying to be more womanly . . . like you said. But I messed it up, I guess."

"Yes. Well," Skye sighs, mollified. "Why don't you try your perfume?"

There's the sound of a bottle being uncapped. Jada's eyes flash to me in a silent plea: *Hurry it up.*

I nod and fly up the last two steps to the second story.

Moving quickly past the door to the master bedroom, I tiptoe past a bathroom and down a narrow hall, straightened paper clips clutched in my hand, going over what must come next: *Pick the lock. Lead Erik out the back and around to the car. Do not let him get in arm's reach of Skye no matter what happens.*

I kneel before the door at the end of the narrow hall, ready to thread the first paper clip through the keyhole, but as soon as I touch the handle, it sinks past the threshold into the dark.

It's unlocked?

I step through the doorway into a room darker than the hall. The stillness is so complete I think I'm alone, the only sound the rain, louder now, hammering the roof overhead. It takes me a few moments to realize the figure in the corner is a person.

Lying on a bed under a sterile reading light, he doesn't move, doesn't seem to breathe. His face, under the tubes and tape, is unmistakable, but I've never seen it so still. The only indication he's alive is the tick of the machines; the blue wavelengths climbing up and down, marking his heartbeat. Half his head has been shaved down to the skin and white stickers with metal diodes are positioned along his scalp, metal clamps with fishtailing leads plugged into a bank of monitors. The waves they emit are almost flat.

Looking down through the mesh of tubes threaded into his wrist, I see the black heart on his finger. I drew it only yesterday and it's already started to fade. I take his hand; it's cool to the touch. My tears spill over then, and I have to cup my other hand hard over my mouth to keep back my sobs.

"Erik?" I whisper. His eye lids don't even flicker.

What the hell have they done to him?

My breath climbs to a pant as I turn on the beige metal cabinet beside us and start taking pictures of all the medications, the rows of pills, the bags of fluid hanging from his IV stand. The monitors, the oxygen tube under his nose, I take pictures of all of it and text it to Dennis along with a line of question marks.

Good grief

Dennis sends back, then: He's in a medical coma.

Chapter Eighteen
Beach Bonfire

∽

I rock forward with the force of my swallowed sob, a ball of rage that wrings pain from my entire body; my vision swims with dark lace. An image of Erik across the fire my first night at camp rises in my memory, from when we were all discussing what would happen to Class As.

"*They would never kill us,*" he'd said. "*That would be inhumane. They'll just drug us to the point where all we can do is watch TV and piss our pants.*"

Skye's laughter floats up from downstairs.

I wish to God I had let Erik kill him.

Deep breaths. *Deep breaths.*

I start looking up the medications on my phone when Dennis sends me another text:

What are you going to do?

Get him the hell out of here.

Is it safe? To take him off whatever machines he's on?

Safer than letting him stay here.

But Dennis is making a fair point. I do some internet research. Every sound floating from upstairs makes me jump, but I look up "medical coma" and the medications I sent Dennis and sum up my findings:

He's not on a ventilator, just oxygen. Internet says he can go off the meds he's on, especially as he hasn't been on them a long time. but he might not be able to stand/walk/talk/be aware of his surroundings for several hours. But please, check my math.

Waiting for Dennis' response, I search the room and find Erik's clothes in a side cabinet, with Skye's dupe phone still in his pants pocket. I flash through the security camera views.

Skye and Jada are still sitting by the fire. As I watch, she reaches for a poker and stabs at the glowing logs until new flames break forth, and Skye's voice echoes up the stairs:

". . . can get another log if you like . . ."

I watch Skye move from screen to screen: past the stairs, out through the kitchen, when my other phone lights up with Dennis' response:

Cross ref'd medications. You're good to unplug him but, yes, you have several hours before he's mentally online. How is Jada? Did Nobody talk to you yet?

Holding her own. Nobody is outside?

As quickly as I can, I peel the electrode stickers off Erik's head. I go slower with the adhesive tape around his IV, but it still leaves a rectangle of red skin. He doesn't even flinch. I unscrew the IV connection and start peeling more electrodes off his chest, bright red circles blooming across his pale skin no matter how careful I am.

I go around the bed and open the window wide, pushing out the screen so it falls through the darkness and into the grass below. The ground seems much farther away than two stories. There's no getting him out this way, but I let the cold air and glittering rain rush in, hoping it will revive him faster. There has to be some way to revive him. How am I going to get him out of the room, if he can't move at all?

Can I even lift him?

I tentatively put an arm under Erik's broad shoulders. I can barely get him high enough to wriggle my arm underneath, gritting my teeth and gasping with the effort.

My phone keeps lighting up on the floor, a firefly dance of blue between it and the dupe, but I can't give any updates to Nobody or Dennis until I know if I can get Erik upright. Even then, the idea of maneuvering him down the stairs without Skye seeing is impossible. This is *impossible*.

No. Nothing is impossible. I just need to keep thinking. Stay calm and keep thinking.

Maybe I can get Jada to take Skye somewhere? Lock him out of the house. He's getting more firewood now—if I hurry, we can lock him out right now.

I pick up the dupe phone and flash through the grid of security screens to make sure. But to my surprise, Skye is in the kitchen, rattling the back door like he can't get it open. I hold my breath listening as his voice floats up the stairs.

"Something is holding it."

The square next to theirs, the one with the fireplace, flickers with a long shadow as someone cuts across the room, just out of range of the security camera.

Someone else is inside the house. Hope steals through me. Did Javier come in? Nobody? What had Dennis said about Nobody?

I pick up my own phone and go back to my thread with Dennis, each text a few minutes apart:

Its been very weird over here
We got the lag current and it turns out Kate is in Pacifica?
Aarush driving that way now
Kate is near Skye's house?
Should I tell Aarush where you are?

"I'll be right back, okay?" I tell Erik, though I doubt he can hear me. His oxygen is the only thing I've left attached. I close the door softly before creeping quickly down the stairs.

"—who would chain the back door closed?!" Skye yells from the kitchen. "Jada, if you had anything to do with this—"

I freeze midway down as Skye stomps across the landing just in front of me, Taser gun in hand.

Below the stairs, I hear Jada groan.

Skye breezes past her and disappears down a short flight of steps into the front foyer.

I rush into the living room. Jada lies on the floor, giggling.

"Jada?" I kneel beside her. "Jada, what happened? Did you . . ."

Her glass is still full. I don't think she's had a sip, but her eyes are like Rose's when she'd come home from meeting Mr. Moody.

"What the hell!" Skye bangs on the front door; he can't be more than twenty feet away. "The front door is chained too!"

"Heyyyy . . ." Jada's fingers reach up to stroke my face. Her little nose crinkles. "Do you smell that? The perfume smells weird but it's . . . it's something else . . . too . . ."

I look to the white stone hearth. There's something on it that wasn't there before. A matted thing, furry and squat like a huddled cat, the fire reflected in its two tear-shaped panels of glass.

I walk over to it and give it a small kick with my ballet flat.

The thing rolls back, its jaw falling open like a purse flap. Not furry but hairy; dark short hair over skin drained bone white. The shapes of teeth stand out, yellow-beige, against the desiccated wormhole of a human mouth.

The smell Kurt carried with him in the bathroom comes out of the head in an angry cloud, like I've kicked a hive and wasps are pouring out. The headless victim from Bridgewood, Kurt had been carrying her head around?

I stare, not quite believing it, as the head settles against the white rug, and its matted shape resolves into Kate's familiar haircut.

Kurt killed Kate and has been carrying her head around. That's why her kill switch keeps turning up wherever she goes.

Kurt is in here, right now.

I scan the room: the long drapes around the tall windows to our right, the shadowy staircase where I hid myself, not long ago.

"Jada—" I crouch beside her again. "Jada, where's your lipstick?"

"Lipstick . . . ?" Her eyes trail my face in jittering arcs. She flails at her pocket. I pull it out with my left hand because of my bandage. Not that I'm great with knives anyway, but I'm also right-handed.

And that's when a bolt of pain severs me from my sight. My breath and brain glitch, I'm dancing sideways on the floor, muscles jerking like they're trying to break free from my bones.

Skye's feet land just beside my face, the Taser snapping right over me. My brain shatters against the tide of pain, thoughts scattering into fragmentary waves; every time I think I'm passing out another wave breaks, my jaw snapping shut on my screams.

"Guess we found the prankster!" Skye cries. "Let me guess, you two hatched some little high school plot to sneak my brother out of here? Well, all three of you are going *nowhere*."

I can't talk, can't get my tongue to connect with my thoughts. I can't even control where my gaze fixes, staring up at Skye from the floor.

But I register the pale face behind him, creeping out from the shadows of the foyer.

I try to warn him but I can't.

Kurt's arm goes around Skye's neck, and Skye makes a guttural choking sound, his blonde head jerks back. Before he can regain his footing a stripe of orange firelight flashes through the air, and Kurt's straight razor presses at the corner of Skye's eye.

There's nothing I can do. My brain can only report: the coldness of the floor under my cheek, the scrape of Skye's heels as he tries to break free from Kurt, the crash of the Taser as Kurt wrestles it from his hand and throws it against the wall.

Kurt's face is stranger than ever, caked grime half-washed by rain ringing his eyes and mouth. The muscles of his forearm stand out sharply as he digs the corner of the blade in the soft skin around Skye's eye.

I try to contort my fingers into fists. They don't respond. One hand lies limply by my face. The other hand, the one holding the lipstick knife, is curled under me.

"Care to beg for your boyfriend's life?" Kurt calls to Jada.

"Not . . . my boyfriend . . . ," Jada yawns.

"Whatever they're offering," Skye wheezes, "I can beat it."

"No, you can't," Kurt says. "They're going to give me the cure."

The *cure?*

Jada curls into herself and goes still, as though falling asleep. I think of the photos Jaw brought in before the judge, me against the shed wall, face slack with the same sick peace.

"They can't give you a cure, they haven't *made it yet!*" Skye shrieks. "We haven't even finished mapping his brain! They don't even know if it will work! They just want my algorithm!" His voice is pure panic. "If you kill me, you're doomed. Because CurtPro will own the algorithm outright and it will be *everywhere*—"

"Bro, if I don't kill you someone else will," Kurt laughs. "So all you're telling me is that I'm definitely going to need that cure."

"You can't cure being a Class A. It's your personality, not a disease—" That's what I try to say, but it comes out as animal groans.

"Cool, Signal, thanks!" Kurt says sarcastically. Then he yanks Skye's head back, and a blurry memory rises up: Janeane's hands around Rose's neck, her face twisting in hatred.

I accept my memories. My past is in the past, it cannot hurt me.

Kurt runs the razor across Skye's throat, a line of red bursting forth, Skye's shrieks cutting short. Kurt lets him drop. Skye falls hard across from me, eyes meeting mine but not really, dark blood seeping through the manicured hand around his throat.

"Did that get you all *hot*, Signal?" Kurt laughs. He sinks down on one knee. He smells unbearable, my brain reports. "I know you like the guys with the highest kill counts. I'm getting up there now!"

He lunges forward then, and with all the affection of shoving someone down the stairs, covers my lips with his filthy mouth. Sour saliva and rancid blood seep through my teeth, into my useless tongue. I can't even flinch back.

A flash of white goes off behind my eyes.

Rose's voice rings in my head, her real, remembered words:

"Just one picture, she's completely out."

Kurt pulls away from me. "Yeah, I don't get what all the fuss is about." He shrugs, stands, and I hear him wipe the razor perfunctorily on his pants. Like he's getting ready to use it again.

With all my will, I try to push myself across the floor, feet circling like I'm underwater, my limp head rolling back. But it's not enough, not even close. The orange stripe of reflected firelight rises above me, then comes down straight at my face, when a red hand shoots out.

The blade lodges hard in a thick whorl of scar tissue.

Nobody stands over me, her hair white strings from the rain, her clothes striped black from her climb up the side of the house, and regards the razor sticking out of her hand curiously.

She takes hold of the handle branching out from her knuckle. Beads of thick blood wind down her wrist, following the ridges of her scars.

"Ouch," she says calmly.

She gives the straight razor's handle a tentative tug, then wrenches it free with a jerk, red blood gloving her hand.

Kurt takes a step back, almost tripping over Skye. Nobody steps toward him, casually wiping one hand on her shirt front, the shining blade held expertly in the other.

Kurt is watching the knife so intently he leaves himself completely open for her to bring down her forehead. So hard and swift I hear Kurt's nose break.

Everything below Kurt's eyes goes dark red, his hands reflexively covering his face as he hunches over in a moan; but then he weaves forward. It's a feint: he catches up Kate's head off the rug like it's a football, and pivots for the fireplace.

The smell is so sharp even Skye stirs in his pool of blood.

Kurt turns, holding Kate's head by its jaw like a kettle ball, and swings her burning hair at Nobody, his smile shining red.

Nobody springs back, but not fast enough.

Kate's hair catches her shirt sleeve and clings, the flames catch, and she leaps backwards, like she could get away from her own arm. The razor falls from her hand and pinwheels across the floor, disappearing in the dark. Kurt laughs as Nobody frantically tries to slap the flames out with her bloody hand, hyperventilating and sinking to her knees. He swings Kate's head again and she curls forward with an animal moan.

It's that gesture that brings it all back.

Like someone turned a light on in the shed.

Click.

Rose's body leaned forward like Nobody's, on her knees. The smell of bleach. The tarp underneath her crinkling rhythmically. Janeane kneeling beside her in a painter's suit and rubber gloves. The single dark curl beside Janeane's blank eye, caught in her sweat, her knee planted in her daughter's back, her whole body swaying back and forth with the motion of the saw.

One last rock forward, and then a strange sigh of trapped breath releasing. The dark matted thing rolled forward. I'd choked, and Janeane started to turn back toward me, the white tie of her blue paper coverall twisting down her back. I'd twitched my eyes closed before she saw, but I could feel her steps thud across the shed floor before she bent down, her breath passing over my face. She lifted my eyelid, raising the curtain on the whole hellish scene: Rose's back. Rose's blood. Rose's stump. The red teeth of the saw across the blue tarp.

Janeane's burning eye had held mine a long moment. I'd pretended I was dead. That I couldn't see at all. So she let my eyelid fall with a grunt.

And I had kept pretending. Had pushed it away, somewhere deep among my dreams and refused to let it surface. Because I had loved Janeane, because I loved Rose still, because I'd rather keep pretending I was dead than accept the reality.

I accept all my memories.

The horror is like an adrenaline shot. My eyes open as wide as they go, a giant gasp of breath filling my lungs. I am not in the shed. I am awake and this is my life. And I want it.

I push myself up, fingers fanning out below me, other hand curling tighter around Jada's lipstick.

In another moment, legs still wobbling, I've cut through Skye's puddle of blood and am scrambling toward Kurt. He's by the window, holding Kate's burning head aloft, the churning flames lighting her collapsed features from all sides as the long velvet curtains catch. Flames fly up their length and the whole room goes bright as noon. Kurt, laughing, turns to see me as I bring the lipstick knife up to his throat.

"Yeah, right." Kurt grins. "We both know you won't kill me."

Below us, Nobody is starting to get her bearings, her sleeve singed but not burning, her panicked breath starting to slow.

I press the tip of the knife in far enough he stops laughing.

"Drop Kate's head."

He lets it fall. It makes a glittering path across the carpet and out of my peripheral vision.

"Why are you hauling it around, anyway?"

"They didn't want her identified before the trial."

"They? Meaning headquarters or CurtPro?"

"They're the same thing."

"Then why would they kill Skye?"

"Because he still *owns* the Wylie-Stanton, even if they know the algorithm now."

"But it's not going to be used anymore! Camp is getting shut down!"

"No, like I told you, Signal. Camp is just starting. But it won't be at Nara-mauke. It will be *everywhere*."

I don't understand, but it's impossible to think with Kurt watching me, waiting for me to slip, to blink. At our feet, Nobody is crawling around, feeling blindly for the straight razor through the smoke. Somewhere, Jada is coughing.

"Nobody, get Jada out of here!" I cry, not looking away from Kurt. Her steps move toward Jada, then Jada's beaded dress swishes across the floor. Kurt smiles at me, knowingly, blood lining the slight overlap of his front teeth.

"Why don't you kill me already, Signal?"

"Because you know things." I twist the knife a little further. "Why was Troy at camp, if he was never a Class A?"

"We made a deal with Dave." His swallow bobbles my knife hand. "Since I didn't kill anyone, and Troy wasn't technically Class A, they took us in as a package. Made up a new term for Troy."

"Class A influenced," I croak. *That's* why they had Kurt kill Donna.

Because she had evidence that proved their basis for "Class A influence" was a pure psychopath who didn't even rank on the Wylie-Stanton. And his inno-cent Class A brother had tried to cover for him.

"Don't you get it?" I plead with Kurt. "They're not going to cure you. They're going to let you finish your list and then take you out as *messy as possible*. You'll be their proof that even the lowest score of Class A is too dangerous to be in society—"

"Everyone *is* dangerous. If they have to be." His eyes narrow. "Even you, Little Miss Innocent. You're not getting out of this room without killing me. But you can't."

My fingers tighten on the pink tube of lipstick in my hand.

"You can't!" He starts laughing. "You can't go through with it, can you, you prissy little bitch—"

I pull the blade from his throat and stick it straight into his eye, the peeled grape burst of it registering down the length of my arm. When I pull the knife back there's something like an overgrown pink tadpole impaled on its end.

I throw the whole mess into the fireplace, and the eyeball twitches on the red embers, its pink nerve tail curling up with the heat before the entire thing bursts into flame, the roasting smell making Kurt howl even harder as he collapses into shuddering spasms of shock.

I grab a poker from the fireplace stand and scrape the last remnants of burning curtain away before swinging it hard against the glass.

It bounces off.

Skye has shatterproof glass installed. But staring at me through the unbroken pane is Aarush.

"The BACK!" I gesture wildly. "NOBODY AND JADA! OPEN THE BACK DOOR!"

"Right, on it!" Aarush says, perfectly audible through the glass, and I realize he's heard everything before he disappears around the house.

And then Kurt's dirty hands clasp my neck.

Chapter Nineteen
No Signal

~

Kurt's horrible smell fills my mouth, his hot blood sputtering in a fine spray across my bare back as he curses me out. I try to swipe him with the poker, then drop it and pull at his filthy fingers, but they dig tighter and tighter, ragged holes growing at the edges of my vision, fine black lace stretching to the point it finally breaks.

Then Kurt lets out a cry and releases me.

I turn to see Skye, staring up from Kurt's ankles, a sheet of glistening red painted halfway down his throat. He's cut one of Kurt's Achilles tendons and is still gripping the straight razor Nobody dropped.

"Get Erik," Skye rasps. "Oxygen . . . explodes."

His eyes roll to the growing black stain on the ceiling, the flames lapping just under Erik's room.

No.

I hobble toward the stairs. In the kitchen, Nobody is holding Jada's hair back as she vomits noisily into the kitchen sink.

"Help me!" I scream.

Nobody leans Jada onto a barstool, then runs over, pulling her bloodied shirt up around her face as we make our way up the stairs, the black hedge of smoke growing thicker every moment.

Below us I can hear Kurt and Skye grappling on the floor. I don't stop to see who's winning.

Erik's room, with the open window, is much clearer than the staircase. I unleash him from the oxygen tank, then decide to drag it along with us, away from the fire, so we aren't surprised by an explosion. Nobody props Erik up and we each get under one of his arms and stumble toward the stairs. Eyes streaming, we maneuver Erik and the long heavy tank down through the billowing black smoke to the landing and into the kitchen.

Through the glass, Aarush's huge eyes go larger still as he sees comatose Erik, then clocks the bloody handprints around my neck, and finally the long, heavy tank.

"Oxygen?" he calls through the shatterproof glass.

I nod.

"Padlocked." He points to the chain wrapped around the double doors. "Set it off." He points at the oxygen tank.

Explode.

"Guys, get all the way across the kitchen from me," I yell to Jada and Nobody.

They wrestle Erik to the counter as I place the tank on the floor, the nozzle pointing toward the doors.

"Other way around!" Aarush screams, and cold sweat breaks out across my forehead as I turn the canister so its base rests softly against the seam between the doors.

"Strike the nozzle off!" Aarush calls, then sprints clear of the doors.

I grab a meat tenderizer from the counter, its steel head so heavy I have to hold it with both hands. I line up the head with the nozzle, bring it up high, and swing it back down.

An instantaneous rush of white, and the tank shoots forward on its side like a rocket, breaking the doors off their hinges and sending pieces of chain into the Pacific as it flies off the cliff and disappears into the stormy horizon. Aarush shouts wildly at the victory, and Nobody and a recovering Jada help carry Erik out into the fresh air. It's freezing, his thin tie-back hospital gown immediately spots with rain, but he still doesn't blink. I'm bundling my raincoat around him when Jada slips out from under his arm and darts back inside.

"Jada! No!" Nobody screams, but she's too spooked by the fire eating away at the house to follow her.

"Here, Nobody, why don't you take Erik to the car and I'll get Jada—" My hoarse voice scrapes at my throat.

"I dropped the keys in the house," she says.

"We can take my car to hospital—it's parked out front," Aarush says, slipping one of Erik's heavy arms around his shoulders. "He's collapsed from smoke inhalation, is that it?"

But as he scans Erik—the red circles from the electrodes, the IV still in his arm, the nasal tubes for the oxygen taped under his nose, his half-shaved head—he looks to me in frank alarm.

"What happened?"

"Skye put him in a medical coma," I rasp.

"Skye *what?* Where *is* Skye?!" Aarush says. "Could someone tell me what precisely is happening—"

An animal wail issues from the house.

Then Skye and Kurt come crashing through the blown-out kitchen doors, so wrapped in white gold fire it's impossible to tell which is which.

Their hands are around each other's throats, but in their cocoon of flame they move in anguished slow motion. They appear almost to be waltzing as they circle through the rain, melded together by fire. Their burning halo of white and gold lights up the entire yard, the side of the house, the carefully trimmed grass, the white cement sidewalk as they veer down the path that leads to the horizon. And then like some strange sunset, they slip from the edge of the cliff and leave us in the dark.

Aarush stares after them, eyes wide, as Jada rushes to the edge. He seems too stunned to notice the half-empty bottle of perfume in her hand. I watch in silence as Jada throws it underhand off the cliff after them, to be swept out to sea by the storm.

"Hey, guys?" Jada calls over her shoulder after a moment. "Who's the third guy down here?"

"*Javier.*"

* * *

Jada and I sprint through the neighbor's yard, down a series of steep switchbacks that lead to the beach. Jada is barefoot, having kicked her shoes off as soon as I said Javier's name, both of us sopping wet from the rain. We fly across the sand toward the arch just below Skye's house, where three bodies lay in the sand.

"Kurt must have knocked him out before he climbed up!"

"What happens if the tide pulls him in?" Jada pants. "If he's knocked out?"

The answer is to run faster.

"JAVI!" Jada yells, "JAVI!!"

She runs straight into the waves dragging his body toward the volcanic rock. He's on his back, thank God, but nothing can protect him from the black heaving ocean, except Jada's small hands. She catches at his raincoat and pulls him back up the slope of the beach before he's driven against the arch of rock.

I run to her side and help catch his other arm. We throw ourselves forward, dragging him just below the cliff. Skye and Kurt's mangled corpses lie twenty feet away, utterly still, burnt flesh audibly hissing in the rain.

"Can you do CPR?" I ask Jada.

She nods quickly, lacing her small hands together and putting them over Javier's heart. She pumps his chest, then covers his mouth with hers. I look away, toward the threatening horizon, until she sits up and starts pumping again. After another few moments Javier coughs, a long wet gasp. His dark eyes, ringed with white, fall open.

I hold very still, not wanting to interrupt what Jada is whispering to him, and then Javier staggers to his feet, Jada throwing his arm over her shoulder.

I let the space grow between us as she steers him down the beach and up the trail. Giving them a moment alone is not the same thing as rehoming an ex, I mentally explain to Nobody. By the time I stagger up to the hill, they're far away.

I scan the dark block. Where are the police? The firefighters? Surely Aarush has called them?

As I stumble across the neighbor's lawn, the orange fire eating Skye's house is leaping above the treetops. The second story, where Erik was, is just black timber and flame.

A warm hand lands on my shoulder. "There you are."

I jump and turn around to see Sonny Desai, face concerned under the black wing of a large umbrella.

"Aarush told me there'd been some trouble here. Are you alright?"

I nod, a prickle rising along the back of my neck. "Where is Aarush?"

"Pacing around on his phone, trying to get the police to hurry up." A smile crinkles the fine skin around Sonny's eyes. "But I happen to know they'll be another half hour at least. I told them we needed a moment to sort things out."

He gestures for me to follow him to the cover of the neighbor's gazebo, out of the rain. I don't have a choice. I worry nervously with Erik's ring as I spot a security guard by the fence between this yard and Skye's. There's another one around the side of the neighbor's house.

"I'll admit, I was a little hurt I wasn't invited to your wedding." Sonny says, closing his umbrella and giving it a little shake.

"Sorry." I swallow.

"If you'd like to make it up to me, do it again. With a big proper reception this time. You could host hundreds of guests at the Wylie-Stanton house. Once you've renovated it, of course."

I blink at him.

"I'm happy to pay for all of it. Even the renovation! If you do me one favor. Have the ceremony before Erik starts treatment. And hold the reception after."

I stare at Sonny through the dark for a long beat. "How much of CurtPro do you own?"

"Thirty-three percent." Sonny smiles, eyes fully approving and completely cold. "Now that Skye is dead, if you take over Erik's conservatorship, you'll have his six percent along with Erik's six, which comes to twelve. Unless you're inclined to sell?" He chuckles in the silence. "I doubt it. You're a smart girl. I'm excited to be partners in this. As his wife you're Erik's best advocate, and your concerns will be front and center going forward."

"Going forward with making him a super soldier?"

"Super soldier?" Sonny looks baffled, then laughs. "Oh my, no. What? What an archaic idea. We have drones for that sort of thing now. Security threats are not external in the modern arena. No, the monster is *inside the house*. The danger to society is human nature. Class As. Thanks to Erik's rather singular brain, we can find them. And once it's fully mapped, we'll be able to cure them."

And now I'm shaking.

"We've assembled the best neurologists in the world. We heightened Erik's chemistry enough at camp to identify ninety-nine percent of the synaptic routes triggered when he exhibits Class A tendencies. The next stage is to simply adjust the medication until those routes don't . . . light up anymore."

"You mean like . . ." My throat sticks. What had Erik said once? A chemical soul. But that's not what this is. ". . . A chemical lobotomy?"

"That's a . . . mischaracterization. If we have someone like you on the team, we can prevent that. But we need someone who really knows him." Sonny steps toward me. "I was always opposed to Skye as Erik's conservator. He didn't know Erik well enough to keep us from veering off the baseline. But now Skye is out of the way, you will be the one dialing Erik in. And what a beautiful ending to your love story! The original Class A clears his innocent wife's name, and she in turn redeems him, saves him from himself. Think, Signal. In a matter of months, you would have an Erik who is always considerate, compliant, loyal . . . and an inspiration for all the millions who've followed your story so far."

The rain drums in the stillness between us, tide crashing doggedly below.

"You don't understand," I say at last. "The algorithm doesn't—find evil people. It just finds—misfits. You can't *cure* being a misfit."

"How many people can read an algorithm, Signal? Aarush can. Dennis can. Most people, no." He shakes his head. "Yet our entire political apparatus has sworn the Wylie-Stanton does what you say it can't: It roots out the bad apples! *And keeps the good ones safe.* Even if everyone is wrong about what the Wylie-Stanton does, that's a very strong brand to fight against. The Wylie-Stanton is here to stay, and it's my belief that we're only beginning to see its impact."

He doesn't step closer, but his security guards—I count two behind him now, another one behind me—sidle up the steps ringing the gazebo.

"I am offering you and Erik your happiest possible ending," he says after a moment. "But perhaps I should go into the consequences if you turn down my offer."

He reaches into his suit pocket and pulls out a little rubber hamburger with googly eyes.

Aarush's thumb drive.

My vision blurs momentarily, like I've been slapped.

"Father?" Aarush calls from between the trees. "Where did you get that?"

Sonny fists his hand, but it's too late.

"That's my thumb drive!" Aarush's footsteps ring hollow under the rushing rain as he leaps up onto the deck. "How did you . . ." He blinks at his father. "Why would you sabotage a case you were paying for?"

"Aarush, I have no idea what you're talking about." Sonny's tone is confident. "Signal and I were discussing next steps for Erik's care, an obviously sensitive discussion—"

I stare at Aarush, bracing myself. Because if Aarush already knows what I'm about to say, I can fully expect the security guards to rush me, to disappear without a trace.

But it is the truth.

"Aarush," I rasp. "Did you know that your dad basically owns CurtPro?"

Aarush's face goes slack, and when he turns to his father again, it's with new eyes. "*That's* why you wanted the algorithm out in discovery . . . ," he says. "So you can take the Wylie-Stanton *public?*"

"Yes, Aarush. This is how we expand. This is how we grow." Sonny nods. "*This* is the future of security. Predictive analytics, AI profiling. This is what we've been pursuing since *Dennis!*"

I take a step back, hand landing on the wooden railing behind me.

"Signal." Sonny turns on me. "You answer me, right now: Where is Erik?"

I stare at Aarush, as Sonny's security guards move up the stairs that lead to the deck from both directions, a trailer park girl with grown-out roots and a bruised neck in a cheap party dress. We both know the answer to that question. Erik is in the back seat of his car, parked right out front.

"Signal," Aarush says, in his old commanding tone, "catch."

And then his keys, the keys to his precious Aston Martin, arc over Sonny's head. I reach out and catch them.

I swing myself over the rail of the deck and roll forward into the slick wet grass as I land, back on my feet before the security guards reach me, sprinting toward the car as fast as I can.

* * *

The Aston Martin is parked in front of Skye's fence, its chassis unmistakable. Nobody, Jada, and Javier are standing around it, watching Skye's house burn. I land just inside the security light of the front drive when the security guard's hands close around me.

"What the hell are you doing?" Jada cries.

"Get off of her!" Javier pushes the guard backwards, Nobody cracking the side of his head with a punch as I scramble into the low leather driver's seat and start the car.

"Skipper! Where are you going?!" Jada calls as I burn out toward the street.

But I can't tell her because I don't know.

Erik is laid out in the passenger seat, which has been ratcheted back almost flat. He looks pale and cold in his hospital gown and my thin raincoat. I have him safe now, but for how long? We're not even married since the license wasn't filed. I have no legal way to shield him, no money, no place to take him Sonny doesn't own.

CurtPro, headquarters, the police—all of whom seem to have some tie to Sonny—they will find me, wherever I go. My lead time is just minutes, and it's already shrinking. I don't have a way to get Erik out of their power, no one does, except. . . .

No.

No, not that, I can't do that. There has to be another way. I can't even reach her!

. . . But of course I can.

I reach into my jacket pocket, and take out Skye's dupe phone.

I let out a sob as I find her number. Surely this is like cutting out your own heart—I'll collapse from the pain before I can go through with it.

"This is it," I say out loud to the muffled drum of rain. "This is how he kills me."

She picks up on the first ring.

"Nadya, don't hang up." I say. "It's me, Signal. How soon could you marry Erik?"

* * *

He sleeps the entire drive to Los Angeles. I get down to fumes before daring to stop for gas, and while the tank fills I ransack the car until I find a tracker, up under the front driver's side wheel. I stomp it flat and throw it into the trash. I buy a bottle of Listerine, and chug and spit until all the smoke and blood is out of my mouth and the tank is full.

Erik doesn't stir at all.

It's not until we get to LA, past the point the highways close in and candy-colored apartment buildings rise from the palm-scattered hills, that his eyes flutter. Maybe it's the dawning light that's brushing the city with pink and turning all the windows gold, but Erik's color seems to be reviving too. His cheeks flush with drowsy heat, and then he turns a little on his side, and my heart tears.

I'm about to try shaking his shoulder when I hear propellers thudding above us. Not helicopters, something smaller and faster. And then two black metal squids with beady lenses, four rotating blades each suspending them aloft, rise in my rearview.

Destech drones.

The road broadens to several lanes. We crawl down an avenue crowded tight with mansions, the drones floating patiently behind, tracking us. I have to lose them.

I scan through a driving map, trying to find a patch of green between us and Glendale, and decide on somewhere called Griffith Park.

I don't slow by the entrance; hoping to throw them, I turn into the park as abruptly as I can, tires bouncing over a low gutter and hitting a speed bump so hard we almost catch air. And this is what wakes him up.

"W—where . . ." Erik's voice, deep and rough. He drags himself upright, bringing up the car seat, and turns to stare at me, his bloodshot eyes greener than spring. "Signal? What are you doing here? Where are we?"

"Griffith Park."

Around us, the trees clear at intervals to reveal families preparing for parties: setting picnic tables, popping open camping awnings, and hanging bunches of balloons. He stares around us with an expression as baffled as though we were flying through space.

He looks down, pulling my raincoat away, to stare at the hospital gown. "I don't understand . . . it was night, like, a *second* ago—"

"You were on Propofol along with some other stuff," I tell him, trying to keep my voice calm. "It's supposed to feel like a time jump when it wears off. You've lost a day. You'll feel out of it for the next several hours."

"And *my hair*?!" He flips down the passenger side mirror. "WHY IS HALF MY HAIR GONE?!"

In the rearview, a blue sedan is trailing us by three car lengths. We've passed a zoo, and now a museum, but still the sedan doesn't turn off.

"I'm sorry if this is disorienting, but we're being tailed," I tell him. "Tighten your seat belt."

He tugs the strap taut across his chest, and I swerve left without signaling onto a narrower road, asphalt giving way to dirt. After a beat the sedan appears in my rearview, terra cotta color blooming behind it in a rooster tail of dust.

Erik is staring at me now. I doubt my appearance is comforting.

"Why are there bruises around your neck?"

"I'm fine." I glance at him. "Everything is fine. We just have to lose these guys real quick."

I hit the gas and we fly forward, the cloud of dust behind us momentarily swallowing the sedan. I bear down a long curve under a grove of old oaks, their branches flashing overhead like black lightning bolts, then put all my weight onto the gas pedal.

The sedan roars behind us as we fly straight uphill, the golden leaves of the white sycamores blurring in the windows, early morning birds diving out of our way and up into the pale blue sky. We're going uphill so fast it feels like we're building to a takeoff, wheels bouncing against the rutted road so the Aston Martin bucks like an unbroken horse. Erik starts laughing, but then the sedan taps my rear bumper and we fly forward.

Erik whips around in his seat, mad-dogging our pursuers.

The driver's face is clear in my rearview: clenched teeth, shoulders braced, eager to run us off the road. His passenger is yelling for us to pull over. Both large men have white curling wires leading down from their ears, like all the Desais' private security.

"They aren't cops?" Erik half-yells over the engine. "Why are they chasing us?"

"They want you!" I swipe at my phone to wake up the screen. The map is still up and the bars are going down fast. Only two little ones to go. I careen left, onto what appears to be a horse trail, branches scraping against the sides of the Aston Martin.

"This isn't a road!" Erik cries.

"We need to get into the green—" My knuckles are white on the wheel. The last bar on my phone is flickering.

The sedan had to pivot to course correct after my surprise turn. My rearview mirror is empty. So I slow down.

"What are you doing?!" Erik turns on me. "Speed up, we can lose them right now—"

"*Just wait.*" The last bar blinks out of existence. "I need them right behind me."

"They are trying to *total this car!*"

"Trust me." I look him straight in his glowing green eyes.

The sedan roars up behind us, branches trembling as it mows through them, but I only continue forward when it starts truly bearing down. Their nose is almost to my bumper, Erik jumping out of his skin, turning in his seat and screaming with frustration as the sedan buzzes us again. The driver grins at me through their windshield as they speed forward—when there's the high sigh of wind through metal.

The two drones tailing us fall down.

The driver's smile disappears behind an instantaneous spiderweb of shattered glass as the first one lands. The second drone impales itself so deeply in their hood the sedan bounces on impact.

Erik stares through the rear windshield, open-mouthed, as I calmly put the car back in gear and start for the closest actual road. He turns to face me then, and finally recovers enough to say: "You are my perfect woman."

And then my phone chirps between us, as all the incoming texts racked up while we were out of range come in. And they're all from Nadya:

Change of plans where to meet
Don't stop by my house, housekeeper says police are pulled up out
    front
My neighbor has a helipad, pin is address

Erik pulls the phone out of its holder, his jaw tightens.

"Sick of me already?" he asks stiffly.

"I wish I was." My tears spill over and run down my face. "I wish I ever could be. But it wasn't Skye we had to worry about. It was Sonny."

"I know," Erik says quietly.

He tells me about the night before. That he'd found Sonny alone in the nerve center and offered to take the last round of Ledrick's injections if Sonny would return Aarush's thumb drive.

Sonny had congratulated him on his discretion, put the thumb drive in his hand, then poured them both drinks to toast our wedding.

The next thing Erik knew, he was waking up in the car beside me.

"Because they never wanted to make you a super soldier. They want to make a cure for being a Class A."

"Is that . . . possible?" Erik looks baffled.

"No! Of course not! It's just a chemical lobotomy. And Sonny wanted me to oversee it! He waved some stock options in my face and said the Wylie-Stanton was the 'future of security'!"

"Oversee?" Erik bites at his nails. "What does that mean?"

"He said if I signed off on pumping your brain full of chemicals, he'd let me dial in your personality. They'd just keep shutting down synapses until I decided you were 'acting right.'" I wipe at my eyes with my fist. "And then we'd probably go on Mary Larland to talk about how *happy we were* so everyone with a Class A in the family would *run out and buy his stupid cure.*"

"And make billions of dollars. He must have been the one seeding all those articles," Erik murmurs. "But you refused?"

"Hell yes, I refused! I got you away from him as fast as I could." I look up at the rearview mirror. "But any minute now another drone will pop up or some cop on his side will turn up and I can't—this isn't *even my car!* I can't protect you from someone like Sonny!"

He watches the map, orienting itself toward Nadya's pin.

"But Nadya can," he says stiffly. "I get it. I get it." He rubs nervously at the back of his neck, ducking his head forward and scanning the blue-white horizon.

"You know this is the last thing I want," I choke.

"Ditto," he says.

I shift the car into a higher gear and veer sharply uphill. There is no laughter now, no joyous sense of flight. Only a complete and focused silence as we clock the numbers of the spaced-out estates and climb higher over the city. Whenever the sirens fade out in one direction, they build in another.

"There!" I cry, spotting a tall white fence with the address number we're looking for, and the young Erik lookalike from the *Outlaws* video comes running out of the house, face pale over a black Nadya T-shirt. He tensely directs me to pull into the garage.

"Helipad is on the roof. We go to the elevator to your right—" he yells the moment my engine cuts, yanking open Erik's door. Erik staggers a little on his feet, and I hurry around and throw his arm over my shoulder. "This way, hurry—" the guy cries.

Blue and red lights are already bouncing through the tall windows as we breathlessly run for the elevator, the whole house a jumble of pink marble, dark wood, and gold molding.

"Here, here, come on—" the lookalike says, rapidly punching the top button, then racing up the fire stairs with a quick explanation that he'll be right back down.

I came to steady Erik, but he's holding me up, his arm around me so tight, and I'm shaking so hard, because I *know* how bad this will hurt.

"Last chance," Erik says softly, "to take Sonny up on it? Become a billionaire?" He looks down at me, his smile wry, but his eyes strangely flat. "Make me your Erik, for real."

"*You are* my Erik. There's nothing about you I would change. Nothing."

"I bite my nails," he says. "They could turn that off. And all my, uh, killing and maiming and evil tendencies."

My eyes blur with tears, but I fight them back. "If you couldn't kill people, I'd be buried under the Star Barn. If you hadn't hacked up Skye, Alice would be dead. And if you didn't bite your nails, I wouldn't know when you're upset. I want all of it. All of you, alright? I'll wait as long as it takes. Just come back as soon as you can."

Erik stares down at me. His heart is thrashing through the thin material of his hospital gown as the elevator audibly lands behind the doors, and I can't help it. I reach up and kiss him with all my heart, and right as the doors sweep open I gently bite his bottom lip before whispering: "*But the next time I see you, I am never letting go of you again.*"

The lookalike reaches out and grabs Erik's hospital gown. "Come on! Come on!"

Erik staggers, almost like he's resisting, and then he's inside the shining golden elevator and turning to me, his face stricken as the doors close between us.

And I'm left across from my own sobbing reflection.

The police are banging on the front door. No one else is going to answer it; if there were any staff, they fled when sirens started pulling up. The helicopter is thudding, rotor blades accelerating overhead as I stumble through the richly upholstered foyer, and then the door goes flying open as the police break in. Officers with clear shields and dark helmets race past me, sprinting for the stairs. I walk into the tall front doorway, the helicopter sound loud enough to register in my chest as it soars above the house.

There are cries of alarm, and the police cars that hadn't parked yet turn to follow it. But they'll never catch him now. I shield my eyes with my hand, stare out into the deep cloudless blue sky, and watch the helicopter shrink over the hills. When something like a little black squid rises straight up behind it.

And another one, and another one, until four little drones are chasing after the escaping helicopter. They seem too close.

I reach out, as though I could brush them out of the way, but there's nothing I can do to stop what happens next.

Two of the drones veer too close and catch in the thudding rotor, one bursting immediately into flames, the other tangling with the central gear. The black helicopter bobs, like a broken elevator.

Then it falls straight down, crashing into the hills.

I lean forward in a scream I can't hear, only feel.

The explosion is the color and shape of a bird of paradise, bright orange fire fanning out across the blue heaven for just a moment. Then it all turns into black smoke as the world turns off.

Chapter Twenty
Wrongful Damages

∽

Monotone beeping. The rustle of the IV tube dragging against sheets. Fluorescent lights and a cloud of muffled pain. I start to sit up, but Mom gently presses me back down again.

"Hey, baby," Mom says gently. "Kids—she's up."

Nobody looms over Mom's shoulder, blue eyes ringed with hot pink. Jada is on the other side of the bed, both her manicured hands wrapped around mine. Javier nods at the foot of the bed and Dennis, in a chair in the corner, leans forward, putting his glasses back on to cover wet eyes.

"You're at UCLA hospital," Mom says. "You collapsed from exhaustion and—the shock, of course."

Dennis makes a strangled sound like a sob.

"Are you guys . . . is everything okay?" My head feels stuffed with cotton, my heart numb. Like someone has kindly cut it out of me and set it aside for now.

"I've asked your friends to stay with us for a while," Mom says. "Since Sonny, um—"

"Kicked us out," Nobody says.

"I still have another month at Sea View." Mom smiles unconvincingly. "Then we'll just . . . figure out what's next, like we always do."

Dennis stands up. I follow his gaze to the door, where Aarush hovers, tightening a rolled-up piece of newspaper between nervously fisted hands.

"Hello, Breann, and everyone . . . ," Aarush says awkwardly. "I believe it's visitor hours, if I could possibly . . . May I come in, please?"

Mom's jaw is set, her hand clenches mine, but I squeeze back reassuringly.

"Yeah, of course," I say, and Aarush steps in. He looks around the bristling room for a beat before addressing me.

"Please accept my condolences and my most sincere apology . . ." Aarush's voice breaks off; he clears his throat. "I came here because I feel I owe you all an explanation. For your abrupt exit from the house, and the unfortunate sequence of events that led up to it."

"Yeah, please," Jada says, arching an eyebrow.

"While I had nothing to do with that last, rather hasty decision, I cannot acquit myself of my father's dealings. Which have involved all of you, in very painful ways. But especially Dennis . . . Dennis, how should I begin?"

Aarush looks to his former coding partner. Dennis doesn't return the gaze, only straightens his surprisingly broad shoulders, and grips his hands together.

"They don't know the full story," Dennis says. "All they know is I wasn't sentenced for any crime."

"Dennis the Non-Menace," Javier says grimly.

Dennis adjusts his glasses, though they weren't out of place. "I told you guys that I asked my computer teacher if I could take the Wylie-Stanton. But I've never told you guys—never told anyone—the real reason why. Aarush and I were doing a lot of white hat hacking competitions at the time. And his father gave us a challenge: Whoever gets access to the Wylie-Stanton first, and can figure out how it works, wins."

"Dennis 'won,'" Aarush says.

"Yeah, well." Dennis shakes his head. "I didn't get a chance to figure out the algorithm because, as you all know, the process is very opaque. There was no opportunity to be alone with a computer—they just scraped my information and ran it through. And when it came out I was a Class A, there were some . . . serious consequences."

Jada gets up and crosses the room to him. She sits on the arm of his chair and places one small manicured hand on his back.

"Which is why I felt obligated to help Dennis turn off the kill switches," Aarush picks up, "and to assist Signal and Erik on their way to Ledmonton. I thought my father and I were on the same page, that he felt as strongly as I did that the Wylie-Stanton was being misused. But since then, I've learned my father's interest in the Wylie-Stanton was entirely self-serving. He bought up CurtPro because he wanted the algorithm, and when he realized Skye owned it personally and couldn't or wouldn't disclose it, he championed Signal's case because he believed the government would have to bring it out during discovery. When they refused, he dropped her case and made the federal suit his priority. *That* is why the thumb drive with the attic rant went missing, Signal."

Aarush has the good grace to look ashamed.

"I had not considered Father as a suspect. But the fact is he was trying to woo Janeane into testifying about camp to bolster the federal case. Her price was sinking yours."

So that's why Sonny had brought me to Janeane at Ragged Point. And no doubt, he tipped Jaw off about the subpoena.

"But he fought so hard to shut down federal use of the Wylie-Stanton—" I shake my head. "If Sonny was looking into a cure, wouldn't he *need* the Wylie-Stanton to keep going?"

"It seems he saw federal use of the Wylie-Stanton as competition. Now that Destech has the algorithm, they are going to upgrade it and license it for private use. People are still terrified of Class As. So Destech will make it as broadly available as possible." Aarush shifts uneasily on his feet. "Instead of classifying felons, it will . . . classify everybody. Employers can run it on employees, universities can make it part of the application process, it can be required for certification of any kind. Like a social credit score. To try and eliminate Class As from society completely."

We all stare at him in horror.

"And the cure?" I lean forward.

"Was the other half of my father's plan. Once Class As were socially untouchable, CurtPro, my father's other major holding, could market a treatment they could take in perpetuity. I'm sure it would've been very profitable. And utterly devastating to millions of people." Aarush looks at me. "But they can't go through with that now, because they don't have Erik. And they never will."

Nobody swallows a sob.

"I didn't know about any of this." Dennis looks at me. "About what Sonny was planning for Erik or the Wylie-Stanton. If I'd had any idea, I never would've steered you guys to Aarush—" Tears roll down from behind his glasses. "But that doesn't change the consequences. So if all of you never want to speak to me again, I get it."

Jada turns to Dennis, cups his wet face in her hands, and stares through his glasses for a long moment before kissing him.

My jaw actually drops.

Dennis' hand grips Jada's shoulder as he starts kissing her back. Javier covers his mouth, eyes going wide, and Mom gasps. When they pull apart for breath at last, Jada laughs nervously.

"Sorry, I just . . ." She blinks at him. "Life is too short. Is anyone here blaming Dennis, for any of this?" She looks around the room. "Yeah, no, I didn't think so. We all love you, Dennis. Me most of all."

Dennis blinks at her in stunned silence, then looks around the room.

"Excuse us." He says, takes Jada's hand, and they walk out into the hall, Jada's head bowed to hide her smile.

"Well . . ." Aarush looks at me, eyes huge. ". . . There's more I need to tell you. About your trial."

I brace myself.

"I made sure Janeane's attic rant, from the thumb drive, was entered into evidence. Clatsop County informed the court all charges against you will be dropped. They are focusing entirely on Janeane as the prime suspect."

"What?" Mom jerks forward in her seat. "You mean—Signal's name is cleared?"

"More than that." Aarush puts down the curled-up tube of newspaper at last, straightening it so I can see the headline:

WA STATE AWARDS GIRL FROM HELL 12 MIL

"Honor and I took the liberty of reaching out to some people about a wrongful conviction settlement," Aarush says as I look from the headline to him and back again.

"You're sure this means me? I'm getting . . ." I squint at the headline, the numbers not making sense. "I'm getting *twelve million dollars?*"

"I was expecting we'd have to go to trial. But apparently the governor had some strong feelings about the case."

I unfold the newspaper, and see a picture of what I guess is the governor of Washington, his wife, and . . . *Feather?*

Feather, the slightly stout, short-haired outcast from Higher Paths, who I invited into my tent when I was "Sunshine." *Feather* is the *governor's daughter?*

"I went to a camp with that girl!" I tell Mom. Then, looking up at Aarush: "Will twelve million cover the loss of your car?"

"You owe me nothing, Signal. In fact," his thick brows come together over his fine nose, "I must offer my deepest and sincerest apologies for not listening to you earlier. About Skye, about CurtPro." His voice breaks, and I shake my head; he doesn't have to go on but he does. "And about Erik."

I reach out and take his hand. He bows his head briefly, then stands.

"I won't trespass further on your privacy." He clears his throat. "I have an appointment shortly."

"Destech meeting?" I ask.

"No. Interviews. I quit Destech and moved out. Now that I understand where my father is taking his company, I can't be a part of it."

"That's a lot to give up," I say.

"I like to think we have the same affliction, Signal." He pauses at the door and gives me a last sad smile. "An extremely loud conscience."

And I'm so touched, I almost want to tell him about where his car really went.

Almost.

But I can't tell any of them yet.

I look back to the newspaper, starting to get sucked in by this bizarre take on my life story. The article leads with our manhunt; how Erik and I went viral. There are several paragraphs about Janeane, the "Mom From Hell." The article discusses Naramauke, and how the settlement has meant the end of the "Naramauke Rehabilitation Program." The camp itself will be shut down, condemned, and swallowed up by the wilderness.

"Is my phone nearby?" I ask Mom, and she fishes it out of her purse.

I dial Lupin, thinking of the forgotten playground where Erik and I used to talk on the swings. The red cabins at sunset. The long field curving around the lake, how pink the water would go before dawn.

"Sunshine!" Lupin answers, a smile in her voice. "How're you sleeping?"

"Better. That's not why I'm calling." I stare down at the newsprint aerial shot of Naramauke. "This is going to sound weird, but I'd like to offer you a job."

* * *

The next few weeks are busy. Making the offer on the land, looking into exactly what we have to do to qualify as a residential correctional facility. Not because I want us to act like one, but because that way, my friends' time there will count toward time served. Their sentences have been reduced, but Nobody, Jada, and Javier all have a few years to go.

"I want to have a super gentle approach, like Higher Paths," I tell Lupin, "with everything Erik loved about that program. The therapy talk and long hikes and share circles, but only for Class A kids."

Since colleges have started including Class A testing for admission, a lot of Class As have dropped out of high school. Or been kicked out.

"So it's just Class As. Like Naramauke was?" my new director asks me.

"Yeah. That was one good thing about camp. We'd all always been the bad kids or the misfits. So when we were together, we had to be something else. We had to be ourselves."

Once all the paperwork is settled, Lupin drives us out to survey our new camp. Dennis, Nobody, Javier, Jada, and I sit in the back of a rented van, not quite believing it until we cross under the towering wooden sign:

CAMP NARAMAUKE

"A new name," Javier says. "That's the first thing we need."

"Absolutely." I mark down on my legal pad: *Rose Rowan Memorial Camp?*

"This is the main cabin, right?" Lupin asks, slowing beside the tin-covered deck with a familiar crunch of gravel. We make our way down to the path, stiff from the long drive, gulping down the clear cold late afternoon air. Little white wheels of pollen float around us, every tree gilded with amber light, every blade of the deep grass traced with a line of sunset red.

"You going to drag the lake for bodies before we open?" Nobody asks the group, and a rare round of laughter breaks out.

"I'm pretty sure corpses in a recreational lake is an OSHA violation, but maybe we'll just pump the brakes on cannonballs and kayaking the first couple of sessions." I tuck my hair behind my ear. "Then, after we've dug up most of the mannequins, we can sneak the real bodies out when no one's paying attention."

"Oh, leave the mannequins where they are, they're not hurting anyone." Javier laughs.

"Mannequins are just big Barbie dolls." I smile at him, remembering how he cut up my mannequin in this same cold grass we're walking through now.

"What are we doing about the obstacle course?" Dennis asks. "Chopping it up for firewood, I hope?"

"The obstacle course was truly the bane of my existence. But I can't deny it actually *worked*." I shrug. "Sometimes it pays to know how to climb a building! But we'll put in nets, of course."

"Well, that's no fun," Nobody sniffs.

We climb up the hill to the towering sycamore tree over the old Arts and Crafts table.

"We should have a memorial here," I say quietly, toying nervously with Erik's ring. "For all the campers lost in and out of camp. And all the targets too." I clear my throat. "And a new Arts and Crafts building." I cut a look to Javier. "How would you feel about being Arts and Crafts counselor?"

"I would love that," he says seriously.

"Can I be Archery?" Jada asks, eyes bright.

"You can be anything you want. We're going to have lots of positions to fill. Group leaders, Sports, Swimming, Games, a proper nurse and doctor, nutritionists, and mental health specialists—"

"Plenty of unemployed Class As to choose from these days," Nobody mutters, her breath just visible.

Now that a Wylie-Stanton 2.0 is widely available through Destech, the list of colleges and corporations barring Class As grows every day. The argument is, it's too much legal liability if you don't run the Wylie-Stanton and someone associated with your school or job or brand is a Class A and hurts someone else. Dennis has plans to invest and build up a savings account for each of the Teen Killers Club members, for when they get out. But where they will go after is murky. I'm hopeful things will get better in a few years. It's hard to imagine them getting worse.

We make our way farther down the winding trail. Past the obstacle course, and then to the forgotten playground. I stop at the swing set where Erik and I first sat together. I reach out and touch the chains just to hear their high, rusted sound. It's funny how clearly the moments in your life that change everything stand out in retrospect. You are drawn to the places they happened, you are haunted by what you should have done, should have said. You become your own personal ghost.

"Will we have Wi-Fi?" Nobody asks, pulling me out of my thoughts as we move out into the open grass behind the girls' cabin. "Because I need my nightly Zoom call with Amy."

"You're such a *clinger*." I wink at her.

"Wi-Fi is number one, hot water number two, for our top priorities." Dennis takes my legal pad from me to make some quick, neat notes. "And considering we'll also need heating, it might make more sense to tear these cabins down and put up new ones with central air."

"Can we still afford to put up more cabins if we do that? I don't want to turn anyone away."

"Easily." Dennis nods. "And if we continue on my schedule of investments, we could get an East Coast location up and running within five years." We all turn to him, stunned. "But that's a whole other discussion."

"Isn't it a wonderful thing, having an actual genius as your CFO?" Jada links her arm through his.

"I'm a lucky girl. How are you with interior design?" I ask her.

"Depends," Jada says. "How does fuschia make you feel?"

We clip up the steps to the main cabin to help Lupin prepare the food we've brought: take and bake pizzas, big clamshell containers of salad and brownies. Javier sets up the fire pit, and Nobody and I bundle under a blanket on one of the logs.

"Stars are coming out," Dennis says, wrapped up with Jada, looking up into the deep blue vault of sky above us, and my heart speeds up.

"Well. This star might be turning in." Lupin stands and moves toward the plank of light that hangs from the main cabin doorway. "I'm exhausted from that drive, so if my staff doesn't mind getting the dishes?"

We promise to clean up and wish her good night. My heart is pounding now. The night birds are starting to sing, their notes clearer the more the world vanishes.

"Is Lupin going to be at the camp year-round?" Javier asks me.

"No." I shake my head. "She still runs Higher Paths in the summer; she has her counseling practice in the winter. She'll be more of an adviser."

"She's a really good counselor, too," Dennis adds, eyes flashing to me.

"It's great. I think it's all great." Jada sighs happily, "I had some misgivings about coming back, but the renovation plans are turning me around. A couple of hot tubs and a pool, this place would be unreal . . ." Jada cranes her neck, making sure Lupin isn't by the window, before pulling a little plastic compass out of her pocket, leaning forward and hissing, "Now will you tell us what these are for already?! The suspense is killing me!"

I gave each of them a compass while Lupin was getting gas this morning.

"Yeah." Nobody frowns. "Why are there no bearings? What's the black heart about?"

There are white stars trembling at the black edges of the farthest trees now. The main cabin is quiet, Lupin is definitely in her room, and my heart is galloping. I pull the tin of cinnamon mints out of my jeans pocket and put one in my mouth. Then I pull out my big square flashlight. I click it on and train its narrow white beam straight up, alongside the line of smoke rising from the fire.

"Everyone put their beam on mine," I say, "and I'll show you."

They each turn their flashlights on and line their beams up with mine. My light alone wouldn't register, but all of us together make a signal strong enough to climb past the towering trees and pierce through the dark.

"Now we wait," I tell them.

*   *   *

The sound is as clear in my memory as it was in the stillness that morning, right after the helicopter explosion. The police and security guards were all racing back to their cars, radioing in to first responders, eyes blank with panic. I was frozen, watching the smoke rise up to the blue sky when I heard the small:

Ding.

I turned with a wobble back to the empty house just as the brass doors opened.

Erik had come stumbling out. Hair a mess, hospital gown hanging half off his bare shoulder, and biting frantically at his nails.

"I came back," he said. "So you can't let me go again. That's the deal, right?"

I could only stare.

"I appreciate you trying to get me on that helicopter, Signal," Erik said, kneading at his face, "but I just . . . I just want to go home." He shrugged. "And that's the seat next to you. Alright?"

My shocked expression seemed to sink in then, because he frowned. "What? What's wrong?"

I was choking on my own sobs as another, smaller explosion went off in the distant hills behind me, the nervous cough of a looming god.

"Whoa, was that—" He stepped forward toward the open door, surveying the fiery grave I'd almost condemned him to, and then turned back to me, the corner of his mouth twitching. "Damn, Signal, I thought you were just going to tear her throat out. Guess you're finally in the Teen Killers Club."

"*Listen to me.*" My voice was shaking. "You're dead right now, as far as everyone else knows." I pulled Aarush's car keys from my pocket, pressed them into his hot palm. "Take the car and go. Go as far as you can. You can sell the car if you need the money. You can sell the diamond too—" I reached for the engagement ring.

"Don't take that off." He shook his head. "Ever. That's yours. You're mine."

"I'll change my email password to Password1234." I clutched his shoulders, needing to feel him, to know he wasn't some fever dream. But the slight scruff along his jaw, the sticky circle of diode adhesive under his collarbone, I would not have imagined these things. "We'll figure out the rest in drafts. But you have to go *now*, you have to go *fast*—"

"Drafts," he'd promised, starting to smile, "drafts."

* * *

A figure in a white dog mask walks out from the black woods, shoulders bowed, summoned by our beacon. Nobody lets out a yell, leaping up from her chair, but not out of fear. She recognizes him even with the mask on, and by the time he pulls it off the entire Teen Killers Club is on their feet.

"Did you really think you could have a club meeting without me?" Erik smiles.

Nobody runs for Erik but Dennis beats her there, and Erik pulls him in for a bear hug that knocks his glasses off. Jada, at my side, pretends it's the campfire smoke making her tear up as she turns and hugs me, both of us rocking back and forth, laughing. Javier even reaches in and clasps hands with Erik before giving me a small smile.

"Will he be a counselor?" Dennis asks, while Nobody snatches the mask from Erik and puts it on, then bends his crew cut head into a noogie. "Should I prepare a salary account?"

I shake my head. "He wants to do his own thing. He *claims* he has a fool-proof plan to take down CurtPro. But he can't let anyone know he's alive for a while, so he'll hide out here."

"Well, look, if we're not going to have kill switches and fences," Javier strokes his jaw thoughtfully, "he could earn his keep by being security. We'll tell the campers not to go into the woods without a buddy, 'cause there's a guy in a dog mask out there."

"And if someone runs off, we know he can track them," Jada adds.

"Logistical question." Dennis frowns. "Where does he live?"

I tap the compass. "With me. Follow the black heart whenever you want to come hang out."

"Maybe walkie-talkie us ahead of time," Erik says, the side of his mouth twitching. "And give us like, I don't know, a week or two to ourselves. We've, uh, got a lot to unpack." He takes my hand and leans away from the campfire. "You ready?"

I hug Nobody and Jada one last time, and then go with him.

We duck down past the glowing windows of the main cabin, hand in hand, flashlights chasing each other across the grass as we hurry past. Then he veers toward the girls' cabin, leading me to its rough wall and standing on tiptoe to peer through the window, before he smiles back at me.

"The first time we ever spoke," Erik says, "I stood right here and watched to make sure you were alone before I came in and told you I'd been following your case."

"Oh, I remember."

"And you were *scared* of me!" He shakes his head and takes my hand again, and we turn and duck into the trees, moving down the trail toward the forgotten playground.

"Oh *please*."

"Terrified. You were *terrified*. Of *me*!"

We walk deeper into the woods, the towering branches of the great oaks describing a space as large as a cathedral.

"And I remember thinking, this girl has *no idea*! I'm the only one who believes her, I'm going to solve her mystery, I'm going to set her free. I'm *her hero*.

And she's terrified of me! She has *no clue*—careful—" His hot hand catches my shoulder and sends a thrill through my whole body. "Watch your step, there's the stream—"

"Are we *crossing the fence* right now?" I tease.

"Finally."

Up ahead, an arrowhead of glowing blue is just visible through the trees. As we get closer, the Aston Martin resolves from the woods, the A-frame of the mini black cabin kit behind it even cuter than it looked online. I knew he'd been putting it together these last few weeks, but he didn't tell me about the bright blue Christmas lights strung along the edge of the A-line roof. And on our door he's hung a paper sign, covered in his impatient, all-caps handwriting:

WELCOME HOME, WATSON

"Erik . . ." I am squeezing his arm so hard.

"But then—" Erik is grinning when I turn to face him, and trembling with excitement. And when my arms go around his neck, it courses through me. "You ended up doing all of that, for me."

I stare into his eyes, the beautiful one and the normal one, too choked up to speak. And when we kiss, his hand gently drifts to my side, and lands just over my scar. I look down and realize there's a black heart on his ring finger, the mark slightly raised.

"Is that *permanent?!*" I cry, delighted.

"God, I hope so," Erik says. "This time I'm carrying you over the threshold."

And he sweeps me off my feet.

Acknowledgments

This series owes its happy ending to the advocacy and insight of my literary agent, Stacia Decker. My sincere thanks to Matt Martz and the team at Crooked Lane Books; especially my editor Melissa Rechter. Thank you Rebecca Nelson, Madeline Rathle, and Dulce Botello for your support and energy. Much gratitude is owed as well to Josh McGuire for his tireless efforts in manifesting Signal Deere in new and exciting forms.

I want to thank my husband Ryan and our daughter Lovey, who tells the best stories, for giving me so much encouragement and support. My parents, sisters, extended family and friends, who have amplified the series in so many ways.

Most of all I would like to thank the readers who have recommended the Teen Killers series in person and online. I end this story deeply grateful that it's just beginning for future readers.